Advance praise for *A Sudden Dawn* . . .

"Inspirational, beautifully written, expertly researched, and highly recommended. I loved it!"

—Geoff Thompson, martial artist, British Academy of Film and Television Arts (BAFTA) award-winning filmmaker.

"I've read thousands of novels, hundreds of terrific tomes, yet *A Sudden Dawn* easily makes my top ten. It does not matter if you know of Bodhidharma, care about martial arts, or can even spell the word "Shaolin," if you have any interest whatsoever in historical fiction you will be captivated by this extraordinary tale. It is as good as James Clavell's *Shogun*, masterfully written, thoroughly enjoyable, and damnably hard to put down. I cannot recommend Powell's book highly enough. It's freaking brilliant!"

—Lawrence A. Kane, martial artist, best-selling author of *The Little Black Book of Violence*

"The story is an absolute delight to read and I was enthralled from our intrepid hero's entry in to the first monastery and his subsequent journey and final arrival at the Shaolin temple.

Martial artists and Buddhists both will be captivated by this tale of the legendary Bodhidharma."

—Nicholas P. Hughes, martial artist, bodyguard

"*A Sudden Dawn* is a wond
fiction. Mr. Powell has don
characters experiences so re
hot breath of battle on you
the temple's damp hallways
Bodhidharma's journey fron

Sudden Dawn is an experience you will enjoy; it is realistic, historically rich, and full of vital and genuine characters. *A Sudden Dawn* is what martial arts novels should be, engaging, matter-of-fact, and packed with beautiful storytelling."

—Kris Wilder, martial artist, best-selling author *The Way of Sanchin Kata*

"Amazing, the book martial artists have been waiting 2,000 years for."

—Chris Crudelli, author of *Mind, Body and Kick Ass Moves*

"*A Sudden Dawn* opens like the petals of the sacred lotus. It is a visually stunning journey through time and through landscape, to capture one man's journey towards enlightenment. The life of the Bodhidharma (Da Mo), is a fluid and fast paced read, not unlike the birth and practice of kung-fu itself."

—Vincent Pratchett, martial artist, author *The Warrior, the Witch, and the Wizard*

"Goran Powell brings the legend of Da Mo and the Shaolin Temple to life in this sweeping epic tale that is exceptionally well-paced and engaging to the very end. *A Sudden Dawn* is an adventurous story that blends history, myth, and legend into a remarkable and enjoyable tale that is seamlessly woven into a fascinating and moving book.

"As a martial artist and someone who's studied Asian ways for over 20 years, I found *A Sudden Dawn* to have just the right mix of martial arts action, history, romance, and philosophy to engage and entertain throughout the entire text. It is a gripping story that I didn't want to finish. Powell's interpretation of these legendary characters draws you into the story from the first page and takes you along for an incredible adventure spanning the Asian continent. It's one of the most enjoyable books I've read in a long time."

—Alain Burrese, J.D., former U.S. Army 2nd Infantry Division Scout Sniper School instructor and author of *Hard-Won Wisdom from the School of Hard Knocks,* and the DVDs *Hapkido Hoshinsul, Streetfighting Essentials, Hapkido Cane,* and *The Lock On: Joint Lock Essentials* series

"A marvelous modern interpretation of an ancient legend! Reading this book opens a gateway to the mythical origins of the martial arts. Goran Powell's vivid writing style takes you through this gateway and fully immerses you in Bodhidharma's world. *A Sudden Dawn* skillfully weaves fact and fiction to produce a powerhouse of a page turner!"

—Iain Abernethy, 5th dan karate (British Combat Association and Karate England) and best-selling author *Bunkai-Jutsu: The Practical Application of Karate Kata*

"A wonderful mixture of philosophy and fun, a great story I wish I had written myself!"

—Arthur Rosenfeld, martial artist, critically acclaimed author *A Cure for Gravity*

"*A Sudden Dawn* is an epic tale of superbly crafted characters that surges with action, intrigue and touching human relationships. I can't remember the last novel that has taken hold of my mind like this one and has kept me up late at night turning pages.

Although this is a book of historical fiction, it is so grand, so rich, and so memorable, that you want it to be true."

—Loren W. Christensen, 8th dan black belt, best-selling author of 40 martial arts books including, *Warriors, Defensive Tactics, On Combat,* and *Fighter's Fact Book.*

"Breathtaking! I read into the early hours of the morning of my karate grading because I couldn't put this novel down! The saying goes that you shouldn't judge a book by its cover, but in the case of Goran Powell's *A Sudden Dawn*, the stunning illustration is a perfect reflection of the imagery this book evokes. Inspiring, enlightening, funny and sad, this beautifully written story and its characters, will stay with you long after you turn the last page."

—Karen van Wyk, author *Sanchin—A Martial Arts Novel*

"*A Sudden Dawn* is an entertaining and exciting blend of history and myth. In the martial arts and Zen Buddhism, the Indian monk Bodhidharma is afforded great respect and the traditional link to the fight art of Shaolin Temple Boxing is a story often told. Goran Powell has added flesh to the bare bones of the tale, and turned often idealized historical figures into human beings."

—Harry Cook, author *Precise History of Shotokan 2nd ed.*

A Sudden Dawn

Also by Goran Powell...

Waking Dragons—A Martial Arts Autobiography

A Sudden Dawn

a martial arts novel by

Goran Powell

YMAA Publication Center
Boston, MA USA

YMAA Publication Center, Inc.
Main Office
PO Box 480
Wolfeboro, NH 03894
1-800-669-8892 • www.ymaa.com • ymaa@aol.com

Editor: Leslie Takao
Cover Design: Axie Breen

ISBN-13: 978-1-59439-198-9
ISBN-10: 1-59439-198-X

20201027

Publisher's Cataloging in Publication

Powell, Goran, 1965-

A sudden dawn : a martial arts novel / by Goran Powell. -- Boston, MA : YMAA Publication Center, c2010.

p. ; cm.

ISBN: 978-1-59439-198-9

1. Bodhidharma, 6th cent.--Fiction. 2. Buddhism--China--History--Fiction. 3. Hand-to-hand fighting, Oriental--History--Fiction. 4. Kung fu--History--Fiction. 5. Historical fiction. I. Title.

PS3616.O878 S83 2010 2010927414
813.6--dc22 1005

Printed in USA.

To my wife Charmaigne, without whom
Bodhidharma would never have left India.

PROLOGUE

Pallava, South India, A.D. 507

The Lotus Sermon

As the sun set over the southern kingdom of Pallava, a vast crowd gathered in a park in Kanchipuram, the elegant state capital. People had come from all over the city. Many more had traveled from the ports and fishing villages of the palm-fringed coast. Some had even journeyed from the remote villages of the interior. They had all come for one reason—to hear the words of the renowned Buddhist master Prajnatara. It had been many years since Prajnatara had spoken in public and the warm evening air crackled with expectation.

However, there was one young man among the throng who had no interest in the ramblings of an old monk. His name, like his father's, was Sardili; and his only interest was in getting home after a long day of training at the Military Academy. He was halfway across the park when he caught a glimpse of a skinny little man sitting apart from the crowd. At first Sardili imagined it was a hermit, come to join in the occasion, but when he noticed all eyes on the little man and heard Prajnatara's name spoken in awe, he realized it was the master himself.

The crowd was waiting for Prajnatara to begin his sermon, but Prajnatara simply held a flower aloft and gazed at it in silent wonder. Sardili paused to see how long the little master would keep such a multitude waiting. People grew restless and called out to Prajnatara urging him to speak, but if he heard them he did not respond. A mischievous young boy went forward and shook the master by the shoulder, but Prajnatara ignored him and continued to gaze at his flower. One of Prajnatara's disciples gently ushered the boy away.

Sardili grew tired of waiting and turned to go, but at that very moment, Prajnatara spoke.

"Sit with me."

His voice was powerful for such a small man, and oddly compelling. Those nearest him began to sit. When those behind saw what was happening they followed, until the entire multitude was seated before him. Then, Prajnatara held up the yellow lotus that he had picked from a nearby pond, and refocused his gaze upon it. Sardili wondered whether some strange magic was about to occur. Perhaps the flower would burst into flame or be transformed into a bird and fly away. He waited. No magic took place. Bored with watching, he rose to leave, but, just then Prajnatara spoke again.

"A thousand years ago, when The Buddha was coming to the end of his life, there was great debate about who would be his successor. Who among his followers understood his wisdom most completely? A gathering was organized to decide the matter, the last The Buddha would ever attend on earth, and it took place in a beautiful park not unlike this one, in northern India."

Sardili sat again, compelled to listen to the master's tale.

"Many thousands of people came to hear The Buddha's final sermon. But instead of giving a lengthy speech as he usually did, he simply waded into a pond and pulled up a lotus. He showed it to his followers and, like you, they wondered what to make of it. Even his most senior disciples were puzzled. Normally, The Buddha spoke for hours and they listened, hoping that if they listened for long enough they would become enlightened like The Buddha. But now, in the most important sermon of his life, The Buddha did not have a single word to say.

"Eventually, some of The Buddha's disciples began to debate and speculate on the meaning of the flower. Hearing them, The Buddha rose and held up the flower to each of them in turn. Each disciple guessed at its meaning, hoping to become The Buddha's successor. The flower was Heaven? The root was Earth? The stem was The Buddha's doctrine, which joined the two? Each tried in turn, offering a new suggestion, until finally The Buddha came to Kasyapa, the last of his disciples, who said nothing and simply smiled at his master. With that, The Buddha gave the flower to Kasyapa and turned to address the multitude. 'All that can be said has already been said,' he told them. 'That which cannot be said has been passed to Kasyapa.' And that is how Kasyapa became The Buddha's successor."

The crowd was silent, awaiting an explanation, but instead, Prajnatara returned to his silent contemplation of the lotus. People called to him to clarify the meaning of his story, but he ignored them and continued to gaze at the flower. Sardili wondered what Kasyapa had seen in the flower to make him smile. He stared at Prajnatara's lotus to see if anything would become apparent. He even smiled as Kasyapa had done, but saw no new meaning in it.

The crowd began to disperse, bemused and disappointed, but Sardili remained with a handful of others watching the flower, intrigued to know its meaning. As darkness fell, Prajnatara's disciples lit torches, while their master continued his silent study of the lotus. Hours passed. Shortly before midnight, Sardili accepted that Prajnatara would make no further revelations. The hour was late. His parents would begin to worry. He rose and left the little master still seated in the park and gazing at his flower as if he were seeing the most precious thing in the world.

Over the following days, the riddle of the Lotus Sermon returned to Sardili many times. Each time it puzzled him more. Days turned to weeks and still the riddle did not leave him. Instead, it grew into an obsession that gnawed away inside him, a terrible itch he could not scratch. He became distracted in his studies at the Military Academy. In lectures he no longer challenged the strategies of his teachers, as he had once done so keenly. In sparring matches, his opponents tagged him with practice blades, something none had succeeded in doing for many years. In training with real swords, his mind wandered to the lotus and he opened a deep gash in his own calf. His instructors grew concerned and visited his father, the renowned General Sardili.

The next morning the young Sardili was summoned to his father's office. It was at the far end of the Sardili residence and away from the distraction of the general's large family. That part of the house had always been kept free of noisy children and chattering servants. Only a steady stream of military personnel had come and gone at all hours of the day and night. Sardili knocked. Normally the general's adjutant would answer, so Sardili was surprised when his father appeared quickly and greeted him with a broad smile.

The general was an imposing figure. He towered over other men, not just because of his size—though he was tall, and built like a bull. There was a certainty in him that bent others to his will. His deep rumbling voice carried effortless authority and his piercing eyes held lesser men captive in their gaze. The general had always towered over him too, but now as he entered the study, the young Sardili noticed he was half a head taller than his father.

"Sit down young man," the general said cheerfully, and Sardili felt himself drawn into his father's irrepressible warmth. It was a side of the general few soldiers had seen, but one he had enjoyed often enough as a boy. "How are you?" his father boomed. "We haven't spoken for some time. I've been preoccupied with affairs of state. You know how it is. My retirement hasn't brought the peace I was hoping for."

"You're too young and fit to retire, father. Everyone knows that," Sardili said dutifully.

"That's good of you to say, but I'm not fit now, not as I once was. Not as you are now." Then the general's face grew serious. "Anyway, enough about me. Let's talk about you, my son. One of your instructors from the Academy visited yesterday. We had a long talk. A good talk. He says you're an outstanding young soldier, the finest the Academy has ever produced. He tells me you're unbeaten in both armed and unarmed combat for the last five years, and at the trials earlier this year, no one lasted more than a few seconds with you in the arena."

The general had been pacing the room restlessly as he spoke, and now he stopped and threw up his hands in defeat, "I must confess, I knew you were talented, but even I was surprised to hear this. You don't think to inform me of your achievements?"

"I'm sorry, father," he shrugged. "I didn't think you'd be interested."

"Of course I'm interested! I like to hear of your progress. No one is prouder of you than I, Sardili. You must know that."

"These things come easily to me," he said modestly.

"That's understandable. You are a Sardili of the Warrior Caste. It's in your blood."

Sardili smiled. He had heard the same thing countless times before and waited for his father to get to the point. The general rarely engaged in idle chatter and Sardili knew he had been summoned to for a reason.

"Your studies are also going well, I hear …"

"Yes, father."

"Good. That is important, too. Soldiering is not all about brute strength you know. Your instructor tells me your understanding of strategy is advanced, and you're well versed in the classics, the Vedas …"

"Yes, father."

"When you graduate at the end of the year, there's a place waiting for you in King Simhavarman's Royal Guards. I served in the Guards myself, as you know. It's the best start any soldier could wish for, the finest regiment in all of India."

"Yes, father."

"Nevertheless, your instructor also mentioned that you have been a little, how did he put it …distracted, recently …" His father paused, giving him a chance to comment, but Sardili simply waited for him to continue.

"I have to say that I have noticed the same thing," his father said eventually. "Would you agree?"

"Perhaps," he shrugged.

"Is something wrong, Sardili? If there is, you can tell me. We're both grown men now, after all. A woman, perhaps …?"

"No," he said, reddening.

"A man, then?" his father laughed, squeezing his shoulder playfully.

"No!"

"Well what is it then? Speak up now boy," the general ordered gently.

"You'll think it strange," Sardili said.

"I have seen and heard many strange things in my lifetime," the general smiled.

Sardili shifted uncomfortably in his seat. "I saw a prophet, a few weeks ago, in the park."

"Which prophet? There is no prophet that I know of in Kanchipuram."

"His name is Prajnatara," Sardili said.

"Prajnatara?" his father snorted, "Prajnatara is just a crazy old Buddhist monk from Magadha. What has he been saying?"

"Very little," Sardili sighed, "but what he did say made me think."

His father waited for him to continue, but Sardili raised his hands, as if to say he could not explain further.

"Made you think about what?" his father persisted.

"Life, I suppose," Sardili said at last, "what we're all doing here . . ."

"Oh son," his father laughed, "these are big questions for one so young and best left for priests to worry about, not warriors. One day you'll lead men into battle. It doesn't pay to dwell on such matters, trust me on this."

Sardili did not reply. He did not want to contradict his father, but the general saw the determination in his son's eyes and his expression hardened.

"Remember what I've always told you. You are a Sardili. You were born to the Warrior Caste. You have trained your whole life to follow in the family tradition. Soon you'll graduate from the Academy with the highest honors and King Simhavarman himself will welcome you to his Royal Guards." His expression softened, "You'll make us all very proud, Sardili. Just keep your mind on your training a little longer and years from now, when you're old and retired like me, you can concern yourself with such questions."

"Yes, father."

"Good," his father beamed, "I'm glad we had this talk and cleared things up. Let's put it behind us and never speak of it again."

But they did speak of it again, and when they did, an argument raged in the Sardili residence unlike any before and hung over the household for weeks like the brooding clouds of the summer monsoon.

Sardili had tried to obey his father, but the mystery of the Lotus Sermon had been too powerful. He had gone in search of Prajnatara to demand an explanation, but Prajnatara had vanished. No one knew where to find him. Sardili had tried visiting local temples and wise men seeking the meaning of the flower sermon, but none had been able to provide the answer. Eventually his father had heard of his absences and summoned him once more to demand an explanation.

It was then that Sardili told his father of his intention to become a monk, and the general's fury had known no bounds. His mother had pleaded with him tearfully, night after night. His uncles and cousins had visited and spoken with him for hours on end. His instructors had come and tried to reason with him, one after the other. He had listened to each visitor in turn, politely, patiently, seriously, but steadfastly refused to change his mind. And finally, when all arguments had been exhausted, a terrible silence descended over the household.

Sardili waited for many days, hoping his father might relent and give him his blessing before he left, but the general refused all contact with his son. He was a warrior who carried the scars of many battles, but his son's betrayal had cut him deeper than any enemy blade ever could.

And so on a bright day in spring, Sardili decided he could wait no longer. He kissed his mother goodbye, hugged his brothers and sisters, and took leave of his faithful servants before walking out of the lofty hallway into the fierce heat of the day.

On the veranda he paused to admire the beautiful gardens one last time, then walked to the gate and turned for a final farewell. His family had gathered in the entrance to see him off and behind them, he noticed a shadow. It was his father. He waited by the gate in silence until his father emerged and walked swiftly toward him. For a moment he thought his father might strike him but the general stopped, two inches from his face, and spoke in a low growl, "You are a stubborn, headstrong boy, Sardili. You always were. Ever since you were a child, you wanted everything your own way. You were never satisfied, always striving, until you got what you wanted. And I admit that I was glad of it, because I knew it would make you into a great soldier. Now you've chosen a different path, one I know you'll follow with the same stubbornness. I only hope you don't waste your life chasing an impossible dream."

"I won't," Sardili said with a certainty he did not feel.

He looked into his father's eyes and saw the love still visible beneath the hurt and anger. He could think of no other words to say and a great sadness welled up inside him. "Goodbye father," he whispered, turning quickly to hide his tears, and walked away from his home forever.

Sardili learned that Prajnatara had gone to Sri Lanka; but when he arrived in Sri Lanka, he was told Prajnatara was in the western port of Kochi; and in Kochi he heard rumors that Prajnatara had retreated to the mountains of the interior. Three years passed and still he wandered in search of Prajnatara. He visited many temples on the way and met with many holy men. He studied the Buddhist scriptures and committed the words of the sacred Sutras to memory. He learned to still his mind in meditation. He begged for food and came to understand the virtue of humility. He starved his body of nourishment and his mind of desire. He grew weak, so weak that he saw visions of startling clarity. Yet he knew they were not the truth but merely illusions brought on by his weakened state.

Five more years passed and Sardili had become a wise and learned monk. Yet, in his heart, he felt no closer to the truth than the day he had left home, and he began to wonder if his father had been right after all.

Still, he wandered in the southern kingdoms of India seeking Prajnatara. Another year passed and he found himself in the jungles of Pallava, less than three days' journey from his home city of Kanchipuram. On the banks of a slow moving river, he met an old ferryman who, on seeing his monk's robe, offered him free passage across the water. As they crossed, the ferryman spoke of a beautiful temple located a short distance upriver and urged him to visit it. He smiled and told the old ferryman that he was seeking a particular temple, and a particular master.

"This is Prajnatara's temple," the ferryman told him.

Sardili had heard countless false stories of Prajnatara's whereabouts, but something about the old man's gentle confidence made him follow the ferryman's directions. At a fork in the river, he saw the pale stonework of a temple, half-hidden by the jungle, just as the old man had described. It was smaller than he had imagined, the point of its stupa barely reached the surrounding trees, yet its lack of grandeur was part of its appeal. The temple was exquisitely beautiful. Sun-bleached walls were carved with scenes of The Buddha's life and inscribed with passages from the Sutras. Flowers and shrubs decorated the temple grounds, and a tranquil bathing pool glistened in the shade of a banyan tree.

The main door was unlocked. He pushed it open. The entrance was empty, but he could hear rhythmic chanting coming from the corridor that led away from the hall. He waited, expecting someone to appear. When no one came, he made his way down the dim corridor. The familiar smell of incense floated on the cool air. He came to a door ajar and peered inside. Young monks were studying the Sutras, and their earnest faces reminded him of a time when he had dedicated himself to understanding the sacred texts. Now he had begun to despise the same texts for their endless contradictions. Not one had revealed the truth to him.

A man appeared at his side. "Can I help you, Brother?"

Sardili was startled to see it was Prajnatara staring up at him, looking no older than the day he had seen him in the park almost ten years earlier. The slight frame and soft features gave Prajnatara an almost boyish look and he stood no higher than Sardili's chest, but there was firmness in his stance that belied his gentle appearance. Sardili bowed and pressed his palms together in the traditional Buddhist greeting.

"My name is Sardili," he said.

Prajnatara waited for him to continue.

"I have come to study here, if you will accept me," he added.

"What is it you seek, Sardili?" Prajnatara asked.

"I seek what every monk seeks—enlightenment."

"And what do you suppose that to be?" Prajnatara asked, his expression puzzled, as if Sardili had brought up a fascinating new topic for discussion.

"To see the world as it truly is," he said, "to know my own mind . . ."

"You don't know yourself, Sardili?"

Sardili shrugged.

"Yet you have studied a long time?" Prajnatara probed.

"Yes."

Prajnatara waited for him to say more, but Sardili had no wish to elaborate. "I ask to be accepted as a student," was all he said.

Prajnatara studied him silently for a minute, then shook his head. "You are too old for this temple, Sardili. All our students are young. You won't fit in. I regret to say the answer is 'No.'"

Sardili had never been refused entry to a temple before and found himself at a loss for words.

"I'm sorry," Prajnatara continued, turning to go, "I hope you haven't come far."

"Wait, please," Sardili stepped closer, "I have come far. It has taken me years to find you ..."

Prajnatara stopped but did not look back, "You won't find what you're seeking in this temple."

"I will do whatever is necessary to fit in."

"It won't help."

Sardili put his hand on the little master's arm. "Please, Master Prajnatara, I beg you to reconsider."

"Take you hands off me," Prajnatara said icily. "One monk must never lay a hand on another in this temple. That is our sacred rule."

Sardili released him and took a step back. This was a disaster. "I'm sorry, truly. Please forgive me, it's just that ..."

Prajnatara turned back to face him, looking him up and down once more as if seeing him for the first time, then slapped him hard across the face.

Sardili was stunned. In all his years at the Military Academy no blow had ever caught him so unaware. His first instinct was to strike Prajnatara down, but he fought the urge. His second was to touch his own cheek, which smarted from the blow, but he refused to show he'd been hurt.

"Now you may join us," Prajnatara said, "if you wish."

Sardili stared in astonishment at the little man who, it seemed, had so little fear for his own safety.

"What do you say?" Prajnatara demanded.

"I thought you said one monk must never lay a hand on another," Sardili said through clenched teeth.

"Did I say that?" Prajnatara asked, his eyes wide.

"Yes you did. I believe you called it a sacred rule."

"Rules are for children, Sardili."

Sardili's eyes bored into the little master's with barely contained violence.

"Make up your mind," Prajnatara smiled, turning and walking

away. He had almost reached the end of the corridor when Sardili, beaten, shouted after him, "I will join!"

Prajnatara hurried back, a broad smile on his face now. He seized Sardili's hands and clutched them to his breast, "You will? Are you sure, Sardili? I am so pleased, especially after I treated you so poorly. You would be perfectly justified in leaving and never returning. But you will stay?"

"I came to study," Sardili said struggling to control his temper, "and that's what I will do."

"Well I'm delighted to hear it," Prajnatara said happily, "but please don't be too determined my dear Sardili, as it can rather get in the way of things. Now, let me think ... You can join the classes, starting from tomorrow. In the meantime I'll get Brother Jaina to show you around and help you settle in. Don't go away. I'll be right back. I'm so delighted that you came to join us, truly I am."

Sardili waited over an hour and when the little master eventually reappeared, he was accompanied by a thick-set monk with a square jaw and a heavy brow. Prajnatara introduced them to one another, and as he did Sardili thought he saw a fleeting look pass between Prajnatara and Brother Jaina. Then Brother Jaina led him away to the tiny monk's cell that would be his home for the foreseeable future.

The room was empty except for a roll of bedding on the floor and a chest for his belongings. When Brother Jaina had gone, he arranged his few possessions in the chest and sat on the floor. A great loneliness came over him, and he vowed it would be the last time he joined a new temple in search of the answers that had eluded him for so long.

The next day began with the dawn call to meditation. At the sound of the bell, the novice monks filed into the cool hall and took their places on rows of cushions. Prajnatara was waiting at the front. When they were all seated, he lit an incense burner and rang a tiny bell to signal the start of the meditation. The sweet chime seemed to go on forever.

When meditation ended, they ate a light breakfast and studied the Sutras with one of the senior monks. With the sound of the temple gong, Brother Jaina arrived and called them outside to exercise before the searing midday heat descended. They performed the yoga asanas, which Sardili knew well and followed easily; but what happened next came as a surprise. The young monks fetched thick reed mats from the temple and laid them down on the hard earth. When this was done, Brother Jaina began to instruct them in wrestling. Sardili noticed they practiced a form that had originated in Kerala, a form now common throughout India.

Prajnatara appeared at his side. "Are you surprised, Sardili?" he asked with a smile.

"I have never seen wrestling in a temple before," Sardili answered.

"We find it helps students to concentrate if they are fit and healthy. Brother Jaina did a little wrestling in Kerala before he joined our order. Tell me, do you wrestle yourself?"

"Once, a long time ago."

"Splendid! Where did you learn?"

"My father taught me."

"How fascinating! Your father was a wrestler?"

"No. My father was a general, but wrestling was his passion. He believed all the battlefield arts could be understood if one could understand wrestling."

"Your family is from the Warrior Caste?" Prajnatara asked, warming to the subject quickly.

"Yes."

"It must have been difficult turning your back on the family tradition to follow The Way."

"It has been a humbling experience," he answered truthfully.

"And do you think your father was right?"

"About what, Master?"

"About understanding many things from one."

"I am not in a position to judge, Master. I gave up such pursuits a long time ago to follow The Way."

"You don't think The Way can be found in strategy?"

"I don't know where it can be found. That is why I am here."

"What do you know, Sardili?"

He saw the mischief in Prajnatara eyes. "I know it's not common to see monks wrestling," he answered stiffly.

"True, but your father sounds like a very wise man," Prajnatara persisted.

"My father was a warrior. The Way is a way of peace …"

"Ah, beware of trying to define The Way with words, Sardili. It goes against the very essence of The Way."

"Then please tell me, what is the essence of The Way?"

"Actions, not words, Sardili," Prajnatara said loudly, clapping the back of his hand into his palm, then shook his head in bitter disappointment. "If only you had listened to your father instead of a lot of silly old monks! It's too late now. You're stuck with us. So come, let us see you wrestle. I will get Brother Jaina to select a suitable opponent for you."

"It would be better if they wrestle among themselves," Sardili warned.

"Oh come, Sardili," Prajnatara laughed, "what are you afraid of?"

Sardili looked into the master's face to see if he was serious and found he could not tell. He stripped down to his loincloth, as the other wrestlers had done, and Brother Jaina welcomed him onto the mat. "Do you wish to warm up, Sardili?" he asked.

Sardili was loose from the earlier exercises and his huge lean muscles glistened with a fine sheen of sweat.

"I am warm, thank you Brother Jaina," he said.

Jaina called out an opponent for him, a big youth as tall as Sardili, though not quite as broad. Sardili smiled at the young man, but the youth simply watched him warily. They circled for a moment, before going into a clinch. The youth moved quickly, pushing and pulling fiercely to unweight the stranger who had appeared on their mat. Twice he attempted a throw, but Sardili was as immovable as a rock. The youth switched suddenly to a standing submission, hoping to lock one of Sardili's arms in both of his own. It was then that Sardili tired of the boy's childish antics. There was a blur, nothing more, as the youth was spinning in the air. It seemed to the startled onlookers that Sardili would drop the boy on his head, but Sardili turned him at the last instant and sent him crashing down safely on his back.

The youth groaned, stunned by the fall. Sardili looked to Brother Jaina, unsure of the rules of the match, but Jaina said nothing. It seemed a submission was needed to end the bout. Sardili knelt beside the boy and waited for him to recover. Slowly the youth rose to his knees and reached out to take hold again. It was a mistake. Sardili seized his wrist and pulled. His left leg snaked around the outstretched limb and trapped it between both knees. He raised his hips. "I submit!" the youth cried urgently.

Sardili released the lock and helped his opponent to his feet, massaging his elbow joint until the pain had subsided and some movement had been restored.

One by one, the other wrestlers came out to face him, each more reluctant than the last. At first, he allowed them a little dignity before defeat, a few moments to attempt a throw or submission. But after a while he tired of their dismal efforts and, without quarter, slammed them into the mat and wrapped them in excruciating locks and chokes. Each opponent submitted to a different hold, many of which had never been seen before, each yelped in pain and tapped frantically to be released. After each match, Sardili took time to treat the area of the body that he had traumatized only moments earlier.

Soon he had disposed of all the young wrestlers and only Brother Jaina remained. Sardili rose to leave the mats, unwilling to expose the young monks' instructor to a humiliating defeat, but Brother Jaina called him back. Prajnatara nodded his approval for the bout and Sardili returned to the center of the mat.

Brother Jaina turned out to be a strong and skilful wrestler, but he was no match for Sardili, who forced him to submit in little more than a minute. To Jaina's surprise, he did not feel Sardili's enormous strength at work, nor his considerable weight. Sardili defeated him with a level of skill that required no strength, skill Jaina had seen only in the greatest wrestlers in the land. He bowed to Sardili while the young monks regarded the newcomer with barely concealed wonder.

In the evening, Prajnatara took Sardili aside and asked him to instruct the wrestling from that day forth. He agreed, and soon became something of a celebrity among his students, who progressed rapidly under his expert supervision.

Sardili enjoyed his new role as a teacher, but as the days became weeks and then months, he grew disillusioned with his life at the temple. The long hours of meditation and study brought him no closer to the enlightenment he sought. He tried discussing his concerns with Prajnatara, but Prajnatara evaded the subject, talking instead of the weather, the flowers in his gardens, or the progress of Sardili's wrestling students. When Sardili pressed him on the subject, Prajnatara struck him hard on the chest and reminded him that he would not find what he was seeking in the temple.

The days grew shorter. Summer gave way to autumn and in those long silent hours of the evening, Sardili came to realize that his quest was over. There was no prize awaiting him in Prajnatara's temple. No treasure to be discovered. No truth. No nirvana. It was time to abandon his fruitless search and dedicate himself to a more realistic goal, though he had no idea what that might be.

The hour was late when he went to inform Prajnatara of his departure. The temple lamps had already been extinguished and only a single candle burned in the corridor. He moved silently to the master's quarters, not wishing to wake the sleeping monks, and knocked softly on the door.

Brother Jaina answered and stepped aside to let him in. Prajnatara was seated at his desk with paperwork laid out before him. He looked up with a smile. "You look concerned, Sardili. Come in. Take a seat. Talk to us. You will be a welcome respite from the tedious business of running a temple. What can Brother Jaina and I do for you?"

"Nothing. I am leaving," Sardili answered.

"Leaving? So soon after arriving? Are you sure about this, Sardili?"

"Yes. I decided you were right. I won't find what I'm looking for in this temple. I have come to thank you for your teachings and your hospitality, but The Way is not for me. It's time I did something different."

Prajnatara turned to give Sardili his full attention." Different in what way?" he demanded with a frown.

"More purposeful."

"The Way is eminently purposeful, Sardili."

"Not if one cannot find it."

"Perhaps you seek it too hard," Prajnatara sighed.

"And perhaps you talk in riddles," Sardili answered, unable to contain his mounting frustration.

"What will you do instead?" Brother Jaina asked.

"I have not decided yet."

"Will you return to your family?"

"Perhaps."

"Do you think your father will welcome you back?"

"That is my business, Brother Jaina."

"It will be awkward," Jaina continued, "returning home after so long with nothing to show for your efforts."

Sardili felt his temper rise, and when he noticed Prajnatara and Jaina exchanging a knowing glance, he could contain it no more.

"I see this amuses you both!" He exploded, smashing his hand onto the table and sending papers flying. Brother Jaina flew to his feet to stand between Sardili and his master. Sardili grasped Jaina's robe and he fought the urge to hurl the smaller man aside.

A splash of cold shocked him. Prajnatara had thrown a jug of water in his face. "Cool down, Sardili," he ordered.

Sardili released Jaina and pointed a warning finger at Prajnatara. "I would advise you not to strike me a third time," he growled.

"I wouldn't dream of it," Prajnatara said lightly, "but before you go, tell us why you're so angry?"

Sardili glared at the little master, searching for the words to adequately describe the depth of his disillusionment. "It's all false," he said finally, his voice little more than a whisper now. "I have wasted so many years chanting, praying, reciting, debating—and all for nothing. You talk of the truth. You claim to possess it. But the truth is you have nothing. A man could waste a lifetime on this charade."

He strode across the room and reached for the door.

"You're quite right, of course," Prajnatara said casually, taking a scroll from a cabinet and crossing the room to offer it to him. "These scriptures really are quite useless. Tear them up if it makes you feel better. Get rid of everything in this entire temple if you wish. None of it is necessary. Not one single thing." He turned and swiped a bowl of incense from a nearby shelf. It shattered loudly on the floor creating a cloud of white dust. Sardili watched in bewilderment. It seemed he was not the only one who had lost his self-control.

"Here," Prajnatara said, taking a carving of The Buddha from his window, "break the stupid little statue into little pieces if you like. It's just a piece of wood, carved in the shape of a man." The master's voice was serious but Sardili still had the feeling he was being mocked.

"Keep your Buddha," he said angrily, striding from the room.

"Sardili wait, please ..."

He ignored the master's pleas and went to his room to collect his belongings. When he emerged, Brother Jaina was waiting for him. "Sardili," he said quietly, "at least wait until morning. You can talk with Prajnatara again, when you're not so angry. Then if you still wish to leave, we will give you supplies for your journey."

"I'm leaving now."

"The jungle is a dangerous place at night."

Brother Jaina was right but Sardili did not care. He yearned for the dark embrace of the jungle and strode from the temple without another word.

"Come back when you're ready," Jaina called after him, but Jaina's words were already lost in the thick night air.

Sardili walked among the gnarled shadows of the moonlit jungle, driven by rage at the monks, the temples, the scriptures, The Buddha, and above all, at himself. He had hurt his father, his mother, his family. He had wasted his youth. Tears of frustration coursed down his cheeks and he left them to fall into the folds of his robe. He walked for hours, directionless, until the sky began to lighten and the first glow of dawn appeared on the horizon. It was only then that he noticed his mouth was dry and his limbs weary.

He stopped in a quiet glade and took a pull of water from his goatskin. By the time he had returned it to his knapsack, a watery sunshine had filtered through the treetops. He rubbed his eyes wearily and rested his head in his hands. His anger had gone, leaving him exhausted. His mind began to replay the events of the previous evening. Prajnatara had reacted strangely to his outburst. He had not disagreed or protested. In fact, he had agreed that it was all pretense. It made no sense.

A dwarf deer wandered into the glade and nibbled on a patch of wild grass, unaware of his presence. Sardili clicked his tongue and the little deer noticed him and darted away. He found himself smiling at the creature's stupidity. One moment it had thought the glade safe, the next, a place of danger. But the glade had not changed. Only the deer's mind had changed.

He wondered if he was the same. Could it be so simple?

He dismissed the idea. It was nonsense. But even as he did, he knew it was true, and his life would never be the same. He rose and walked in circles, checking and rechecking his revelation. Was there a flaw in his thinking? A gap in his logic? There was no flaw, no gap. This was beyond intellect or logic. It was something more profound, a simple acceptance that needed to be made. It was the truth about himself.

Until that moment, he had been like the deer, seeing things as he had wanted them to be rather than as they truly were. He had been demanding the truth when it had been under his nose all along. He had been searching for miracles when the miracle of life had been playing out before him every second of every day.

He thought of the Lotus Sermon. How simple the answer seemed now. The flower had been just that—a flower, nothing more, nothing less. It was perfect as it was. To attempt to describe a flower was laughable when its beauty was on display for all to see. Yet only Kasyapa had understood the inadequacy of words. No wonder he had smiled at The Buddha's little stunt. No wonder The Buddha had handed the lotus to him.

Sardili felt a burning excitement in the pit of his stomach, a delicious secret he now shared. He was walking on air, his mind alive, his senses alert. He had seen the true nature of his own mind, and with it, the true nature of all things. He began to laugh, long and loud, at his own stupidity. His thoughts turned to Prajnatara and his laughter turned to a long howl of shame. How ridiculous he must have appeared to the little master; and how rude, shouting and thumping the table like a spoiled child, manhandling poor Brother Jaina! He had to return to the temple and beg for forgiveness.

He would go soon, and quickly, but not immediately. First, he wanted to continue through the trees and wander beside rivers and streams, fields and flowers, seeing everything in this new and perfect light. He wanted to climb high hills and look down on the earth with new eyes, to visit the towns and villages of India and talk with old men and children, beggars and noblemen, Brahmins and Untouchables. And he wanted to do these things with all the breathless excitement of a newborn child entering the world for the very first time.

It was midnight, some days later, when Sardili returned to the temple. An attendant monk was dozing in the entrance. He woke at Sardili's appearance and welcomed him back with the news that his room was waiting for him, untouched. Sardili slept peacefully that night, and in the morning he visited Prajnatara in his study once more. He found him sharing breakfast with Brother Jaina and stood before them, wringing his hands in shame.

"Welcome back Sardili," Prajnatara said with a broad smile, unsurprised to see him.

Sardili took a deep breath. "Master Prajnatara, Brother Jaina … I hardly know where to begin. I behaved disgracefully and I am truly sorry. I have come to beg your forgiveness."

"There is nothing to forgive, Sardili," Prajnatara said, holding out his hand to him. "Come and sit with us."

"I wish to make amends," he said, taking the master's hand gratefully.

"Then join us, and have some food."

"I can't believe I said such things …" he said, shaking his head, only his dark beard hiding the depth of his embarrassment.

"Think nothing of it. We have each been through the same things. I am just delighted you came back, and if I'm not mistaken, you seem a little happier too?"

"I am, Master."

"Excellent. It must have felt good to get a few things off your chest."

"It was stupid of me. Thoughtless."

"Nonsense, it is forgotten. Now eat," Prajnatara ordered.

Sardili helped himself to some fruit from the master's table and rolled it in his huge hands as he spoke.

"When I was away, I was able to think more clearly than I have for a long time. I decided that I would like to stay at the temple after all, if you will take me back."

"Of course," Prajnatara said, his face suddenly serious, "but only on one condition …"

"Name it, Master."

"You must teach wrestling again. I'm sure Brother Jaina won't mind."

"Not at all," Jaina said. "After all, Sardili's skill is far greater than my own."

"If Brother Jaina will assist me," Sardili said.

Jaina nodded his consent.

"Then it is settled," Prajnatara beamed. "Now take some rice too, Sardili. You have a busy day ahead of you."

And so Sardili returned to the daily life of the temple. Each morning he taught wrestling to the young monks and their skills improved quickly under his expert tutelage. Prajnatara watched from the shade of the banyan tree, enjoying the atmosphere created by the strange monk who had returned from the jungle like a man reborn.

Until one day, when the lesson had finished, he touched Sardili gently on the arm. "Come, walk with me by the river. It's quiet down there."

They strolled to the water's edge in silence and turned to follow the course of the river through the trees. In the shade of a great banyan Prajnatara stopped and spoke. "You can stay at the temple as long as you wish, stay forever if you like, but why waste any more time?"

"I'm not sure I understand," Sardili said with a frown.

Prajnatara took him by the arm and they continued along the riverbank. "We both know you have arrived at the truth, Sardili."

"That is not for me to say," Sardili replied, his voice husky, barely more than a whisper.

"No, it is for me to say, and I say it to you now."

Sardili halted and his eyes filled with tears. No words could pass his lips. Prajnatara took his hand and gave him time to weep, then led him along the river's edge once more, as if holding a child in danger of falling, until Sardili finally found words.

"I have never spoken of this before, but I saw you once, many years ago, in Kanchipuram."

"Kanchipuram?" Prajnatara exclaimed. "A wonderful city. I have not been there in many years."

"I was little more than a boy at the time," Sardili said. "You gave a sermon in the park. You held up a flower."

"The Lotus Sermon?"

"Yes."

"I remember," Prajnatara smiled. "It's one of my favorites. It always gets people thinking."

"You could say that," Sardili said with a bitter laugh. "It certainly got me thinking. More than that, it bewitched me. Consumed me. The riddle of what Kasyapa saw in the flower made me give up everything to find the answer."

"And did you find your answer?"

"No."

"Why not?"

"Because it wasn't a riddle."

"What made you think it was?" Prajnatara probed gently.

"My mind."

"The mind never tires of playing tricks on us," Prajnatara said with a shake of his head.

They walked in silence until they reached the fork in the river and Prajnatara stopped, his expression suddenly serious. "Sardili, once you have discovered The Way, there is no need to keep rereading the signs. There are countless souls waiting to be enlightened. You must go out and help to awaken them from delusion. This is your destiny."

"What about the temple?" Sardili asked.

"Don't worry about the temple. We will continue as we always have. Brother Jaina can teach the wrestling. His belly will grow big if he allows you to do all the work."

"But I will miss it here, Master. It's so beautiful."

"And the temple will miss you, Sardili. But there is important work to be done. What has been passed to you must now be passed onto others."

"How will I do that, Master?"

"How do any of us do it? It's a difficult task Sardili, but The Buddha has set down his wisdom in the scriptures and rituals that we follow."

"I don't think I can teach like that," Sardili said guardedly, "Scriptures, rituals, they are not the real truth."

"Perhaps not, but scriptures are useful in pointing The Way. Rituals are an important discipline. What will you do instead?"

"I will point directly at the truth."

"That's a very ambitious method, Sardili."

"I will make people see."

Prajnatara's eyes looked into his and for a moment, Sardili had the feeling they were seeing past his flesh and bones to a place far beyond the soft waters and rich jungles of Pallava. When they returned, they held him in their steady gaze.

"Yes, I believe you will Sardili," Prajnatara said, smiling broadly and clapping him firmly on the shoulder. "I truly believe you will."

密林

PART 1
JUNGLE

Bodhidharma

The monk followed the jungle path beneath towering rosewood and teak, past tamarind trees laden with ripe fruit, and banana trees with giant leaves reaching out to the morning sun. He stopped at a mango tree and picked the ripest offerings for later in the day before continuing into the dark heart of the jungle. Here the trees grew so close that they formed a dense canopy over the earth. Only the occasional ray of light found its way through the mesh of leaves, to dance on the jungle floor or illuminate one of the flowers that grew in that hot dark world. And when it did, the monk considered himself blessed to see such wonders.

He moved quickly, carrying few possessions: a blanket, a bowl, an iron pot, and a pair of old sandals that hung from his walking staff and swung in time with his step.

The jungle's carpet of twigs and leaves felt good beneath his feet and the scent of spice trees and decaying undergrowth filled his nostrils like a rich perfume. Fallen fruit littered the jungle floor, shaken down by the wind and the monkeys that jumped and shrieked overhead. Now and again a new piece of fruit would fall, narrowly missing his head. He would scowl up at the treetops and shake his staff at the monkeys, ordering them to show some respect to The Buddha's messenger. The monkeys would screech in reply and turn, showing him their tails in a gesture that spoke as clearly as any words.

By late morning the jungle had begun to thin. Soon he left the shade of the trees altogether and emerged into the blinding light of the open country. It was springtime in the kingdom of Pallava and the distant hills were a startling blue. The kurinji was in bloom. It was a good omen because the kurinji flowered only once in twelve years. The monk considered making a detour to sit among these rarest of flowers, but time was against him and he pressed on.

He picked up a country road that twisted through fields of wild flowers and sharp elephant-grass. Hoofprints in the dried mud told of oxen that had walked the same path some time before. He followed their plodding footsteps until the shadows disappeared and the sun was directly overhead. Then he laid down his staff in the shade of a purple jacaranda and prepared to drink tea and meditate.

He collected a pile of twigs, which burst into flame at the first spark of his flint, then set a pot of water to boil. While he waited, he laid out his ingredients: tea leaves hand picked from the wild bushes that grew in the region, sugar crystals, cardamom, and cinnamon bark. When the water boiled, he added the ingredients to the pot and set it aside to cool before taking a sip. The tea was just as he liked it: strong, sweet, and fragrant.

He closed his eyes and inhaled deeply, emptying his mind of all thought, fixing on nothing, until he was free to take in everything. The eye of his mind filled the sky and looked down on the green earth below before departing to explore the heavens. Moving freely in the farthest reaches of the cosmos, he occupied galaxies and worlds beyond description or knowledge, until his awareness filled the entire vast emptiness of the void. And then it was still. Neither moving nor seeking, unaware of self or other, it was one with all things, simply being.

By late afternoon, the monk had reached the banks of a slow-moving river. Reeds grew so tall that they obscured his view. He stepped among them, sweeping them aside until he saw what he was looking for, a rickety old jetty that stretched out into the brown water. He continued along the riverbank, enjoying the music of the reeds and the water, until a new melody reached his ears, the tinkling laughter of children.

A boy and girl were standing waist-deep in the water. The boy was young and bright eyed, with a ready smile. The girl was older, almost a woman. She was washing her brother's hair and his dark curls glistened as she massaged coconut oil into his scalp. Her own hair had already been washed and combed, and hung long and straight down her slim back. She bowed to the monk and prodded her little brother to do the same.

"Greetings Master," she called.

"Greetings, child."

The boy bowed too, but there was mischief in his eyes. "Master, I have a question," he shouted.

"Then ask it," the monk said.

"Why don't you wear your sandals?"

The girl prodded her brother angrily. It was bad karma to poke fun at monks, but this monk answered good-naturedly. "I like to feel the earth beneath my feet."

"Then why carry them at all?" the boy asked, ignoring his sister's efforts to silence him.

"Sometimes the ground is covered in sharp stones or thorns. Then I wear them."

"If I had sandals, I would wear them all the time," the boy said.

"Then your feet would grow soft," the monk laughed, "and you would be afraid to feel the earth against your skin. And that would be a sad day because you would forget how good it feels."

The boy was about to say more, but his sister pushed his head under the water and rubbed his hair vigorously. The monk chuckled to himself as he continued on his way to the jetty.

The old ferryman sat in his usual place, watching the river go by, as he had for so many years. A tremor in the jetty's ancient beams told of a new passenger approaching. The old man did not turn to see who it was, preferring instead to try and guess from the footsteps. These were unusual, and for a moment he could not place them. They were not the steps of one of his regular passengers, of that he was certain. The tread was light and balanced, yet the jetty swayed under a considerable weight. He could recall such an effect only once before, when he had rowed a tall young monk across the water.

"Sardili!" he said, turning with a smile.

The figure on the jetty was not the young monk he remembered. A tangle of black hair fell onto immense shoulders. A thick beard hung down over a threadbare black robe. Worn leather sandals swung from the end of a gnarled walking staff. The stranger would have been a fearsome sight, were it not for the eyes that twinkled with mischief and laughter.

"Is that you, Sardili?" the old ferryman asked, shielding his eyes from the sun.

"Yes, my friend," came the answer.

"I hardly recognized you," the ferryman said with a frown, "Whatever happened to that clean-cut young man who passed this way before?"

The monk grinned and spread his hands. "He has been wandering."

"Wandering? That doesn't sound like him. He was such an earnest young fellow when I met him—so full of purpose. Did he lose his purpose?"

"On the contrary. I think he found it."

"In Prajnatara's temple?"

"Yes."

"Well I'm pleased to hear it," the old man said, slipping into his boat. "Come, climb in. We can talk as we cross."

Sardili obeyed and the old ferryman began to row, his strong, steady strokes belying his advanced years and the skeletal thinness of his body.

"You're visiting Prajnatara again?" he asked.

His passenger nodded.

"I'm sure he will be delighted to see you, if he recognizes you, that is, Sardili."

Sardili smiled. No one had called him by that name for a long time.

"You have a new name?" the old man asked, as if reading his thoughts.

"I do," he smiled.

"Tell me."

"I have been given the name Bodhidharma."

"Bodhidharma?" the old man chuckled to himself. "Well well, to be called 'Teacher of Enlightenment' that is quite an honor."

"And quite a burden."

"Perhaps, but Prajnatara is no fool. If he gave you such a name, you must deserve it. I will call you by that name from now on, Bodhidharma." Then the old man saw the sadness in the younger man's eyes and his tone softened. "Go and see Prajnatara again. He will help you, like he did before."

Bodhidharma put his fingers in the warm brown water, then raised his hand and watched the golden droplets return to the river from his fingertips. "I should have visited him long ago," he said softly.

"They say that to enlighten someone can take countless lifetimes, or a single moment," the ferryman smiled, "so what's your hurry?"

"You were a monk yourself?" Bodhidharma asked.

"I have been many things in my life," the ferryman answered, steering the boat expertly to the shore and securing it against the blackened timbers of the jetty.

Bodhidharma stepped ashore. "What do I owe you?"

"Nothing," the ferryman said with a wave of his hand.

"You said that last time you rowed me across."

"Do you think I want bad karma by taking money from a penniless monk?" the ferryman asked testily.

"You don't care about karma," Bodhidharma said, looking down from the jetty, "I have never seen anyone as happy as you are here on this river. You would row the whole world across for free if you didn't need to eat."

"We all need to eat," the old man said with sad smile.

"I guess we do," Bodhidharma said, bending to grip the old man's hand in silent thanks before entering the waiting jungle.

A parrot screeched a greeting and he returned its call without breaking stride. His thoughts were on the message he had received from Prajnatara and his fingers closed on the paper that he had kept in the folds of his robe. The hastily scribbled note had requested his presence at the temple. The tone had been casual and friendly, but Prajnatara never did anything without reason, and as Bodhidharma made his way to the little master's temple, he wondered, not for the first time, what that reason might be.

Yulong Fort, China

Kuang's breath came out in strangled gasps. Snot hung from his nose and a rich, thick phlegm gathered in his throat. He wanted to stop and hawk it up but that would mean giving up his slender lead over the other runners, and that lead was too precious. Corporal Chen was waiting for him at the top of the hill. By the time he reached him, Kuang's thighs felt fit to burst, but he was still first and hoped for a word of praise from the corporal.

"Too slow, hurry up," the corporal snarled, pushing him on down the shingle slope.

Two more soldiers were close behind. Kuang lengthened his stride to get away from them and fought the urge to look behind. It would only slow him down. The crunch of their footsteps told him they were only a few paces back. The temptation was too strong. Unable to resist, he stole a glance behind. They looked as tired as he was. It was good to know.

He reached a deserted farm building and scrambled over the outer wall. Earlier he had vaulted the same wall in a single leap, but this was his second lap of the training ground and this time he was forced to grit his teeth and haul himself up slowly. He lay across the top of the wall for a moment, wondering breathlessly how much longer he could keep up his furious pace.

The next two runners began to help one another to climb the wall. He despised them. He did not need help. He would be first, the best, the only one to get round the course unaided. He jumped down and set off again through thick mud that sucked at his feet, sapping his strength with each step. A pool of black water came into view. The stench pierced his nostrils. The place had once been a cesspit. More recently it had been allowed to fill with rainwater and Corporal Chen had thrown in rocks and tree branches to make it more difficult to cross.

Kuang jumped in up to his waist and felt his feet sink into the sludge. By the time he had reached the center of the pool, the water was at his chest and the stench had become unbearable. The first time he had crossed, he had succeeded in holding his breath, but this time he was too tired. He took a gulp of the foul air and retched. Nothing came up except a streak of yellow bile. He had not eaten for hours.

Corporal Chen was waiting on the far side of the pool. Kuang could see him beckoning and hear the insults ringing out across the water: he was too slow, too lazy, a disgrace to his parents, his ancestors, and all the soldiers who had served in the imperial Chinese army throughout the ages.

Was it true, he wondered? He was trying his best, like most of the others in his troop. They had not asked to join the army. They were not the elite cavalry that was winning glorious victories against the barbarians on the steppes. They were conscripts, little more than boys, stationed in a remote fort on the border with Tibet, a thousand li from civilization. A thousand li from home.

Corporal Chen was still shouting insults in his ear as he dragged himself from the water and stumbled along the gravel path to the remains of an old barn. The building had burned down years ago, leaving only crumbling outer walls and blackened timbers of the roof. He scaled the wall and climbed the first roof strut, ignoring the splinters that dug deeply into his hands. By the time he had reached the main crossbeam, the two soldiers behind him were at the wall. From their grunts and groans, he could tell they were suffering too, and smiled grimly to himself. They would not catch him. Not today.

He was near the end of the crossbeam when he noticed four dark shapes passing beneath him, four soldiers, crawling on their hands and knees to avoid being seen by Corporal Chen.

"Hey, you're cheating!" he yelled, searching frantically for Corporal Chen, but the corporal was nowhere to be seen.

He jumped down and chased after the four who had stolen his lead. He saw them by a pile of logs at the bottom a grassy slope. The soldiers hefted a log onto their shoulders and set off up the hill. He grabbed a log of his own and hurried after them, his curses lost in his deep gasps for air. Soon he began to catch the last of the four. When he was close enough, he drove his log into the soldier's back, sending him sprawling. The soldier lay in the grass, too weary to get up, his log rolling down the hill.

"You'll pay for that, Kuang," he snarled.

Kuang ignored him and hurried after the next man, who he

recognized as Tsun. Tsun was big and powerful. During his short time in the barracks, he had already begun to intimidate the weaker conscripts. Kuang had kept out of Tsun's way, but he now was too angry to care and jammed his log into Tsun's knee.

Tsun stumbled and dropped his log with a curse but recovered instantly, spun around and smashed his fist into Kuang's face. Kuang fell. His log landed on top of him. The punch had caught him on the nose and his vision misted over. He struggled to get to his feet, but was dazed by the punch. Tsun kicked him hard in the ribs. He rolled away, hoping to make some distance and let his head clear, but Tsun was too quick and pinned him on his back against the hillside. He saw Tsun's black outline against the white sky, his fist pulled back for the first of many punches.

They never came.

Corporal Chen wrapped Tsun's arm expertly behind his back and dragged him off. "Plenty of time for that later," he said grimly, shoving Tsun away to fetch his log. Then he turned to Kuang. "I saw what you did, Kuang. Do fifty push-ups here and another lap of the course. Then rejoin us at the bottom of the hill."

Kuang was about to protest, but the look on the corporal's face changed his mind. He turned on his front to begin his push-ups. He was exhausted, and after five, his arms began to tremble. He gritted his teeth and continued to ten. Corporal Chen stood over him, waiting for him to stop or rest. "Why were you cheating, Kuang? It brings you no reward. I see everything you do. You have only disgraced yourself and dishonored your parents, your ancestors ..." The corporal continued, but his words faded into the distance as Kuang slipped away to a place where nothing could reach him. He was too proud to stop or rest, and with the corporal standing over him, he would do all the push-ups. At any other time, fifty would be easy, but now, with his strength gone, he knew the pain would be immense. The only way to get through it would be to take his mind somewhere far away.

He lowered himself to do another push up. A blade of the coarse mountain grass pricked his forehead. He turned to the side, but as he lowered himself again, it tickled his cheek. It reminded him of a place and a childhood he had left behind, and all but forgotten. He followed the memory until it led him to another hillside far from the barren wilderness of Yulong Fort. He was back in the rolling green landscape of his homeland in Hubei. His friends were there, at the top of the hill, beckoning to him. He set off up the slope to meet them, but as he did, they turned and ran away. He could no longer see them, but he could hear their laughter on the wind. He ran hard to reach the brow of the hill and see where they had gone. He pushed harder, counting each step up the slope: twenty-seven, twenty-eight, twenty-nine ... he was on high ground and the wind roared in his ears ... thirty-two, thirty-three, thirty-four ... The sun appeared over the brow of the hill and shone so brightly that he couldn't see. Still he pushed on ... forty-five, forty-six, forty-seven. Time slowed. His counting slowed, almost to a stop, but not quite. Forty-eight. His nostrils were filled with the smell of the grass, a scent so powerful it cut off his breath. Forty-nine. His eyes were screwed shut against the sun and he was running blind. He was almost there.

Fifty. He had reached the summit.

His vision returned slowly. He rolled onto his back and stared up at the white sky, then sat up and looked for Corporal Chen. The corporal had gone, and only his voice could be heard in the distance, cursing the other soldiers. Kuang rose and walked up the hill slowly, his arms limp by his sides. When he reached the top he realized something was missing. He had left his log behind. If Corporal Chen saw him without it, he would only add to his punishment. He went back to retrieve it.

When he reached the top again, he saw the others had finished the course and the corporal had marked out a square on the ground. The soldiers had removed their tunics and were wrapping their hands in rough strips of sackcloth. He made his way down the hill to join them, wondering what was happening. When he arrived Corporal Chen yelled at him furiously. "What are you doing here, Kuang? Go round the course again like I told you. I'll be watching you. Move!"

Some of the soldiers jeered as he went past. They hated him. He knew that. He had made no effort to fit in. He had always tried to be better than the rest, and they despised him for that. He did not care. In his heart, he knew he would leave them all behind one day. He would become a great soldier. This was just a test that had to be endured.

A different voice cut through the jeers. "Keep going, Kuang." It was Huo, who had the bunk above his own in the barracks, "I saw who cheated."

Kuang gave Huo a small nod of thanks before setting off around the course once more.

"The rules are very simple," Corporal Chen told the gathered soldiers. "No biting. No gouging. No attacks to the groin. China needs her soldiers to produce more little soldiers." He smiled, but no one shared his grim humor. "You can punch, kick, and wrestle. You win when your opponent is knocked out or submits. You stop only when I say. There are no other rules." He scanned the pale faces waiting around the makeshift square. "Wan and Lei, you are first."

The two fighters stepped into the square and circled each other warily.

"Hurry up!" he bellowed.

They charged at one another, flailing wildly, neither in control, until a wild punch from Wan connected with Lei's chin. Lei's legs buckled and his punches grew weaker. Wan sensed victory and landed another hard punch on his opponent's nose. Bright streaks of red splashed Lei's chest. He doubled over, shielding his face with his arms.

Wan looked to Corporal Chen, hoping he had done enough to win, but the corporal stared at him impassively. Wan shrugged and drove his knee toward Lei's head to finish him. Lei moved his arm at the last moment and Wan's knee connected with an elbow instead. He gasped in pain and held his knee tightly. Still dazed, Lei rose from his crouch to see what was happening. Wan could not afford to let Lei recover. Ignoring the agony in his knee, he rushed forward, grabbed Lei behind the head, and pulled him onto his left knee. This time the blow connected hard and Lei crumpled to the ground with no more than a sigh.

Kuang had been watching from the top of the hill. He had done a little wrestling at the training camp in his hometown, but this was far more serious, and he was already exhausted. Whatever happened, he knew he was going to get hurt. He made his way around the course slowly, hoping to regain a little energy before having to fight. Corporal Chen's voice could be heard barking orders at the soldiers, and the dull thudding blows of the fights echoed around the stony training ground.

By the time he rejoined the rest, the other soldiers had recovered their energy. Some were limbering up and stretching in preparation for their turn in Corporal Chen's brutal matches, while others stood nervously waiting their turn. He collapsed beside them, hoping to rest. His hopes were quickly dashed when the corporal ordered him into the square, scanning the others for a suitable opponent. Even before the name was called out, Kuang knew who it would be.

"Lung!"

Lung was easily the biggest soldier in the garrison, a farm laborer from Hunan, and hugely powerful. Though not vicious by nature, Lung had the look of a seasoned brawler, and Kuang prepared for the worst.

They stepped into the square and Kuang's eyes locked onto Lung's for the first time. The small, round eyes were impossible to read, but he knew he could expect no mercy. He stayed at the edge of the square and fiddled with his hand-wrapping, waiting for a little freshness to return to his limbs. Lung figured out what he was doing and crossed the square with a roar, launching a barrage of punches at his head. He slipped to the side and struck at Lung, but the bigger man's power drove him back. He stumbled and covered his head with his hands. Heavy punches smashed his arms and shoulders. He threw two more punches of his own and felt his fists make contact with Lung's face, but Lung was unstoppable.

He skirted the edge of the square, hoping for a moment's respite, but Lung was on him, catching him with a hard punch in the stomach that doubled him over. Lung smashed a knee into his body. Ignoring the pain, Kuang threw his arms around Lung's legs to tackle him. Lung sprawled, throwing his legs behind and out of reach. His great weight bore down on Kuang's back and he pounded vicious punches into his sides. Kuang drove forward to get a better grip on Lung's legs, but Lung was too strong. Something had to change.

He dropped to his knees and twisted suddenly. Lung lost his grip for a moment, but regained control by falling on top of him. Now he was trapped beneath Lung's bulk. He pushed and struck out with his elbow, catching Lung in the face, stunning him for a second. It was the chance he needed to squirm out. He stood and aimed a kick at Lung's head, but tiredness had made him slow. Lung caught his leg and threw him to the ground, landing squarely on top of him and driving the air from his body. Now he was pinned securely, and Lung began to strike at his head with the base of his fist.

He turned away in desperation. It was a mistake. He had given Lung his back. Lung's massive arms wrapped around his neck and drew a strangle hold in tight. He heard a roaring in his ears, felt the prickling redness behind his eyes. The world was closing to a small dot. With the last of his strength, he stood up with Lung on his back before blacking out.

When he woke, the pressure was gone. For a moment, he thought the fight was over and he had been carried to the side. But then he saw the eyes of the other soldiers on him and saw he was still in the square. Lung was beneath him. The throbbing on the back of his skull told him what had happened. His head had flown back when they had fallen and struck Lung hard in the face.

He spun and found himself on top for the first time. Lung's nose was broken. Blood was running into his eyes from a deep gash and his hands were rubbing frantically at his eyes. Kuang felt a stab of pity for the big man. It lasted for just a moment—the fight was not over yet—Lung was a formidable opponent and could recover in an instant. He stood over him and raised his foot to stamp on Lung's head. Corporal Chen stepped forward but Kuang was beyond waiting for the order to stop. He dropped to one knee and began punching steadily, until he felt two soldiers dragging him off his beaten opponent.

He stood with his hands on his knees, gulping in deep lungfuls of the thin mountain air, grateful for the respite, but his ordeal was not over. Corporal Chen nodded to Tsun, who was ready and waiting with his hands wrapped. Tsun rushed at him. Kuang raised his hands in futile defense. A huge punch found its way past his guard and caught him on the temple. He crashed to the ground. Then Tsun was standing over him, kicking at his head and ribs. He curled into a ball to protect himself and rolled away, scrambling to get to his feet. Tsun followed and kicked at his head, clipping him on the jaw. He fell again, badly dazed. Tsun pinned him on his back and straddled his chest. There was no escape. Vicious punches began to fall. He fought to push Tsun off, but Tsun's weight was planted firmly on his chest. He parried Tsun's punches and moved to prevent them from connecting hard. He struck back, but from his position on his back his punches had no effect. Tsun gripped his wrists and pinned his hands to his chest, then moved forward to sit on them and finish him off. As Tsun shifted his weight, Kuang bucked hard with one huge final effort. It was enough to lift Tsun a fraction and he slipped out between Tsun's legs.

Tsun spun and seized him. Kuang felt a knee smash his ribs. The stunning pain made him feel faint. He threw his arms desperately around one of Tsun's legs, but was too weak to take him down. Tsun resisted easily and struck at his head with hard punches. Too dazed to think any more, Kuang clung on grimly as Tsun punched him. All sense of time left him. After what seemed like an age, the blows became lighter. Tsun was still striking him—now he was using his palms instead of his fists. The blows registered faintly, somewhere in the distance. He guessed Tsun's hands were too damaged to hit hard and he clung to Tsun's thigh with a satisfied grin.

At last Corporal Chen sent two soldiers to pry him off. They dragged him from the square and laid him on his back, staring up at the empty sky. He did not move. His eyes closed and he drifted into a dreamless sleep.

Some time later, he did not know how long, he was dimly aware of more matches going on nearby. Then the sounds faded and he heard nothing. When he woke again, the sky was grey and the air cold. He began to shiver uncontrollably. Each new breath sent a stab of pain through his side. His head was pounding. His lips were swollen and there was a metallic taste on his tongue. He tried to stand but a searing pain ripped through his body and he fell back, groaning.

He considered calling for help, but his pride prevented him. He closed his eyes and waited, wondering if he would get back to the barracks before nightfall. Eventually he heard the crunch of footsteps on the shingle track. He tried to sit up and see who was coming. It was too painful. Instead, he raised his head, breathing hard with the effort. The approaching figure was nothing more than a silhouette in half-light. He laid his head back, exhausted, and waited. Finally a head appeared above him, but he could not make out the face against the darkening sky.

The Temple in the Jungle

Bodhidharma followed the narrow jungle path until he saw the fork in the river. The temple was near. Soon it came into view, its pale stonework gleaming in the mottled sunlight between the trees. A lone figure was working in the gardens and he recognized the slight frame at once. It was Prajnatara, tending the flowers. He called out a greeting and Prajnatara turned, shading his eyes from the sun. At the sight of his old student, the little master let out a cheer and hurried through the the trees, beaming with delight.

"Bodhidharma! I knew you would come. Did you get my message? Of course you did, you're here, aren't you? Well, well, let me look at you. You look ..." Prajnatara paused, looking him up and down disapprovingly, "... quite different from the last time I saw you. Heavens, yes. It's understandable. You have been on the road a long time and traveled a great distance to be here. I heard you have been wandering all over India. But listen to me chattering on like an old fool and keeping you standing out here in this dreadful heat! Come inside, my dear Bodhidharma. Come into the shade and cool off. You must be tired, hungry, thirsty?"

Prajnatara led him to his private chamber and rang a bell. A novice monk appeared and Prajnatara ordered refreshments for his special guest. "It's so good to see you again," he continued breathlessly, "I hardly recognized you after all this time. I see you no longer wear the orange robe of the order. And you certainly have a lot more hair ..."

Bodhidharma shrugged apologetically.

"Well never mind, it's of no real concern how a master dresses, and besides, you always were a bit of a special case. I remember the day you first appeared at our temple, how you showed us your wrestling skills. What a time that was! The young monks still talk about it today. Brother Jaina still reckons you're the finest wrestler he's ever come across."

"How is Brother Jaina?" Bodhidharma asked, taken aback by the master's overwhelming warmth.

"Oh, he is fine, and looking forward to seeing you, but all in good time, all in good time. First we must talk; or rather, you must wash, and eat, and then we can talk. Where is that boy?" He grumbled. Just then the novice appeared with a basin of water for their guest and Bodhidharma washed his hands and bathed his tired feet.

"I see you still wear your sandals on your staff," Prajnatara said, handing him a vial of warm oil to massage into his feet.

"I'm saving them for a special occasion," Bodhidharma said with a grin.

"Then keep them nice and clean," Prajnatara said.

Bodhidharma raised an eyebrow inquisitively, but Prajnatara changed the subject quickly. "You look as strong and fit as ever. Even bigger than before if I'm not mistaken, and all muscle by the look of it. You still exercise?"

"Every day," Bodhidharma answered.

"Splendid! I'm delighted to hear it. Fitness is very important, a lot more important than people realize."

The novice reappeared with refreshments and Prajnatara had him set the tray down before his guest.

"Please have some first," Bodhidharma insisted. Prajnatara was about to decline, but knowing his former student would not eat until he had taken something first, he helped himself to a small handful of rice, leaving the rest untouched.

"When I got your message ..." Bodhidharma began, but Prajnatara held up his hand to silence him. "First eat," he ordered.

Bodhidharma was hungry. He obeyed. The food was simple but tasty, just as he remembered it. He lifted a handful of rice and vegetables in his fingers and nodded his appreciation, his mouth too full to speak.

"We have a new cook," Prajnatara smiled. "I have been instructing him personally. Now I think he's even better than the old one."

Bodhidharma ate quickly, sensing Prajnatara's eagerness to talk. He also sensed it was a matter of some importance, despite Prajnatara's attempt at small talk. As soon as he had finished, Prajnatara leaned forward and squeezed Bodhidharma's arm affectionately. "Forgive me for coming to the point so quickly. I asked you here because I have a very important request to make of you."

"There is nothing to forgive, Master," Bodhidharma said, "I should be the one apologizing, not you. I should have visited long ago. I have been remiss. And whatever request you have, consider it done."

"It is kind of you to be so understanding," Prajnatara said, "but please hear me out before agreeing to anything."

Bodhidharma was about to protest but something in his former master's face made him sit back in silence and let him speak.

Prajnatara waited, seemingly unsure how to begin.

Bodhidharma could feel the little master testing different opening lines in his head, and he wondered what sort of request could cause Prajnatara to hesitate so. All at once the answer seemed to come to Prajnatara and he spoke breathlessly, as if relating the latest temple gossip to an old friend. "Recently I have been in correspondence with The Venerable Ananda, you know who he is, of course..."

Bodhidharma nodded slowly. "Of course, The Venerable Ananda is the Buddhist patriarch, the living embodiment of Buddha on Earth. Every Buddhist knows this."

"Quite so," Prajnatara said. "He is also a wonderful man. He was my master when I was young. I studied with him for many years in Nalanda. It was Ananda who enlightened me and showed me The Way. Now he is the patriarch and Grandmaster of Nalanda, and no monk has ever been more deserving of such a title. Since taking up that position, Ananda has worked tirelessly to ensure the transmission of the lamp."

"The lamp?" Bodhidharma asked, determined to follow Prajnatara's rambling speech.

"Yes, the transmission of The Buddha's teachings! Once the flame of enlightenment has been lit, it must never be allowed to go out. Ananda's efforts have been rewarded. Already the teachings have spread far beyond the five kingdoms of India—west into Persia, north into Central Asia, and east into China, where they are proving to be immensely popular. Recently we learned that the emperor of China himself is an avid follower of Buddhism."

"That is encouraging news," Bodhidharma said.

"It is excellent news. Excellent news. The Venerable Ananda has made it his life's work to ensure people around the world are not denied the perfection of The Buddha's teachings.

"He must be very happy," Bodhidharma said.

"He is, but in his most recent correspondence he also intimated that he is gravely concerned." Prajnatara paused, his brow knotted in a frown. "He writes of visions that appear to him with great regularity and clarity. They tell him that the future of The Way lies in the East, in China. The importance of bringing the teachings to the Chinese people cannot be overstated."

"And this concerns him, you say?" Bodhidharma said, hoping to steer the little master toward the point of the conversation.

"Yes, most gravely, because China is vast, Bodhidharma! It stretches from the Himalayas in the west to the eastern Ocean, from the tropical jungles in the south to the frozen steppes of the north; and the population outnumbers all the five kingdoms of India put together. The journey to China is long and perilous. Only a handful of teachers are prepared to make it, or capable of enduring the hardships along the way."

"I see."

"I'm glad you appreciate the situation," Prajnatara said solemnly.

A brief silence followed. It seemed Prajnatara was waiting for a reply.

"These are very important matters," Bodhidharma offered, wondering what the master was expecting to hear.

"Vitally important! They are the key to the very future of The Way. So what do you say, my dear Bodhidharma?" Prajnatara demanded, the first signs of exasperation creeping into his voice.

"What do I say about what?" Bodhidharma asked, more bewildered than ever.

"About what we have been discussing …"

"I'm sorry Master, I have no idea what you're talking about," Bodhidharma said with a frown.

"About going there, of course."

"Going where?"

"Oh, by the Buddha's bones!" Prajnatara shouted. "To China, where else?"

Bodhidharma stared into his eyes and saw that he was serious. He let out a roar of laughter that shattered the silence. "You want to send me to China?" he asked, his body still shaking with mirth.

"That was what I had in mind," Prajnatara said coolly, "and I don't consider it a laughing matter."

"Oh please forgive me Master," Bodhidharma begged, wiping the tears of laughter from his eyes, "and please don't think me rude. I'm flattered, really I am. I'm only laughing at the irony of it all, because, well, I haven't told you yet, but I am a hopeless teacher. In the five years that I've been away, I've achieved nothing. I'm ashamed to say I have no disciples, not even a single student. The longest anyone has stayed with me has been six weeks, and this is teaching Indians, my own countrymen, people who speak the same language as me. So you see, I couldn't possibly go to China and enlighten the Chinese. It would be a wasted journey."

"I see," Prajnatara said slowly.

"I'm the last person on earth you should want to send," Bodhidharma said with a apologetic shrug.

Prajnatara sat quietly for a while, considering his words carefully before speaking. "Why do you think you failed, Bodhidharma?"

"My methods don't work."

"And what methods are those?" Prajnatara probed.

"Pointing directly to reality."

"That is a very ambitious method, as I think I told you before."

"You did Master, and I must admit you were right. But you know my thoughts on the matter. I don't believe in debating scriptures and following rituals. For me it's just so many empty words and empty practices. I would be a hypocrite if I started doing all that now. I hope you understand."

"I understand more than you think," Prajnatara reassured him. "You see The Way clearly Bodhidharma, but you don't see how to illuminate it, yet. That is another skill you must learn."

"You think I should teach scriptures and follow rituals?"

"I think students need something to grasp. You can't simply snap your fingers and set them free. Things are never that easy, not for a teacher nor for a student."

"Maybe you're right," Bodhidharma conceded. "I seem to be getting nowhere by trying to take a shorter path."

"There is no shorter path. There is only the path. Each person must be allowed to tread it in their own time."

Bodhidharma nodded glumly, "I guess you are right, as usual."

"It's never easy to break the spell of desire," Prajnatara said. "Don't be too hard on yourself. Remember how long you yourself toiled under the yoke of delusion before you saw the truth."

"I remember all too well," Bodhidharma said with a bitter smile.

"Try to be a bit more patient, with yourself and your students. I imagine you drive them quite hard."

Bodhidharma stared at the floor without comment.

"Brother Jaina tells me you're renowned all over Pallava," Prajnatara continued, "The villagers call you the warrior monk. I think they're perhaps a little afraid of you."

"What are they afraid of? They have nothing to fear," Bodhidharma said indignantly.

"Of course not, but give people a chance to get to know you. Remember, not everyone is born to the Warrior Caste, as you were. Take them one small step at a time and they will make the final leap when they are ready."

The old ferryman had been right. Prajnatara was wise and Bodhidharma felt he had been enlightened all over again.

"Don't misunderstand me," Prajnatara smiled, "I admire your conviction, really I do. You're not wrong when you say scriptures and rituals are not the true Way. Still, they point in the right direction. And besides, the methods themselves are not the real issue."

"They're not?"

"No. It's the discipline required that is important. Even students who reach enlightenment may falter if they're not strong. You have that strength—I saw it in you when you arrived. It's in your blood. I knew that if you grasped the subtle beauty of The Way, you would never stray from the path, and nor have you. I did not give you the name Bodhidharma for nothing. You will be a great teacher one day."

"When you gave me that name, I thought it was the greatest honor a man could have," Bodhidharma said with a heavy heart. "Now it hangs around my neck like a curse."

"It is neither a blessing nor a curse," Prajnatara said. "It is simply your destiny. The name Bodhidharma will be known throughout the world. I have seen it in a vision, and these things cannot be ignored."

"You are too kind, Master."

"Nonsense," Prajnatara waved his hand dismissively, "and besides, your disdain for the scriptures will not be an issue in China. In fact, it will be something of a blessing. I'm told there are very few translations of the Sutras into Chinese, and those that do exist are of dubious quality. Your "direct methods" as you call them will be a useful way to spread the teachings, at least at present."

"You still want me to go to China?" Bodhidharma asked, astonished.

"Of course."

"Even after everything I told you?"

"You are the perfect envoy," Prajnatara said, nodding vigorously, "Trust me on this. And besides, I have already mentioned you to The Venerable Ananda and he agrees."

"He does?"

"Completely." Prajnatara hesitated, examining his fingers before continuing. "There is another reason why you were chosen for this task, a rather more pragmatic reason. You're young and strong, and like I said, the journey is long and arduous."

Bodhidharma was finally beginning to see why he had been chosen for such a mission, "Long and arduous?" he repeated slowly, I believe "long and perilous" were your exact words, Master."

Prajnatara's pained expression returned. "They were? Yes, well, perhaps I did say that. Look, I won't lie to you Bodhidharma. I'll give you the facts as I know them." He paused to clear his throat. "The Venerable Ananda did inform me that several monks who went to China seem to have disappeared."

"Disappeared?"

"They have not been heard from again."

"How many, exactly?"

"How many what?"

"How many monks have never been heard from again?"

"Well I'm not sure of the exact figures. I suppose The Venerable Ananda might have some more precise statistics ..."

"Just approximately," Bodhidharma persisted.

"I believe four masters went to meet with the emperor of China in recent years. None succeeded."

"Why did they fail?"

"Two were quite old, and the journey is very demanding. There are mountains of dangerous cold, treacherous rivers, endless deserts. It's thought they perished on the way. On top of that, there are bandits and brigands in the hills. One may have been killed, or captured and enslaved. The fourth went by sea, a very long route. I believe his ship was either lost at sea or attacked by pirates."

"I see."

"The Venerable Ananda and I felt that a monk with a background like yours would be the ideal candidate to succeed in such a mission," Prajnatara said lightly, as if giving an answer to a simple puzzle. "If your skill with the bow and the sword is even half as good as your wrestling, you should have nothing to fear. In fact, heaven help any bandit who tries to stop you!"

"You make it sound easy," Bodhidharma scowled.

"It is not easy. Not at all. But then, the path never is. It is simply the path. And this is your path. Surely you can see that?"

Bodhidharma stared at him coolly.

"Besides," Prajnatara continued, "it's not all doom and danger. Think of the adventures you'll have, the places you'll see. You can go north to Magadha and bathe in the sacred waters of the Ganges. Make a pilgrimage to Bodh Gaya and meditate beneath the Tree of Enlightenment like The Buddha. You can visit Kapilavastu, Sarnath, and Kusinagara. And after all that, you can go to Nalanda, the greatest temple in the world, where The Venerable Ananda will be expecting you. He will help you prepare for your onward journey. You will climb the Himalayas and stand on the roof of the world. I climbed those mountains myself when I was young. They are so beautiful. I only wish I could see them once again before I die, but my place is here now. And then you will see China! Just think of it, an unimaginable land, known to the rest of us only through myth and legend. How I envy you."

He stopped abruptly to gauge the reaction of his disciple.

"It sounds like the two of you have it all planned," Bodhidharma said.

Prajnatara laughed. "The Venerable Ananda and I have written many times on the subject, that much is true. He is very excited about the possibility of your mission, very excited about you. But there is no need to answer right now, Bodhidharma. Think it over. Take as long as you wish. I know you will make the right decision."

"There is no need to think it over," Bodhidharma said quietly. "I will go."

Prajnatara's face lit up. "You will?"

"I will. If you say it is my destiny, then I will follow it."

"How wonderful!" Prajnatara clapped his hands in delight. "The Venerable Ananda will be so thrilled when I tell him."

"I would not want to disappoint the living embodiment of Buddha on Earth," Bodhidharma said with a grim smile.

"Oh Bodhidharma, you could never disappoint him, nor me! But I'm so happy that you have accepted. It is your path. I have seen it in a vision, and these things cannot be ignored." Prajnatara poured a little water for himself and took a sip. "On a more practical note, you will need more than your bowl and sandals for this journey. I will give you funds and provisions to help you reach Nalanda, and Ananda will help you from there. But we can make all those arrangements later, much later. First we should relax, and you can tell me where you have been wandering and preaching, and why you have waited so long before coming to visit us. I am very angry with you, young man, very very angry ..."

And so it was that Bodhidharma set off for an unknown land beyond the Himalayas, a place he could only imagine from a painting he had once seen, long ago, in the library of a temple he had visited. The painting had been unusual, most unlike the richly colored art of India. With just a few bold strokes of black ink on stark white paper, the artist had created an enormous winged serpent coiled around sharp towers of rock. Angry white water seethed beneath it, and a fine silver mist hung in the air. Curious markings ran down the side—Chinese writing, he had been told—though no one had any idea of their meaning. The effect had been startling; an alien world filled with unknown dangers. It was a land that could not have been more different from the warm flat jungles of his homeland, a place that was now both his destination and, if Prajnatara was to be believed, his destiny.

Kuang Returns to Barracks

Huo bent to help Kuang to his feet. "Come on, you fool," he sighed, straining to lift him, "let's get you back to the barracks. It's going to be freezing out here tonight."

Kuang struggled to stand. His body was wracked with pain. He took two faltering steps supporting himself on Huo's shoulder, but the pain was too great and his legs buckled beneath him. Huo caught him and lifted him in his arms like a baby, ignoring his groans. "No need to thank me," he said.

Huo had a fat lip and his left eye was black and swollen, despite which, he appeared in good spirits. He had clearly fared better in Corporal Chen's brutal training fights than Kuang had. "Why did you come and get me?" Kuang demanded sullenly.

"Corporal Chen sent me."

"He did?"

"When I told him you hadn't come back, he ordered me to come and get you."

"That's very caring of him."

"Try not to annoy him, Kuang. Just keep your head down and don't get noticed. That's what I do. It's the best way."

"I don't want to be like you."

"Good. I don't want to be like you, either."

They continued in silence until they reached the torch-lit compound inside the fort. Commander Tang's residence stood before them. The commander was the officer in charge of the fort, and as they drew nearer, Kuang twisted in Huo's arms.

"You can put me down now," he said.

"Don't be stupid, we're almost there."

"Put me down."

"Shut up," Huo laughed, "or I'll drop you here and leave you on the floor."

"Come on, put me down, please ..."

Huo gave in and put him down and Kuang walked despite the pain. Huo wondered why his friend was so determined to walk. Perhaps he didn't want Commander Tang to glance out of the window and see him being carried like a baby. When Huo noticed movement on the terrace outside the commander's residence, he guessed the real reason for Kuang's reaction. Weilin was outside.

Weilin was Commander Tang's daughter and often came out in the evening to tend her flowerpots or read a few pages from her book. Like all the soldiers in the fort, Huo watched her hungrily, from a distance. She was young and pretty. She was also the only young, pretty woman in the fort. But when it came to his chances with Weilin, he knew she may as well have been on the moon. Not only was she the commander's daughter, she was also betrothed to Captain Fu Sheng, a cavalry officer who was stationed on the northern frontier. The captain visited the fort only rarely, but his reputation was enough to deter any young man who might have been foolish enough to make advances to his fiancée.

Tonight, Weilin was reading by lamplight. The flame flickered in the sharp mountain wind, catching the soft curve of her cheek, the ripe lips. Her eyes were buried in her book. As they passed by, Huo was surprised to see her look up. Normally she ignored the soldiers coming and going around the fort but this time he saw her gaze follow Kuang as he passed. In a sudden flare of the torchlight, he was even more surprised to see a look of concern cross her face at the sight of Kuang's bruised and swollen face.

Kuang turned to hide his face from Weilin and hobbled toward the barracks as quickly as his aching legs would carry him. Huo hurried after him. "Hey, Kuang!" he whispered urgently, "don't even think about it!"

Kuang ignored him and continued in silence.

"Seriously, Kuang … I mean it. I really mean it."

"I don't know what you mean," Kuang said tersely as he mounted the barrack steps on stiff legs.

"Yes you do. You know exactly what I mean," Huo persisted.

Kuang ignored him and went inside. Huo looked back toward the commander's house. The flicker of the lamplight could still be seen in the distance. He waited a moment, watching the light play against the dark setting of the surrounding mountains, and then followed Kuang out of the cold night air and into the warm, stuffy embrace of the barracks.

A Pilgrim in Magadha

Bodhidharma crossed many rivers on his journey to the northern Kingdom of Magadha, but none stirred him like the Ganges. In the clear morning light, the vast expanse of sparkling brown water filled his vision. The river was the birthplace of a civilization and the artery that pumped life through the Buddhist heartland of Magadha. The Buddha himself had lived and preached all his life in this fertile plain. As Bodhidharma sat by the waters edge, he pictured The Buddha bathing in the sacred waters, speaking softly with his disciples, the river clean and uncrowded.

Things were very different now. Hundreds of people were gathered at the water's edge and standing in the shallows, washing their hair, their teeth, their clothes, cupping their hands to drink the sacred waters of the Ganges hoping it would endow them with eternal good health. The swollen corpse of a goat float by, followed by the body of an old woman. Bodhidharma filled his goatskin from the murky waters, but did not drink. He would use it later for tea. He knew the difference between truth and myth.

He had crossed the Ganges once already on his way to Kapilavastu, the birthplace of The Buddha, and from here he had visited the other sacred sites where The Buddha had lived and died. Now he prepared to re-cross the river for the final destination of his pilgrimage. He waited on the riverbank until a boatman noticed him and steered toward him. The boat was already filled with passengers, but there was always room for one more, especially if that person was a holy man who would bring good karma.

Bodhidharma stepped into the boat and sat beside a young boy, who cowed away from him and nestled closer to his father.

"You are going to Bodh Gaya, Master?" the boy's father asked.

"Yes, I am."

"To see the Bodhi Tree?"

"Yes," Bodhidharma smiled, "I have read about it for many years but never seen it."

"It is a very special place," the man assured him.

"Why do you want to go and see a tree?" the boy asked, forgetting his fear of the fierce-looking stranger.

"The Buddha was sitting beneath that very tree when he became enlightened," Bodhidharma answered.

"What happened to him?"

"He saw the true nature of things."

"And what was it?"

"That is a good question," Bodhidharma laughed.

"Have you seen it too?"

"Perhaps."

"What did you see?"

Bodhidharma leaned closer so only the boy could hear him. "What I saw was not important. It was the light that I saw it in."

"What sort of light?"

"A very clear light."

"If I become a pilgrim, will I see it too?"

"Maybe one day," Bodhidharma smiled, "I certainly hope you do."

The dusty road to Bodh Gaya was crowded with pilgrims. Some were tall and slender with light skin from the north of India. Others were dark, with round eyes and tight black curls from the south, like him. Still others had come from beyond the Himalayas. There were white-skinned men with brown hair and green-eyed women in colorful costumes who, he imagined, had traveled from Persia or another unknown land far to the West. He passed a group of traders with smooth skin and almond eyes. Their features brought to mind descriptions he had read of Chinese people but when he asked their origin, he discovered they were from Burma.

A busy market had sprung up on the road to the Tree of Enlightenment. Stallholders sold paintings, tapestries, statues, and carvings of The Buddha seated beneath the Bodhi tree. A throng of wagons and carts had become hopelessly jammed. The drivers shouted angrily at one another while their mules and oxen twitched their tails against the swarming flies. Bodhidharma passed single-humped camels from the deserts of Arabia, and two-humped camels from Bakhtar beyond the Hindukush. On the edge of the market, a group of mahouts stood in a tight circle and joked among themselves while their elephants munched on mountains of leaves and looked down on the chaos before them with laughing eyes.

The market gave way to a park with a low limestone wall around it and cultivated gardens on either side. In the center was an expanse of dry grass filled with pilgrims, and rising above them all, a giant fig tree. A steady stream of pilgrims was walking round the tree, chanting prayers. Their endless footsteps had formed a rut in the ground that had baked hard in the sun. Other pilgrims lay prostrate toward the sacred tree, and yet more sat facing it in meditation, rigid and determined, as if waiting for a miracle. Some had clearly been there for many days and were on the edge of exhaustion.

Bodhidharma found a space near a group of hermit monks who were seated in a circle. Their matted hair and beards hung to the ground. Their skeletal bodies had been smeared from head to foot with grey ash. One of them noticed Bodhidharma through half-closed eyes, and turned to take a closer look. He watched as Bodhidharma lit a fire and prepared to make tea and heat a generous portion of flat bread and spiced vegetables. Finally he caught Bodhidharma's eye and gestured to him. "May I join you, Brother?" he called out. His companions glared and whispered to him urgently, but he ignored them.

"If you wish," Bodhidharma replied.

The hermit rose with difficulty and took a few faltering steps toward him, unsure of his balance. He bent to sit down, but his legs gave way beneath him and he slumped in a heap on the ground beside Bodhidharma.

"What is it that you are doing, Brother?" he asked, breathless from the exertion of moving from his seat.

"Drinking tea," Bodhidharma said.

"We drink only the water from the sacred River Ganges," the hermit said, shaking his head disapprovingly.

"The river may be sacred," Bodhidharma said, "but the water is dirty."

"The water of the Ganges is the water of life," the hermit said, his dark eyes boring into Bodhidharma's.

"The river contains death as well as life. Take a look next time you're on the riverbank."

"So where did you get the water for your tea?" the hermit asked triumphantly.

Bodhidharma looked at the hermit who was grinning broadly now, his broken teeth huge inside his fleshless skull. "From the river," he sighed.

"Ha ha!"

"The fire rids it of the spirits of the dead."

"You believe that?" the hermit scoffed.

"I do, and it also makes good tea. Here, try some," Bodhidharma said offering him his cup, "it's very refreshing."

"I cannot accept, but thank you," the hermit said.

"Why not? Is it because you might grow to like it?"

"The Buddha told us to free ourselves from earthly desires."

Bodhidharma took a sip of tea and smacked his lips appreciatively. "He did. But did he not also say that to deny oneself life's pleasures is wrong too? Did he not speak of a middle path?"

"Maybe so, but where exactly does that path lie?"

"A good question," Bodhidharma smiled, setting his flat bread to heat over the fire.

"And what is your answer, Brother?" the hermit demanded.

"In a place that cannot be named."

"Then does it exist at all, one might ask?"

"Yes."

"That is what you believe," the hermit said, "but are you certain?"

"I am," Bodhidharma said with a smile.

The hermit stared at Bodhidharma for a moment then looked around at the park of Bodh Gaya. He noticed his fellow hermits glaring at him and turned back quickly to the stranger in the black robe who was sipping his tea contentedly.

"If you are so certain of things, then why are you here?" he demanded.

"I am making a pilgrimage on my way to Nalanda,"

Bodhidharma told him.

"You wish to study at Nalanda? I must warn you, it is very difficult to get in. They will turn you away at the gate."

"I have an introduction," Bodhidharma told him.

"An introduction, you say? From whom? They are very particular in Nalanda."

"Prajnatara."

"Prajnatara, you say? Master Prajnatara is your master? Why did you not say so before? Prajnatara is very famous here in Magadha, although I heard he went south many years ago to teach."

"He is, and he did."

"He must think very highly of you, to send you all the way to Nalanda."

"He is sending me a lot farther than that," Bodhidharma smiled. The hermit's eyes darted over the body of the dark monk and examined his face, determined to take in every detail. "May I know your name, Brother?" he asked finally.

"Bodhidharma."

"Bodhidharma, you say?" the hermit's eyes widened in wonder, "and you were given this name by Prajnatara himself?" He shook his head urgently from side to side, "I should call you Master instead of Brother! Please forgive me."

"You're free to call me anything you choose," Bodhidharma said, removing his flat bread from the fire and setting his pot of vegetables on the flame.

"I shall call you Master Bodhidharma," the hermit said, pressing his palms together with a smile, "and I am honored to meet you. My name is Vanya."

Bodhidharma reached for his bowl and began to fill it from the pot on the fire. "Would you like to share my food, Brother Vanya?" he asked.

Vanya's face fell in dismay and he shifted uneasily where he sat.

Bodhidharma smiled. "Maybe later," he said, "I can see you have no appetite at present."

"Yes, thank you, Master," Vanya said with relief. "Please don't think me rude."

Bodhidharma began to eat noisily, shoveling mounds of spiced vegetables into his mouth with hunks of flat bread and washing it down with slurps of hot sweet tea. Vanya watched uneasily. He wanted to look away, but felt the eyes of his fellow hermits on his back and did not dare to turn in case one of them should catch his eye. "Forgive me for being so forthright," he said finally. "You eat and drink in a holy place."

"I'm hungry," Bodhidharma said.

"You cook for yourself, which is forbidden by the Buddhist law."

Bodhidharma shrugged.

"And I see you carry possessions."

"I am on a long journey, Brother Vanya."

"How can a man who is truly free of worldly desire do such things?"

Bodhidharma looked at Vanya's wasted body, the grey skin stretched painfully thin over protruding bones, the sunken eyes and festering sores that remained untreated on his limbs. "The Buddha once did as you do, Brother Vanya," he answered. "He denied himself and starved himself for many years. In the end, he abandoned that path saying the true Way lies neither in denial nor excess."

"But to put oneself above the suffering of the great Lord Buddha, that could be considered pride, one of the greatest of all sins," Vanya said.

Bodhidharma rinsed his cup and bowl and set about packing his knapsack, but Vanya had not finished. "Detachment, that is the key to all things. That is what The Buddha said. Freedom from desires and cravings. Freedom from revulsion and loathing, until even death no longer holds any fear for us."

Bodhidharma rose to his feet and slung his knapsack over his shoulder. "Your mind is made up Brother Vanya, and my path takes me elsewhere. I wish you well."

"Detachment is freedom from the wheel of birth and death," Vanya said repeating a mantra that he and his companions lived by.

Bodhidharma planted his walking staff firmly in the ground. "Quite right!" he said, and then bent low so none but Vanya could hear. "Just beware of attaching yourself to detachment."

He walked swiftly through the throng of pilgrims, surprised by the strength of his sudden anger. The hermit had studied for many years, yet he was still so blind. Not for the first time, he wondered if he had the strength to enlighten a single person, let alone the emperor of China. His furious pace took him quickly through the crush of the marketplace, and by the time he had reached the road to Nalanda his anger was replaced by a sadness that reached deep into his bones. His pace slowed and his knapsack felt heavy on his back. Finally he stopped and closed his eyes in despair.

Suddenly, there was the sound of urgent footsteps behind him.

"Wait, Master, please!"

It was Vanya, gasping for breath as he spoke, "I would like to walk with you, if I may. Please, wait a moment. I wish to follow The Way as you do. Let me travel with you as your disciple."

"No," Bodhidharma said, setting off again on the road.

"Wait just a moment, I beg you," Vanya spluttered.

"I'm sorry," Bodhidharma said without looking back. "My path takes me far from here. I suggest you find a different teacher."

"But you said you were going to Nalanda," Vanya said, urging his wasted legs to go faster and catch Bodhidharma.

"I am going a lot farther than Nalanda."

"How much farther?"

"To Nanjing."

"I have never heard of it. Is it far?"

"Very."

"Let me go with you, at least as far as Nalanda. I have so many questions for you."

Bodhidharma walked. Vanya stumbled along beside him, his head so full of questions that he could not think of a single one, and soon he was too tired to utter a single word. Bodhidharma's relentless pace quickly became too much for him and he fell behind. But Vanya knew the way to Nalanda and kept Bodhidharma in sight, far ahead in the distance.

When darkness descended and Bodhidharma stopped to rest, Vanya joined him by the fire, just as his little pot of water began to boil. Too exhausted to speak, he simply smiled happily at Bodhidharma, as if they had been traveling companions for so long that words were no longer needed. Bodhidharma handed him a bowl of rice and a cup of hot, sweet tea and this time Vanya ate and drank without protest.

Flowers on the Balcony

"Come on, my friend," Huo said, pulling on his overcoat and heading for the door of the barrack room. "Let's go to Longpan. We'd better hurry up, or all the pretty girls will be gone."

Kuang remained on his bed and stared at the bunk above. "I'm not your friend, Huo, and I'm not going into that stinking town."

Huo turned back and walked over to the bunks. He noticed Kuang's face had almost healed from Corporal Chen's brutal training session. The scab on his lip had all but disappeared and his left eye had reopened. The ugly swelling had gone down and only a little yellow bruising showed around his cheekbone.

"If I'm not your friend, then who is?" he demanded.

Kuang ignored him.

"Anyway," Huo continued, "why are you sulking? It's the end of the week. We need to relax. Come on, it'll be good to get away from the fort. There's nothing for you here." He paused to let his meaning sink in. Still Kuang didn't answer.

"Don't be an idiot, Kuang!" Huo said finally.

"What do you mean?" Kuang said.

You know what I mean. I saw the way you were looking at Weilin."

"She was looking at me!"

"She's just bored—don't flatter yourself. Weilin is Commander Tang's daughter and she's engaged to Captain Fu Sheng."

"What about it?" Kuang said.

"Fu Sheng would tear you apart if he even suspected."

"I'm not afraid of Fu Sheng. Besides, it's none of your business."

"I'm trying to help you, you idiot!" Huo said.

Kuang glared at Huo, his temper rising. Then he remembered how Huo had carried him back to the barracks when he had been too weak to walk, and the anger left him. "I'm staying here," he sighed. "You go to Longpan. You don't need me."

"Have it your own way," Huo shrugged and made for the door.

"I never did thank you for the other day," Kuang called after him.

"No, you didn't."

Huo stood in the doorway as Kuang searched for the right words, then gave up waiting. "Never mind," he said, stepping out of the barracks and into the dusk. "There really is no need."

Kuang sprang up and checked his face in the polished brass that served as a mirror. He wondered whether to wait another week, but when he thought of Weilin's pretty eyes and slim waist, he decided he had waited long enough.

He left the barracks and crossed the compound, keeping to the shadows. When he reached the commander's house, Weilin was not in her usual place on the terrace. He wondered what to do. He could not stand around idly. Someone would soon notice him. Perhaps he would go into Longpan after all, get some food, a few drinks, perhaps a girl—someone to pass the time with until he could have the girl he wanted. He turned to go. He had only gone a few paces when he heard the faint click of a door opening behind him. Weilin was on the terrace. She glanced at him for a moment, then set about rearranging her flowerpots.

He sauntered over to her and stood in the shadows nearby. "Is something the matter, Miss?" he asked with a smile.

"Perhaps I should ask you the same thing?" she answered without looking up from her work.

"What do you mean?"

"It's not me who is skulking in the shadows," she replied without turning to look at him. "Is there something you want, soldier?"

"You don't know my name?" he asked.

"Why would I know your name?" she asked icily.

Things were not going as he had hoped and he began to wonder if he had made a mistake after all. "I know your name," he continued lightly. "You're Weilin. I'm very pleased to make your acquaintance. My name is Kuang, from Hubei."

"In that case, I do know your name," she said. "In fact, I have often heard it mentioned in my father's house, usually when trouble is discussed. Now I can put a face to the name."

"Then at least you know my face," he smiled, hoping to seize a small victory.

"Who wouldn't know your face? It stands out from the rest, even among the battered faces I see here every day."

He touched the remains of the scab on his lip before he could stop himself. He was getting nowhere. She clicked her tongue and busied herself with her flowerpots, picking out dead leaves and pouring a little water into each.

"I know your face," he said finally. "It stands out too, but for a different reason."

She ignored him.

"You're very beautiful," he said, almost to himself.

She looked at him then, waiting for a further remark, but there was none.

"That's kind of you to say," she said at last, "but I don't think so."

"Oh, it's true," he smiled, "believe me."

"What is it you want, exactly, Kuang?"

"I came to tell you that you're the most beautiful woman in the whole of Yulong Fort," he said with a mischievous smile. Her face hardened. It was hardly a compliment, considering the age of the few other women who lived in the fort. Then, seeing the humor in his eyes, she relented and laughed despite herself.

He stepped up to the balcony rail with a broad grin and she saw how handsome he was beneath the cuts and bruises. "If someone sees you here, there'll be trouble," she warned.

"No one will see me. Besides, we're only talking, nothing more."

"Why aren't you in Longpan this evening like everyone else?"

"There's nothing for me in Longpan."

"I'm sure there are plenty of pretty girls."

"None like you."

"You're out of your mind, Kuang!"

"Maybe," he said, reaching over the rail for her hand and drawing her to him slowly, drawing her so close he could only see the curve of her cheek and the top of her lip. He leaned forward to kiss her. To his surprise, she did not resist. When a lingering moment later she pulled away, he drew her back and they kissed again.

"This is a bad idea," she whispered urgently. "You shouldn't be here. If someone sees you, there'll be serious trouble."

"There's no one around," he assured her. He vaulted the balcony rail and pulled her body to his, pressing his lips to hers. His hands cupped her neck lightly, then smoothed down her back, settling on her slender hips. His knee found its way between her thighs. Her body tensed. He wondered if he had gone too far when he felt her press into him, her small hands pulling on his shoulders.

A sound came from inside the house—a door closing—footsteps in the hall. Kuang vaulted back over the rail and darted into the shadows. Weilin returned to her flowerpots. They waited, breathlessly, but no one appeared. He returned to the terrace, but she put her hand on his chest to prevent him from jumping over the rail. "I'm betrothed, Kuang! I'll be married soon. And don't forget to whom. You know what Fu Sheng would do if he found out."

"I'm not afraid of Fu Sheng. I'm not afraid of anyone."

"You should be. He would kill you. He would probably enjoy it," she shuddered.

"But where is Fu Sheng now? Out in the steppes, more concerned with killing Turks and Uighurs than with being with you. If I was him, I would never leave you on your own."

"Fu Sheng has important duties."

"Your father arranged the marriage?" Kuang asked.

"Father did what's best."

"Best for who?"

She looked so sad that he did not know what to say next. Instead he kissed her and she did not resist.

There was another noise from the house. He leapt away into the shadows just as Weilin's mother put her head out.

"Are you out there, Weilin?" she called.

"Yes mother, I'm tending the flowers."

"You've been out a long time. It's cold tonight. Come inside and sit with me. Keep me company."

"I'm coming, mother."

She looked at the shadows where Kuang was hiding, turned away, and was gone before he could say anything.

He waited for a minute, before returning to the barracks. The empty room was cold and silent. He lay on his bunk and closed his eyes, thinking of Weilin. Kissing her again. It was a dangerous game he was playing but he did not care. Whatever happened, he had to find a way to be alone with her again.

Monks Enter Nalanda

"There it is, Master," Vanya cried, "Nalanda!"

The point of a giant stupa rose over the treetops, glinting gold against the blue sky, and Bodhidharma felt his heart quicken. He had read many descriptions of Nalanda and seen its golden tower in countless paintings, yet nothing had prepared him for the sight of it rising before him. Nalanda was the jewel in the Buddhist crown, a monastery the size of a city, the greatest temple on earth. Monks came from all over the world to sit in its lofty lecture halls and study in its libraries, which, it was said, housed over a million books and scrolls. The stupa towered over everything, dwarfing the trees that grew nearby, reminding all living things of their place in the world—they were a mere speck in the universe, their lives as temporal as that of an insect, over in the blink of an eye.

Nalanda's outer wall was high enough to defend a fortress. A row of brightly colored flags fluttered in the warm breeze and palm swifts darted overhead. At the entrance, two guards stood by enormous doors of black wood and iron. The doors barred the way inside save for a small gap between them. There was a young man talking with the guards and as they drew nearer, Bodhidharma could hear them discussing a passage from the Lankavatara Sutra. He turned to Vanya for an explanation.

"They do this, Master," Vanya whispered loud enough for all to hear. "They ask questions about the scriptures. It's a test. You can't enter Nalanda unless you know the answers." He lowered his voice so that only Bodhidharma could hear, "I have tried several times myself, but they were never satisfied. I think it's because I'm not of noble birth."

Moments later, the young man was turned away by the guards and brushed past them in obvious distress. Then the elder of the guards glanced at the two waiting figures. "State your business at Nalanda," he said curtly.

"I am here to meet with The Venerable Ananda," Bodhidharma said.

The guard glanced at the wild-looking monk, taking in the shabby robe, the bare feet, and the skin beaten black by the sun. He was little more than a beggar. "The Venerable Ananda does not give an audience to casual visitors," the guard said.

Bodhidharma had only to produce Prajnatara's letter of introduction, but he did not. Instead he planted himself firmly before the guard. "He will see me."

"On what business?"

"No business of yours, Brother," Bodhidharma answered, "and before I see him, perhaps you can enlighten me on this practice of turning away young monks who wish to study and barring the gates of a monastery to visitors?"

The younger guard stepped across to stand by the shoulder of his companion, who was about to answer when Vanya hurried forward and spoke quickly. "Brother Guards, it appears you have failed to recognize Master Bodhidharma! He is a disciple of Master Prajnatara himself and has traveled all the way from Pallava to meet with The Venerable One." He leaned closer to the guard, speaking in a whisper, "You're keeping him waiting at the gate like a novice. Do you think that wise?"

The senior guard hesitated.

"Perhaps you want to debate the scriptures with him?" Vanya smiled.

"No one is allowed into Nalanda without the correct papers or authority," the junior guard said. "Those are our orders."

"You are following orders. That is very commendable," Bodhidharma said, keeping his gaze fixed on the senior guard, who looked more closely at the stranger before him. This time he noticed the expanse of hard muscle beneath the threadbare robe. The man was built like one of the wrestlers who competed in the arena at Rajagriha. His bulging forearm suggested many years of wielding weapons and the calloused fist that gripped the walking staff was that of a Vajramukti master, able to shatter bone as easily as snapping a twig. The guard looked into the fierce black eyes and saw that if the stranger wished to enter, two guards would not delay him for more than a heartbeat. At that moment, Bodhidharma smiled.

The guard made up his mind. "I will escort you personally," he said, hushing the objections of the younger guard with a frown.

He led Bodhidharma into the monastery and Vanya hurried after them before anyone could object. In the broad courtyard, monks and nuns strolled in pairs, deep in conversation. Novices hurried to their lessons with scrolls under their arms and senior monks sat with one another in the shade of the many trees. The guard led Bodhidharma and Vanya down a wide avenue that ran between the many lecture halls, libraries, and temples of Nalanda. They entered a beautiful garden with fruit trees and flowerbeds of orange, purple, white, and yellow. Young monks bathed in tranquil pools of spring water. Towering above them all was the great stupa of Nalanda, so high that from where they looked, its top disappeared from view.

They entered a great hall lit by a wall of lamps and decorated with exquisite tapestries depicting scenes from The Buddha's life. A gong as tall as a man stood in the entrance and reflected the flickering lamplight in its gleaming surface. An attendant monk emptied incense from a burner and ghostly clouds of white dust caught the lamplight and swirled up toward the ceiling.

The guard spoke privately with the attendant before bowing to Bodhidharma and taking his leave. The attendant introduced himself and led the two visitors down a maze of dark halls and passages. They climbed several long flights of stairs and Vanya became breathless with the exertion. On the upper floors, the corridors were brighter and the ceilings higher. These were the living quarters of the senior monks and sunlight poured in through high windows, falling on bookshelves filled with scrolls and manuscripts, comfortable seating areas and quiet rooms for private study. They passed a little meditation hall that housed a beautiful gilded shrine, complete with offerings to The Buddha and freshly cut flowers from the gardens.

At the end of the corridor, they came to an ornate screen door and the attendant tapped it once. After a brief wait, the screen opened a crack and another monk appeared. They spoke quietly and the screen door slid shut again. Vanya walked in circles impatiently while Bodhidharma took his time examining the paintings on the wall. Finally the door slid open and an older monk appeared with a smile. He invited Bodhidharma inside and instructed the attendant to show Vanya to his quarters.

Bodhidharma found himself in a lofty chamber with high windows. The walls were decorated with silk tapestries crafted with an artistry he had never before encountered and intricately carved panels gilded in silver and gold. The air brought a faint waft of incense, mixed with a subtle floral scent that reminded him of his homeland.

An old man was seated by the window at the far end of the room. He wore a simple orange robe like any other monk and no visible adornments, but The Venerable Ananda emanated power and Bodhidharma knew him instantly. He went closer, pressing his palms together in greeting and bowed low. The grandmaster looked up, noticing his visitor for the first time, and squinted to get a better view. With a yelp of delight he rose on unsteady legs and hurried forward until he was one step away. Here he stopped to examine the unkempt monk from head to foot, his mouth working silently as he did, before bowing long and low.

When Ananda straightened, he was beaming with delight. He extended his hands in welcome and Bodhidharma took them. Ananda squeezed, shaking them gently, his grip surprisingly strong, then released them and embraced him warmly. "Bodhidharma," he said, his voice light and reedy, "you are exactly as I imagined you! Prajnatara describes you perfectly. It is wonderful to meet you at last. I am so very happy that you have come."

"It's a pleasure to be here. I have dreamed of seeing Nalanda for many years," Bodhidharma said. "Master Prajnatara sends his regards. He always speaks most fondly of you."

"Ah Prajnatara, what does he know?" the old man laughed. "Prajnatara is young and foolish, easily impressed, but at least he was right about one thing. He told me you would come, and you did! Come and sit beside me, Bodhidharma. Let us sit by the window, where I can see you properly. My eyes are not good any more."

Bodhidharma helped Ananda lower himself onto his seat and they sat in silence for a moment. Ananda's face filled suddenly with concern. "You have traveled a great distance to be here. You must be exhausted! Have they given you refreshments? A room? Have you had time to rest?"

"There will be plenty of time for resting," Bodhidharma assured him.

"If you're sure," the old man said, still uncertain. "After all, I forget that you are still young and strong. Nevertheless, you must eat and take some juice to restore yourself." He summoned his assistant and asked for refreshments to be brought, then sat back once again and fixed his watery eyes on Bodhidharma.

"You have only just arrived. You have not had a chance to see everything that we do here in Nalanda. Did you know we have over ten thousand monks, over five hundred teachers. Monks come from all over the world to study with us. They come in such numbers that recently, we have been forced to turn most of them away.

"I saw such an instance when we arrived," Bodhidharma said.

"You did?" Ananda's brow creased in concern.

"Yes, a young man was turned away at the gate."

"Oh how tragic," Ananda cried. "It saddens me greatly to deny the blessing of an education to anyone, but there is simply no more room here, Bodhidharma. No room at all! The dormitories are already overcrowded. Each single room is already occupied by two and sometimes three monks. This is why we are striving to open new centers of learning where people can go and study The Way. Masters from Nalanda have traveled all over India to open new temples. Prajnatara went to the South long ago, as you know. Others have gone into the Himalayas and beyond, to Persia, Samarkand, and Khotan. Some have even reached China, where there are millions of souls waiting to be freed." He paused. His mind was drifting and he needed a moment to collect his thoughts. "However in recent years, I regret to say, the missions to China have not been so successful."

"I heard," Bodhidharma said evenly.

"Yes," Ananda said, "the journey is testing in many, many ways. That is why, when Prajnatara wrote and told me about you, Bodhidharma, I knew you were the right person for this mission. I am so delighted that you have answered your calling."

"I only hope I can fulfill your wishes."

"Oh come! You must have faith in yourself, Bodhidharma. You are young and strong, still in your prime. No one is saying it is easy. Remember how The Buddha himself struggled before his own enlightenment and how hard he worked afterward to spread his wisdom. It took him his whole life ..." His old eyes glistened with emotion and he paused to collect his thoughts. "Have you visited the sacred sites yet?"

"Yes, I made a pilgrimage before coming here."

"That is wonderful! Let it inspire you," he said, squeezing Bodhidharma's shoulder, "and it also means we can start preparing for your journey right away. China is a long way, and we are going to help you in every way we can."

He paused, nodding to himself, and leaned in as if divulging a secret to a close friend, "There is someone I would like you to meet, a monk who will be of great assistance to you. He has been with us for eight years now. He is a skilled teacher and an inspiring orator. In debates, he is more than a match for even the most senior of monks. His knowledge of the Sutras is unequalled. He would make the perfect traveling companion for you. There is only one problem. He is so happy here, I fear he will be reluctant to leave."

"I don't want to drag anyone away from the joy of their studies," Bodhidharma smiled.

"Do not concern yourself with that. One could easily spend a lifetime debating the finer points of doctrine, but there comes a time to pass the basics on to the next generation, don't you agree?"

"I do. To keep it all to ourselves would be a little selfish,"

Bodhidharma answered with a grin.

"Selfish?" Ananda said, looking up in surprise. "Yes, indeed, it would be selfish," he said nodding seriously. "In fact, it would be more than selfish. It would be a sin!" His old face creased with laughter and he tapped his own leg in delight, dabbing at the tears that ran down his cheeks.

Bodhidharma waited in silence until the old man had recovered his composure.

"Now what was I saying?" Ananda mused, still shaking his head in mirth. "Ah yes, well, I am sure this monk can be persuaded, once we put the argument to him. I will arrange for us to meet with him in due course."

Bodhidharma waited to hear more about the mysterious monk, but Ananda's assistant appeared with refreshments and once they were served, Ananda demanded to hear of Bodhidharma's journey from Pallava and his pilgrimage to the holy sites. Next he insisted on knowing every detail of Prajnatara's temple in the jungle, so that he could visit it in his mind whenever he wished. They talked on and as the shadows lengthened Bodhidharma saw the old man had grown weary.

"I think my journey has taken its toll, Venerable One," he sighed. "I hope you will forgive me if I retire to rest."

"Of course you must rest, dear Bodhidharma," Ananda smiled, ringing the bell for his assistant. "We must both rest. My assistant will show you to your room. You will find everything in order."

Bodhidharma's room was spacious. Crisp, clean white bedding lay on the floor and a plump new cushion had been set out for his meditation. In the corner was a chest for his possessions, and two small paintings hung on the wall. In one, The Buddha was descending a staircase from Heaven. In the other, an elephant was kneeling at The Buddha's feet. On the window was a beautifully carved statue of The Buddha seated in meditation, and beside it a tray of incense, a burner, and a small vase of flowers. Someone had taken a good deal of trouble to prepare the place for their new guest.

"I hope the room is to your satisfaction," the assistant said.

To a wandering monk who spent countless nights under the stars, it was untold luxury. "It is perfect," Bodhidharma answered. "Thank you."

"Please summon me if there is anything further you need," the assistant said with a smile, then pressed his palms together in the traditional Buddhist greeting and bowed low. "Welcome to Nalanda."

A line of orange robes lay neatly folded by the edge of the bathing pool. A group of novices were washing in the water, their smooth limbs and shaved heads glistening in the bright sunlight. They laughed and splashed each other gently, not wishing to earn a reprimand from one of the more senior monks. Unruly behavior was frowned upon in Nalanda.

One of the boys froze abruptly, his mouth agape. The others followed his gaze to the giant form at the water's edge, etched in black against the bright sky, a dark demon from an ancient scroll. As the stranger stepped into the water, the boys could see his hair, face, and limbs were streaked with grey dust from the road, which added to his unearthly appearance. They shrank back as he waded into the deeper water. When the water reached his chest he set about washing himself thoroughly, applying oil to his hair and beard and massaging the mass of muscle in his neck and shoulders, before dipping below the surface to rinse himself clean.

When he emerged, he snorted a fine spray from his nostrils, like a buffalo at the riverbank. Murmurings rustled through the group of novices. One of them snorted, and the rest began to giggle. Meanwhile, the dark stranger floated on his back, ignoring their antics. The boy snorted again and the others laughed helplessly. Suddenly the stranger stood, eyeing them coolly, then sank beneath the surface and disappeared.

Swimming and diving were strictly forbidden in the bathing pools. These were sacred places created for the cleansing of the body, not frivolous enjoyment. The boys watched, bewildered, as the water settled and all trace of the dark man disappeared. A minute passed and he did not appear. When a second minute passed, they became concerned. They swam around the surface of the pool, looking, but there was no sign of him. Should they call for assistance? Would anyone believe them if they said a huge black stranger had washed in the pool and then disappeared without trace? A third minute passed and they began to wonder if he had existed at all. A chill of fear took hold of them. Had it been a demon after all, who would drag them under too?

Suddenly the water exploded around them and a giant shape rose in their midst. The stranger seized one of them and raised him high above the water. It was the boy who had snorted. Now he was shrieking with fear. The demon spun him in the air, round and round, until the boy began to laugh uncontrollably. The others grew bolder and began to splash the stranger, shouting at him to put their companion down.

"You want me to put him down?" he roared.

"Put him down! Put him down!"

The boy was hurtled through the air and landed in the middle of the pool. The others jumped at Bodhidharma. He threw them, one by one, until the commotion began to attract the attention of other monks nearby. Then he settled in the cool water to relax. The novices gathered around to speak with the strange monk from the south who was so unlike their usual teachers.

Soon, they were joined by another equally strange monk. Vanya's skeletal form shivered uncontrollably as he removed his robe and entered the cool water.

"I have some good news for you, Master," he smiled as he sat beside Bodhidharma. "I have discovered the whereabouts of Nanjing."

"You have?"

"Yes, and I know what you did not tell me. You are traveling to China."

"I told you it was far."

"You did, and now your journey will be shorter because I will be traveling with you."

"You think you can cross the Himalayas on these skinny legs?" Bodhidharma said, gripping Vanya's thigh and squeezing until Vanya winced in pain.

"These legs have walked the length and breadth of Magadha," he said indignantly, puffing his chest out as far as it would go. "I have not always been a hermit, you know. I was once a great hunter, a warrior, like yourself."

"Vanya," Bodhidharma sighed, "I'll be leaving soon. You're too weak to travel with me."

"Who says I'm weak?" he shouted, "I'm as strong as a tiger." He jumped up from the shallows and threw wild punches, roaring and grimacing. Bodhidharma watched unmoved.

"You don't react very quickly for a warrior," Vanya said, panting from the exertion.

"I only react to a threat," Bodhidharma said gravely.

"You were very lucky, Lord," Vanya said, shaking his head at the thought of the damage he could have inflicted. When he turned to sit down again in the water, Bodhidharma scooped him up and held him high in the air. Vanya roared his defiance but it was no use, and the next moment he was flying through the air.

He emerged from the water with a curse and sat apart from Bodhidharma.

"If you really want to travel with me, you need to make yourself strong," Bodhidharma said from across the pool.

Vanya scowled. "I am strong," he said half-heartedly.

"If you can climb to the top of the stupa, then you are strong. Do it before I leave and you can come with me. If you can't, I'll ask The Venerable Ananda if you can stay here and study in Nalanda. It's what you wanted, isn't it?"

"It was, but not any more. Now I want to follow you."

"Why?" Bodhidharma demanded.

"I wish to know my own nature, as you do."

"You can learn that in Nalanda."

"Perhaps, but I am certain I will learn it from you."

Bodhidharma stared at Vanya, and Vanya saw that his request had pleased the master.

"The journey is long and dangerous," Bodhidharma warned.

"I'm not afraid," Vanya assured him.

"You intend to cross the Himalayas with me?" Bodhidharma asked seriously.

"Yes, as your disciple," Vanya said eagerly.

Bodhidharma's eyes hardened. "Then you'd better get to the top of the stupa," he said with a finality that brooked no further discussion, and Vanya knew he must meet the challenge.

The Scholar

"Today you will meet a very special monk," The Venerable Ananda told Bodhidharma, "an interesting character, one of the most learned masters at Nalanda. He has studied the scriptures in great depth and is able to debate them with consummate skill. Yet he has been unable to attain the simple beauty of The Way."

"Why is that?" Bodhidharma asked.

"He does not trust his own judgment."

"That is a difficult step."

"A terrifying step," Ananda nodded seriously, "and I believe you are the one to help him take it."

"I'm afraid you're wrong. I have had no success in the past," Bodhidharma said.

"Well you will have plenty of time to perfect your methods," Ananda smiled. "It is a long way to China. If we can persuade this monk to accompany you, he will be of great help to you. Let me introduce you to him."

He rang a small handbell and his assistant entered, followed by a short monk in a simple orange robe. The monk's head was shaved like the others, yet there was something unusual about his appearance. As he came into the light, Bodhidharma saw the same almond eyes that he had seen in the Burmese on the road to Bodh Gaya, but this man's skin was as smooth as silk and shone pale silver in the dim light. The monk was Chinese! Bodhidharma was surprised he had not considered the possibility.

"Brother Yin Chiang," Ananda said warmly, rising unsteadily, "how wonderful to see you. Thank you so much for coming to meet with us at such short notice. I hope we are not keeping you from your studies."

Brother Yin Chiang was unsure how to answer, and the sight of the wild-looking man beside The Venerable Ananda did nothing to ease his concern.

"Let me introduce you to our special guest," Ananda continued, ignoring Yin Chiang's obvious dismay. "This is Master Bodhidharma, from the Kingdom of Pallava. He was born to the Kshatriya, which, I'm sure you know, is India's ancient Warrior Caste. He is an invincible warrior, but he is also a Buddhist master. His name is most apt, since he brings enlightenment wherever he travels."

Vanya turned to Yin Chiang, "And this is Brother Yin Chiang, who has come all the way from the Chinese city of Changan. Brother Yin Chiang has been a resident in Nalanda for eight years, I believe, and in that time he has translated many of the most important Sutras into Chinese."

"Delighted to meet you, Brother Yin Chiang," Bodhidharma said with a bow, "though The Venerable One exaggerates more than a little when he speaks of my abilities."

"Nonsense," Ananda said beaming with joy. Yin Chiang stared wide-eyed for a moment longer until he recalled his manners and returned Bodhidharma's bow. "It's a pleasure to meet you, too, Master Bodhidharma," he said in perfect Sanskrit.

His words had a pleasant timbre that Bodhidharma had never heard before and it delighted him to hear the sacred language spoken so well.

"Now please sit, both of you," Ananda urged, "so we can talk more comfortably. There is much to discuss."

Once seated, Ananda smiled and waited a moment before beginning.

"Master Bodhidharma is only visiting Nalanda for a short time, in preparation for a far greater journey. Soon he will be leaving to bring the sacred teachings to China. As you know, Brother Yin Chiang, it is our duty to offer enlightenment to all living beings. There are many millions in your homeland, so I am sure you appreciate the enormity of this task."

Yin Chiang remained lost for words, so Ananda went on. "I know you planned to return to China one day when you felt ready, but this is a chance we cannot miss. My dear Brother Yin Chiang, we have delighted in your company and I know you have enjoyed being here, but Bodhidharma's arrival is a sign that we cannot ignore. I ask you to consider returning to China with him now and sharing in his divine mission of enlightenment."

He waited, giving the little Chinese monk time to compose himself.

"It is a great honor to be considered for such a task," Yin Chiang answered at last, "but I fear I am not ready to leave Nalanda. There are so many scriptures that I have not translated, so many questions left unanswered."

"Brother Yin Chiang," Ananda said gently, "there is a limit to what you can learn from the Sutras. To grasp the true nature of life you must look beyond the scriptures. I believe Bodhidharma can help you in this. In return, you can teach him about the wonders of China and your delightful Chinese language. He is an excellent linguist."

Bodhidharma had to suppress a smile at this, since Ananda had no way of knowing his ability.

"There is another reason why you must go," Ananda continued cheerfully. "After meeting Bodhidharma, I was visited by the spirit of a Bodhisattva who showed me a wondrous scene. I saw monks sailing on a river inhabited by an angry dragon. The journey was filled with danger, but the monks were protected by the Bodhisattva who appeared to them in many different forms. At the end of the river, they came to mist-covered mountains. I saw them enter a beautiful temple of red and gold, set in an emerald forest. I have had the same vision each night since Bodhidharma arrived. It is surely a sign, and when a Bodhisattva points the way so clearly, it is destiny."

Yin Chiang did not answer.

"Take some time and consider my request at your leisure," Ananda said gently, though Bodhidharma knew that behind the softness of Ananda's words, there was no doubting the force of his request.

"In the meantime," Ananda continued, "perhaps you could tell

Bodhidharma of your journey to Nalanda. I believe it was as difficult and dangerous as it was magnificent, and he is certainly going to need your expert advice."

This was a subject that the little scholar felt far more comfortable with, and no sooner had he begun to speak than Bodhidharma saw the tension in Yin Chiang's shoulders melt away.

"Most Chinese pilgrims travel northwest on the trade routes through Central Asia, skirting the Taklamakan desert and entering India through the mountain passes of the northwest. This route avoids the Himalayas, but it is very long and in recent years, it has also become extremely dangerous. The Huns have occupied the passes and prey on travelers. There is an alternative route, by sea, but this goes countless li away from the right direction and is also dangerous, with treacherous waters and equally treacherous pirates."

"You came by a third route, did you not?" Ananda asked, though he knew the answer well enough.

"Indeed, there is a third way, a route which I discovered while visiting a remote temple in Yunnan in southwestern China. There I met a hunter who knew the mountain country far to the West. He told me of a wild region of hidden valleys and primitive warring tribes, each with their own customs and language that no outsider can understand. Some are not even fully human but part animal. Some have two heads and eat the flesh of their enemies. The mountains are also home to demons and deadly serpents, and the rivers contain angry dragons that drag unwary travelers to their doom. The hunter told me of a direct route through these mountains to India, a route few believed existed. He assured me that in just two months one could reach the borders of Assam. I checked with local guides and they confirmed that the journey was difficult, but not impossible. I asked the hunter to take me but he refused, saying it was too dangerous. It was only when I offered to pay him a staggering sum that he finally agreed. We waited for the snow to melt on the high ground and then set off, following the course of the Yangtze River into the mountains. When we reached the high ground there was no air and I could scarcely breathe. I became ill and was forced to rest for several days before I was strong enough to continue. It took us many more weeks to reach a Tibetan village. Here the hunter entrusted me to local guides who, for many more pieces of silver, took me through endless high wastes of Tibet. We crossed the upper reaches of the Mee Kong River and the Salween. The rapids were so fierce that I feared for my life many times. Finally, we reached the Tsang Po, which we followed into Assam, where it becomes the Brahmaputra. Here I paid yet another guide, an Indian this time, to take me to Nalanda."

"You endured great hardship and made great sacrifice to come here, Brother Yin Chiang," Ananda said, "and I hope the return journey will be easier for you. We will arrange for trustworthy guides to take you to the farthest borders of Assam and give you ample supplies and silver to smooth your path."

Ananda rubbed his eyes and put his hands on his knees to help him rise, "Now I hope you will excuse me. I am weary and must retire for the evening. Please stay and make use of this chamber as long as you wish. There must be many things you wish to discuss."

Once Ananda had gone, Bodhidharma turned to Yin Chiang eagerly. "I must commend you on your knowledge of the holy language, Brother Yin Chiang. You speak so fluently. I only hope that one day I might master your language in the same way."

"Thank you," Yin Chiang said. "If I can be of assistance, please let me know. I will do my utmost."

"The Venerable One says you are an excellent teacher."

"He is too kind."

"He is also far too generous in his praise of me," Bodhidharma said. "Nevertheless, if you're willing to instruct me, I would like to begin learning Chinese as soon as possible."

"I would be delighted," Yin Chiang said. "Simply let me know when you would like to begin."

"Tomorrow," Bodhidharma said.

"Tomorrow it shall be."

"Perfect," Bodhidharma said happily. "Now please tell me more of your journey. Did you meet any warriors with two heads?"

"I met a warrior with five heads," Yin Chiang smiled mischievously.

"Tell me every detail," Bodhidharma insisted, hungry for information, and by the time they finally retired, the lamps of Nalanda had long since been extinguished and a new friendship had been bonded.

Soldier Helps a Lady

"You're very quiet," Huo said.

Kuang shrugged.

"I can guess why."

"Leave it, Huo!"

They had been standing guard at the entrance to Yulong Fort for an hour and there was another hour to go before their shift would finish. Kuang looked out over the barren wilderness that surrounded the fort, the sharp rocks, coarse mountain grass, and white-tipped peaks in the distance. The only man-made feature on this desolate landscape was the rough track that led to Longpan.

"You're thinking about Weilin," Huo said. Kuang ignored him. "No good will come of it," he continued. "I'm only trying to stop you from making a big mistake."

"Shut up Huo! I'm warning you!" Kuang snarled.

They returned to a long silence.

"So you won't be interested in the whereabouts of a certain young lady, then?" Huo said finally.

"Which young lady? What are you talking about?"

"Nothing, I shouldn't have said a word."

"You'd better tell me now."

"No, it's nothing."

"Tell me!"

"Alright, alright, calm down," Huo laughed. "It's just that I saw a girl leaving the fort a few hours ago."

"Which girl?"

"Didn't I mention her name? It was Weilin."

"Where was she going?"

"Well since you ask so nicely, she was with a maid and they were going into Longpan to pick up some medical supplies."

"And why are you telling me this?"

"Because I think I can see her now, coming this way."

Kuang looked up and saw that Huo was telling the truth. Two figures had appeared on the road to the fort. When they drew a little closer, he could see they were both carrying bags.

"Perhaps we should help them," he said. "Their bags look heavy."

"We'd be deserting our post," Huo said. "You go. I'll cover for you."

"Fine," Kuang said, and loped down the track to help the women with their burdens. When he reached them, he saw Weilin's cheeks were red from the effort of walking and the harsh mountain wind. Stray strands of her hair had escaped from her bonnet and fluttered in the air. She had never looked lovelier. He smiled and held out his hand to take her bag.

"There is no need, thank you," she said curtly.

"Forgive me Ma'am, but I was ordered to help you by the duty officer," he answered. She frowned. Kuang ignored her and held out his hand for the maid's bag, which the maid handed over gratefully. Then he reached for Weilin's bag, and this time she relented and gave it to him.

The women followed him up the track in silence. When they reached the fort, Huo bowed smartly to the ladies and saluted Kuang. Weilin knew enough about military life to know one trooper did not salute another and glared at him, but Huo looked straight ahead and avoided her eyes.

"If you tell me where the bags need to go, I will deliver them for you," Kuang offered.

"My bag has medicines for the hospital," Weilin said. "The other has supplies for the house."

"Then please don't concern yourself. I'll deliver this one to the hospital for you."

"There's no one there," she replied. "The doctor and all the orderlies are out with the cavalry. Someone will need to show you where the medicines go. They have to be stored correctly."

"Then one of you can come with me," he smiled.

"I suppose I had better go," Weilin said to the maid, "since I know where things are kept. You go back to the house. I'll be there soon."

As soon as the maid was out of earshot, Weilin turned on Kuang angrily. "What are you up to, Kuang?"

"What are you up to Weilin? You don't come out in the evenings now."

"That's no concern of yours."

"Yes it is. I've been waiting for you."

"I told you before. It's not safe. Someone will see us. Fu Sheng will find out and kill you. He would probably kill me too, if it weren't for my father."

"Then come away with me. We can leave this place and go to

Hubei."

"Oh, Kuang," she sighed.

"Let's do it," he said seriously, opening the door to the hospital.

"You're insane," she said, shaking her head in frustration as she followed him inside.

The deserted hospital was cool and dark. It consisted of little more than a cramped entrance hall, which served as a waiting area, an operating theatre with three tables, a ward of a dozen or so beds, and a storeroom where the medicines were kept. At the back of the hospital was the doctor's private room where he stored the most powerful drugs, which he prepared himself, and which he kept permanently under lock and key.

Kuang carried the bag through to the storeroom and began to hand over its contents to Weilin, who started stacking the medicines and provisions on the appropriate shelves. Once the last of the supplies had been stored, she rearranged the new jars carefully until everything was neat and tidy for the doctor's return.

When she had finished and left the storeroom, Kuang was waiting for her in the main ward. He stood before her, barring her way. She did not step aside. Slowly, wordlessly, he took her in his arms and drew her in. She allowed him to hold her despite herself, and when he pressed his lips to hers, she did not resist. Instead, she let him kiss and caress her—hating herself for her weakness—and loving him for his foolishness and his bravery and for being so handsome and for wanting her so badly that he would risk everything to be with her.

Kuang began to undress her. She closed her eyes and raised her arms so he could remove her clothing more easily. He folded her robe carefully and placed it on a nearby bench. Then he gathered her in his arms like a child and laid her gently on one of the hospital beds. In the dim light her pale skin looked perfect and unblemished against the rough mattress. Her eyes never left his—whether seeking trust or simply because she did not want to see his nakedness, he could not be sure. He undressed slowly, not wishing to appear too eager, not wanting to frighten her—not now. He placed his clothes neatly beside hers on the bench and stood beside the narrow bed.

There was no room to lie beside her, so he leaned over and placed his knee between hers, grazing her lips softly with his own as he did. He felt her warm breath on his cheek and felt the tension in her thighs melt away. Pushing them apart gently, he knelt between them, his mouth never leaving hers, and she enveloped him in her arms. He felt his head swim, intoxicated by the delicious softness of her body against his, a feeling made all the more exquisite by the contrast with their surroundings. The sensation of her warmed him to his core, bringing back memories of home and comfort and laughter around the hearth, a feeling he had not felt since he was a child.

He nuzzled her breasts and circled her hard nipple with his tongue, then took it in his mouth and pressed it firmly against the roof of his mouth. She sighed, stirring beneath him. He moved to her other breast and a low moan escaped her lips. All thoughts of home left him. He needed her now, urgently, and pressed himself into her. He felt her hand between his legs, feeling for him, guiding him inside her, and watched as she bit her lip to suppress a cry as he entered her.

He moved slowly at first, his eyes on hers, waiting until he saw the subtle change from fear to desire. As his movement quickened, her lips parted and her brow knotted in concentration. Her breathing grew louder with his, and her lips urged him silently onward. He felt her tiny finger dig deep into the skin of his back and clasp the hair on the back of his head. When he felt her nails sink into the flesh of his buttocks and heard her cry out, he could wait no longer and within moments he had spent himself inside her.

They lay still for a short time and she caressed the back of his neck, but then the tension returned in her. He climbed off her swiftly and sat at the foot of the bed. She rose instantly and hurried to fetch her clothes. He watched her dressing in the dark.

"There's no mirror in here," she complained, running her fingers through her hair and flattening it down hastily.

"Let me see you," he said.

"She turned and stood before him. He straightened her robe and adjusted her collar. "You look fine. Beautiful."

"I don't feel beautiful," she said, turning to go.

He reached out and caught her by the wrist. "Meet me here again tomorrow night?"

"I can't, Kuang."

"You can. The troops won't be back for another five days. No one will know."

She tried to pull away. He gripped her more tightly and saw her wince in pain. He let go instantly, sorry for hurting her.

"Tomorrow at midnight," he called after her retreating form. "I'll be waiting for you. Will you come?"

She did not answer.

"Weilin?"

Light flooded into the hospital for a moment as she opened the main door to leave, then the place returned to the dim light of before. He rose to get his clothes, unsure what to make of their encounter, and wondering if she hated him now or whether she would be there again tomorrow.

The Golden Stupa

Vanya woke in a sweat. The sun had not yet begun its assault on the day, and already excitement and fear gathered in the pit of his stomach. He would not be free of either until much later.

He dressed quickly and slipped out into the dark corridors of the dormitory. An attendant monk in the entrance hall noticed him, but said nothing as he passed. Outside the air was cool. A faint glow behind the buildings of Nalanda was the only indication of the coming dawn, but in the cloudless sky, the moon provided ample light to guide him to the stupa. He stood before it and looked up. The tower disappeared above him into the darkness. He muttered a short prayer and went inside.

After two paces, he found himself in complete darkness. Keeping one hand on the wall, he stepped carefully until he came to the staircase at the back of the entrance hall. He began to climb slowly, feeling his way in the darkness. He came to a window that let in a trace of moonlight. Here he waited, reluctant to plunge himself back into the darkness. It was not long until daybreak, but with the light would come the heat of the sun. He decided to press on.

At the second window, he stopped again to catch his breath before stepping once more into the dark. By the time he had reached the third window, his legs were heavy and he wondered how much farther he could go. A weak spray of sunlight seeped into the stairwell, bathing the grey stone in an unearthly glow. He rose and pressed on to the fourth window, where he stopped to look out over the surrounding jungle.

Could he really travel to China, he wondered, and cross the highest mountains in the world? He attempted the next flight, but his wasted legs would take him no farther. He sat on a step and tears of frustration welled in his eyes. He feared he could not even make it back down the staircase alone. The thought of being rescued was too much to bear and it drove his descent on trembling legs.

Outside in the courtyard he counted the windows of the stupa. There were thirty-three.

He made his way miserably to the dining hall and a novice monk set a bowl of rice-gruel before him. He left it untouched and hung his head in sadness. A heavy hand touched his shoulder.

"You are not yourself this morning, Brother Vanya," Bodhidharma said, taking the seat beside his. "Is something the matter?"

Vanya shook his head from side to side in bitter regret. "I am very much afraid I will not be accompanying you on your journey to Nanjing."

"Really? Why not?" Bodhidharma demanded.

"I tried to climb the stupa this morning and was easily beaten."

A novice appeared quickly by Bodhidharma's side and served him with a bowl of gruel, which he began to eat noisily. "That is your reason?" he asked between mouthfuls.

That was the condition you set for traveling with you," Vanya said.

"It seems your desire to travel with me is not so strong after all," Bodhidharma said.

"I want to! I tried my utmost, but I couldn't go any higher than the fifth level and there are thirty-three in total!"

"Maybe so, but I am not leaving today, Brother Vanya. There is still time. You can't become strong overnight. You need to build your strength gradually. If you really want to climb the stupa, I will help you."

"You will?"

"Of course. You can start by eating properly," Bodhidharma said, pushing Vanya's untouched bowl toward him. "Then you can walk in the countryside and do exercises. In the evening, you can climb stairs. Not too many, just enough to grow a little stronger each day. Then, when your body is ready, you can attempt the tower again."

Vanya's face transformed from sorrow to joy and he hugged Bodhidharma.

"I will do as you say, Master," he promised, and spooned down his breakfast with new resolve.

While Vanya was exercising, Bodhidharma spent hours learning Chinese with Yin Chiang and the little scholar was delighted with the progress of his new student. When Yin Chiang announced that he would return to China with Bodhidharma, The Venerable Ananda was duly informed and was overcome with joy.

In the cooler hours of dawn and dusk, they walked far across the countryside with Vanya. In shaded clearings they performed squats to prepare their legs for the hardships ahead; and when they had finished and returned to the monastery, Bodhidharma went deep into the dark forest to practice alone long into the night. After three weeks, Vanya climbed the tower again and reached the eleventh window.

Summer was approaching and word from the mountains was that the snow was melting at the high passes. A team of guides was found to take them to the farthest borders of Assam and detailed travel plans were made. Vanya redoubled his efforts. Ten days before their departure, he reached the twentieth window. The next day, Bodhidharma ordered him to rest and massaged his thin legs with warm oil until they were able to bear his weight once more.

Their preparations continued until three days before their departure, when all three monks had agreed to attempt the giant stupa. They rose at dawn and climbed together. Vanya slowed after twenty flights, but refused all help. Bodhidharma and Yin Chiang continued without him, until Yin Chiang was forced to rest and ease the cramps in his legs.

Bodhidharma continued alone, placing one foot ahead of the other with no thought of the searing pain in his limbs. When he reached the top, breathless and drenched in sweat, he went to the window and looked out over the green landscape below. To the west he saw steaming jungle, to the south and east scrubland and desert, and to the north a soft haze blurred the horizon—the warm damp air of the Ganges.

Some time later Yin Chiang appeared at his shoulder, too breathless to speak. They stood side by side and gazed out over beautiful Magadha in silence. Somewhere beyond the northern mist, they both knew the mountains awaited them, soaring peaks so high that the stupa of Nalanda was no more than a thorn in a green carpet that lay at the mountains' feet.

Vanya appeared on the staircase, grim-faced and determined, and hobbled slowly to the window. Bodhidharma put his arm around his shoulder to steady him and together they looked out over the verdant landscape below. No words were spoken. None were needed. Tears of joy pricked Vanya's eyes at the sight of such beautiful country, followed some time later by tears of sorrow at the thought of leaving his beloved India to venture into an unknown land with his new master.

Cavalry Charges

The troop of Chinese cavalry had ventured far beyond the protection of The Great Wall and onto the endless steppes that belonged to none but the nomads. By day, the wind bit through their leather and armor and slashed at their faces with sharp desert dust. By night, the temperature plummeted far below freezing and any horse or pack animal that strayed from the herd was dead by morning.

Their leader, Captain Fu Sheng, rode at the front of the troop, accompanied by his second-in-command Lieutenant Pai. Pai had served under Fu Sheng for almost two years, but still found himself uncomfortable in the young captain's presence.

"This is how I imagine the edge of the world," Pai said, trying to make conversation, "Who would want to live in a place like this?"

"Our fight with the nomads is not about land," Fu Sheng said. "It's about teaching the barbarians to respect the emperor's power."

"Yes, Captain," Pai replied smartly. It seemed Fu Sheng was in no mood for small talk.

"You're clear about your orders?" Fu Sheng demanded.

"Perfectly."

"Then await my signal."

They had been tracking a Uighur warband that had been plundering Chinese settlements on the frontier. The attacks had begun when the emperor had decreed that all trade with the nomads should cease. The decree had deprived the tribesmen of essentials like rice and salt, as well as the luxuries they had grown accustomed to: spices, elixirs, teas, and silks. What they could no longer acquire through trade, they had begun to take by force.

General Lo in Changan had been alerted about the raids. The general had learned the lessons of the steppes the hard way and did not even consider sending infantry to deal with the tribesmen. The speed and mobility of the Uighur riders made them invulnerable to foot soldiers. Instead, he sent the newly-formed cavalry unit that had been commissioned to deal with just such incidents.

The captain in charge of this unit was Fu Sheng, a young man who was fast becoming a legend on the frontier. Little was known of his origins, though it was said he was from humble beginnings, the son of a petty official from Shandong Province in the east. Fu Sheng had first come to the attention of his superiors for his skill with the sword. He had been unmatched in swordplay throughout his military training and wielded a blade as naturally as others moved a hand or limb.

When the formation of an elite cavalry was announced, Fu Sheng had volunteered, eager to see action on the frontier. Though he had never sat on a horse before, he took to the saddle as naturally as he wielded a sword. Soon he found himself in charge of a small platoon that patrolled the northern border around Lanchou on the Yellow River.

In between skirmishes with the fierce tribesmen, he spent his time studying their methods of war. He read histories and military records, pored over maps of old battlegrounds, and spoke to the officers and men who had faced the horsemen on the plains and survived. He filled journals with notes and sketches of the maneuvers, feints, and ambushes they had used to defeat the Chinese infantry; and he found himself filled with a grudging admiration for these savage men who practiced the art of war with such perfection.

He taught himself some of their harsh Turkic language, and during periods of truce, spent time in their settlements on the pretext of trading horses and supplies. While there, he observed their daily lives and rituals, their customs and manners, and how they trained for battle. He saw young Uighur men, little more than boys, shooting hares at full gallop and snatching up their carcasses from the ground without slowing a pace.

No amount of training could make his Chinese riders equal

to the tribesmen in the saddle, that level of horsemanship took a lifetime to learn—time he did not have—but he did have one advantage. The tribesmen fought when the mood took them, forming loose alliances, looking for quick victories and easy spoils. Their leadership was often shared by the heads of several tribes. There was rarely a strong, central command, and once their bloodlust had been satisfied they were keen to return to their flocks and their women. In short, they lacked the iron discipline of the imperial Chinese army.

It was this discipline that allowed Fu Sheng to drill his cavalry for weeks without respite, until every formation was perfect, every maneuver precise, every command and signal known, understood, and instantly obeyed. He spent countless days on the plains, re-enacting the tactics that the tribesmen had used against the Chinese in the past: charging, flanking, retreating, even scattering in mock panic before regrouping for a deadly new charge. He drilled his troops relentlessly, until formations of man and horse moved as one, and he wielded his cavalry as effortlessly as his sword.

When new unrest erupted to the west, Fu Sheng had been sent out with a troop of cavalry to investigate, and he led them to a stunning victory against a far larger warband. It was the first of many victories, and he had been promoted quickly. By the time he had reached the rank of captain, he had taken personal control of the training of an entire company. It was the finest cavalry unit in the empire.

His men revered him for the skill and power he had bred in them and the victories he had brought them. With him at their front, they were invincible. But they had also witnessed his savagery on the battlefield. They had seen his youthful face lose its mask of serenity, replaced by a demon that dealt out death on all sides with a bloodlust that made even the most hardened veteran turn away.

Now Fu Sheng was tracking a huge warband, over a thousand riders led by the powerful warlord Gulnar. After ten days on their trail, his scouts had caught sight of the Uighurs on a dark plain of rock and shale, where the only feature to punctuate the flat landscape was a row of black hills in the west. His troops had been in good spirits despite the hardships of the terrain, but the Uighur force was larger than expected—considerably larger than their own—and seeing the enemy in such numbers was making the men nervous. The savagery of the Uighurs was well known and every Chinese soldier knew he would rather die than be captured alive.

Now that the enemy had been sighted, the riders milled around uncertainly, wondering why the order to form-up was not given.

Fu Sheng ignored their concerns. "Go now, Lieutenant," he ordered Lieutenant Pai, and Pai wheeled around and galloped away alone in the direction they had come, disappearing quickly into the dust.

The men were eager to charge, but Fu Sheng made them wait. He was asking a lot of them, he knew. The line between bravery and panic was much thinner than most people realized. If they did not engage the enemy soon, there was a danger they might turn and flee instead. But he had trained his men personally and knew them well. They would wait, at least a while longer. He rode among them, smiling, talking earnestly with his men, discussing the fine details of the weather conditions, the ground and the direction of the prevailing wind, bristling with confidence. He was a man who knew that victory was assured, and his mood was infectious. The troops steadied their mounts and waited for the order to charge.

Two li to the north, the Uighurs organized themselves in a loose formation. Three figures in black armor and furs rode to the front. Their helmets were decorated with gnarled antlers, and they carried high the banner of their tribal crest—a fierce black bird, with a hooked beak and sharp talons, that fluttered in the desert wind. The largest of the three was Gulnar; the others were his sons, Bayanchur and Kul.

Gulnar called his sons to him and they conferred. With a terse nod he broke away and rode along the battle line of horsemen, the bloodlust visible in his eyes. His riders cheered as he passed, raising their weapons in the air—crossbows, axes, swords, and war-clubs. Gulnar shouted to them promises of blood, victory, and spoils, and they rose to his cries. He turned and began the advance toward the Chinese position. A roar went up along the ragged line as they set off after him.

The Chinese heard the distant roar and saw the barbarians approaching. Still they waited for the order to form-up and advance, but it did not come. Instead, Captain Fu Sheng gave the order to fall back in a loose formation. There was a moment's delay as they waited, wondering if they had misheard, but he repeated his order loudly and they turned as instructed and rode away.

Gulnar looked across to his elder son, Bayanchur. "A trap, you think?"

"I have never seen any Chinese retreat before," Bayanchur shouted to his father.

Gulnar had seen Chinese generals put infantry in front of a river to block their retreat and force them to fight. He had seen them order a paltry force of Chinese cavalry to charge directly into a superior force. But he had never known them to retreat. He himself had no such objection to it and often used a retreat to lure the enemy into a fatal ambush. Perhaps the Chinese leader was doing the same? He scanned the terrain ahead, but there was no obvious advantage for the Chinese in fighting farther down on the plain. He noticed their retreat had grown disorganized. Some of the troops had already lost formation. He encouraged his horse into a canter, hoping to scatter the Chinese into a panic that would make them easy prey for his riders. Then he noticed a lone horseman approaching with a white banner. It seemed the Chinese wished to talk. Perhaps they wanted to surrender?

Gulnar held up his hand to halt the advance. He smirked at his sons. They would amuse themselves with this messenger first, before sending him back to the Chinese with no eyes, ears, or tongue. That would be their answer. The approaching messenger wore the uniform of a captain, but he looked too young for such a rank. He was almost certainly a decoy, Gulnar decided. Chinese leaders never went near the front lines, preferring to guide the battle from a safe vantage point at the rear.

The messenger halted before them. He appeared perfectly calm and Gulnar wondered if he was too inexperienced even to be afraid. Gulnar's younger son, Kul, whipped out an arrow and loaded it into his crossbow, but Gulnar raised his hand to stop him. They would have some amusement first.

The messenger, still oblivious of the danger he was in, began to address them in a high, ceremonial voice. He seemed to be reciting an official Chinese message with all the dignity he could muster. Gulnar could not understand the exact words, but the meaning was clear enough. The messenger was demanding his surrender. He grinned at his sons, who began to circle the messenger as he spoke, riding so close that their horses brushed against his. It had no effect on the pompous young man and he continued with his long speech. He appeared to be laying down the terms of their surrender in great detail. As he spoke, he did not look at them directly, but instead gazed into the distance behind them. It was all rather comical. Gulnar allowed him to continue. Impatient, his riders began urging him to dispense with the messenger so they could set about the business of slaughter.

He was about to allow his sons to have their fun with the messenger when the messenger seemed to sense his time was up. He raised his hand, as if to say he was not finished yet. Gulnar found this highly amusing. It bought the messenger a few more seconds of life. But Kul had tired of the man's arrogance and began to spit angry words in his face. Still the messenger continued, until Kul drew his short, razor-sharp sword and made several cuts in the air. Still, the messenger's eyes remained fixed on the horizon.

Furious, Kul raised his sword high and struck at the messenger with such force that he overbalanced in his saddle. Gulnar watched in surprise as Kul slumped forward—his son had not been unseated from a pony since he was a small boy. Then the awful truth dawned on him as Kul's body hit the ground and his head fell away at a grotesque angle. Gulnar had not seen the messenger move, but somehow a sword had appeared in his hand and bright blood dripped from its blade.

An eerie quiet fell over the plain. Even the incessant wind seemed to stop for a moment, until a roar from Gulnar and Bayanchur broke the silence. They spurred their horses forward and drew their weapons in fury. Fu Sheng slipped from his saddle and stood behind his horse. They circled to reach him, but he slipped beneath the horse and reappeared on the other side. Gulnar smashed at the horse with his war-club to get it out of the way while Bayanchur rode around the screaming animal to reach his brother's killer. The horse reared up, kicking furiously. Gulnar saw the messenger pass unscathed beneath its thrashing hooves and emerge at Bayanchur's flank. A deep gash appeared across Bayanchur's thigh, while his horse, pierced in the belly, bucked wildly. Bayanchur had to dismount before it fell. He roared in agony as his wounded leg buckled beneath him.

Gulnar dismounted to help his son. As he did, the messenger appeared from nowhere and cut his bicep to the bone. Gulnar's war-club slid from his useless fingers and he waited for the next cut—the killing blow.

It did not come.

Instead, the messenger surveyed the scene around him. Gulnar heard the cries of his men and saw arrows falling on them from the rear. He realized they were facing cavalry on two sides. His front ranks were already swarming forward to assist him, while those at the rear did their best to wheel around and face the enemy behind them.

Amidst this chaos, the main Chinese force began its charge. Satisfied that everything was going as planned, Fu Sheng turned his attention to Gulnar and his son once more. They were side by side now, observing the destruction of their warriors helplessly. Gulnar picked up his war-club in his left hand and Bayanchur drew his axe grimly. They were both afraid of the messenger now; he was a demon and not of this world, but they had no choice but to attack. Gulnar began to swing his lethal war-club. The deadly spikes whirred brutally through the air. In two turns, Fu Sheng had picked up his rhythm and anticipated the crude path of the approaching club. He slipped through its arc effortlessly, cutting as he passed, opening a deep wound across Gulnar's abdomen. Bayanchur swung his axe with savage force. Fu Sheng evaded it with a graceful twist of the shoulders and circled, keeping father and son in a line to prevent them from attacking on both sides.

Bayanchur was nearer, but he hesitated, fearing the messenger would kill him. Fu Sheng sneered at him, mocking his fear. The insult was too much for the son of a Uighur chief and he lunged forward, his axe whirring in the air. Fu Sheng read the crude cadences of his attack easily and severed his arm. Gulnar attacked through a fountain of blood, but he was weak. Fu Sheng slashed his left arm so deeply that it hung limply from his side.

The front ranks of the Uighur horsemen were almost upon him, but he could not resist one more lingering look at the broken figures before him. Their eyes spoke of the horror of Kul's severed head, the agony of their wounds, the dread of their own deaths, a heartbeat away. It was a sight Fu Sheng would treasure as one of his most exquisite memories.

He took two heads with two swift cuts and strode to Kul's horse, which was standing riderless nearby. The Uighurs shot their arrows as he urged the horse into a gallop. He hung from its side to shield himself. The horse was hit, it stumbled and fell, but it did not matter. The oncoming Chinese cavalry reached him and parted in perfect formation to go around him. They had seen what he had done to the Uighur leaders and seen the red banners appearing at the enemy's rear. Their captain had returned to them, miraculously unscathed. A roar of battle joy went up among them as they charged into the barbarians. There would be no stopping them.

They tore into the Uighurs with unbridled savagery. Leaderless and surrounded, the tribesmen quickly fell into confusion and panic. The slaughter was swift and cruel. Some of the Uighurs died fighting. Others threw down their weapons and tried to surrender, but no prisoners were taken that day. When the killing finally ended, a hellish silence hung over the plain, punctuated only by the screams of dying horses and the groans of the few Chinese casualties.

The doctor and his orderlies tended to the wounded quickly, as they had trained to do, while the soldiers pitched their camp for the night. Only when the perimeter was secure and all the wounded had been treated did Fu Sheng give permission to collect the spoils of war. The bodies of the dead were stripped of armor and weapons and searched for gold, silver, gems, and any other items of value. The Uighurs' supplies and mule carts were added to their own and their horses rounded up and led into a makeshift corral.

The battle had been easier than expected, but there was little celebration among the soldiers. The bloodlust had left them now and they were weary to the bone. Some spoke in hushed voices of the captain's exploits and shivered in the icy wind of the plains. What they had witnessed filled them with a gnawing unease. No ordinary man could have done what he had, and some whispered that a spirit from the underworld walked among them.

Fu Sheng sat apart, cleaning and resharpening his sword. Even his officers left him alone as he tended to his blade with infinite care. Only Lieutenant Pai approached to inform him that his tent was set up and his meal was ready to be served.

"You took your time today, Lieutenant," Fu Sheng said without looking up.

"We came as quickly as we could Captain, I assure you."

"You didn't stop in a tavern on the way?"

Lieutenant Pai waited in silent dread until he saw the smirk playing on the captain's lips.

"We searched, because we were parched, but there's nothing in this godforsaken place," he said dryly.

"You did well today Lieutenant," Fu Sheng grinned. "It will be mentioned in my dispatch to General Lo."

"I was only doing my duty, Captain."

"Nevertheless, it will be noted."

"Thank you, Sir."

Fu Sheng wondered about inviting Pai into his tent to dine with him. They could discuss the battle and savor their victory together. But Pai was uncomfortable in his presence, that was clear. No, he would dine alone and compose his report to General Lo instead. It was better that way. Better to be feared than to be loved.

A Second Vision

The Venerable Ananda's assistant brought juice for him, as he did every day at that hour of the evening. He found the old master sitting in his favored spot by the window and set the juice down beside him. Normally The Venerable Ananda never failed to thank him and often exchanged a few pleasantries too, but this time he was silent, lost in some deep reverie. The assistant left quietly, not wishing to disturb the great man over a trifle.

However, when he returned an hour later, he found the juice untouched and his master's eyes wet with tears. He touched Ananda on the shoulder, concerned, and inquired if he was unwell. Ananda turned slowly, seeing him for the first time, and assured him that he was fine. The assistant was reluctant to leave him in such a state, but Ananda insisted, so the assistant complied.

But The Venerable Ananda was not fine. The vision he'd spoken of to Bodhidharma and Yin Chiang had changed, and ever since their departure, a new vision had taken its place. It returned to him each day, entering his mind during meditation and invading his dreams when he slept, and each time the vision was more vivid than the last. In it, he saw his greatest desire would be fulfilled. Bodhidharma would bring The Way to China. But far from making him happy, the vision filled him with dread.

He could still make out Bodhidharma's powerful figure on a slope of startling green in a place that could only be China. Bodhidharma was walking with two companions. They were entering a monastery together, the same little red monastery he had seen before. Everything was as it should be.

But then the eye of his mind descended from the sky, and settled closer to the gates of the monastery. From here he could see that Bodhidharma's followers were not the same two who had left Nalanda with him. Ananda stretched his mind, hoping for a glimpse of their faces, but that much he could not see. All he knew was that the Indian hermit and the Chinese scholar were no longer with Bodhidharma. He searched for them on the green mountainside and followed the rocky road from the temple to the main highway, all the way to the long river that cut China in two, but there was no sign of them. He searched the countless towns and cities of the Empire, the vast grasslands and endless deserts, the high mountains and the deep lakes, hoping to find them, but he searched in vain.

And finally, he prayed for them, and wept for what he had done.

山巒

PART 2
MOUNTAIN

Monks Go East

The monks washed the dust of the plains from their bodies in the cool waters of the Ganges. Nearby, on a makeshift quay of tattered planks, a longboat was being loaded with baggage and supplies. It had been chartered to take them to the highland waterways of Assam. The craft was old but in good repair, and, if the captain was to be believed, had made the long journey on more than one occasion. A compact sail hung neatly rolled on the low mast. Oars and poles had been stacked on each side for use during the difficult upstream passage of the Brahmaputra.

Bodhidharma and Vanya languished in the shallows enjoying the caress of the sacred river, but Yin Chiang washed quickly and hurried away to supervise the loading of his baggage. He watched anxiously and urged them to be careful as the crew struggled to bring on board his heavy box of scriptures and translations. They succeeded without mishap or complaint.

When all the baggage had been safely stowed, the captain demanded a price five times higher than originally agreed, claiming the load was too heavy. The head guide argued furiously with him for almost an hour, until a small increase was agreed, and they were ready to set sail.

The longboat eased downstream into the gentle breeze and moved swiftly, helped by the occasional stroke of the oars. They continued southeast for many days, until the Ganges met the Brahmaputra in an expanse of water so vast that it filled the horizon like a brown sea. Here they turned northeast up the Brahmaputra into Assam. After many more days, they left the marshland and mangrove swamps of the delta behind and entered rolling green hills thick with jungle. The air was filled with the howls of monkeys and the cries of colorful birds. All manner of creatures came to the water's edge to drink: water buffalo and the enormous gaur that stood taller than a man, sambar and wild boar, dogs and jackals, civet and leopard. Herds of wild elephants splashed in the shallows and the monks delighted in their antics. When the crew learned that elephants did not exist where Yin Chiang came from, they tried to convince him that the elusive unicorn also inhabited the jungles of Assam. Vanya nodded seriously, assuring him it was true, and Yin Chiang kept one eye on the shoreline as they traveled.

He spent most of the day teaching Chinese to Bodhidharma, who learned with astonishing speed. He had never heard an Indian speak Chinese before and it filled him with an inexplicable joy. Soon they were able hold a simple conversation, and before long they were ready to begin the painstaking work of translating the Sutras.

They spent hours discussing the meaning of important passages and grew accustomed to paring down the elegant Sanskrit prose to its essence for ease of translation. Yin Chiang found himself surprised at Bodhidharma's interpretations, which were often quite different from his own and those generally accepted by Nalanda's intellectual elite. He began to wonder if this wild-looking monk from the jungles of Pallava was up to the academic challenge of penetrating their depths. Yet The Venerable Ananda had spoken most highly of him and that was praise of the highest order. Yin Chiang did not know what to think.

At dusk, one of the crewmen called him urgently to the prow and pointed out a giant beast in the shallows. "Unicorn," he announced with a broad grin.

There was a horn protruded from the beast's head, but it was certainly no unicorn. Its skin was as thick as an elephant's and its eyes small like a pig's. Yin Chiang glared at the crewman while the rest of the crew fell about laughing helplessly. Vanya held his sides with mirth and even Bodhidharma could not suppress a smile.

Yin Chiang cursed them all in words that only he could understand and returned to his translations. But that night he lay awake, lulled by the gentle rocking of the boat, and thought of the joke that had been played on him. His mind went back to what The Venerable Ananda had said to him, that Bodhidharma might yet enlighten him; and finally he smiled to himself. Perhaps he did take things a little too seriously, after all. Perhaps a rhinoceros was indeed a unicorn.

The next day he chose a passage from the Diamond Sutra that had puzzled him for many years and set about translating it with Bodhidharma. As they worked, he found himself taken by the boldness of Bodhidharma's interpretations and his willingness to ignore conventional wisdom. Soon, he began to marvel at the simplicity of Bodhidharma's approach. A new excitement ran through his veins as he leafed through the pages of his manuscripts and scrolls looking for further challenges for his new teacher.

That evening, when the longboat had pulled into shore and the smell of frying fish was drifting from the charcoal stove, Vanya joined them with a question of his own.

"I have been reading the sacred scriptures too, and I'm worried that we are not following The Buddha's law correctly. He tells us to burn incense each day, to scatter flowers, and light lamps in his name. How can we reach nirvana if we don't do these things?"

"A good question," Bodhidharma said earnestly. "What do you think, Brother Yin Chiang?"

"I must confess, I miss the daily rituals of temple life. They are very calming. However, we are on a journey, so I think we can make allowances. Besides, I don't believe these practices hold the key to nirvana."

"And what do you say, Master?" Vanya asked.

"Do you really think that burning incense and harming plants will help you reach nirvana?"

"I guess not," Vanya said dejectedly, "so why does The Buddha tell us to do it?"

"He was using metaphors, but all over the world monks concern themselves with rituals and ceremonies instead of what they symbolize. Burning incense means keeping our own awareness alive. Scattering flowers means spreading the teachings. Lighting lamps means passing on enlightenment to others. There is no mystery."

Bodhidharma saw the disappointment on his disciple's face and continued more gently. "Brother Vanya, you were once a hermit. You fasted, as The Buddha did once. The hunger you experienced was not designed as a punishment for the body but rather an exercise for your mind. You learned to combat the cravings of hunger. That took strength. That is why I encouraged you to join me."

"Encouraged me? You did everything possible to dissuade me!"

"If that is what you think, then you are deluded," Bodhidharma laughed, clapping Vanya on the back. "Once we stop eating the food of delusion, then we are free!"

"In that case, I face a dilemma," Vanya said quietly.

"What is that, Brother Vanya?" Bodhidharma asked, his face a new picture of concern.

"The fish, cooking on the charcoal … it's fresh from the river. I watched them catch it less than an hour ago. It smells delicious and I'm looking forward to eating it. But that's bad because it's a desire, a craving. So now I'm wondering: should I eat it or shouldn't I?"

"Another weighty matter," Bodhidharma said earnestly, "which must be given due thought and consideration. What do you say, Brother Yin Chiang?"

"It all depends how badly Brother Vanya desires the fish," Yin Chiang said with a frown. "If he wants it to fill his belly, it is understandable. But if he wishes to indulge in sensuous pleasures of the palate, then it is most certainly a sin."

"And if he lies about it, that is another sin," Bodhidharma said.

"Assuredly."

Vanya looked from one to the other in dismay, until they could conceal their laughter no longer.

"Come, my dear Vanya," Bodhidharma chuckled, "let's go and eat fish. You'll need all your strength for the mountains, so eat plenty. Those mountains are not far now."

The river began to narrow and the current quickened. Soon the entire boat crew was needed to row against the powerful current. Villages appeared less frequently in these wooded highlands. When the longboat stopped for supplies, the local tribes spoke in unfamiliar tongues that the guides struggled to understand. They wore striped loincloths and headdresses of colorful plumage with protruding antlers or boars' tusks; they worshipped unknown deities, snake gods and mountain spirits; and each new village seemed stranger than the last.

White peaks appeared over the hilltops and by the end of the day, masses of dark rock and ice loomed, blocking out the sun. Late the following morning they arrived at a village in a bend of the river and the boat pulled into the bank. The head guide spoke briefly with the longboat's captain and returned to inform the monks that they had reached the end of their river journey.

Men from the village came to the water's edge to help unload the boat. After a short discussion with the head guide, a local boy led the monks to a hut where they could stay until the next part of their journey began. The hut's pointed roof was made of reeds and there was a heavy blanket across the entrance. Inside, more blankets had been piled on the floor and hung from the walls. Cushions of leather and fur lay scattered around and a small stove smoldered in the center.

The head guide came to inform them that a party of Tibetans had been sent for to take them through the mountains. He could not say when, but assured them it would be soon. The three monks explored the village followed by a gaggle of curious children, then walked beside the river, heading upstream until they came to rapids that no boat could ever hope to pass. In the evening, they joined the villagers in a large communal hut to share a meal and drink the sharp local wine. By the time they retired to their own hut, the outside temperature had fallen to a level neither Bodhidharma nor Vanya had experienced before and they hurried inside and cocooned themselves in thick blankets and furs.

A week went by and there was no sign of the Tibetans. On the morning of the eighth day, they woke to find a band of men in heavy woolen coats with fur hats hung by a string on their backs. Their coats were wide open despite the chill of the morning air, and they appeared flushed and red-faced. Two of them were involved in a heated discussion with the Indian guides, with one of the villagers acting as a translator.

Even stranger than the men were the huge shaggy beasts that had arrived with them. The animals had long curved horns and matted black hair that flowed almost to the ground. They stood in a ragged line, flicking their tails and munching grass from the hillside. Vanya went to take a closer look. One of the beasts snorted loudly and he jumped away, much to the amusement of the Tibetans.

"I see you have never encountered the great horned bear of the Himalayas," Yin Chiang chuckled.

"What are these creatures?" Vanya asked warily.

"Don't worry, they're harmless to humans. Unless provoked ..."

"You're joking, I take it."

"They're almost as rare as the unicorn of Assam," Yin Chiang said, relishing his chance at getting his own back.

"Seriously, what are they?" Vanya asked, "I have never seen anything like them. Are they some sort of oxen?"

"They are yaks," Yin Chiang said, "and actually quite common in the high country. The yak is to the mountains what the camel is to the desert. They are the main form of transport in the Himalayas, if not the only one, and serve all sorts of other purposes too. In fact they are truly remarkable creatures, as you will soon discover."

"We will?" Vanya asked.

"How else do you expect to cross the Himalayas, Brother Vanya? No other pack animal can survive up there."

Vanya looked at the imposing white peaks and the enormity of the journey ahead struck him for the first time.

"How will we survive?" he asked, almost to himself.

"The yaks will help us. You'll see."

They went to join the head guide who was still arguing with the Tibetans. When the Tibetans caught sight of Bodhidharma, all discussion ceased. He towered over them and the sturdy little mountain men gazed up at him dumbly. The translator quickly explained that this was the holy man who wished to cross the mountains into China, and the Tibetans began to talk quickly among themselves.

"Is there a problem?" Bodhidharma asked.

"They are demanding more money than usual," the guide answered. "They say the journey is more difficult because there have been landslides during the winter and several passes are blocked. They will need to take a different route."

"Have they seen the landslides with their own eyes?" he asked.

There was a rapid exchange of words and the answer came back via the translator. "They say it is true."

"Tell them there is no more money than what we are offering," Bodhidharma said, fixing one of the older Tibetans with his gaze. There was another furious exchange of words. More of the Tibetans gathered round and the atmosphere grew tense. Some appeared ready to accept the money on offer, but the older man, who seemed to be their leader, was standing firm. Bodhidharma held up his hand for silence and pointed to him.

"What is this man's name?" he asked the translator.

"Khandro," came the answer.

"Ask Khandro how he plans to make the journey when he is in so much pain?"

The translator spoke quickly and Khandro replied angrily, glaring at Bodhidharma. "He demands to know what you mean?" the translator said.

"His back is locked on the lower left side. It has been that way for some time. Does he seriously intend to carry a heavy pack?"

As Bodhidharma's words were translated, Khandro could not hide his astonishment and his companions were stunned by the monk's insight. They had all seen their leader suffering in silence for many days, too proud to acknowledge his injury or reduce the weight in his pack.

"Come with me," Bodhidharma ordered, extending his hand to Khandro. There was no need for any translation. Khandro hesitated for a moment, then obeyed, and Bodhidharma led him away to the hut where they had been staying.

Inside he gestured for Khandro to remove his clothes while he lit a stove and arranged a pile of blankets into a thick bed. As Khandro took off his tunic and lay down, Bodhidharma took a vial of warming oil from his knapsack and rubbed it vigorously into his hands. Soon his powerful fingers were prodding the knotted muscles on the Tibetan's back, seeking out the source of the tension and working the dense tissue relentlessly until he felt it relax. Khandro could not help grunting with appreciation, but his pleasure turned to fear as he felt a great weight pressing down on the center of his back. A violent jolt forced the air from his lungs and he heard a loud crack. For a moment he feared his spine had been snapped, but when he sat up, he found he could move easily and the pain in his back had all but disappeared.

Bodhidharma laid him down once more and turning him on his side, laid his hands on Khandro's shoulder and hip. Again Khandro felt a great weight bearing down on him until, with a jerk, there was another crack and Bodhidharma released him. He tried to rise but Bodhidharma placed a hand on him gently, and turning him onto his front, covered him with a thick layer of blankets. "Sleep," he ordered, closing his eyes so Khandro would understand.

Khandro began to protest. He was far too busy to sleep. Bodhidharma held him down gently and spoke in a low and monotonous voice. Though he could not understand a word, Khandro felt compelled to obey. He was aware of Bodhidharma rising to fetch something, but did not have the energy to see what it was. A sharp smell penetrated his nostrils. The Indian was mixing a pungent paste in a wooden bowl. Khandro's eyelids grew unbearably heavy. He wondered if the paste was for him—it was the last thing he thought before falling into a deep sleep.

When he awoke an hour later, the Indian was still seated beside him. Embarrassed to have fallen asleep, he rose quickly expecting a sharp pain in his back from the sudden movement. It did not come. Instead, he felt flexible and more filled with energy than he had for a long time. Bodhidharma handed him the fiery paste he had mixed earlier. He accepted it and sniffed it curiously before setting it aside. Then he took Bodhidharma's hands in his own and turned them over to inspect them. They were the hands of a powerful healer, but the heavy calluses told him healing was not their only power. He thanked Bodhidharma in words Bodhidharma could not understand and they left the hut together to return to the others.

Khandro crouched down beside the Tibetans and spoke rapidly, then rose and bent this way and that to demonstrate his new mobility. His companions were duly impressed and conferred for a moment before summoning the translator. The translator listened to them in surprise, then spoke with the head guide, who in turn spoke to the monks. "I don't know how you did it," the guide said with a bemused smile, "but now, the Tibetans are willing to take the holy man wherever he wants to go."

Kuang Waits in the Dark

The last of the torches had been extinguished and Yulong Fort was silent and still. The only sound in the barracks was the snoring of the other recruits. Kuang rose silently from his bunk and slipped out into the cold night, crossing the compound by the faint light of the moon.

The storeroom inside the hospital was usually kept locked, but Weilin had a key and they had taken to meeting there at midnight. The room was damp and dark. He took a blanket from one of the shelves and wrapped it around his shoulders, then waited miserably for over an hour.

This time she did not appear. He was about to leave when he heard the click of the door and her silhouette appeared in the entrance. She stopped, hesitant to come inside. "I'm here," he called softly.

She came to him and he reached for her, putting his hands on her hips. She gripped his wrists. "Hey," he laughed, trying to free his hand so he could touch her, but she held him with a strength he didn't know she possessed. "What's the matter? I've been waiting for you, Weilin."

"Weilin is not coming tonight, or any other night!"

It was spoken in a harsh whisper. He recognized the voice of Weilin's maid.

"You are such a young fool Kuang," she hissed. "Yes, I know your name, and who you are! I'll be watching you very carefully from now on. Did you really think the two of you were invisible? Count yourself lucky that it was me who spotted you, and no one else. You can never see Weilin again. Never come near the commander's house. Never speak even a single word to her, or I will see to it that you suffer."

She was so angry that she struck at his head with her clenched fists and Kuang was too dumbstruck to resist. The blows caught him on his ears and around his temples. He did not care. He knew he would not see Weilin again, and the thought made him numb to the pain.

Finally the maid pushed him aside and picked her way out of the cramped storeroom leaving him alone in the dark.

Yaks Carry Scriptures

The monks' baggage was arranged outside the hut in a neat row and the Tibetans examined each piece before loading it onto the yaks. The Indian guides had prepared the monks well, with neatly packed supplies, thick blankets, winter clothing, and fur-lined tents. Each piece was loaded on the yaks without comment until one of the Tibetans came to Yin Chiang's chest. He looked inside and seeing the rolls of tightly packed paper, dragged the chest to one side.

"That is coming too," Yin Chiang said.

The guide shook his head. The translator from the village could not be found, so one of the younger Tibetans who spoke a few words of Chinese was summoned.

"This box must be brought," Yin Chiang told him.

"Too heavy," the young man said.

"The papers are very important."

"It will not balance," the young man explained. "The yaks walk on narrow paths, very dangerous. All baggage must balance. Paper is no use on the mountains, except for fire," he smiled apologetically.

"What is your name, young man," Yin Chiang demanded.

"Rinchen."

"Well, Rinchen," he began, but more guides had gathered

around them and began talking to him loudly in Tibetan. Then Bodhidharma appeared by his side and Yin Chiang looked at him imploringly.

Bodhidharma smiled and put his hands on the box. "Very important," he said to the Tibetans. At this the other baggage was quickly unloaded and painstakingly rearranged so the chest could be carried by a single yak.

When the Tibetans were satisfied all the yaks had been loaded correctly, the monks said a grateful goodbye to their guides and the local villagers, and the yak train began its slow ascent of the mountains. The delay had meant a late start and the animals were suffering in the heat. The Tibetans pushed the pace, eager to get the heavily laden yaks out of the low-lying hills and into the mountains before the midday sun cleared the surrounding peaks.

The trail climbed relentlessly and after several hours Vanya began to fall behind. The Tibetans did not slow and soon Yin Chiang fell back too. Only Bodhidharma seemed able to keep up with the relentless pace of the Tibetans and their yaks, who, despite their enormous loads, picked their way along the narrow path as easily as a pony on a country lane.

By midday the air had begun to thin and the monks struggled to breathe. Vanya and Yin Chiang were both sick. Soon after, Vanya became dizzy and disorientated and sat down helplessly on the mountainside. Yin Chiang was about to call for help when Rinchen appeared with a cup of steaming liquid for Vanya.

"What is it?" Vanya demanded weakly.

"They call it tea," Yin Chiang said, "but it's nothing like Chinese tea, or even Indian tea. Nevertheless, you should drink it. It will revive you."

Vanya looked warily at the red-brown liquid, and sipped it cautiously. He grimaced. "It is even sweeter than Bodhidharma's tea," he complained.

"Drink it all," Yin Chiang insisted.

Vanya complied miserably and felt his head clear almost at once. The sweetness gave him a little extra strength and soon he was ready to rejoin the others in their never-ending climb. They walked throughout the day, until the forested hills were left far behind and only hardy shrubs and mountain grass grew on the stony ground at their feet.

Darkness came early on the mountain. As soon as the light began to fade, a cry went out along the yak train and they wheeled into a stony clearing to pitch camp. The Tibetans unpacked swiftly, working in perfect unison and Bodhidharma had never seen a camp set up so fast. By the time Yin Chiang and Vanya joined him, their tent was pitched and Rinchen had an urn of water sitting over a fire. One of the older Tibetans was pumping air into the flames from the strangest contraption Vanya had ever seen.

"What on earth is he doing?" he asked.

"There is less air up here," Yin Chiang explained, "the fire needs air to breathe."

"But what is he using as bellows? It looks like a dead animal!"

"It is," Yin Chiang smiled, "it's made from a yak skin."

Vanya feared he was the butt of another joke, but Yin Chiang assured him it was true and, taking the bellows from the old man, held it out for Vanya to examine. Vanya was forced to admit it was indeed made from a yak. The old man spoke to Rinchen, who translated for the monks.

"Old Dorje says you should try it."

"I tried it last time I was in the mountains," Yin Chiang said. "It's a lot more difficult than it appears," and try as he might, Vanya could get no air from the giant bag of skin. The fire began to splutter and he was forced to hand back the bellows to Old Dorje.

When the water in his urn began to boil, Rinchen added a brick of red tea, two fistfuls of sugar and a generous sprinkling of salt.

For his finishing touch, he reached for a sheep's stomach used to store rancid yak's butter and, to the monks' dismay, squeezed several lumps of the glistening white pulp into the brew.

With the tea complete, he opened a sack of barley pellets and the Tibetans gathered around with their bowls. Rinchen poured tea into each of their bowls and they helped themselves to the pellets, which they softened in their tea before eating. Some had brought extra food, butter, cheese, meat and dumplings, since each man was responsible for his own supplies.

Rinchen handed a bowl of tea to Bodhidharma, who regarded the grey liquid gloomily.

"Don't touch it, Master," Vanya warned. "It will make you sick."

Bodhidharma put it under his nose. It smelled rancid. He handed it back as politely as he could. The others refused too and made their own tea as they always did, much to the amusement of the Tibetans. Rinchen offered them barley pellets, but they refused these too and unpacked the food they had brought from the village: rice, bread, spiced vegetables, and fruit. Rinchen heated it for them on his fire and they ate heartily, hungry from the exertions of the day.

Later, they sat around the fire together and the Tibetans passed around a bottle of liquor that burned the throat and warmed the belly. Conversation livened as the fiery drink loosened their tongues. Rinchen taught the monks how to say "yak," "tea," and "tsampa," the barley pellets that were the staple diet of the Tibetans. Yin Chiang tried to work the yak-skin bellows once more, without success, much to the amusement of the Tibetans. When the bottle was empty, they retired to their tents, where, despite the freezing temperature and howling wind outside, the monks drifted quickly into a deep and untroubled sleep.

They were awakened at dawn by a cry that echoed around the camp. By the time they had emerged from their tent, the camp had all but disappeared onto the yaks. The cooking pot had been packed away, but Rinchen gave each of them a leather bag filled with food provisions, which, he explained, they could eat whenever they felt hungry.

The Tibetans were keen to get away early and soon the yaks were moving off and climbing ever higher into the mountains. Despite the sunshine, the temperature continued to drop and even the Tibetans wrapped their coats tightly around themselves. The air grew so thin that every step became slow and labored. Vanya fell behind again and Yin Chiang walked with him, grateful for the slower pace.

The Tibetans halted the yaks at midday and soon an urn of tea was boiling on a fire. They gathered around and dipped tsampa pellets into their tea. Khandro made a space by the fire for Bodhidharma and offered him a bowl of tea. This time he accepted, and the Tibetans watched as he raised the tea to his lips. Old Dorje tapped his fist against his own chest, then pointed at the tea.

"It makes you strong?" Bodhidharma asked in Chinese, grimacing at the harsh flavor of the tea.

"Yes, strong!" Rinchen nodded eagerly.

"I can imagine," Bodhidharma said, forcing the foul liquid down with a gasp, much to the amusement of his audience. Suddenly he clutched his throat and began to shake violently. The Tibetans watched in horror until he turned and winked at them, causing much amusement among the taciturn mountain men.

When it was time to continue, they unloaded one of the yaks and redistributed its load among the other animals. A makeshift saddle was placed on its back and the exhausted Vanya was lifted onto the animal. To his surprise, he found it easy to balance on the yak's broad back and rode happily for several hours that afternoon, until it was time to swap with Yin Chiang, who was also struggling to keep up.

They were approaching the first of the high mountain passes.

The sun shone so brightly that their skin blistered and burned until a shift in the trail took them into the shadow of a giant peak and their limbs numbed with cold. The wind threatened to blow them into bottomless ravines or smash them against the rocks of the cliff-faces that they hugged. Even the air itself played tricks on their eyes, revealing pristine views one minute, then shrouding them in cloud the next.

Herds of unusual creatures roamed freely in this remote wilderness: wild yaks, large and fearsome; long-necked asses called kyang; four-horned sheep and mountain goats that perched on impossible ledges; and mottled snow leopards that watched impassively from their rocky lairs. Wild dogs followed the yak train from a distance, their coats so shaggy that they could be mistaken for bears, and wolves howled mournfully each day with the onset of dusk.

The Tibetans kept their crossbows at hand in case a predator should attack one of the yaks, and used them to shoot any passing game that could supplement their rations. At night by the campfire they told stories of giant bears, invisible panthers, and restless spirits that roamed the mountains, leaving tracks in the snow that led the hunter to his doom.

They followed a trail that snaked among the majestic peaks, crossing dazzling glaciers, furious streams, and narrow mountain passes. On a high plateau they skirted a salt-water lake so vast that it was called a sea. Ice packs floated close to the shore, cracking and groaning in the wind. The ground was made up of no more than sharp stones, rocks, and shifting shale, yet even here the yaks found vegetation to graze on and despite walking all day under enormous loads, needed nothing more than what they found as they went along. They were at their best in the bitter cold of the morning and the evening. The Tibetans rested them at mid-day, allowing them time to graze and drink from the clear mountain streams. In return, the yaks provided for their masters: meat, milk, butter, lamp oil, leather, fleece. Their coarse outer hair made rope, blankets, and even coverings for shelters; their blood was a powerful medicine, and in a place where no wood grew, dried yak-dung was a ready fuel for the fire. Yin Chiang told Vanya that he had even seen boats made from yaks, but Vanya steadfastly refused to believe him and nothing he could say would change his mind.

One morning the monks awoke to find the camp engulfed in a cloud so thick that it was impossible to see an arm's length in front of them. The Tibetans packed slowly, hampered by the icy cold and lack of visibility. When the yaks were finally loaded they waited, unwilling to move forward into the white void. When it became clear the cloud would not pass quickly, Rinchen lit a fire and they gathered around to drink tea, unable to make out anyone but the person beside them. The conversations around the fire were muffled by the dense vapor, creating the eerie effect of voices murmuring in a dream.

The cloud remained throughout the morning, long after the Rinchen had extinguished the fire and packed the last of his things onto a waiting yak. Then in a turn of the head, it dissolved to reveal row upon row of splendid peaks, gleaming white and gold against a sky of fathomless blue. A cry went out along the waiting line to move off but Bodhidharma remained where he stood, transfixed by the beauty of what he saw before him. Yin Chiang appeared at his shoulder and they admired the peaks together.

"I had no idea we were camped in such a magnificent setting," Bodhidharma said with a shake of his head.

"There is no end to the surprises of mountains," Yin Chiang said happily. "It's a line by one of China's most famous poets."

"How true," Bodhidharma smiled. "My master, Prajnatara, told me of this place. The Roof of the World, he called it. He said it was incomparable, but I could not appreciate his words until now."

"There is nowhere else like it," Yin Chiang said quietly.

"The Tibetans too, and their animals. They are fascinating—so suited to their environment."

"If only people in the world below could be the same," Yin Chiang said.

"What is stopping us?"

"Maybe we don't believe life can be so simple."

"Can it?" Bodhidharma asked.

"You consider this nirvana?" Yin Chiang demanded, intrigued.

"I consider it a blessed existence to be at one with the world."

"Blessed, perhaps, but this world is harsh. The scriptures make nirvana sound blissful, wonderful ..."

"People who write scriptures don't climb mountains, Yin Chiang."

Yin Chiang looked hurt and Bodhidharma took his hand and grasped it firmly.

"Look at this place. Despite the hardship, would you miss it for anything in the world?"

"No," Yin Chiang conceded with a smile, "I would not."

"Nor I, Brother, nor I. And in truth, what more is there to say?"

A Night in Longpan

Dusk enveloped Longpan. The tavern owners lit their oil lamps and stoked their charcoal fires in preparation for the soldiers arriving from the fort. The smoke mixed with the early evening mist to create a fog that hung in the narrow streets and alleyways and stung the eyes and nostrils of the town's visitors.

Kuang had arrived early, eager to get away from the barracks and blot out all thoughts of Weilin, but it was too early to start drinking in a tavern, or to find a woman for the night. He came to a canteen by the side of a canal where he remembered eating once before. The soup had been good. It would make a welcome change from the slop they served at the fort.

A young waitress showed him to a corner table with a smile. She was pretty, but not as pretty as Weilin. Now that he could no longer have Weilin, he could not get her out of his mind and craved her with a passion he could not understand. The waitress took his order and went to the kitchen, where a heavyset man was chopping vegetables, his hand moving in a blur. An older woman was cooking beside him. The waitress spooned a generous portion of noodles into a bowl and the cook poured broth over them, steam rising around her as she did.

Kuang grunted his thanks as the waitress served him. "It looks good."

"Mother's soup is renowned," she smiled.

"The cook is your mother?" he asked.

"Yes."

"And the other cook, is he your father?"

"No, that's Uncle Chin. He helps out here."

"So, what's your name? Mine's Kuang, by the way."

"Nice to meet you, Kuang," she smiled.

"What time do you finish tonight?" he asked.

"Oh, we're open until late."

"Maybe we could meet afterward?" he said with his most winning smile.

"I have to stay and help with the cleaning-up," she said apologetically.

"I'm sure mother and Uncle Chin can manage without you for one night?" he persisted.

"Tonight is a very busy night," she said, turning away.

"You never told me your name," he called out after her, but if she heard him, she did not answer.

A new group of diners had arrived and she turned her attention to them with a smile. Kuang saw her smile fade when she saw who had entered. He followed her gaze and was dismayed to see it was his old enemy Tsun and his three followers.

Tsun called out to the waitress loudly, "Is your father here?"

"He's away on business," she answered.

"When will he be back?" Tsun demanded.

"Next week, I think."

"If the old man's not here, we'll talk to your mother instead," Tsun said menacingly, and Kuang saw a look of dread pass across the waitress's face.

"I'll check," she mumbled. "Father may have returned early."

She hurried into the kitchen and Tsun took a seat at an empty table. It was then that he noticed Kuang sitting in the corner and glared at him. There was a score to settle between them, but now was not the time. Tsun was busy with other matters.

Kuang held his gaze, masking his concern that he was trapped in a canteen with Tsun's gang, until a tall man emerged from the kitchen. Kuang guessed it was the waitress's father. He carried a long-handled axe by his side. The chef, who the waitress had called Uncle Chin, followed one step behind with a meat cleaver which he spun expertly in his fist. The two men strode to Tsun's table and stood over the seated soldiers.

"What is it you want, exactly?" the owner demanded, tapping the head of his axe lightly on the floor.

"We're only here for a bowl of your fine soup," Tsun smiled like a trapped snake.

"There's no more soup," the owner said.

"You must be mistaken. Comrade Kuang over there has a fresh bowl and it looks very tasty."

"That was the last of it," the owner said.

Tsun shrugged. "There is one other small matter, the money you owe me from the game we played last week. You can give it to me now, if you like."

"I don't owe you any money," the owner said evenly. "You and your friends were cheating."

"You can pay me later if you like," Tsun continued to smile.

"You're getting nothing, and you need to leave now," the owner said, his fingers playing lightly around the axe handle.

The soldiers rose from the table and Tsun stared hard into the owner's eyes as he passed. "We'll see you again soon," he warned.

The owner shut the door behind them and locked it, waiting with his axe ready in case they should try to force their way back in. Meanwhile Uncle Chin hurried through the kitchen and locked the back door.

"It's not over yet," the owner said to no one in particular.

The waitress and her mother stood in the kitchen, holding each other to stop themselves shaking. Kuang finished his soup quickly, and reached into his pocket to pay. He was eager to get away before Tsun and his gang returned. He did not think Tsun would let such an incident pass. The owner waved his money away. "No need for that. I'm sorry your dinner was disturbed. Please, wait just a few more minutes before I open the door. Do you know those men?"

"Unfortunately, yes," Kuang answered.

"They have been demanding money, a gambling debt, they claim, but they were cheating."

"I can believe it," Kuang said."

"I have reported them to the magistrate, but he says it's a matter for the military."

"Have you tried speaking to someone at the fort?" Kuang asked.

"Yes, but I was sent away. The army doesn't care about us. We're not even Chinese as far as they are concerned. No officer would ever take my word over that of a Han Chinese."

There was a soft knock on the door.

The owner took up his axe in both hands and stood his ground.

"Hey, open up!" called an old voice.

"It sounds like Old Cheng!" The owner said to Kuang. "Is that you Cheng?" he shouted through the door.

"Of course it's me!" came the answer. "Who did you think it was?"

"Are you alone?"

"What sort of question is that? I've been alone for over twenty years!"

"I mean is there anyone with you, outside?" the owner shouted, emphasizing each word so the old man would hear.

"Who would I bring with me?" Cheng shouted. "What is going on? Why are you closed at this hour?"

The owner unlocked the door and opened it a crack to make sure Old Cheng was alone, only then did he open the door to allow him inside.

"What sort of a greeting is this?" Old Cheng grumbled, looking at the axe in the owner's hands.

"I was chopping wood," the owner smiled reassuringly, leaning his axe against the wall.

Cheng looked about at the troubled faces. "Why do you all look so worried?"

"Just come inside," urged the owner.

"Why all the questions?"

"No reason," the owner said, ushering him inside. Cheng came in and put his bag down in the doorway. The owner picked it up quickly and put it inside.

"Come into the warm, and sit yourself down."

"But it's not cold. What's the matter with you tonight?"

The owner swung the door shut, but it would not close. He pressed it again, but there was something wedged in the doorframe.

Too late, he saw it was an iron bar.

The door flew open and old Cheng was flung aside. The owner lunged for his axe, but Tsun was upon him before he could reach it. The other soldiers rushed in with sticks and knives. One stopped to help Tsun overpower the owner, while two others lunged at Uncle Chin. Chin had left his meat cleaver in the kitchen. He barged past the frozen waitress to retrieve it. Her mother began to scream, her hands fluttering wildly in the air, waving away a nightmare. She was in the kitchen between Chin and his cleaver, too terrified to move. He lifted her aside, but the delay cost him dear. The first soldier smashed the back of his head with a stick. Chin turned, staggering, badly dazed. The second soldier struck him a crushing blow across the temple and Chin's lifeless body crumpled to the floor.

Meanwhile the owner shielded his head with his arm as Tsun's iron bar descended with sickening force. The sharp crack of splintering bones rang around the room. The waitress watched in horror as the bar rose and fell on her father, who grew smaller and weaker with each blow until he was almost part of the floor. She blinked furiously, hoping to wake from the living nightmare before her, and all at once, it seemed she had.

The steady rhythm stopped. A figure had appeared behind Tsun and she watched him turn slowly, bewilderment widening his eyes. He was about to ask a question, but no words came from his lips. Instead a crimson line opened across his throat and glistening blood spilled onto his chest. He slid to the floor, still looking up in surprise at the man who stood over him.

It was Kuang.

The other soldiers stopped and stared too, shocked into stillness, and for a moment an eerie hush reigned in the canteen. Kuang's eyes took in the faces around him—the other three soldiers staring at him in disbelief and the mother whose eyes were screwed tight shut—before coming to rest on the pretty waitress. She looked back with revulsion in her eyes, revulsion at what he had done. Revulsion for him. He stepped over Tsun's body and walked out slowly through the fast-pooling blood. It was only when he was far outside the canteen that he heard the screaming begin.

The Small King of the Nagas

The yaks followed the trail through the last of the high passes and down, into a long verdant valley that ran between jagged peaks. The air was infused with warmth and sweetness. Green woodlands returned to the slopes and hardy mountain grass appeared beneath their feet.

They had entered a world hidden from all but the most determined travelers. The Tibetans told them of the fierce Naga tribes that inhabited these remote valleys, relating gruesome tales of headhunters, cannibals, slaughter, and witchcraft. Smoke drifted upward on the far side of the valley and the sound of furious drumming could be heard in the distance. This, the Tibetans explained, meant a battle had been fought and the victorious tribe had taken many heads. The drumming was a warning to other tribes not to face them in the future.

On the third day in the long valley, Vanya was lagging at the end of the yak train when he felt something moving behind him. Several times he turned back to check, but there was nothing there. He hurried to catch up with the group, wondering if a tiger was stalking him, checking over his shoulder as he ran. Around a bend in the path, he found himself face to face with a beast from another world. The height of man, it had the body of an ape and the pointed face of a devil with sharp feathers for hair. It carried a spear in its claw-like hand, and a long machete hung from its hip. Its naked, hairless body bore the markings of a snake on its chest and arms. Around its waist hung skulls too large to be from monkeys.

Vanya had scoffed when the Tibetans had spoken of were-tigers—humans in animal form. He was not laughing now. He waited, frozen with fear as the man-eater looked him up and down and grunted in an unearthly tongue. It sounded almost human, but Vanya could not understand. It came forward and walked around him, inspecting him. Once it was satisfied that Vanya was not armed, it reached up and removed the mask from its face. He was shocked to see the face of an old man, with red watery eyes, wrinkled brown skin and blackened teeth that gave his mouth a terrifying grimace when he spoke.

"An empty face," the old man said, his words clearer without the mask, though his accent was so strange that Vanya wondered if he had understood him correctly.

"Did you say empty?" he asked.

"No warrior's face," the old man sneered.

"I am a monk," Vanya said indignantly.

"Why do you come here?"

"We are on our way to China."

"Here is a dangerous place for monks."

"We come in peace," Vanya said, his eyes flicking down nervously to the skulls.

"Five monks came this way last year, in peace," the old man replied, brushing the tops of his skulls with his fingertips. Vanya stared in horror, until the old man let out a roar of laughter and clapped him on the shoulder.

"You're frightened! Good. You are right to be afraid. I have taken many heads in my time, but only from my enemies. Not from skinny monks with empty faces."

"Empty?" Vanya asked again.

"No marks of battle on your face."

Vanya saw the livid scars all over the old man's face and body.

"I see," he smiled.

"I am Banyang, Small King of the Konyaks. Tell me your name, skinny monk."

"My name is Vanya. I am from Magadha. We are traveling with a party of Tibetans."

"I know your Tibetans. We trade with them sometimes," Banyang said.

"Good," Vanya said with relief. "Trade is good."

"Trade is for women," Banyang said fiercely, then continued more evenly, "but there are some things my village needs from the Tibetans."

"Then come and trade with them," Vanya offered, "and I'll introduce you to my companions. They will be delighted to meet you."

Fugitive Runs

Kuang ran, twisting and turning in no particular direction, lost in the evening fog of Longpan, his only thought to put distance between himself and Tsun's lifeless body. When he reached the outskirts of the town, he turned to check behind. There was no one following. He crouched in the shadows behind a clump of bushes and tried to think, but the image of Tsun's bloodstained body forced its way into his mind. He turned and vomited. He forced the image away. He needed a plan. He would not get far without one.

Giving himself up was one idea, but he dismissed it instantly. He knew he would be executed without a trial. Even if he got a trial, it would be his word against that of three soldiers. There were rumors that Tsun's family had powerful connections back east, and if this were true, he would have even less chance. The word of the canteen owner and his family would count for nothing, even if they agreed to testify. They were not true Chinese.

No, escape was his only option. His best hope would be to reach his home province of Hubei, where he knew people who could help him to disappear. But Hubei was hundreds of li to the east. If he ran now, he could get a night's head start, but with no money or supplies, he would not last long in the wilderness. Instead, he forced himself to consider the most difficult option of all: returning to the fort. He guessed Tsun's companions would delay reporting the incident because they would have to agree on a story first. It would give him a little time before the alarm was raised, but he had to be quick. He made up his mind in an instant and set off at a fast loping pace for the fort.

When he neared the front gate, he forced himself to stop and catch his breath. He did not want to draw attention to himself. He checked his appearance. To his surprise, the knife that had killed Tsun was still in his hand. He cleaned it on a clump of grass by the roadside and replaced it in his waistband. There were dark red splatters on his tunic and trousers, but in the darkness they were barely visible. He would have to risk it. He called out a slurred greeting to the sentry, who opened the gate without a word. There was nothing suspicious about a soldier returning drunk from Longpan.

The barracks were deserted. Kneeling beside his bunk, he dragged out the chest from beneath it and emptied its contents onto his bed. He pulled on his overcoat and threw his goatskin, flint and a sharpening stone into a kit bag. Taking the blanket from his bed he rolled it up and pushed it through the strap, then took the sheet, too. It would be useful for wrapping the food that he was going to get from the kitchens. Lastly he pried up the floorboard beneath his bunk and picked up the pouch of coins he kept hidden there. It wasn't much, but it would have to do.

Outside, he filled his goatskin from the well and hurried toward the kitchens. There was no one about, no sign of a commotion. The alarm had not been raised. He skirted the edge of the compound, keeping to the shadows and was almost at the kitchens when he heard voices. Two soldiers were coming. He waited motionless in the shadows, hardly daring to breathe, until they had passed. The door to the kitchen was locked. He considered smashing the lock, but it would make too much noise. Time was running out. There was only one alternative. He went to the rubbish dump behind the kitchen, where food waste was covered by heavy boards to keep out scavengers. He lifted the boards aside and held his breath. There were still some scraps on the top that he could salvage. He gathered handfuls of rice, half eaten bones and wilted vegetables and rolled them up in his bed-sheet.

The outer wall of the fort was just a few paces away, but he fought the urge to scramble over it into the protection of the night. There was one more thing he needed to do first. He made his way to Commander Tang's house, scaling the stone wall silently and creeping close to the ground, until he was beneath Weilin's window. He tapped softly. Nothing. He wondered where she could be at that time of night. He tapped again. A sound came from inside and the shutters opened a crack.

"Is someone there?"

"It's me! Are you alone?"

"Kuang! What are you doing here? I thought you were in the town tonight?"

"There's no time to explain. Something happened. I have to leave right now."

"Leave? Why? Where are you going?"

"I want you to come with me."

"What do you mean? What happened? Just tell me," she pleaded.

"There was a fight, in Longpan. I have to get away! Come with me, Weilin. We can go together. I know people who can help us, but you have to come with me right now."

He waited for her answer, but she was silent.

"Weilin..." he urged.

"You can't ask this of me Kuang," she said finally, her voice trembling, "I can't run away with you in the middle of the night."

"I know what I am asking sounds insane, but you have to trust me. If you don't, you'll never see me again."

"You're crazy, Kuang. Just tell me what happened! I can speak to my father."

"I'll tell you later, I promise. Just come with me now."

"You know I'm engaged to Fu Sheng, I can't leave with you. There must be another way."

"There is no other way," he said, louder than he intended, then continued in a whisper. "I have to go. I'm sorry to have asked this of you. I have missed you, Weilin, I will miss you ..."

She watched his shadow slip across the garden and over the wall. Then he was gone. She waited, hoping he might return, that it might be a bad joke, but she knew he would not, and that she would never see him again. What had happened in Longpan, she wondered. She pressed her forehead against the window and stared out into the night, too shocked to cry, at least for the moment.

The Headhunters

Banyang led the yak train of monks and Tibetans across the valley to his village. They passed through dense woodlands and skirted fields of rice and taro, until they came to the first sign of the Konyak village. It was a graveyard filled with ornate grave-markers, each one carved from hardwood and polished so it gleamed in the sunlight. The Konyaks honored their dead. They continued around the outer stockade of sharp bamboo spikes until they came to the village entrance, a narrow gateway carved in the center of a giant banyan.

Inside, the visitors were greeted by a row of four stakes, each holding a rotting human head. The stench was overwhelming and the monks struggled not to vomit, but Banyang seemed oblivious and sauntered happily toward the center of the village. Villagers began to emerge from their huts. Most were naked except for necklaces and bracelets and a narrow strip of cloth between their legs, though some of the older members of the tribe wore a blanket around the shoulders. The adults had blackened their teeth like Banyang, which gave them an unearthly grimace when they spoke.

Banyang led them past pens of pigs and chickens, black buffalo in sturdy paddocks, and half-wild mithan, with their long horns and fierce tempers that had been tethered securely to the stockade. He stopped outside a large wooden building set on ornate pillars and decorated with wild boar skulls. A long wooden gong stood in front of the house, created from the hollowed-out trunk of a tree. Inside the monks could see more human skulls.

"This place is the Morung," he explained. "Young men and boys live here under the guidance of their seniors. You will all sleep in here tonight. There is plenty of room. A hunting party has gone out for a few days."

"What are they hunting?" Vanya asked, dreading the answer.

"Heads," Banyang barked.

Vanya had no more questions.

The monks took their packs into the Morung while the Tibetans began the serious business of trade, laying out their wares for the locals to see: medicines from India and China, bundles of colorful silks, precious metals, gem-stones, spices, and salt. The villagers arrived with woven mats and baskets, jewelry carved from the finest hardwood, soft leather, brightly colored inks and dyes, local wine and liquors, and the potion that, when consumed, took away all pain and allowed the drinker to see the future.

In the evening, they all gathered around a roaring fire. Plates of hot food were graciously served and wine flowed freely. Banyang urged his guests to eat and drink their fill. As they ate, a party of young men returned to the village shouting and singing. Young women emerged from the neighboring Morung to greet the blood-ied warriors and admire the trophy they had with them—a human head, too bloodstained to tell its age or even its sex.

"What happens now?" Vanya asked miserably, draining his wine cup in one gulp to steady his nerves.

"The head will be put in the gong for drumming. The noise loosens the skin," Banyang explained. "It helps it to come away from the skull. Then the children will be encouraged to play with it for a while, and after that it will be put on a spike with the other heads."

"Children play with it?" Yin Chiang asked incredulously.

"It makes them strong and fearless," Banyang assured him.

"Surely no child would touch it?" Vanya said.

"At first, some cry and hide behind their mother's legs," Banyang smiled patiently, as if explaining to a child, but we make it a game for them and they soon learn to be strong. After that, we boil the head until the flesh falls away. Then we leave it to dry, so it can be decorated. Decorating the skulls is an art form. I have a fine collection in my home. Would you like to see them?"

Perhaps tomorrow," Vanya answered warily, finishing another cup of wine.

"You don't have the stomach for skulls, Brother Vanya?" the old man laughed, refilling his cup for him.

"Do you eat the flesh of your enemies," Vanya asked, too

intoxicated now to worry about offending his host.

"Of course," Banyang said triumphantly, "and so do you!"

Vanya stared in horror at his dish, until he heard the sniggers from around the campfire.

"I am joking with you, Brother Vanya!" Banyang chuckled. "No, we do not eat human flesh. Not usually …"

"But sometimes?" Vanya ventured.

"Only in times of great need. It pains me to speak of such times."

"I'm sorry, I did not mean to …"

"No matter, Brother Vanya," Banyang said sadly, "no matter."

There was a long silence around the campfire. Then Banyang began to speak in a voice so quiet that Vanya was forced to lean forward to hear him.

"It was a terrible time, the worst in the history of our people. First, there was rain. Endless rain. Terrible floods washed away everything from our valley. Crops were ruined. Livestock drowned. Huts and grain stores swept away. In one storm, ice fell from the sky like rocks, killing anything that was out in the open, man or beast, anything that could not find shelter. The wind blew so hard that what was left of our huts disappeared into the sky. By the time the storm tired itself out, over a hundred people had died in this village alone. All livestock had perished. A terrible famine followed. Many more villagers died. Those that remained became too weak to hunt or search for food. We ate tree bark, wool, and leather to stop the pain in our stomachs, but it was no use. My family was dying before my eyes."

"What did you do?" Vanya whispered.

"In the end, my wife and I decided there was only one answer."

"What was that?" Vanya asked, his voice thick with dread.

"We had three children, Brother Vanya. Three beautiful children. The eldest was in his teens, a strong and able boy, useful in the fields, a good hunter. The middle child was a girl, not much use around the house, but quite beautiful. I was looking forward to a good marriage for her in due course. The youngest was still a baby, a girl who cried all night long from the hunger pangs. My wife could not feed her and she was growing weak." Banyang swallowed hard. His eyes glistened with emotion as he continued. "In the end, there was nothing else for it. We had to eat one of the children. But, which one? We could not decide."

He paused, overcome with grief at the memory, and then forced himself to go on. "I suggested we should eat the baby since it had the tenderest flesh, and besides, we had not grown as fond of it as of the older children. But my wife, who is very wise, pointed out that there was not much flesh on the baby. We would probably have to eat another child soon afterward. This made us think again. We considered the eldest child. A sturdy boy, his flesh would last us several weeks, perhaps even months, if we rationed ourselves carefully. It made the most sense. I decided to kill him. But then my wife asked who would do all the hard work in the fields when we were old? Who would mend the leaks in our roof, chop wood for the fire, and drive our oxen to market? I realized she was right. So we settled on the middle child, the girl, for in times of famine a girl who can't cook is even less use than before."

He sighed deeply. "So I waited until the middle of the night, when the children were asleep, and reached for my dao. I stood by my daughter's room. I was about to kill her when a great sadness came over me, for although she was not a clever girl, nor very hard-working, she was beautiful and I loved her dearly. But I remembered my duty to the rest of my family and, with a heavy heart, I plunged the dao deep into the side of her neck."

There was silence around the campfire. The listeners held their breath as Banyang continued, his voice quavering with grief. "My wife could not bear to touch the flesh of her dead child, so it was left to me to cook the girl. This I did, and in the morning I woke my wife and children and served a dish of freshly roasted meat to my starving family."

There was a long silence.

"How did …"

"You want to know how she tasted?" Banyang hissed, his blood-red eyes boring into Vanya's.

"No!" Vanya stammered, "I was going to ask how did you feel?"

"I'll tell you how she tasted," Banyang said. "Considering she was a lousy cook, it was the tastiest dish she ever made."

Vanya stared open-mouthed. Laughter erupted around him and he threw his cup down in disgust. Banyang beckoned one of the young women nearby and she sat beside him. "My daughter," he beamed, taking her hand, "she has returned from the dead!" He gnawed playfully on her arm, until even Vanya could not help laughing.

"We are headhunters, not cannibals, Brother Vanya. There is a big difference. To take a head is the mark of a happy man. A warrior. Whoever is prepared to kill his enemy is never worried or depressed. To take a head in battle is the highest honor among the Konyak people. That has always been our way. There are some tribes who take the heads of women and children, believing one head is much like another. They say any head contains magical powers. It's not true! Those hunters are no stronger than women and children themselves. Some even buy slaves and slaughter them, like animals, just to get heads for their rituals. That is the act of a coward, not a warrior. No power will come to them from such things."

He ordered one of the boys from the Morung to serve more wine. "You think of us as savages, Brother Vanya. You too," he said, pointing to Bodhidharma and Yin Chiang, "but our ways have kept us strong and happy for generations. Tomorrow, I will prove to you that we are not completely uncivilized. You will see Konyak justice at work."

"We will?" Vanya asked warily.

"Yes, there will be a trial."

"Who is on trial?"

"One of our villagers."

"May we know what he is accused of?" Yin Chiang asked.

"He lit a fire which went out of control and damaged his neighbor's property. The neighbor complained to the village council, who agreed to put the careless villager before a panel of judges."

"What will happen if he is found guilty?" Yin Chiang asked with concern.

"Oh, he is guilty, that much is certain. It will be a short trial."

"What will his punishment be?" Vanya demanded, fearing the worst.

"He will be fined."

"That's all?" he asked, relieved.

"Yes, that is the verdict," Banyang said.

"With the greatest respect," Yin Chiang said carefully, "how can you know the verdict before the trial has taken place?"

"Simple, I am on the council," Banyang said.

"But what about the trial and the panel of judges?"

"I am also the Chief Judge," Banyang answered with a grin. "The verdict is assured. Trust me on this, Brother Yin Chiang. Justice will be served."

The trial took place the following morning outside the Morung just as Banyang had promised. The monks woke to discover a crowd had gathered on the steps outside and Banyang sat with four tribal elders at a low table. The judges were in place, but there was no sign of the accused. No one seemed to mind. Both the judges and the crowd chatted among themselves while they waited for the accused to show up. After several minutes, a small, thin man appeared before the judges' table with a basket of husked rice on his shoulder and a pig under his arm. He set them down before the judges and disappeared again, returning soon after with two large jugs of wine. Banyang stood and formally accepted his offerings. Then the accused watched dispassionately as Banyang took a spear and skewered the pig at his feet.

The carcass was carried away and the crowds dispersed. The trial was over and Banyang sidled over to where the monks were sitting.

"Now you have seen Konyak justice at work," he said proudly.

"Who gets the pig and the rice and wine?" Vanya asked.

"The council, of course. We will share it out tonight," Banyang answered.

"What compensation does the plaintiff receive?" Yin Chiang asked.

"The plaintiff?" Banyang asked, puzzled by the question.

"The man whose house was damaged in the fire," Yin Chiang explained.

"He gets nothing," Banyang said, shaking his head in amusement at the thought. "Only the council receives compensation."

"Forgive me King Banyang, but how can that be justice?" Yin Chiang demanded.

"You fail to see the wisdom of our method," Banyang grinned. "Think about it. If that man gets compensation, then everyone will start accusing his neighbor over the slightest thing. We would be swamped with trials. This way, there are very few trials, and people are still careful."

Vanya looked at Bodhidharma and then to Yin Chiang. "There is a certain logic to it," he admitted finally.

"It is quite ingenious, don't you think, Brother Yin Chiang?" Bodhidharma laughed.

"It's preposterous!" Yin Chiang said. "It would never work in a civilized country." Then he remembered where he was and smiled at Banyang nervously and said, "or rather a big country, with many complex layers of society."

"Big countries are far too foolish to see the beauty of our system," Banyang said sharply, silencing Yin Chiang's arguments instantly. Then his expression softened and he revealed his black teeth in a broad smile, "But come, let us take breakfast together. The trial has already wasted enough of the day, and I think your Tibetan friends are eager to get going."

After they had eaten and the yak train was loaded, Banyang accompanied them to the village entrance, stopping only once to pat the head of a child who was playing with a ball on a length of vine. The monks noticed the ball bounced oddly as the child ran. Then as the ball spun around, they saw a nose and gaping mouth, opening and closing with each step. It was the head that had been brought in the night before. They exchanged glances and continued silently toward the exit.

It seemed Banyang had not been teasing them about everything, after all.

Kuang Changes his Uniform

The moonlight was just strong enough for Kuang to scramble across the rocky wasteland that surrounded the fort. He went north, heading for the East Road that ran along the next valley. The road would take him to the Yangtze, which in turn would lead him home. He reached it in less than an hour and broke into an easy run. His aim was to cover a good distance before dawn, when the fort would send search parties.

He ran throughout the night, keeping up a steady pace and

thanking Corporal Chen for the punishing exercises he had put him through. When the first rays of watery sunshine lit up the bleak valley, he left the road and returned to the rough country, where he could hide more easily at the first sign of soldiers. Keeping the road in sight, he ran between sparse trees and rocks, through low gullies and along the base of dark cliffs.

Soon the sun bathed the valley in a warm glow and the temperature rose. Exhausted, he stopped at a stream to drink and refill his goatskin. He wondered if the stream flowed all the way to the Yangtze. If it did, he could follow it, instead of the more obvious East Road. He decided to take that chance and followed the course of the bubbling water. By midday he was staggering with tiredness and knelt by the stream to splash its icy water on his face. It was not enough. He put his head under and listened to his heartbeat, pounding loud as a drum.

After another ten li, he discovered a cave behind a clump of bushes. He needed to sleep, if only for an hour, and went inside. Away from the sunlight, the cave was freezing and his sweat-soaked tunic clung to him. His teeth began to chatter, but he dared not light a fire in case the smoke alerted his pursuers. He wrapped his coat and blanket around himself and ate a little of the food he'd collected from the rubbish dump before closing his eyes.

Despite his exhaustion, sleep would not come. He shivered uncontrollably as images of Tsun's final moments assailed him: the pallor of his skin, the unspoken question on his lips, the crimson line across his throat, the screams of the waitress. He forced the images away, thinking instead of Weilin and their nights in the hospital together. He reached out to her, his hands on her narrow waist, but as he did, she changed and the angry maid scratched at his face in fury. All at once he was back in his barrack room. The slow breaths and heavy sighs around him told of sleeping soldiers, the thick air of too many bodies in too close a space. Huo snored contentedly above him. Everything was as it should be. He looked over to Tsun's bunk. It was hard to see in the darkness, but there was a shape there. Could Tsun be alive? He lay frozen for a long time gathering his courage, then he crossed to the huddled form. His hand hovered by Tsun's shoulder, hesitating to touch him. He drew back the cover. Tsun rose and turned to him, the same question still on his lips, the same ugly line across his throat, opened to a silent roar, accusing him. He fell to the floor, screaming. The other soldiers woke and gathered around him, their voices distant and garbled. He became aware that he was in a nightmare of his own making and woke with a start.

He was alone in a cave, but there were voices outside. Real voices. This was no dream. A new panic surged up from his belly. The soldiers had caught up with him already. He was trapped! He listened, praying they would leave without searching the cave, and he heard laughter. The voices did not sound like soldiers. They sounded more like children.

He peered cautiously from the cave and saw a flash of orange by the stream. A group of novice monks was preparing to bathe. They removed their robes and folded them neatly on nearby rocks. One of them was already wading out into the icy water and his companions were urging him to go deeper, laughing.

Kuang watched from the bushes. With their shaved heads and white loincloths, it was hard to tell the monks apart. They were like little soldiers, stripped of their individuality. He crept toward them, moving silently behind rocks and trees. The monks had their backs to him, all except the first, who was now waist-deep in the stream, facing the others. They were urging him to dip himself in the stream, but the water was icy cold and he was delaying. They called him names and challenged him, but he refused to plunge in. Kuang waited, forcing himself to be patient. At last the boy ducked himself into the water. He came up quickly, gasping from the cold, then soaped himself methodically before squatting and rinsing himself clean. He ducked his head under once more to get rid of the last of the soap and rose with glee to laugh at the others. Now it was their turn.

One by one they, too, entered the icy water and bathed until, after several minutes, the first of them reminded his fellows that they were taking too long. The senior monks would be displeased if they were late. They rinsed themselves and hurried to get dressed. In their haste, there was some confusion over whose robe belonged to whom. In the end, it became clear that a robe was missing. One of the boys stood shivering in only his loincloth. The others helped him search, clambering among the rocks and exploring the whole area, but there was no sign of his robe.

Half a li away, Kuang stopped at a tranquil rock pool and sharpened his knife to a fine edge, testing it with his fingertips until he was satisfied; he began to shave his head, working slowly to avoid creating distinguishing marks or scars. Fortune had given him this chance. He did not want to waste it. When he had finished, he ran his fingers over his scalp and checked himself in the surface of the rock pool. It was done.

He took off his army uniform, wrapped it in a bundle and weighed it down with heavy stones. He considered adding his knife to the bundle since a monk would never carry a weapon, but he could not be without it in the wilderness. The bundle sank into the dark water without a trace. The monk's robe fitted perfectly and he slipped his knife into the back of his waistband. Leaning out over the pool once more, he was surprised to see a young Buddhist monk staring back at him. He turned his head from side to side, wondering what Weilin would make of him now. The thought of her sent a stab of pain through his belly. It was no time to be thinking of Weilin, but her pretty face forced its way into his thoughts. He forced himself to his feet and pushed himself onward, growing more angry with her with each step for refusing to come with him.

Anger was good. It spurred him on.

He broke into a run, still following the course of the stream toward the long river that promised to take him home.

Yaks Swim

The stony path descended into the valley and the roar of the white water grew louder, echoing in the surrounding rocks. With a final twist, the path landed them on a shingle beach beside a fast-flowing river. The Tibetans gathered for an urgent discussion and from their grim expressions, it seemed they were concerned about something. Yin Chiang went to investigate.

"There was a bridge here," Rinchen explained, "but it has gone."

"What happened to it?" Yin Chiang asked, fearing the answer even as he did.

"Washed away by the current," Rinchen answered, "during the winter."

"We need to cross?" Yin Chiang said almost to himself.

"Yes, we will try to ford it here," Rinchen said, his laughing eyes deadly serious for once. "This is the best place."

He waded into the water up to his waist to test the current. It was strong, but not impossible. He shouted to the others to let them know and the decision was made. They would cross.

The Tibetans unloaded the yaks and the monks watched as they opened bundles of bamboo poles, leather sheets and bladders that, like everything else, had come from yaks. The bladders were inflated and sealed, and in little more than an hour, six makeshift rafts were complete.

Yin Chiang was worried that his scrolls would be left behind, but they were secured to one of the rafts along with the rest of the baggage and supplies.

"How will the yaks get across?" Vanya asked.

"They swim," Yin Chiang replied. "Yaks are good swimmers. Once the lead yak goes in, the others will follow."

Rinchen stripped to his undergarments and tied a rope around his waist. Two of his companions held the other end while he picked his way along the rocky bank, moving upstream for a hundred paces before wading out into the freezing water. His arms and shoulders worked hard to keep him upright. His companions paid out the rope, watching his every move, ready to haul him back if he should be swept away. Near the middle of the river, the water was at his waist. The current was too strong to stand. He dived and swam with strong, steady strokes toward the opposite shore. The current flung him downstream at an alarming rate. He was soon past the point where the others stood. Their shouts of encouragement were lost in the roar of the water. But his steady strokes paid off and he neared the opposite bank. Seeing he was not in trouble, his companions paid out more rope, and after two attempts, he stood in the water and waded onto the shore.

When he had secured his end of the rope to a solitary tree stump on the bank, they pulled the rope taut and tied it around a heavy boulder. The yaks waited patiently in the shallows while the rafts were tied to their harnesses. Then the lead yak was urged into the water. Soon it was swimming strongly, and with prompting from their drivers, the other yaks followed. Next the Tibetans set about crossing, holding the rope for safety, until only the three monks remained ashore.

Yin Chiang ventured into the fast water and took hold of the rope. Vanya followed, and Bodhidharma watched as he gripped the rope, grim-faced.

"You don't swim, Vanya?" he asked.

Vanya shook his head.

"It doesn't matter. Just move along the rope. I'll be right behind you."

Yin Chiang moved steadily across, hand over hand, and Vanya and Bodhidharma followed close behind. In the center of the river, their feet were swept off the bottom and the current dragged at their bodies and limbs as they struggled to move along the rope. Suddenly they heard shouting from the Tibetans; a warning. A fallen tree was hurtling downstream, its branches reaching out to ensnare all before it. A branch hit one of the swimming yaks and it went under. It re-emerged a moment later, but the branch became tangled in the raft and pulled the animal away downstream.

"Cut the raft!" Khandro roared.

The nearest man took a knife from his belt and leapt after the yak.

"No!" Yin Chiang shouted. The raft carried his scriptures and translations, but his protest, if heard, was ignored, and the Tibetan freed the yak and swam with it to the shore. The raft was carried downstream on the fierce current and soon disappeared around a bend in the river. Yin Chiang closed his eyes tightly and groaned in anguish.

"We need to keep moving," Bodhidharma shouted, but Yin Chiang ignored him.

"We'll search downstream."

"It's no use. They'll be ruined. A lifetime's work, gone," Yin Chiang cried.

Vanya clung grimly to the rope, his strength failing quickly. Bodhidharma felt his own muscles cramping. They could not stay where they were.

"Move on now, Yin Chiang," he ordered, but Yin Chiang was frozen.

He moved around Vanya and, taking Yin Chiang's head in his

arm, pulled him close, until his mouth was at Yin Chiang's ear. "Wake up and move along the rope!"

Yin Chiang started, shocked by the menace in the master's voice. He stared at Bodhidharma for a moment, as if emerging from a trance, then put one hand over the other and moved on.

That evening Bodhidharma found Yin Chiang sitting away from the campfire. Vanya was beside him, silently sharing his grief. They had searched downriver for several hours, until Yin Chiang himself had seen the futility and called off the search. Bodhidharma put a blanket around Yin Chiang's shoulders and sat beside him in silence until Yin Chiang spoke.

"The loss of the scriptures doesn't sadden you?" His voice was little more than a whisper.

"It does," Bodhidharma answered, "but your loss saddens me far more. I know how you treasured those scrolls."

"I copied many of them myself, from the sacred Sutras at Nalanda, the Heart Sutra, the Lalitavistara Sutra, the Diamond Sutra … I translated all the key passages into Chinese. They would have been invaluable in spreading the teachings to my people."

"We'll send for replacements when we reach China," Bodhidharma assured him.

"What will we do in the meantime?"

"We will teach just as before. You are the teacher, Brother Yin Chiang, not the scriptures."

"But the scriptures contain the wisdom of The Buddha."

"The scriptures are simply words. When a child is young, it doesn't understand words. It copies the actions of its mother and father. Now you will be mother and father to the monks of China, and they will be your children. They will learn by your actions."

"That's a difficult way to teach," Yin Chiang said, his voice faraway.

"The most difficult way of all," Bodhidharma nodded. "Far more difficult than reading from the scriptures."

"Do you think it was destiny that took the scrolls from me?" Yin Chiang asked.

"No, it was bad luck."

"But the Tibetans didn't want to bring them. It was as if they knew."

"The Tibetans were just being practical. What do they know of scriptures?"

"Yet they are wise, in some ways, are they not?"

"They lead a simple life. It's easy for them to be wise. We live in a complicated world. Things are more difficult for us."

"But the scriptures teach us how to live, do they not? They show us how to follow The Way."

"Of course, that is their role."

"Now you argue for the scriptures, earlier you argued against them!"

"The scriptures have their place. But for you, Brother Yin Chiang, the thing you seek can no longer be found in the scriptures."

"Then how shall I ever find nirvana?"

"Let the scriptures go and trust your own mind."

"You make it sound easy."

"No! It is not easy. It is the most difficult thing in the world."

"Why?"

"Because delusion is so comfortable."

"Yet it is possible for me?" Yin Chiang asked, stared into the flames of the fire where the Tibetans sat.

"Very possible," Bodhidharma said gently. "Now come, let's join the others and warm ourselves by the fire."

Yin Chiang rose and the Tibetans made room for the three

monks around the fire. Their mood was subdued. They knew how much the papers had meant to the little Chinese monk. But they could not remain somber for long, and when the fire began to splutter, Rinchen took the yak skin bellows from Old Dorje and offered them to Yin Chiang.

"First, show me how it's done," Yin Chiang implored.

"Don't ask me," Rinchen laughed, "I have never been able to make the stupid thing work. Only old Dorje can do it. Why do you think we bring him along?"

Yin Chiang took the bellows and tried for several minutes to get them working without success. He passed them to Bodhidharma, who had no luck either, much to the amusement of the Tibetans. With an oath, Bodhidharma conceded defeat and handed the limp bellows to Vanya to try.

No one was more surprised than Vanya himself when a breath of air, little more than a sigh, emerged from the bellows. Soon he was producing air almost as expertly as old Dorje himself. The sight of the skinny monk pumping the bellows, delirious with joy, made them all forget the events of the day, and even Yin Chiang could not help joining in the laughter.

Captain Visits Yulong Fort

In the final hours of the night, a freezing fog crept down from the mountains. Huo cursed his luck for drawing the night shift on guard duty. The hours went slowly without Kuang to talk to. The other soldier on duty with him had fallen asleep, which was against the rules, but nobody checked up on them at this hour. If it spared him from feeling the cold, Huo did not see the point of waking him.

He pulled his tattered cloak around himself more tightly and paced up and down to keep the numbness from his feet. It did nothing to keep out the cold that reached into his bones. He wondered why a guard was needed at all. There was no one outside the fort in these conditions, except perhaps Kuang. He wondered if his friend was still on the run, or whether he had been captured yet, or killed.

It had been almost a week since news of Tsun's death had hit the fort and the search parties had gone to get Kuang. Since then, there had been no news. Nobody knew what had happened in Longpan. Tsun's friends said Kuang had gone berserk, beating the owner and the chef with an iron bar. When they had tried to intervene, Kuang had cut Tsun's throat in cold blood. Huo did not believe a word of it, but nonetheless Tsun was dead, and Kuang had been involved. He hoped Kuang would be captured alive, so he could at least give his version of events.

There was a muffled noise in the fog: the clatter of hooves on the stony path, a flare of torchlight. He kicked the other guard awake and shouted a challenge. A dark horse appeared through the fog. He recognized its rider instantly. It was Captain Fu Sheng, the cavalry officer engaged to Weilin.

"Welcome to Yulong Fort, Captain," he said smartly, hurrying to open the gate.

A troop of men appeared behind the captain. Huo swung open the heavy wooden door and watched them file past into the fort. They were dirty and exhausted from their long journey, but rode upright and proud. At the end of the column was a mule cart laden with Turkic armor and weapons taken from the enemy dead. The barbarians, it seemed, had lost another battle to Fu Sheng.

Weilin lay frozen on her bed, listening to the captain's footsteps in the hallway, pressing her cold hands to her face. She knew she should go out and greet her fiancée, but she could not bring herself to do so. Not yet. She knew her faithful maid would never tell of her affair with Kuang, but she feared she would betray herself in some way. Fortunately she knew Fu Sheng would want to speak to her father before seeing her. He was ever the dutiful soldier. She had time to compose herself.

When she heard his footsteps entering her father's study, she pulled a shawl around her shoulders and went outside. A heavy frost lay on the ground. It covered the terrace and the rail where Kuang had once stood with a stupid grin on his face, where they had once touched and kissed. It all seemed so long ago. She moved the flowerpots out of the shade and into the watery sunlight, wondering whether Kuang had been out in the open at night, hoping he had found warmth and shelter.

She waited on the terrace until Fu Sheng emerged to join her. He looked tired and drawn, but his eyes shone bright and he smiled when he saw her. His long face and smooth skin gave him a boyish appearance. He was quite handsome, but there was an icy indifference behind that smile, and deeper still, something nameless and ugly lurking in him that terrified her. He came forward to embrace her and bent to put his lips to hers, but she turned aside.

"Welcome back Captain," she said with all the warmth she could muster.

"There is no need to call me Captain," he chided her gently, "call me Fu Sheng, please. It's good to see you, Weilin. I've been away on the frontier too long. I'd forgotten how pretty you are."

"You flatter me," she said, still avoiding his name.

"No, it's true."

"I heard you had a great victory against the barbarians," she said.

"Yes, we did. One day I will tell you all about it."

"No!" Her voice trembled. "I don't want to hear about it. I'm sorry, but I can't abide bloodshed."

"I don't care for it either," he smiled, "but sometimes, it's the only way to protect the things we hold dear."

"As long as we're safe, that's all I care about."

"That is how we stay safe, Weilin."

She rearranged her flowerpots, turning them so the sun reached all the leaves. She could feel him watching her. "How long will you be staying here?" she asked.

"A little while longer than I had anticipated. The northern frontier will be quiet for some time and there's a matter I need to attend to here."

"What is that?" she asked casually.

"Your father informed me of an incident involving some of the recent conscripts. One of them was murdered and his killer has escaped."

"I heard about it, a terrible business," she said.

"Yes, and the idiots who have been tracking him have found nothing. It seems our fugitive has vanished like a ghost."

"He's not been caught?"

"No, and the murdered soldier comes from a well-connected family. Your father is worried they'll take the matter to General Shou in Nanjing if we don't catch their son's killer. Your father's reputation is at stake, so I've offered to oversee the matter personally."

"What do you know about the man who did it?" she asked.

"His name is Kuang. Apparently a bit of a loner. It seems there was a grudge between him and the other soldier, Tsun, which erupted into a fight while they were on leave in Longpan. According to his corporal, Kuang is a strong and determined young man. It seems he's also more resourceful than anyone gave him credit for. He's managed to evade capture for over a week."

"You think you'll find him?"

"Of course," Fu Sheng said with certainty, "It won't be difficult, once we start searching properly. A sketch has been drawn and we'll post a ransom. Someone will turn him in before long."

He took a roll of paper from his jacket and read from it, "Kuang is of medium height and build, no distinguishing features." He shrugged, "it doesn't matter. He'll give himself away—one way or another. It's just a question of knowing what to look for."

Weilin took the sketch from him and held it at arm's length. "I recognize this soldier," she said lightly, "he was always in trouble with Corporal Chen. The likeness is good, although I think he had a moustache."

"Are you sure?" he asked.

"Perhaps I'm wrong," she shrugged.

"I will have it added to the sketch," Fu Sheng said, taking it back from her.

She remained on the terrace long after Fu Sheng had taken his leave. A cloud had covered the morning sun and the air remained bitterly cold. She drew her shawl around her shoulders and shivered. The house was warm and inviting, but she did not want to go in.

Soldier Learns to Beg

Kuang felt himself growing dangerously weak. He had not eaten for many days, not since he had caught a fish in his hands, more by luck than skill, and eaten it raw. The other fish in the stream had evaded him ever since. The roots he had tried to eat were too tough to swallow and the bitter berries he found made him sick.

As night fell, he came to a village nestled in dark hills and skirted the outer dwellings until he came to a thicket of trees where he could hide. Even with his blanket wrapped around him he was soon stiff with cold, and hunger pangs kept him awake throughout the night. By morning, he had made up his mind to go into the village in search of food. If he could steal a chicken, he could cook it. He had a knife, firewood and a flint.

The thought of roast chicken made his mouth water as he approached the first rough farm buildings on the outskirts of the town. There were pigs in one of the pens. Roast pig would be delicious. He chose a small one that would be easy to carry, but as he took a step forward, a farmer appeared. Kuang stopped in his tracks, convinced guilt was written all over his face, but the farmer gave him a friendly wave. It took him a moment to remember he was dressed as a monk. He waved back and turned to continue into the village.

The next small holding had chickens in the yard. He was about to enter when a black dog began to bark furiously. Perhaps the dog had seen through his disguise, where the farmer had not. He hurried on until he came to an area of open ground where rubbish had been piled and searched for something edible. The stench was unbearable. He turned and fell to his knees. Tears of despair filled his eyes and he sat back on his heels and wept.

A bush moved. There was something inside. Whatever it was, bird, rat, mouse, he would eat it. He parted the bush carefully and discovered a little grey cat inside. He had not considered a cat. "Here little one," he coaxed, holding out his hand to it, "I have a surprise for you." The cat was mesmerized. He let it sniff his hand and felt the tiny whiskers brush his fingertips. It cowered to the ground, but did not run. In a flash he snatched it up and squeezed its neck hard, shutting off its spitting protest swiftly, ignoring the tiny needle-like claws that dug into his skin. A sharp cry came from behind. He spun around to see two boys watching him, aghast. He smiled at them and slackened his grip on the cat. "Don't worry," he called out to them, "I'm only checking his coat for fleas. The little fellow's fine."

The boys scowled at him. He stroked the cat, and placed it gently on the ground. It sank its razor-sharp teeth into his finger before vanishing into the undergrowth.

An older girl came out of a nearby house to see what was happening. "Are these boys bothering you, Brother?" she asked, concerned.

"Oh no, the boys are no bother, Miss," he smiled.

It was the first time he had spoken for many days and the words felt foreign in his mouth. His voice did not belong to him any more. The boys muttered something to the girl while he did his best to maintain a benevolent smile.

"You stupid boys," she scolded, "monks care for all living things, including cats. How dare you insult a monk? You'll bring bad karma on us all. Go inside and fetch alms, quickly now!"

As the boys hurried inside, Kuang did his best to hide his delight. "Please don't be hard on the children," he smiled. "They're good boys. They thought they were protecting a helpless creature. It was a simple mistake."

"Nevertheless, you must forgive us."

She shouted to the boys to hurry up and they appeared a moment later with a small bundle of food wrapped in a leaf.

"What's this?" Kuang asked, unable to believe his luck.

"Rice and fruit," the bigger boy said.

"There is no meat, since you do not eat meat," the smaller boy said earnestly.

"That is true, young man, but I'm visiting some very poor families later on, and they need a proper meal." The words hung in the air until the girl got their meaning and sent the little boy back inside. He returned with a meager portion of stewed pork and two small fish wrapped in another leaf.

"Bless you," Kuang said, "and may good karma be upon you."

The girl regarded him with the first traces of suspicion on her face. He did not know what monks normally said when they received alms, but it seemed it was not that. It was time to go.

He bowed and walked away slowly until he was out of sight, then raced into the nearest bushes and devoured the offerings in a frenzy. His hunger slaked, he lay back against a tree and rubbed his belly, which groaned with the onslaught of the unexpected food.

After a quick nap, he walked into the center of the village where he found a bustling market. No one paid any attention to the young monk who wandered among the stalls; they were all too busy to notice him. He sat on a stone wall at the edge of the market, wondering how to obtain more offerings, when a shadow fell over him. He looked up in fear, but it was only an old woman.

"Did I startle you, young man?" she laughed.

"I'm sorry, Grandmother, my mind was far away," he answered with a smile.

"Well that's only to be expected, you are a monk, after all," she said. "I have some dumplings for you, if you like. Where is your bowl?"

"My bowl?" he asked dumbly.

A look of pity settled on her face. You don't have a bowl?" she asked, speaking very slowly, as if talking to an imbecile, "Every monk needs a bowl to collect alms."

Kuang decided to play along. It was worth the humiliation if it got him some more food. "I used to have a bowl but it was stolen from me by thieves. But please, let me accept your kind offerings like so," he smiled, holding out his cupped hands.

"They stole a monk's bowl?" She shook her head sadly, "they will have bad fortune."

"I hope not," Kuang said piously.

"You are too forgiving," the old woman chided him, "but that is your way, I know. Let me see what I can do," she said, searching under her stall until she found what she was looking for.

"Here, take this," she smiled, handing him a battered wooden bowl with a crack in it. "It's old, but it's better than nothing."

"Thank you," he said, touched by her generosity.

"A monk needs a bowl," she smiled, "and something to put in it," she said, adding two dumplings.

In the course of the afternoon, more stallholders added food to his bowl until, with food in his belly and supplies in his bag, he was ready to make his way onward toward the Yangtze, toward his home.

By evening the road had taken him into a rocky hollow. The waning sun disappeared behind a craggy ridge and a distant rumble grew louder with each step, until it became a deafening roar. Soon the earth began to shake beneath his feet. Kuang slowed, wondering what place he had strayed into. A mist shrouded him like the icy breath of a great beast and his robe grew clammy and stuck to his skin. The road disappeared, leaving only a stony path a little wider than a man that twisted through steep walls of rock. The mist lifted momentarily to reveal giant cliffs above him, blocking out the sky, then returned to engulf him once again. He continued blindly into the whiteness until something made him stop abruptly and he found himself teetering on the edge of a precipice. Through the swirling mist, he caught a giddying glimpse of the river far below. Snarling water tumbled through the jagged canyon. He filled with despair. This was not the river that would take him home. This was an angry dragon, waiting to devour anyone foolish enough to come close to its snapping jaws.

He turned onto a makeshift path that had been cut into the side of the precipice and followed it downriver. The smooth rock was slick with vapor and treacherous. He was forced to test each step as he went. The opposite cliffs seemed impossibly close, as if the two sides of the gorge had clashed just moments ago.

He hugged the side of the gorge for several li until he came to a shallow cave beneath an overhanging rock where he decided to stop for the night. Lighting a fire was out of the question, the meager sticks he had collected were hopelessly damp. He ate a little food from his bag and lay back on the hard rock, but sleep would not come. Tsun's ghost was hungry for revenge and each time he closed his eyes the white face assailed him. The red slash across his throat. The eyes wide in surprise. The unspoken question. Should he have walked away? He wondered. It would have been shameful to let Tsun beat the canteen owner to death, but perhaps it would have been the wisest thing to do. He could have been a witness, spoken up for the man. He might have tried to wrestle with Tsun, but Tsun was strong—he knew how strong—and with three comrades to help him, Kuang knew he would have been overpowered, beaten, perhaps killed.

But he had killed Tsun.

He remembered how the pretty waitress had looked at him after he had done it—the horror and disgust in her eyes, even though he had saved her father's life. Had he done wrong? He did not know the answer. He was a soldier, he told himself. It was his job to take life. But even as he did, he knew it was not true. He had not killed an enemy in battle. He had ended the life of a fellow soldier, a recruit from his own platoon, a young Chinese man much like himself. And now, hopeless and alone, it seemed he had effectively ended his own life, too.

In Yulong Fort, Lieutenant Pai waited outside Captain Fu Sheng's office. The captain summoned him inside and Pai strode boldly into the room, his jaw set firmly to hide his apprehension. Pai could never tell what his captain was thinking or what he would do next. It was what made Fu Sheng such a formidable soldier. But Pai had seen his captain's bloodlust on the battlefield, and despite the captain's warm greeting, he could not help feeling a sense of dread in his presence.

"Sit down, Lieutenant," Fu Sheng said with a casual wave of the hand. "I was speaking with Commander Tang earlier today. He told me of an incident that took place recently in Longpan."

Pai remained standing. "The garrison town outside the fort, sir?"

"Yes, a fight between two conscripts. One of them was killed with a knife. Perhaps you have heard of it?"

"Yes, there has been talk."

"Good, I see your ear for these things is as well-developed as ever," Fu Sheng smiled, but the smile disappeared quickly. "The commander is concerned. The killer was a conscript named Kuang who has been on the run for over a week. All efforts to track him down have failed. The whole incident is threatening to become an embarrassment. I have offered Commander Tang our assistance. Our riders can help to widen the search. I will coordinate efforts from here, but I want you to take charge of the main search party."

"May I ask what has been done so far?" Pai said.

"Thirty riders have searched in all directions for over fifty li. There have been no sightings of Kuang, no word whatsoever. Over two hundred people have been questioned. No one has seen him."

"Maybe he stole a horse and got far away?"

"No horses have been reported stolen, but we can't rule out the possibility. If a horse is missing, we need to know. However, he is not a rider, as far as we know, and there are few horses in these parts. So let's assume he's still on foot."

He handed Pai two sheets of paper.

"Here's a sketch of Kuang, and a list of all the towns and villages that have already been searched. They should all be searched again, properly. Someone in the area might be sheltering him. Interview the soldiers from his barracks. Find out all you can about him. See if he has friends or relatives nearby."

"Yes, Captain."

"He may have disguised himself by now. The idiots who have been searching have probably been looking for a soldier. He could be a farmer, a shepherd, a merchant. Question anyone of the right age who is remotely suspicious—any young man traveling alone."

"Yes, Captain," Pai said smartly.

Fu Sheng sat back in his chair. "Now tell me, if you were him, where would you go?"

"Where is he from?" Pai asked.

"Hubei, I believe."

"Then I would go to Hubei and hide out with friends or relatives."

"You don't think he would go somewhere else, somewhere less obvious? Hide out in the wilderness perhaps?"

"It's possible," Pai nodded. "What do we know of his background?"

"His father was a blacksmith. Kuang trained as a blacksmith before he was conscripted."

"A blacksmith from Hubei wouldn't last long in the wilderness. There's nothing to eat except rocks unless he happens to be an expert hunter."

"Commander Tang tells me Kuang is untrained in weapons. There has been a shortage out here. So, where else might you go?"

"I might try to hide out among the local people. He could still be hiding out in Longpan."

"Perhaps, but it's unlikely. It appears he came back to the barracks and picked up his possessions before he disappeared."

"Quite methodical, then."

"Yes, and the commander tells me the town has been searched twice. Kuang has no known contacts in Longpan. The canteen owner's house has been searched regularly. It doesn't look like he's there, and if he is, the reward will soon get people talking."

"Then if it were me," Pai said, "I would head for home, after all, and travel day and night to get there as quickly as possible. It would be my best chance of success in the long run."

"I agree," Fu Sheng said, nodding approvingly. "Corporal Chen says Kuang was the fittest of all the new conscripts, so he could be traveling fast. He left the fort around midnight. The search parties waited until dawn before going after him."

"He could have covered fifty li by then."

"True, but if our guess is correct, finding him will be easier now. There's only one way to find your way to Hubei if you are stuck in the wilderness."

"He'll be making for the Yangtze," Pai said. "I will begin my search there."

"Do it," Fu Sheng said. "And take some riders from the fort, some soldiers who will recognize him."

"Yes, Captain."

"Keep me informed."

"Of course," Pai nodded.

Outside, the cold air felt good on Pai's face. He inhaled deeply as he walked away. Fu Sheng had been civil as usual, almost friendly, but Pai knew he had to find Kuang. Dead or alive, it did not matter. All that mattered was that he did not fail.

Tiger Leaping Gorge

Sunlight flooded the gorge, illuminated the shallow cave where Kuang had been resting. He stepped out onto the path carved into the cliff face to find a very different scene from the night before.

The mist had lifted, and only the finest traces of vapor remained, glittering in the air around him. The cliffs rose into a sky of pure blue, while the river below danced, sparkling white and green in the sunshine.

There was another path on the opposite side of the gorge. He noticed a line of men and pack animals moving steadily downriver. The animals were yaks and doubtless suffering in the heat. He guessed the men were Tibetan traders and wondered idly what they were bringing into China on their shaggy beasts.

His own path took him down the gorge and he followed it for an hour, descending ever closer to the level of the river. The growing thunder filled his senses, making him giddy, while the current performed tricks for his eyes, doubling back on itself, circling in eddies, rising, then disappearing to reveal vicious rocks that had been lurking beneath the surface.

A rope bridge came into view, spanning the river at the narrowest point of the gorge. A town had sprung up on either side of the bridge, and the path led inevitably toward it. Soon Kuang was in a busy square filled with stores selling silks and cloth, spices, wines, and medicines. Cooks fried aromatic dishes in blackened pans and grilled skewers of meat over charcoal. The sweet smoke made him hungry, but food could wait. He was no longer starving.

He went to inspect the bridge. Four lengths of rope held it in place across the gorge. The gangway was made from wooden planks, dark and waterlogged from the constant spray of the river. He crossed the bridge, looking down the gorge as he went. The river ran between low banks of sharp rocks and boulders. Half a li downstream was a spit of land and a small jetty where several boats were moored. In the middle of the river a single sampan, heavily laden and low in the water, fought its way across. The lone boatman worked hard against the current but seemed to be getting nowhere. Kuang crossed to the other side of the gorge, but there was little of interest on that side so he turned back for the market.

In the main square, he walked among the shops and stalls with his bowl collecting alms, when a flash of orange caught his eye. A line of monks was coming across the bridge. He counted six orange robes. His stomach turned over. Were they the same monks who had been bathing in the stream? He glanced at their faces. He did not recognize them. Even the color and style of their robes was not the same. He sighed with relief. One of them noticed him and smiled. He nodded in reply. The monk stopped and pressed his palms together in greeting and Kuang did the same. For a moment, neither knew what to do next. Then the monk approached him.

"I have not seen you here around here before, Brother. Have you come to visit our monastery?" he asked.

"No," Kuang stammered, "I'm just passing through."

"From your accent I would say you're from the East. You're a long way from home."

"That's right," he smiled, "I'm from Hunan. I have been delivering a message."

"To the Fire Mountain Monastery?"

"No, a different monastery," Kuang replied lamely.

"There are not many monasteries in these parts," the monk said, puzzled.

"It's many days farther to the west," Kuang said stiffly.

"If you're going to Hunan, you have a long journey ahead of you. Can we offer you hospitality?"

Kuang was about to refuse, but the thought of a warm place to sleep and hot food was too tempting. He accepted gratefully.

"We are from the Fire Mountain Monastery," the monk explained, pointing to the peaks on the far side of the gorge. "It's fifteen li from here, but we come to this town to tend the shrine in the local monastery. It's small, but we can find room for one more. You can help us in our work if you want to gain merit."

"You are very kind," Kuang smiled.

"It is nothing. By the way, my name is Lieh," the monk said.

"Kuai," Kuang said, choosing the name of a young monk he remembered from his hometown.

Lieh led the way to an iron gate in a high stone wall built into the cliff face and Kuang followed him into a neat garden. Flowering vines tumbled down the cliff-side, creating a waterfall of bright colors, and glossy black stones had been placed in an array on white pebbles. The stones could have only come from the river, and Kuang wondered at the power that could polish rocks until they shone like mirrors.

At the end of the garden stood a shrine with a red tiled roof and behind it a small grey monastery, no bigger than a modest house. As the other monks set about tending to the gardens, Lieh took Kuang inside and showed him to the dormitory. "Leave your things in here Brother Kuai," he said. "They'll be perfectly safe. Now, do you wish to help us work and gain merit? Or perhaps you would rather rest?"

"I will help you," Kuang said with a smile, not wishing to arouse suspicion from his new host.

"Splendid," Lieh beamed. "We can tend the shrine together and it will be done in no time."

On the far side of the gorge, the yak train stopped on the edge of the precipice and Bodhidharma looked down at the river far below. "What is this place?" he asked.

"It is called Tiger Leaping Gorge," Yin Chiang answered.

"What a wonderful name."

"It originates from long ago," Yin Chiang explained, "when a group of hunters was tracking a tiger. They chased it into the gorge and thought it trapped, but at the narrowest point in the gorge the tiger leapt across to the other side and escaped.

"You have been here before?" Bodhidharma asked.

"On my way to India," Yin Chiang answered. "There is a town, farther along by the bridge, and a small monastery where we can get shelter."

"A roof over our heads?" Vanya said with enthusiasm.

"The first of many," Yin Chiang smiled. There is something else you should know," he continued more seriously. "This is as far as the Tibetans need to take us. We are at the Yangtze now. If we follow its course, the river will lead us all the way across China to the emperor's palace in Nanjing, more than three thousand li to the east."

The Tibetans unloaded their baggage from the yaks and Yin Chiang paid Khandro, who took the money without comment. After many weeks on the mountains, the monks and their guides had grown close and relaxed in each other's company. Now that it was time to part ways, there seemed little to say. A few words of farewell were exchanged, inadequate words for men who had crossed the Himalayas together. They embraced silently, and then the Tibetans wheeled the yaks around and headed back in single file toward their high mountain home.

Bodhidharma and the Chinese

The young monks had gathered in the monastery's communal hall and Brother Lieh was reading aloud a passage from the Heart Sutra. When he had finished, he looked around at the faces before him and his gaze rested on Kuang's. "Are you familiar with the Heart Sutra, Brother Kuai?" he asked.

"It is new to me," Kuang answered warily, "I don't believe we study it in our monastery."

"Really? I find that quite surprising," Lieh frowned. "It is considered one of the most important of all the sacred texts."

"Perhaps here, but it is not considered so important in Hunan," Kuang answered lamely.

"Fascinating," Lieh said, his eyes wide, "I did not realize there were such differences across the country. Which texts do you hold to be most sacred in Hunan?"

Kuang shifted uncomfortably on his seat. "It has been such a long time since I was at the temple ..."

The gentle chime of a bell in the entrance hall saved him.

"It seems we have more visitors," Lieh said with a smile.

"I will see who it is," Kuang said, jumping up. "Please, continue without me." He made his way to the entrance hall, relieved to be away from Lieh's questions, but his relief was short-lived. The cramped entrance hall was filled with three strangers in ragged mountain clothes. The nearest, still holding the little hand-bell, was Chinese; but the other two were barbarians unlike any Kuang had seen before. Both were tall and black-skinned, covered in long hair, with hooked noses like birds of prey, and round, piercing eyes. The first was gaunt and hungry, the second a giant the size of two men and carrying a gnarled walking staff in his fist.

"Greetings, Brother," the Chinese man said. "I am Yin Chiang and these are my companions, Master Bodhidharma and Brother Vanya.

Kuang did not know what to say.

"Despite our attire, we are monks," Yin Chiang assured him. "We have been traveling for many days in the mountains. We have come all the way from India," he added with a friendly smile.

Kuang stared at the hairy barbarians. He scanned the thin one quickly before looking the giant up and down, from the boots to the black fingers that clutched the heavy staff, to the wild hair, and the eyes that seemed to see right through him to his dark truth.

Kuang tore his eyes from the Indian master and looked at the Chinese monk. He had no idea what to do. "Wait a moment please," he muttered and hurried away to fetch Brother Lieh.

Yin Chiang repeated his introductions to Brother Lieh, but at the sight of the Indian monks, Brother Lieh was also dumbstruck.

"I stayed in this very monastery many years ago on my way to India," Yin Chiang said pointedly, "I remember it well ..."

Lieh was still silent.

"I presume it is still customary to offer hospitality to fellow monks on a long journey," he added deliberately.

"Oh yes, yes of course," Lieh said, finding his voice at last, "please forgive me. You are most welcome. We are honored. Come inside and I will arrange sleeping quarters for you. You can share our food and tea."

"You have tea?" Bodhidharma asked.

Lieh was shocked into silence once more. The Indian spoke Chinese! He had believed only the Chinese could understand their own language.

"Yes, we have tea," Kuang said having recovered from his surprise a little quicker than Brother Lieh.

"Tea? Yes, of course," Lieh said, "we have tea."

"Then lead the way," Bodhidharma urged with a smile.

Lieh showed them into the communal hall and called the other monks to attention. "Brothers, we have visitors," he announced. "Three monks who have traveled all the way from the Western Heaven: Brother Yin Chiang and his companions ..."

He stopped and turned to Yin Chiang for assistance.

"Brother Vanya and Master Bodhidharma," Yin Chiang said with a benign smile.

The young monks pressed their palms together in greeting and bowed. A novice was dispatched to the kitchen and he returned quickly with a pot of tea and three tiny cups. He served Bodhidharma first, who lifted the tiny cup to his nose to sniff its contents. "It has a strange color," he observed.

"This tea is very common in China," Yin Chiang assured him.

"It's green," Vanya said.

"It's young tea," Yin Chiang explained, "and very refreshing."

Vanya took a sip and his mouth turned down in disapproval. "It's bitter." Bodhidharma took a sip and Yin Chiang waited eagerly for his verdict. "It is a little weak," Bodhidharma said.

"This is how we drink tea in China," Yin Chiang said brightly.

"It's better than Tibetan tea," Vanya said, "although I was getting used to it toward the end of the journey. It was good for keeping out the cold."

"Tibetan tea is mountain tea," Yin Chiang smiled. "Chinese tea is for civilization."

"It needs a little something," Bodhidharma said, reaching for his pouch of sugar crystals and spices. He offered it to Vanya, who helped himself to a generous portion, before passing the spices to Yin Chiang. Yin Chiang refused. "Chinese tea requires no additional spice or sweetness." He took a loud sip.

"It's very good," he said loudly, nodding his approval to the young monks.

"Would anyone else care to try it with sugar and spices?" Bodhidharma asked, taking the pouch from Vanya and offering it to the assembled monks, "You perhaps, Brother Lieh?"

"No thank you," Lieh said uncomfortably.

"Anyone?" he asked, amused by the look of terror on their young faces. "Does no one prefer sweet tea? You perhaps, Brother Kuai?"

Kuang started. He did not remember introducing himself to the Indian.

"Come, help yourself," Bodhidharma urged, offering the pouch to Kuang, "I insist!"

Suddenly all eyes were on Kuang. He could not refuse. Slowly he added sugar and spices to his tea, then sipped it cautiously. He did not like tea at the best of times, and this tea tasted particularly bad.

"What is your verdict, Brother Kuai?" Bodhidharma asked eagerly.

Kuang swallowed the tea with difficulty.

"You don't think it's good?"

Kuang was about to answer truthfully when he noticed Lieh's pained expression and hesitated. He guessed it would be rude to criticize the Indian master's tea, even if it was foul. He shifted uneasily in his seat, wishing he had never entered the monastery.

"Don't worry, you don't have to answer!" Bodhidharma laughed. "Some things are best left as they are, don't you agree Brother Kuai?"

"As you say Master," Kuang said with relief.

They sipped their tea in silence until Lieh ventured to speak again.

"Perhaps you would instruct us while you are here," he asked Bodhidharma, "We have never met a master from the Western Heaven, until today."

"I would be honored," Bodhidharma said happily, "but I must begin by saying that the Western Heaven is not a Heaven at all, but simply a land, very different to this one, it is true, but a land nonetheless, with men and women, towns and cities, palaces and poverty, beauty and ugliness, like every place in the world."

The monks listened, expressionless. He smiled, hoping to lighten the mood. "I myself come from the Pallava in southern India, where we are particularly fond of long names. My home town is Kanchipuram, and I can tell you that even Brother Yin Chiang, who speaks perfect Sanskrit, has trouble in pronouncing it."

"Kanchipuram," Yin Chiang said indignantly.

"*Kanchipuram*," Bodhidharma corrected with a mischievous smile.

"That is what I said, "Yin Chiang cried, throwing up his hands in resignation.

"The nearest port to Kanchipuram is Mahabalipuram," Bodhidharma continued, warming to his theme. "Now who would care to try and say that? You perhaps, Brother Lieh?"

Brother Lieh made a valiant attempt, and soon the young monks were laughing happily as Bodhidharma chose more Indian words for them to say. Only one was silent. He had no wish to draw any more attention to himself than he had already. The Indian master unnerved him. The laughing black eyes seemed to see everything, and Kuang had the feeling they had already seen past his disguise and looked deep into his soul.

Later in the evening, the monks gathered in the meditation hall for further instruction. Bodhidharma lit a stick of incense and waited until they were settled before beginning. "Tonight we will not meditate in the usual way. There are many methods of meditation but they are merely different paths to the same destination. This destination I call the Mind."

The students stared at him blankly. He sighed inwardly before continuing. "This is not the mind you know, but rather your original mind, or Buddha Mind. Like the mind of a newborn child, or a wild creature, it does not concern itself with doing good or evil, judging right from wrong. It is not aware of itself, but simply acts in accordance with The Way, which is always natural and correct."

He glanced at Yin Chiang, who nodded encouragingly, though privately Yin Chiang doubted the monks understood a word of what Bodhidharma was saying.

"Our ordinary minds are filled with a never-ending stream of thoughts which cloud the Buddha Mind," Bodhidharma continued. "These are the creations of base desires and cravings, prejudices and fears that possess our minds like evil spirits. We act on these thoughts, rather than from the pureness of the Buddha Mind. Each of us is born with a Buddha Mind. We must simply learn to listen to it. To do so, we begin by clearing our minds of random thoughts until it is quiet. Then we can hear. It may sound simple, but it requires much hard work."

He clapped his hands. "Close your eyes and focus on your breath. Think only of your breath."

He counted ten breaths and told them to open their eyes again.

"Did you think of breath?"

The monks nodded.

"Did anyone think *now I am thinking only of breath?"*

Some raised their hands.

"You see the problem?" he smiled. "It is very difficult to control our own minds. Thoughts come and go without our consent. Let's try again."

He rose and walked among them, correcting their postures as he went. Kuang's legs ached from his seated position and he began to fidget. Bodhidharma put a steadying hand on his shoulders and another on his back, and pushed him gently into a more upright position.

When he clapped his hands for them to stop, Kuang stretched out his legs gratefully. "How many different thoughts did you have?" Bodhidharma asked, pointing to Brother Lieh.

"Three," Lieh said, dejected.

"And you?" he asked, pointing to another monk.

"Seven."

He asked each monk in turn.

"Four."

"Five."

"Three."

"And you?" he asked, pointing to Kuang.

"One," Kuang answered defiantly.

"It seems you are a master already," Bodhidharma smiled, "but you others needn't worry. You too will learn to master your thoughts in time, just like Master Kuai. And since he is such a fine example to you all, he can sit at the front, beside me."

Bodhidharma beckoned to Kuang and with all eyes upon him, Kuang could not refuse. He rose slowly and took his place at Bodhidharma's feet.

"If an endless stream of thoughts can invade our heads without our consent, who is really in charge?" Bodhidharma asked. "What controls our actions? Is it really us, or these unbidden thoughts? All we see, hear, touch, feel, smell, and understand is known in the mind. How do we know if what we believe to be true is really true, and not just one of our unbidden thoughts, deceiving us? The truth is we cannot, until we are able to empty our minds of unbidden thoughts. Then we can recognize the difference between truth and delusion. Let's practice again."

The monks closed their eyes and counted breaths while he walked among them, correcting their posture until their bodies were aligned and balanced over a firm seat; since to sit firmly was to be connected to the earth, and to feel this was to be connected to heaven, in this way body and mind worked as one.

As the evening wore on, the monks grew tired and began to slouch. Kuang grew uncomfortable in his seat. His legs had gone to sleep.

"Think only of breath," Bodhidharma ordered, standing behind him.

Kuang could not steady his mind. He felt sure the Indian knew what he had done. He could not think of breaths. He was in the canteen. Tsun was turning to face him, blood spilling onto his chest. Then silence. Then screaming. It was the same scene that haunted his dreams each night, but now he noticed something new, a dark form watching from the shadows at the back of the kitchen. It was the Indian monk! He felt panic rising in his chest. He couldn't breathe. He tried to stand, but a clap of thunder exploded in his ears and a shock traveled down his spine. Bodhidharma had slammed his palms down hard on Kuang's shoulders and was pressing him firmly into the ground.

"Sit still, little master."

Kuang twisted away and sprung to his feet, spinning to face the dark monk.

"Calm yourself," Bodhidharma ordered.

Kuang moved for the door, but Bodhidharma held his arm. He tried to break the Indian monk's grip, but it was surprisingly strong.

"Wait a moment, Brother Kuai."

The Indian was enormous, but he was only a monk, and monks were not fighters. Kuang's fist flew toward his jaw. He felt nothing on his knuckles, but his punch must have landed because the monk had disappeared. He must have fallen. Too late, he realized he had not fallen but was beside him. Iron arms spun him around and snaked around his neck in one fluid move. Before he could begin to struggle, a terrible throbbing began in his temples. A roaring in his ears. The air turned red. His legs gave way to blackness.

Kuang woke on the stone floor. The Indian was standing over him. The other monks had gathered around and were staring at him. He rose slowly to his feet. The Indian was still between him and the door. He could not fathom the look in the strange black eyes, but the Indian had humiliated him, and now he stood between him and freedom. His hand reached into his waistband.

"Calm yourself, Brother Kuai," Lieh cried, but it was too late. The knife was already in his hand.

"Brother Kuai!" Yin Chiang implored him. "There's no need for this. Please, I beg you, put the knife down and let us talk like monks."

Kuang ignored them both. He was determined to teach the Indian a lesson he would not forget. He stepped forward, flicking the knife left and right, the blade glinting in the lamplight. The monks shrank back in horror, all except the Indian who waited, still as a stone. Kuang knew his next cut would reach him, slice through his skin, hurt him.

He struck.

Somehow his blade went wide, guided away by a force that was not his. Something hit his neck—too hard to be a hand; it must have been some object of wood, or iron. The Indian had his wrist. A shocking pain ran up his arm. The knife was levered from his grasp and pressed to his throat. Cold eyes stared into his, black and merciless. He was about to die, and to his surprise he felt no fear or panic. Instead, he was simply struck by the irony of his final moments. He had escaped the wrath of the Chinese army only to be killed by a monk. He closed his eyes, waiting for the cut.

It did not come.

He opened them again and saw the black eyes had changed. They were perfectly calm once more. He felt himself propelled through the entrance hall and the front door and out into the garden, to freedom. He stumbled through the iron gate into the main square, where a busy night market had sprung up. Walking drunkenly, his mind still bleary from being choked unconscious, he was dimly aware of musicians playing a slow melody. They sounded far away. An old man was fixing a wheel on his cart. A woman was roasting meat on her charcoal grill. Nobody took notice of the monk wandering haphazardly across the square.

He fought to regain his composure. He had to think! His bag was still in the monastery. It contained all his possessions, but he could not go back for it. He would need to steal new clothes, a blanket, an overcoat and a flint if he was to survive in the open again. And he would need a new disguise. The army was bound to hear of the incident and be on the lookout for a monk.

As the lamps of the marketplace faded behind him, there was only a faint moon to light his way. He considered sleeping in the town and continuing his journey at first light, but something told him to get away now. He had tried to kill a monk. It would be all over town very soon.

Was he really a murderer, he wondered. The Indian was not a brute like Tsun, but a man of peace. A monk. An emissary of The Buddha himself. The Indian had had the power to kill him, and after the knife attack he'd had reason, too, but he had spared him.

Kuang stopped on the street that led to the edge of the town, uncertain about going into the wilderness without his knife. It would be a struggle to build even the most basic shelter or protect himself against the humblest of predators. His hand reached to his waistband where the knife had once been. To his astonishment, his fingers closed around the hilt. He withdrew it and turned it over in his hand, feeling its reassuring weight in his palm. The Indian must have returned it to him before throwing him out. He shook his head, trying to clear the confusion as he headed for the darkness at the edge of the town.

Lieutenant Pai led his weary troop toward the inn in the center of the town. The dimly lit road was almost deserted. A lone child played with pebbles. An old woman pulled a cart of melons with infinite slowness toward the night market. A lone monk approached, lost in his reverie, unaware of the soldiers until they were almost upon him. The monk glanced up and stopped in his tracks, his frightened eyes looking directly into Pai's. Pai cursed inwardly. If monks spent less time daydreaming and paid more attention to where they were going, they would not be taken by surprise.

The monk bowed his head quickly and hurried past. The lights of the inn twinkled up ahead. They were almost at the entrance when Captain Fu Sheng's words echoed in his ear: *He may have disguised himself.*

Pai turned in his saddle and, more out of curiosity than suspicion, called after the monk. "One moment, Brother."

The monk did not stop.

"You there," he repeated louder, "wait a moment!"

Still the monk did not stop. Pai nodded to the last two riders in his troop. They wheeled around and trotted after the monk, who continued with his head bowed. Pai tried to recall the monk's face; the eyes, the mouth, the jawline. He snatched the artist's sketch from his saddlebag and studied it quickly. It was the same face. Only the hair was missing.

"Damn it. It's him! It's Kuang!" he roared, turning his horse. "After him. He mustn't escape!"

Kuang darted into a narrow passage between two huts. Two horsemen followed while the others split up to cut off his exits. He hurled himself through the alley, leaping over baskets and boxes, heading for the maze of narrow streets near the monastery where he would have the best chance of losing his pursuers. He could never hope to escape them in the open. They would run him down in seconds. The horses were close behind, but the animals were too big, and low roofs and washing lines blocked their path. The riders dismounted to give chase on foot, losing valuable seconds. He sprinted on, pulling down any obstacles he could find, startling the animals that foraged for food in the back alleys. There were shouts and the blasts of horns coming from the main streets. The soldiers were alerting each other of their location. He turned right, then left and scaled a wall in a single bound. Dropping into long grass on the other side, he crouched in the shadows, listening. The soldiers ran past. He had lost them. He slipped over another wall and into a different alley. The soldiers knew they had lost him and began retracing their steps. He kept going, following the roar of the rapids that would lead him toward the center of the town. At the end of a new alleyway he saw the night market. He was close to the monastery and the maze of alleys around the main square. He crouched in the shadows once more, listening. The sound of the soldiers and their horns seemed far away. His plan had worked.

"There he is!"

Two soldiers had spotted him from the other end of the alley. He headed into the main square, darting among the crowds, twisting this way and that to get across the square and into the darkness of another alley. A hand grabbed his sleeve. He turned to attack.

"Brother Kuai, wait! We've been looking for you." It was Brother Lieh from the monastery.

Kuang tore free, but couldn't get away; he was surrounded by orange robes. What did they want with him? He did not care. They would make a useful diversion while he tried to slip away.

Lieutenant Pai surveyed the scene from horseback. There were young monks all over the crowded square. In the dim light, it was impossible to tell them apart.

"Seal off the square!" he shouted, "Don't let any monk leave. Hold them all."

Kuang saw horsemen above the crowd, coming toward him. The soldiers dismounted and pushed through the crowds to reach him. He saw them seize Brother Lieh and wrestle him to the ground. A mounted trooper raised his baton and Kuang watched it fall on another young monk. The soldier dismounted and raised it again. Kuang waited for the sickening sound of the baton on flesh and bone. The baton fell, but not on the monk. A dark form appeared beside the soldier and the baton flew from his grasp. It was the Indian. His staff had moved so quickly that Kuang hadn't seen it, but the soldier's hand was smashed and he cried out in agony. Two more soldiers dismounted to help their stricken companion. A third drew a crossbow and aimed at the Indian.

Yin Chiang reached up to wrestle the crossbow from the soldier. "Don't shoot! He's a monk! Put down your weapons, this is madness!"

Another mounted soldier appeared. Kuang recognized Corporal Chen. Chen rode behind Yin Chiang and struck him on the back of the head with the flat of his sword. The little Chinese monk collapsed. The soldier with the crossbow took aim again, but his target was obscured by the frenzy of the panicked crowd. He dismounted and drew his sword.

Vanya rushed to Yin Chiang's lifeless body and cradled his head in his lap, calling out his name.

Three soldiers advanced warily on Bodhidharma, swords drawn, ready to attack. He circled to prevent them attacking all at once. One lunged forward, thrusting. Bodhidharma parried and struck him hard across the neck with his staff. As the soldier fell, Bodhidharma spun him around and drew his limp body across his own as a shield. The second soldier's sword flashed, and his blade buried itself deep into his comrade's shoulder. As he wrenched it free from his comrade's flesh, a sharp blow on his back left him struggling to catch his breath. He sank to his knees. The outline of a young monk hovered over him, a bloody knife in his hand. Have I really been stabbed by a monk, the soldier wondered? The monk knelt beside him. For a moment the soldier thought the monk might tend his wound and his life might be saved. Then he recognized the face of the fugitive, it was Kuang, the killer. This monk wanted only his sword. He felt it being pried from his grip. It was the last thing he felt.

Bodhidharma heard Vanya's voice crying out above the noise of the crowd.

"He's dead! They killed Yin Chiang!"

He saw Vanya's kneeling form, the body of Yin Chiang in his arms, and watched helplessly as another trooper rode past, slashing through Vanya's neck, killing him instantly.

Slowly Bodhidharma laid down his staff and picked up a sword from a fallen soldier. He inspected the quality of blade and the workmanship on the hilt. It was a cheap sword and crudely made, but the blade was steel and sharpened to a fine point. It would serve its purpose well enough.

Kuang stood beside him, sword in his hand. Their eyes met in grim understanding; there was no time for words as more soldiers pushed through the crowd, encircling them. They were almost surrounded. Kuang heard a roaring in his ears. He shook his head, but the noise would not stop. He glanced at the Indian. If he was as skilful with a sword as he was with a stick, they would take many more lives before they were overpowered. The roaring in his head would not go away. He could not let a monk kill for him. It was too much.

The noise was not in his head. It was real. It was the rapids in the gorge. He gripped the Indian's arm and looked him straight in the eye.

"Follow me!"

Without waiting for a reply, Kuang launched himself through a gap in the ring of soldiers. There was no time for thought. Bodhidharma followed.

Two soldiers swung their swords as he passed, so close that they shredded his robe, but he was free and running headlong behind Kuang. Kuang threw his sword aside and Bodhidharma did the same. The soldiers gave chase, but kept their swords, which slowed them. Others remounted and galloped to head off the fugitives at the next street.

Kuang rounded a corner and they raced along the riverbank together. Mounted soldiers appeared from the opposite direction. They were trapped, with soldiers front and rear, their only escape across the bridge. In that moment Bodhidharma knew Kuang's plan. It was insanity, but he did not slow down. Kuang veered onto the bridge ahead of the chasing soldiers and he followed. The bridge's planks jumped wildly beneath his feet. The soldiers were just two steps behind, causing the bridge to sway even more violently. When Kuang reached the center, he put his hand on the thick rope and vaulted over the side, turning in mid air to survey the scene behind him. Bodhidharma saw the trace of a smile on his lips as he disappeared into the foaming water. He let out a guttural roar and followed Kuang over the side. It was suicide, but better to end his life in a river than at the hand of an ignorant soldier. The Yangtze might even carry his remains to Nanjing, a fitting end to his disastrous mission, and as he plunged into the freezing darkness, his mind was almost serene.

Monks Ride the Dragon

Kuang was tumbling helplessly in icy blackness. He had no idea in which direction the surface lay. He kicked, but was at the mercy of the reckless currents. The shocking cold had taken his breath away, and his empty lungs offered no strength to his limbs. Panic filled him and he clawed feebly at the darkness, struggling to the last. He was tired, so tired that he felt himself dreaming of sleep. The river would be his final resting place. He kicked lamely, one last time, and his foot struck something hard, a stone. It was the riverbed. He knew where he was. He knew the way to the surface. He kicked with new determination, fighting his way toward the air. Water filled his lungs and he began to drown. There was a moment of stillness, an emptiness that was death itself, and then his head cleared the surface. His mouth gaped wide, screaming for air, for life. He coughed and gasped before sinking back beneath the water. But the fight had returned to him. He kicked again for the surface and this time he remained above the water. His troubles were only just beginning.

He had reached the first of the rapids and rocks loomed ahead. He searched for the Indian monk, but there was no sign of him. A smooth rock brushed against his leg like a giant creature lurking beneath the surface. A head cleared the water. The Indian had surfaced surprisingly close and fought to sweep the long hair from his face. "Prepare for the rapids!" Kuang shouted, though he had no idea if he could be heard. "At the end, swim left."

Bodhidharma saw Kuang being swept into a chute between two rocks and catapulted into a wall of white water. He struggled to get his own feet to the front as he, too, was sucked down. He was falling, unable to breath in the blinding froth. Then he was plunged into deeper water once more, his legs bumping on giant rocks. The current dragged him over stones worn smooth by eons of relentless water. Just when he thought he would not make it, he cleared the surface and saw Kuang's head bobbing in the waves ahead.

A vicious wave picked Kuang up and dashed him against a rock, holding him there for a moment before sucking him under. Bodhidharma was smashed against the same rock moments later, and dragged beneath it. He was caught, going nowhere, unable to surface. Reaching out in the darkness, searching for something to hold onto, his hands slipped on the smooth rock. The current turned him upside-down. He reached once more and felt a fallen branch trapped under the rock. His hand closed on it and he used it to pull himself past the rock. The current pitched him downstream once more. He resurfaced halfway down a stretch of wild water, gasping desperately. There was still no sign of Kuang. White foam obscured his vision. Waves spun him until he was giddy. He lost all sense of where he was. He felt himself descending the rapids backward. The water threw him between two giant rocks and he found himself stuck there. He rested for a moment, still searching for Kuang, and thought he saw him some distance ahead. He held onto the rocks, breathing hard, until another giant wave pushed him off and cast him into a new channel of fast water. In a calm between the waves he saw Kuang clearly, swimming hard for the left bank. There was a small spit of land and behind it a jetty where several sampans rocked in the quieter water. He remembered what Kuang had shouted, what seemed a lifetime ago, and kicked hard for the left bank.

Kuang swam hard to reach one of the boats but the current swept him past. His fingertips brushed the bow of the last of the sampans, but he couldn't hold on. He kicked and lunged in a desperate attempt. His fingertips hooked over the stern. He clung grimly to the little boat. His strength was almost gone. The sampan was his only chance of survival. He pulled with his last remaining strength and hauled himself into the sampan.

Bodhidharma swam hard to reach him, but the current had thrown him into the center of the river. He saw Kuang's mouth moving but heard nothing above the roar. He thrashed in the water, trying desperately to reach Kuang's outstretched arm. Their fingertips brushed, but he was dragged away by the seething river.

The effort had sapped the last of his strength. The power of the water was too great and he could fight it no longer. With his end close, his mind filled with grief for his disciples, his friends. He had led them to their death on his disastrous mission. He thought of his beloved master, Prajnatara, who had such faith in him, and The Venerable Ananda, who had believed him capable of illuminating The Way to all of China. For a short time, it had seemed their faith might be rewarded. Now, in the space of a day, all hope had vanished.

He slipped beneath the surface and his mind turned to his own death. He was determined to face it correctly, without regret. Death itself held no fear for him—he was simply returning to the place he had come from—only the transition would be painful. He prepared for his final experience of life and gave up his body to the river.

The river accepted him. His lungs filled with water. He fought down the panic and welcomed the river, examined it, experienced it, loved it, as he had loved all other aspects of his life. But the river had not finished with him yet. It hurled him to the surface and dashed him against a rock. The impact smashed the water from his lungs. He drew new breath.

The river was toying with him now. It held him high against the rock, then eased him slowly back into the water. He was caught in a whirlpool that sucked him under. If the river did not want him, perhaps it was a sign? He swam, fighting once more to reach the surface, and his hand struck something solid.

It was not a rock.

He reached for it again. It was wood. Through the churning water around him, he saw the blurry vision of a monk, standing above the river. A Bodhisattva had come from the Heavens to welcome him to the next life. The Bodhisattva rode in a chariot above the waves and held out a branch to him. He grasped it, and the saintly figure hauled him into the chariot. Bodhidharma marveled at his strength. He was overcome with love for the gentle being. He tried to speak, but gagged on the water in his lungs and, to his dismay, spewed brown water and bile into the chariot. He tried to apologize, but could not stop coughing. The saint spoke loudly to him. He could barely understand, confused and in shock, choking in his own vomit. Finally, his lungs cleared and he drew in deep, pure air. His vision cleared.

He was not in a chariot. He was in a sampan and the figure beside him was no saint.

"Take the paddle and row or we'll be smashed to pieces!" Kuang roared, inches from his face. The boat was being pounded against jagged rocks and he was fighting to hold them off. Bodhidharma snatched up the other paddle from the bottom of the boat and together they pushed away from the rocks and back into the mainstream.

"Turn!" Kuang screamed, but it was too late. The boat was going backward. Water gushed in over the stern. They struggled to turn in the fuming water before they reached the next rapids. The boat turned halfway around. It was the most dangerous position of all. The waves struck the side of the boat and rocked it violently. Kuang pointed to a chute of water disappearing between rocks. They heaved once more on the paddles and the front came around just in time to disappear down the rapids.

Then they were airborne.

The sampan landed with a sickening thud and filled with water.

"Keep paddling," Kuang urged. They fought their way out of the rapids to a stretch of calm water bathed in pale moonlight and rested a moment, still knee-deep in water.

"We should keep going," Kuang said, "until we reach the next set of rapids. The soldiers will be searching. We need to get far away."

They paddled on for another five li, carried swiftly by the current. When the noise of the next set of rapids called from the darkness, they pulled into shore and dragged the sampan onto the shingle beach, then turned it upside down to empty it of water.

"The soldiers won't reach this place before dawn," Kuang said, collapsing onto the pebbles and staring up at the starless sky.

He glanced at Bodhidharma, who sat motionless, staring at the rocky ground before him. Kuang sat up and cleared his throat. "You helped me against the soldiers tonight. Thank you."

Bodhidharma said nothing.

"Your disciples ..." Kuang continued, then stopped, unsure how to go on. A biting breeze came off the river, passing through his sodden clothes and seeping into his bones. "I'm sorry for their deaths."

The words seemed so inadequate. He tried to think of more to add, but there was nothing else to say. He stole another glance at the Indian, who continued to gaze at the stones of the beach. Kuang wondered if he had even heard him.

He closed his eyes and tried to sleep but it was far too cold. He lifted the rim of the up-turned sampan and climbed beneath it to shelter from the wind.

"Join me under here if you wish. It will be warmer," he offered, but Bodhidharma did not answer.

Much later, Kuang drifted into a fitful sleep, only to be woken moments later by new dreams of blood and slaughter. He found himself shaking so violently that he feared his heart might stop. He lifted the sampan to check on the Indian and saw him seated exactly as before, oblivious to the cold, lost in some unknown reverie that took him far from the riverbank. Kuang lay back inside the sampan and prayed for dawn and the warming rays of the morning sun.

The Sampan

When dawn came to the shingle beach beside the Yangtze, the night sky was replaced by a sheet of solid grey clouds. There was no sign of the sun. Kuang struggled from his bed of stones beneath the upturned sampan and went along the riverbank to assess the rapids ahead. His limbs felt stiff and useless. He hobbled toward a rocky outcrop and climbed up until he could see the course of the river.

When he returned to the sampan, Bodhidharma had not moved. Kuang squatted beside him.

"The rapids ahead don't look too dangerous," he told him. "We came through a lot worse last night, and now we have the daylight. I think we can make it."

Bodhidharma was silent.

"The soldiers will be hunting you too now," Kuang continued.

"We need to get away. Let's keep going downriver. We can carry the boat past the big rapids. In between, we'll be moving fast, faster than even a soldier on horseback can travel in this country. If we work together, I think we can make it."

He waited for Bodhidharma to reply, but Bodhidharma stood and took one end of the sampan without a word. Kuang took the other, and together they slid the boat back into the water.

Soon they were hurtling down a stretch of white water. The spray soaked them quickly and gathered in the bottom of the boat, swilling around their feet. They steered between rocks and around whirlpools, seeking the smoothest course. The river snaked between sheer cliffs that cast icy shadows over the water. There was no sign of life, no sound, save the slapping of the current echoing around the rocks. A movement caught Kuang's eye. A black spot on the riverbank. For a moment he feared it was an arrow, but when the spot came closer, he saw that it was a bird. It flew close to the sampan, darting across the top of the waves, then, it was gone. He turned to look at Bodhidharma. He too had noticed the bird.

Around the next bend, they emerged from the shadows of the cliffs and saw clearing skies ahead. After a few more strokes of the paddles, the sun emerged from nearby hills and bathed them in its warming glow. Kuang took off his soaking robe and laid it out to dry in the sampan.

"Not so cold now," he said cheerfully.

Bodhidharma removed his robe too and Kuang noticed the immense strength in his arms and shoulders. Not for the first time, he wondered what sort of monk it was who fought like a warrior. The Indian was not at all like the gentle, bookish priests he saw in Chinese temples.

A thunderous roar rose in the distance. Soon the water began to froth around them and they steered into the side of the river. There was no beach, only sharp rocks thrown together by the wild water. The sampan slammed into a boulder and Kuang clung to it as Bodhidharma clambered out. He scrambled up to join him and help him to haul the heavy sampan from the water.

Ahead, a crushing mass of water cascaded between steep limestone cliffs. There was no other option: the boat would have to be carried. They began their slow descent of the rocks beside the waterfall, working together to carry the sampan down the near vertical slope. At the steepest part, Kuang needed both hands to climb down to the next ledge, and Bodhidharma held the entire weight of the boat alone until Kuang could take it again. The spray made the smooth stones as treacherous as ice. Sharp rocks shredded their hands and feet, and their blood stained the dark wood of the sampan.

After a painstaking hour, they reached the tiny beach beneath the waterfall and collapsed. Kuang closed his eyes for a moment and woke some time later to a gnawing hunger in his belly. He sat up and found the Indian sitting nearby.

"We need to find food and shelter."

Bodhidharma rose without a word and they returned the boat to the river. Paddling beneath darkening skies, their strokes grew weaker until they barely had the strength to steer. Their eyes scanned the riverbank for signs of life, any place where they might find food and warmth. Just when they had almost given up hope, they saw something moving on the riverbank.

A sheep.

Two more quickly appeared beside it. They disembarked near the animals and hid the sampan in a clump of bushes. At the top of a grassy hill, they spotted a shepherd and set off up the slope to beg for his help. They had no other choice. The shepherd was small and so weather-beaten that it was impossible to know his age. He stood by a pile of wood covered with canvas to keep off the rain. An axe hung loosely from his hand.

"Greetings, friend," Kuang smiled, "perhaps you could help two travelers? We have been attacked and robbed. All our possessions were taken. We haven't eaten for several days."

The shepherd replied in a dialect that even Kuang struggled to understand. He began to repeat his request, but the shepherd raised his hand and took a sack from beneath the canvas covering. Inside were four buns. He offered them to Kuang and Bodhidharma, who took one each and gulped them down in seconds. The shepherd, seeing their hunger, offered them the remaining buns too.

"We can't take all your food," Kuang said, eyeing the buns greedily. The shepherd waved away his protest and pressed the buns on them. They ate quickly. The shepherd pointed at Bodhidharma and asked where he was from. Kuang explained he was a monk from India and this seemed to satisfy the shepherd, who led them down the other side of the hill to his cabin. Inside the cabin was bare except for some crude furniture, a stove, and a bundle of rugs and blankets, but Kuang noticed it was well stocked with supplies. The shepherd lit the stove. Soon the smell of roasting mutton filled the cabin and the shepherd piled their plates with meat.

"Do you eat meat?" Kuang asked, as Bodhidharma reached for a piece of mutton.

"No," Bodhidharma answered.

"But this is meat!"

Bodhidharma ignored him and ate. The shepherd urged them to eat until they could eat no more, and only then did he take a little for himself. When they had all finished, he opened a bottle of rice wine and warmed the rough liquid over the fire. They finished the bottle quickly and he warmed another. Then he sat back contentedly and began to sing a mournful song in a dialect neither of them could understand. When he had finished, he pointed to Kuang and demanded a song. The wine had gone to Kuang's head and he sang a song from his childhood, a cheerful tune, and highly inappropriate given the events of recent days, but it was the only one he could think of, and he did not want to disappoint his host.

The shepherd was delighted and clapped along as Kuang sang. Bodhidharma sat still, seemingly lost in his own thoughts, but when Kuang had finished, he struck up a tuneful melody from his homeland without prompting. His rich voice formed the strange sounds in a pleasing way and his companions listened throughout the many verses of his song. When he had finished, the shepherd clapped his hands in delight and warmed another bottle of wine, rubbing his throat to show that it was good for soothing the voice. The singing continued long into the night, until Kuang could not stay awake any longer and fell into a sleep so deep that for once, no ghost could penetrate it.

He awoke in a fog, wondering where he was. His eyes were dry. His head throbbed. He looked around the empty cabin and slowly it came back to him: the shepherd, the food, the wine, the singing.

It was morning already. The Indian and the shepherd were outside. He stumbled out to join them. The shepherd had packed a sack of provisions for them and was tying it with string. Kuang noticed he had also given them blankets, a flint, and an old pot so they could heat food and water.

He tried to thank him but the shepherd waved away his thanks and began speaking seriously to him. Despite his unfamiliar dialect, it was clear he was talking about the river, and Kuang followed his meaning well enough.

"There's a river port downstream," he explained to Bodhidharma, "three days from here. There are rapids on the way, some passable, others too dangerous. We'll have to carry the boat around those, but the journey can be done. At the port, there's a junk that sails all the way to Wuhan in my home province of Hubei. The captain is called Luan Po. The shepherd says he might help us."

"How shall we find this captain?" Bodhidharma asked.

"His is the only junk that comes this far upriver. If it's at the port, we will see it."

The shepherd walked with them to the riverbank and watched as they dragged the sampan back into the water. Kuang thanked him. Bodhidharma took the shepherd's hands in his and held them to his own chest. The shepherd smiled at the giant monk from across the mountains and reached up to touch his throat.

"Yes," Bodhidharma said, "it is a little sore from singing."

The shepherd held an imaginary cup to his lips.

"Warm wine," Bodhidharma smiled, touched by the man's kindness, "I will remember."

The shepherd held the sampan steady as they climbed in and handed them the sack of provisions, which Bodhidharma secured in the middle of the boat. They pushed off from the shore. The current snatched them up and the little figure of the shepherd disappeared quickly into the distance behind them.

A Change of Names

Bodhidharma found himself captivated by the passing landscape. A dazzling array of flowers grew in the stark hills. He had never seen such variety of color and form in one place. He thought of Yin Chiang and what he had told him of the Yangtze's geography, beginning in the Himalayas and flowing the length of China before emptying into the eastern ocean. He could not imagine such a river, but Yin Chiang had been a most precise scholar. If he had said it, it was sure to be true. He knew how much Yin Chiang would have relished their journey together on the river and felt a new wave of sadness surge inside him.

His thoughts turned to Vanya, who had given up everything to follow him and braved the Himalayas in search of nirvana. Instead, he had been led to a violent death by his master. The riverbanks closed in, squeezing the river, creating angry, pounding water. Tall cliffs rose to block out the sky. He pushed the past from his mind. He did not dare dwell on it. The sadness threatened to drown him more completely than the river ever could. He had to keep going. He had already failed too many people.

Instead, he studied the young man in the sampan who was now his only companion in this forbidding land. The impostor-monk had tried to kill him, but then had saved his life, not once but twice. He had also saved him from using a sword against the soldiers. Bodhidharma wondered if the young man knew how much that meant to him. Probably not, he decided.

They pulled into the bank to rest. Kuang opened the sack of provisions and saw that the shepherd had included a small bundle of tea leaves for them. He lit a fire and handed the tea to Bodhidharma. "Make it as you wish," he said, "but you'll have to drink from the pot. We have no cups."

Bodhidharma prepared his tea in silence.

"I'm afraid I have forgotten your name," Kuang said.

"Bodhidharma," came the reply.

"Bo Da Mo?"

Bodhidharma did not correct him but sipped his tea instead.

"The other monks called you "Master." Were they your servants?" Kuang asked.

Bodhidharma glared at him with eyes so cold that Kuang felt he might kill him with one blow. "No," Bodhidharma answered, "and from your question, it is clear that you are no monk. So tell me who you are?"

Kuang swallowed hard. He had no more stomach for deceit.

He would trust the Indian. "I was a soldier once. I'm not even that now."

"And your name is not Kuai."

"No, my name is Kuang."

Bodhidharma tipped his tea away and handed the pot over. "Warm the food. We need to get going."

"Tell me one more thing," Kuang said as he waited for the food to heat, "what type of monk are you, exactly?"

"Just a follower of The Way."

"Would you teach me your Way?"

"What is it that you wish to learn?"

"To fight like you," Kuang grinned.

"Then the answer is no," Bodhidharma said coldly, and from the hard set of his jaw, Kuang saw it would be dangerous to press him further.

Around a sweeping bend in the river, they passed a hut built on stilts, sitting out above the water. More buildings began to appear and by nightfall they had reached a bustling river port. Boats of all sizes were moored on the bank: canoes, dugouts, bamboo rafts, sampans, floating houses, and giant storage barges. Shops and warehouses lined the waterfront. Oil lamps cast their long reflections across the water and charcoal fires mixed with the smell of pungent fishing nets.

The quay was crowded with boatmen loading cargo, and fishermen bringing their catch to the night market, mending nets, or scrubbing down decks. But there was no sign of a junk. They searched past the main quay, until only a few boats were moored on smaller jetties, and returned to the busiest part of the port to make enquiries. Here the boats were moored two or three abreast against the quayside.

Kuang spotted a narrow gap between two enormous barges and

they paddled toward it. As they glided into the quayside, he noticed the giant head of a woman looking down at him. She was carved on the prow of a long boat that had been concealed behind the barges. A mast and sails stretched up behind her. It was a junk.

A man's head appeared beside the woman's, dark-skinned, with a thatch of graying hair and a broad grin. The man had been drinking and his voice boomed out across the water. "Well look what the river has thrown up!"

"Who speaks thus to The Buddha's servants?" Kuang answered quickly, hoping to hush the man before the entire port heard him.

"By my ancestors! It is the captain of this vessel, if you must know, and in all my days on this river I have never seen such strange servants of Buddha as these."

"That is only to be expected," Kuang replied, steering the sampan toward the junk, "since one does not meet a master from the Western Heaven every day, nor his most faithful disciple."

"That man is a Buddhist master, you say?" the man demanded loudly.

"Yes, the renowned Master Da Mo from India no less, traveling to meet with the emperor himself."

"Is that so?"

"It is, Captain, and since we have introduced ourselves, perhaps we might know your name?"

"I am Luan Po."

"In that case, we have heard of you, Captain."

"You have? What have you heard?"

"That you have the fastest junk on the river for over a hundred li."

"I have the only junk for over a hundred li!" he chortled. "But it's true, she's fast. Your Indian is hoping to go to Nanjing?"

"Yes."

"You'd better tell him there's still a long way to go."

"We are aware of that Captain," Kuang said, guiding the sampan to the junk's prow. "That is why we wished to enquire about passage aboard your fine ship."

"I only go as far as Wuhan." The captain said.

"Wuhan is fine."

"You can pay?"

Kuang smiled up at the captain. "Those who help the Buddha's servants gain extraordinary merit."

"Merit is not a currency that holds much value on this river," the captain laughed. "How much silver do you have?"

"We were robbed by bandits. We were lucky to escape with our lives."

"Robbed, you say? You and the barbarian."

"Please Captain, there is no need to be disrespectful to a great sage. This man was sent by The Buddha to bring enlightenment to China."

Bodhidharma stood and put his hand on Kuang's shoulder to silence him.

"Good evening, Captain," he said in perfect Chinese, "I am delighted to meet you. Please excuse my disciple. He is a little over-eager at times."

He fixed the captain with a broad smile and for a moment, the captain was lost for words. "Is it true, what the young man says?" he spluttered at last.

"Truth is a rare currency, Captain," Bodhidharma laughed, "Rarer even than silver, or merit for that matter. But he is not lying when he says we are going to meet the emperor, or that we seek passage downriver."

"You have no money?" the captain said suspiciously.

"None at all, I'm afraid. That much is also true."

The captain stared at the Indian for a long time. "Are you hungry?" he asked.

"We are."

"Then come aboard. You can eat with me and keep me company. Most of the crew is in the town. Tonight is our last night here. We sail in the morning."

Kuang tied the sampan to the junk, whispering urgently to Bodhidharma as he did. "I have just realized I need a new name. What shall I call myself?"

"Anything you like."

"I can't think!"

"You are running out of aliases?"

"My mind has gone blank."

"Where did the name Brother Kuai come from?" Bodhidharma prompted.

"He was a monk from my village." Kuang clapped his fist into his palm in delight. "That's it, I have a name. I will be Hui Ko! He was Brother Kuai's master, and a very wise man."

"Perfect," Bodhidharma said dryly, as they went up the gangplank to meet with the captain.

"I can't think of anything else."

"Then Hui Ko it is."

And from that moment on, Bodhidharma was called Da Mo, and Kuang became known as Brother Ko to everyone, including himself.

江河

Part 3
RIVER

The Goddess Yao Chi

"Let me begin by introducing you to someone important," the captain said as Da Mo and Ko came aboard. He led them to the woman carved on the prow. "This is the Goddess Yao Chi. The ship is named after her."

Above the gentle face and coiled hair sat a crown of red, green, and gold. A little of the paint had peeled away, no match for the harsh conditions of the river, revealing many layers beneath. The head had been valiantly restored and repainted many times.

Below the Goddess were more heads of women, although smaller, and beneath them all, a dragon whose serpentine body trailed away below the waterline. The hull was marked with deep gashes, as if the boat had been attacked by a great beast.

"The other women are her eleven handmaidens," the captain explained. "In ancient times, they helped Yao Chi to quell twelve angry dragons that lived in these mountains and caused havoc with the river. When their battle was won, they turned themselves into twelve mountains to guide boats safely down the river. They can be seen at the Wu Gorge. It is one of the most beautiful stretches of the Yangtze.

The captain turned to Da Mo. "Tell me what do you make of our Goddess, Master Da Mo?"

"She sounds like a Goddess of great compassion," Da Mo said with a smile.

"She has not failed me yet," the captain said seriously. "Do you have such gods in your religion?"

"We have Bodhisattva saints to guide and protect us," Da Mo answered.

"Are they powerful?"

"Powerful enough to get me here from India," Da Mo said.

"Though not so safely, eh?" the captain said mischievously.

Da Mo did not answer. He had no stomach for such a debate, not after what had happened to his disciples, and the captain did not seem to mind. "Come, let's eat," he said, "and you can tell me more about your religion. Buddhism has become very popular in China recently, although I don't know why. We already have our own beliefs, which are the best in the world."

They climbed out onto the raised upper deck at the rear of the boat and sat on low benches outside the captain's cabin. He filled three cups with crude rice wine and handed them around without enquiring whether they drank.

"Our chef is in town tonight along with the rest of the crew. You'll have to put up with my cooking," the captain said, pulling a stool between his knees and gutting a fish expertly in two quick cuts. "So, Master Da Mo, you're traveling to Nanjing to see the emperor? Do you think he will see you?"

"I have heard he is a keen follower of Buddhism, so I hope he will," Da Mo answered.

"Why the emperor should need anything more than The Analects is a mystery to me," the captain said. "They maintain order. Order is the most important thing in a country like ours."

"You mean The Analects of Confucius," Da Mo said.

"Yes, you know of our great sage?"

"I heard about him from a Chinese scholar whom I met in India."

"What is your opinion of him?"

"Unfortunately, there are no records of his works in India, but I intend to study his writings while I am here."

"That is unusual," the captain said with a grin, "for a priest to be interested in doctrines other than his own."

"The wisdom of the sages is rarely so different, once you see past the different words used to convey it."

"Maybe so, but their followers rarely look that far. Look at the

Taoists these days, wasting their time trying to be immortal. Life is hard enough without prolonging the misery, don't you agree? Now the Buddhists come along offering an end to suffering. Don't they know there can be no end to suffering? Haven't they seen what people do to each other?

The captain lit his stove and heated oil in a blackened pan before continuing, "There are brigands and pirates on this river who would gut you like a fish just for the pleasure. Perhaps monks in remote monasteries are unaware of the cruelty that goes on in the world?"

"We are fully aware of it," Da Mo answered, "but The Buddha spoke of the suffering of the mind rather than the body, which is the cause of much pain in the world. He told us that suffering comes from fears and cravings, which make us lose our real minds. When one fear is overcome, a new one takes its place. When one desire is fulfilled, another fills us with new longing. The way of The Buddha is to desire nothing, and fear nothing. That is true peace."

"No offense, but that's nonsense," the captain said cheerfully, sprinkling his fish with hot spices, much to Da Mo's delight. "It's natural for us to seek certain things and fear other things. It helps us to survive. If we didn't hunt animals and cultivate land and desire women, what would happen? We'd all be dead! There'd be no food. No children. No future. To stop seeking would be to give up on life."

He took three bowls and shared out the sizzling fish, then refilled their cups with wine. "Even fear is important. It teaches us to respect danger and keeps us alive."

"True, Captain, but there is a subtle difference," Da Mo said, warming to the debate at last. "The wise man still acts with purpose, he is simply not blind to what makes him act. His actions are not governed by emotion, but rather by truth."

"What difference does that make in practice?"

"He acts in accordance with his true nature, rather than the twisted imaginings of his mind. Such a person is called a Buddha and lives each moment in bliss. He does not cling to comforts that cannot last. He does not run from difficulties that must be faced. He does not hope to live forever, but rather to live each moment to the fullest. This way he escapes the torment of The Wheel."

"The wheel?"

"The endless cycle of birth and death."

"I have yet to meet such a man who does not fear death," the captain frowned.

"The Way is difficult. Those who tread its path must practice diligently for many years to strengthen their resolve."

The captain turned to Ko. "It seems your master expects a great deal of you, young man. You have many battles ahead."

"I believe so," Ko said with all the sincerity he could muster.

"Of course you do!" the captain said, suddenly filled with good humor. "Practice hard, young man. You have a chance to escape The Wheel. Take it! It's too late for me. I'm destined to continue in this hellish life on the river." He laughed and refilled their cups.

"Now listen, Nanjing is many days from here. I have made the journey many times and let me tell you, it's long and dangerous. You can't do it in a sampan. We sail for Wuhan in the morning with a full cargo to trade. You can travel with us, if you wish. It will give you a chance to persuade me of your arguments, but I don't think you'll succeed."

Da Mo accepted gratefully, and they remained talking with the captain until the sky began to lighten and Ko found himself swaying with tiredness. Only when Da Mo rose did Ko retire to his bunk to be lulled to sleep by the gentle rise and fall of the river.

They were awakened early by heavy footsteps overhead and the curses of men who had drunk a lot and slept little. Soon the gentle rocking of the waves gave way to a more persistent shuddering and the boat's timbers began to creak and groan. They emerged on deck to see the port already disappearing upriver. The captain had lost his good humor from the night before and was shouting furiously at the pale-faced crew. Da Mo and Ko kept out of the way of the sailors and watched the riverbank go by.

For the first time in months, Da Mo had some time to himself and decided to attend to the knotted muscles in his back and legs, and the shoulder he had wrenched in his flight down the river. He found a quiet area of the deck, bathed in warm sunshine, and began to stretch his tired limbs. Ko watched from a distance. The Indian's flexibility was astonishing, like that of a young child, and when he had finished, he sat cross-legged and placed his feet in his lap to meditate. Ko wondered if the Indian really could control his own mind. He sat beside him and watched the bleak scenery go past.

"I have a question," he said finally.

"Ask it," Da Mo said without shifting his gaze.

"I wish to learn The Way."

"The Way is not for you."

"I'm not talking about fighting. I wish to learn your Way, as you teach it."

Bodhidharma turned and looked into his eyes, and not for the first time, Ko felt him looking directly into his soul. He fought to hold Da Mo's fierce gaze.

Da Mo looked away and returned to his meditation.

"How shall I begin?" Ko asked, delighted that at least this time, Da Mo had not refused.

"One step at a time," Da Mo said.

"What is the first step?"

"You have already taken it."

"Then what is the second step?" Ko asked eagerly.

"Shut your mouth and open your eyes," Da Mo said. "Watch

the river go by without missing a single thing and you will be following The Way most perfectly."

Ko saw the sky change from grey to blue, to white, to red. He saw swirling mists veiling the tall surrounding peaks. He saw rain fall so lightly that it was little more than a vapor, and black cliffs rise and sink in the water. When the sun emerged from behind the clouds, he saw shadows dancing on the rocks, playing tricks on his eyes, forming the shapes of frozen gods and gnarled giants. He saw animal forms carved on cliffs in places so inaccessible that no human could have reached them: a bull, a bear, a phoenix. He saw stone steps climbing a cliff-face, leading nowhere, their end shrouded in silver mist. He saw brightly painted temples clinging to the cliffs like jewels and the mouths of a hundred honeycombed caves; and in the middle of the river, a rock with a perfectly smooth circle in its center.

When he was not watching the river, he sat cross-legged and counted his breaths as Da Mo had shown him in the temple in Tiger Leaping Gorge. After an hour, he stood to stretch his aching legs before resuming his posture. When the river was calm and the breeze contained a hint of warmth, he found his mind growing quiet enough to stay with his breaths. But soon the water called for his attention once more.

They had entered a narrow gorge. The captain called to Ko and Da Mo, pointing to a row of peaks ahead. "There are the twelve goddesses that I told you about, and if you're very lucky, you might even see the rhinoceros watching the moon."

Ko searched for the rhinoceros. The captain pointed to a rock formation fast approaching.

"I don't see it," Ko said, wondering if the captain was making fun of him.

"Keep looking!"

The boat passed by the rocks and Ko stared hard. There was no rhinoceros. It made no sense. Then he saw it—a horn pointing toward a crescent, a thick body beneath. An eye. An ear.

"I saw it!" he beamed.

"You did?" the captain asked in surprise. "Really? I have never been able to see it myself. Are you sure?"

"I'm sure," Ko nodded vigorously.

"Did you see anything, Master Da Mo?" the captain asked.

"No," Da Mo said, who was standing close by.

"Nor I, but it appears your disciple did."

Ko looked from one to the other. Were they mocking him? He could not tell, and he did not care. He had seen the rhinoceros, if only for a moment, and the image was still perfectly clear in his mind.

"I saw it," he repeated.

"I believe you," laughed the captain.

"And you Master Da Mo, do you believe me?" Ko asked.

"Of course I believe you," Da Mo grinned. "How could I doubt a fellow monk?"

"I saw it," he repeated, almost to himself, and sat once more to count his breaths.

The banks closed in and towering cliffs blocked out the sky. Giant whirlpools turned masses of floating logs and debris in endless circles. Murderous shoals lurked beneath the surface, threatening the Goddess Yao Chi as she passed.

And suddenly, the river appeared to come to an abrupt end. A cliff blocked their way. The captain shouted urgent orders to the crew as the junk sped toward it and summoned Da Mo to help him on the steering oar. The cliff was perilously close. "Pull!"

he ordered, and Da Mo helped him drag the oar suddenly to the right. The junk leaned dangerously as it swung around a sharp bend in the river, then righted itself and continued along a new channel. Above the pounding of the current, the voice of a giant echoed in the cliffs.

"What is this place?" Da Mo asked, shouting to be heard above the noise.

The captain's answer was drowned out by the thunder of a booming drum. Then Da Mo saw an unimaginable sight: a junk, sitting at the top of a rapid and pointing upstream, attached by ropes to over a hundred powerfully-built men.

"Trackers," the captain shouted. "How do you think we get the junk upriver?"

Da Mo watched as the trackers heaved, then swarmed around the boat like an army of ants at work. Some stood on the banks or in the shallows, waist-deep in the water, wearing nothing more than a loincloth and a thick harness on their broad backs. Their ropes stretched back to the junk like a giant web. Others were standing on the boat and pushing against the riverbank with poles. Their leader stood on the prow with a drum by his side, waving his drumstick in the air wildly as he yelled his orders. The men on the boat worked in two gangs. One held the boat steady while the other secured their poles further up the rapids and prepared to push. When they were all in place, the leader struck up a new rhythm on his drum and the trackers heaved. A giant groan echoed around the cliffs and the junk moved up the rapids. The prow rose above the white water. The tempo of the drumbeat increased to a frantic pace. Another groan from the trackers, a final heave, and the junk had cleared the rapids. An immense cheer went up among the trackers. Then they chanted in unison, a prayer of thanks to the river, their words resonating through the gorge like thunder.

Ko had been counting his breaths for several hours. When he rose to stretch his cramped legs, Da Mo appeared by his side. "Do as I do," Da Mo ordered.

He squatted low and pushed his hands forward, breathing deeply. Ko followed. Da Mo moved through a series of stances and positions, twisting and turning, extending and contracting like a great cat slinking through the trees of the forest. Ko found himself unable to emulate Da Mo's smooth transitions. He struggled his way back to the first position. They repeated the sequence until Ko could remember it, then Da Mo left him alone. As the junk continued down the Long River, Ko repeated the movements in between his long hours of meditation and felt himself growing stronger each day. On occasion, Da Mo would reappear by his side and correct his exercises, or adjust his seated posture without a word, as if words would break some unspoken agreement between them.

One day when heavy rain fell, Da Mo sent Ko below deck to help the crew bail out the hold. When Ko returned to the deck, he sat beside Da Mo with a grin.

"The hold is full of interesting things," he said.

"I don't doubt it," Da Mo replied.

"Would you like to see it? It contains specialities from all over China which you might find interesting."

Da Mo looked at Ko and considered his suggestion. "Show me," he said at last.

Ko led the way to the cramped store room in the hold and showed Da Mo shelves stacked with rolls of Chinese silk, wool, and leather. They examined sacks of beans and grains that Da Mo had never seen before. There were animal skins, furs, pig bristles, iron, and copperware, sacks of coal, salt, boxes of herbs, and spices from all over the world. In the driest area, on a high shelf, were row upon row of medicine jars. Ko opened the nearest jar and sniffed it, wondering what miracles it contained. A bitter scent stung his nostrils. He handed it to Da Mo who put his nose to the jar. Da Mo recognized the scent, but it had been mixed with other ingredients that he could not place. He made his way along the shelf, testing the entire collection, recording the contents of each jar in his memory before moving to the next one. With the master lost in his new work, Ko moved into the front of the hold where general provisions were stored. He opened a box and took out a handful of leaves.

"Look," he called to Da Mo, "they have dark tea leaves, the kind you like."

He took the tea to Da Mo who sniffed the leaves appreciatively. "It smells good," he smiled.

"I'll take some for you," Ko offered.

"There is no need, thank you."

"No one will know," Ko assured him.

"I would know, and so would you."

"I wouldn't mind," Ko said with a shrug.

"The tea would taste bitter," Da Mo said bluntly, turning away to examine the jars of medicine once more.

Ko stared at his master's back. He had been trying to please his new teacher, but somehow he had managed to disappoint him instead. He returned the tea to the box miserably. His teacher was a difficult man to please.

Captain Fu Sheng Receives His Report

Lieutenant Pai hurried to Fu Sheng's office and was ushered in without delay. "You've been away a long time, Lieutenant," Fu Sheng said, "I trust you have made progress?"

"Yes, Captain," Pai replied, breathing deeply to steady his nerves as he prepared to report the bad news. "We found Kuang. He was disguised as a monk. He had been hiding with a group of novices at a monastery in Tiger Leaping Gorge. There was also an Indian monk at the monastery with two disciples, one Indian, the other Chinese. Kuang was trying to leave town when we spotted him. We attempted an arrest but he ran into a crowded night market. When my men tried to apprehend him, some of the local monks intervened. It was dark, there was a lot of confusion."

"What sort of confusion?"

"A skirmish."

"You fought with monks?"

"We were under attack, Captain. Kuang killed one of my men. The Indian was deadly with his staff."

"How many dead?"

"One soldier dead and two wounded."

"And monks?"

"Three dead, Captain."

"Fu Sheng's eyes narrowed.

"Only one was from the monastery," Pai continued quickly. "The other two were the disciples of the Indian monk. They were strangers."

"And Kuang?"

"We had him trapped along with the Indian, but they threw themselves into the river."

"At Tiger Leaping Gorge?"

"Yes. The rapids are murderous there. No one could have

survived."

"You recovered the bodies?" Fu Sheng asked.

"We searched the riverbank for thirty li downstream, Captain. There was no trace of them, but they could not be alive."

Fu Sheng walked to the window of his office and looked out onto the courtyard. Pai waited, struggling to keep his nerves in check.

"This whole incident has caused nothing but embarrassment. A soldier is murdered. His murderer, a simple conscript, evades capture at every turn. Now monks are killed in a bungled arrest and there is still no evidence that this Kuang is dead. We need to bring the matter to a close."

"May I suggest we inform Commander Tang that Kuang fell in with bandits who were impersonating monks," Pai said. "We tried to arrest him and they fought back. An innocent young monk lost his life, a tragic consequence of their cowardly actions. Kuang and the bandit leader perished in the river rather than face justice."

Fu Sheng stared out of the window silently while Pai waited for him to reply. He could sense the captain's immense displeasure, but when Fu Sheng finally spoke, his voice was perfectly calm.

"Let's hope the matter will end there. If you hear any reports of Kuang or this Indian, inform me at once."

"Yes Captain."

"Dismissed."

Moments later, Fu Sheng went to Commander Tang's residence to make his report and waited impatiently in the hall outside the commander's study. Weilin emerged from a side door with a fixed smile. "Captain Fu Sheng," she said breathlessly, "I trust you are well?"

"Very well, thank you Weilin."

"You're here to see my father?" she asked, before he could

enquire after her own health.

"I am."

"Anything of importance?"

"Not particularly, just some news about that soldier we were tracking," he said.

"He's been captured?" she asked.

"No, he drowned escaping arrest."

Weilin turned to hide her face, afraid he would see her grief.

"You seem upset," he said, suspiciously. "I didn't think you knew him?"

"No, I didn't know him well," she said, struggling to keep the emotion from her voice. "It's just so sad, that a young man should drown."

"He was a murderer."

"I know. Forgive me, I'm just being foolish."

She smiled at him, but Fu Sheng could see her face was a mask. Just then the door to the commander's office opened and Fu Sheng was summoned inside. He regarded Weilin for a moment, then turned without a word, and went in to make his report.

When he left the house an hour later, he heard faint sobbing coming from Weilin's room and felt a cold fury overtake him. It was a fury that, one way or another, would be released.

The Silkmakers

The waters of the Yangtze became crowded with sampans, rafts, river junks, and barges. On the banks, the fields of crops and orchards gave way to warehouses, factories, and busy wharfs, where all manner of vessels were loading and unloading their cargo into the port of Wuhan.

As the light began to fade, the captain steered them into the main quay. Even before they had secured their lines, smaller boats rowed out to meet them. Merchants and traders called out prices from the water as the crew unpacked the cargo from the deck and brought up boxes and sacks from the hold.

Da Mo and Ko waited below for news from the captain, who had gone to arrange their onward passage to Nanjing. They waited long into the evening, until the trading outside had ceased and the cargo hold was safely locked and under armed guard. The rest of the crew had gone to enjoy the many delights of Wuhan.

The captain appeared sometime after midnight, looking tired and drawn. "Word travels quickly on this river," he told them grimly. "Fortunately, I know people who hear all sorts of rumors. There are stories of two monks being sought by the army, an incident up-river in Tiger Leaping Gorge. Nobody knows any details yet."

"Captain," Da Mo began, but the captain held up his hand to silence him. "There's no need to say anything, Master Da Mo. It would be best if you left tonight. My crew can't be trusted not to talk, especially once they have a drink or two inside them. If questioned, I will simply say we offered passage to two wandering monks out of charity, but I can't arrange onward passage for you on another vessel. It would be too dangerous."

"That is understandable," Da Mo said.

"Instead," the captain continued, "I've arranged for you to be taken somewhere where you can stay until these rumors have been forgotten."

"There's no need to risk yourself for us, Captain," Da Mo insisted.

"It's no risk if you go now," the captain said, "bring your possessions and come with me. My nephew is already waiting on the quay."

He led them off the boat to an ox cart parked in the shadows and spoke quietly to the young driver. The monks bid the captain a grateful farewell and climbed into the back of the cart where they lay among the sacks of supplies. The driver threw a rough canvas sheet over them and set off slowly through the dark streets of Wuhan.

They dozed through the night despite the jarring ride and woke in the morning to find themselves in a flat green landscape of woodlands and meadows. "Where are we going, my friend?" Ko called to their driver.

"Far."

"How far?"

There was no reply.

By the afternoon they had entered a bamboo forest and by evening, they had come to a cluster of wooden buildings in a grove of pale mulberry trees. The driver lit a lamp and led them into one of the smaller buildings. It was a workshop of sorts, with rows of shelves filled with boxes and trays, but in the dim light it was impossible to make out what was produced there.

"What is this place?" Ko asked, but the driver ignored him and pointed to two rolls of bedding in the corner.

"You can sleep here. Madam Wang will come by in the morning," he said before disappearing.

Ko took the lamp and looked around. He discovered a stove. There was a well outside so he filled his cooking pot and lit the stove. Then he reached into the sack of supplies that the captain had given them and unwrapped a bundle of tea leaves.

"Don't worry," he said quickly before Da Mo could object, "Captain Luan Po ordered me to take provisions for our journey. I said you were partial to tea and he insisted I should take some for you. I told him you liked sugar and spices, and he insisted I take some of that, too." He looked at Da Mo boldly, "Did I do wrong?"

Da Mo glared at him for a long moment, then sighed, "You'd better let me make it. You'll ruin it."

"It's already ruined, if you ask me," Ko muttered under his breath.

Da Mo made the tea and handed a cup to Ko. "You can have some, too, since you went to so much trouble to get it."

Ko took the cup without comment. They waited for the tea to cool, the only sound the gentle rhythm of rain on the roof.

"That's so strange," Ko said, "the sky was clear when we arrived. I could see the stars."

"What is strange about that?" Da Mo asked.

It's raining, can't you hear it?"

"You don't know where we are?" Da Mo asked in surprise.

"I have no idea. I didn't see any crops outside. It looked like there was an orchard of some sort, but I haven't seen any fruit around the place. There's no sign of any livestock, either. Do you know what this place is?"

"I believe I do," Da Mo said.

"What is it, a farm?"

"Of sorts, but their livestock is very small."

"Chickens?"

"Smaller than that. Small enough to fit on the tip of your finger."

"Now you're joking," Ko said warily.

"We'll see. Drink your tea."

Ko took a sip and grimaced.

Da Mo sipped his own tea and smacked his lips loudly. "He who does not appreciate tea can never appreciate wisdom."

"Is that a saying from The Way?" Ko asked.

"No, I just made it up."

Ko waited a moment, unsure, then snorted with laughter and took another sip of the tea. It was not so bad after all.

But later when he tried to sleep, the strong tea kept him awake and he lay in his strange new surroundings, listening to Da Mo's snoring and the relentless patter of the rain.

He woke to the sound of women's voices outside. Light was flooding into the shed through gaps in the wall planks. He sat up and rubbed his eyes. Da Mo's bed was empty. He threw on his tunic quickly, tidying himself as best he could, and hurried outside. It was a bright morning and he squinted, waiting for his eyes to adjust to the sun. There was something strange about the place, but for the moment, he couldn't decide what it was. Then he realized that he could still hear rain. He looked up at the sky and held out his hand. It wasn't raining.

"What is that noise?" he murmured to himself.

"You must be Brother Ko," a woman's voice said behind him. He turned to find two women eyeing him curiously. One was his age, perhaps a year or two older, with gentle eyes and soft features. Her dark skin suggested she worked outdoors for much of the day. The other was older, and quite beautiful, her skin smooth and pale, her hair tied back in a tight knot. Both were dressed in the finest robes and were clearly ladies of distinction.

"Tien says you needed somewhere to stay," the younger of the two said with a smile.

Ko stared uncomprehendingly.

"Tien is my husband," she added, "he brought you here last night in his cart."

"Ah, yes," Ko said, finally regaining his composure, "that is correct. My master and I were traveling east, but we ran into a little trouble on the river. Captain Luan Po was kind enough to offer us help."

"Captain Luan Po is my uncle," the young woman explained.

"Luan Po often encounters trouble on the river, most of it of his own making," the elder woman said, "but since he is my brother and he has promised you assistance, I won't refuse."

"That's very kind of you, Ma'am," Ko smiled.

"Besides, I suppose it will be useful to have two able-bodied men around, even if they are only monks."

"We are happy to work," Ko assured her.

"I'm very pleased to hear it," she said coldly, "now where is this other monk with the strange name?"

"You mean Master Da Mo?"

"Yes, Da Mo. What sort of a name is that?"

"Master Da Mo is from the West..." he began, but she cut him off.

"What curious names they have in Sichuan," she said. "Well I am Wang Liu and this is my daughter Hua. So, where is this so-called master from Sichuan? Dozing somewhere, I imagine, as most monks do, and calling it meditation."

"Master Da Mo is not from Sichuan..." he began again, but it was too late and Da Mo rounded the corner before he could finish. Da Mo had been bathing and he was naked to the waist. His long wet hair and beard hung in ragged curls and thick black hair glistened on his chest. The women shrank back at the sight of him.

"This is Master Da Mo from India," Ko said hurriedly, "he has come to bring the wisdom of The Buddha to China."

Da Mo smiled broadly and bowed to the horrified women.

"This is Madam Wang," Ko continued quickly, "and her daughter, Hua."

Da Mo threw on his robe and smoothed his hair. "I apologize for my appearance," he said, "I was bathing. The water from your well is very sweet."

"Is he speaking Chinese?" Wang asked, turning to her daughter in surprise.

"I believe so," Hua said, gazing wide-eyed at the huge man.

"Master Da Mo speaks many languages," Ko told them. "He is on his way to meet with Emperor Wu himself."

Wang looked him up and down with disdain. "Well, he is a very humble ambassador for his religion if he needs to stay here."

"We were robbed by bandits..."

"There's no need to explain," she said quickly, holding up a hand, "I have no wish to hear of it."

There was a short silence, and then Ko turned to Da Mo. "I have informed Madam Wang that we are willing to work."

"Naturally," Da Mo smiled, "it's the least we can do to repay her kind hospitality."

"Although I must confess, I have no idea what work is needed," Ko said.

"I believe they make silk," Da Mo told him.

The women looked at one another in surprise and Ko could see from their faces that it was true.

"What is that noise?" he asked, "I can still hear it. It sounds like rain."

"That's how silk is made," Hua smiled.

She was about to say more but Wang held up her hand. "It's best if they don't know the details."

"But if they're to help around the place..."

"The secrets of silk-making are best kept for the Chinese," Wang said pointedly. "In the West, they still believe silk is scraped off the leaves of a mulberry tree."

"Perhaps in some countries," Da Mo said, "but I must inform you that in India, the secret of silkmaking is already known."

"Impossible," Wang scoffed.

"I'm afraid it's true," he smiled apologetically.

"So what is the secret?" Ko asked.

"The rain you hear is the sound of worms munching on leaves,"

Bodhidharma informed him.

"Now you really are mocking me!" Ko said indignantly.

"No, they eat the leaves from a particular tree, out there in the grove. I believe it is called the Mulberry."

Wang and Hua exchanged another glance. The Indian was right.

"But the sound went on all night," Ko protested.

"Those grubs are hungry creatures."

Ko eyed him suspiciously.

"It is true," Hua said, unable to suppress another smile. "Perhaps I can show Brother Ko," she asked, turning to her mother, "since the secret is already out?"

Madam Wang paused, struggling to control her annoyance. "It is not right. Silk-making should be reserved for Chinese, and for women."

"But we're so short-handed, Mother," Hua said gently.

Wang eyed the monks suspiciously. "I suppose so," she said at last, "since we need to increase production this year. The price of silk is falling. Soon everyone in the world will be wearing it. If other countries start making it in earnest, the market will drop even further."

"Do not concern yourself unduly," Da Mo said, "Indian silk is not the same quality as Chinese."

"Foreign silk is naturally inferior," she said, "but people don't appreciate quality any more. They will buy anything as long as it is called silk."

"I believe quality always makes a difference in the end," Da Mo said.

"What do you know of quality, Master Da Mo?" she asked, her chin jutted out in annoyance.

"Only what I see from the garments you wear," he said lightly. 'The shimmer of the cloth and the beauty of the embroidery are quite extraordinary. Even an ignorant monk can appreciate such quality."

Wang stared at Da Mo coolly. "Let us hope others share your view. Now if you will excuse me, I have things to attend to. Hua will show you around, and get you started."

Hua began their tour in the feeding shed where they had slept the night before. "The Wang family is one of the oldest and most famous silk-makers in China," she explained. "Our robes are worn in the royal court and even by the emperor himself. Since father died, mother has been in charge of production. My husband Tien tends to the buildings and the mulberry grove. Grandmother Ao dyes the finished cloth. She used to embroider it, too, but her eyes are not good any more. Mother and I do the embroidery now. We employ women from the local town to weave the thread."

She led them to the first row of shelves and stopped beside a box of trays.

"A silkworm moth can lay five hundred eggs over five days. The eggs are very delicate, so we keep the shed warm to encourage them to hatch. When they do, the babies have big appetites. They eat only mulberry leaves, and feed every half-hour, day and night, until they grow big and fat." She pulled out a tray covered in ragged mulberry leaves and held up a leaf for them to look at. Ko peered closely at the fat worm feeding on it. Then he heard it munching.

"It's true," he cried. "It sounds like rain!"

"Not so loud," she whispered urgently, "the grubs don't like noise. The shed is kept dark and quiet to keep them happy. It makes for better silk."

She took them to where mulberry branches had been propped against the wall at the far side of the shed. "The babies grow to a thousand times their original size in a month, and then we put them on these branches where they weave a cocoon."

Taking a white ball from one of the branches, she held it up to the light and spoke softly. "If you look closely, you can see it has been spun from a single filament. After eight or nine days, the cocoon is ready to be unwound. The grub inside has become a moth. If it's allowed to hatch, it will break the strands, so we steam the cocoon to kill it."

"What a pity," Ko said, "they never get to see the silk they created."

"A few are allowed to break out, so they can lay more eggs," she smiled. "Then the cocoons are dipped in hot water to loosen the filament, which is unwound onto a spool. Several filaments are twisted together to create a single thread. That is what makes them very strong. Most of this is woven into cloth, but some becomes silk paper, which is used by some of the country's most renowned calligraphers. Imperial edicts and decrees are written on our paper. Some are used to string musical instruments. So you see, silk is very versatile. Now, if you will come with me, I will show you the mulberry grove, where you will be spending most of your time."

Ko rose an hour before dawn each day to perform the exercises he had learned from Da Mo. He continued until Grandmother Ao appeared with rice gruel and, if he was lucky, some fruit from the garden. Then he took a ladder and a basket and joined the other workers in the mulberry grove. Here he plucked leaves until his basket was full and ready to take to the grubs.

Soon he was responsible for four rows of shelves, and the grubs on those shelves were his. Each afternoon he transferred them from one tray to another, removing their droppings and the skin they had shed, and making sure the fire was lit to keep the shed warm. Cow dung was used instead of wood because wood created too much smoke. When supplies ran low, he took Tien's mule cart and went to collect more from a nearby farm.

Da Mo gave his basket to Ko and Ko filled it too, working twice as hard as the experienced pickers in the mulberry grove, while Da Mo disappeared into the surrounding forests to meditate. In the evening Ko would drink tea with Da Mo in preparation for a long evening of meditation, and Ko would sip his tea and wait for it to revive his tired limbs.

While the monks sat in quiet contemplation on the other side of the yard, the silkmakers sat together for their evening meal. Hua served soup to her husband, Grandmother Ao, her mother, and finally to herself, in silence.

"What do you think of the monks?" she asked once they had all begun eating.

"Ko seems like a hard-working boy," Tien said, slurping his soup loudly.

"Ko is quite helpful," Wang agreed, "but the Indian is bone idle! He does nothing but sit and day-dream all day in the forest while his poor disciple breaks his back in the grove."

"Oh mother!" sighed Hua, "what have you got against him?"

"He treats the boy like a slave."

"He seems very friendly," Hua said.

"He washes every morning, but I swear I can still smell him. I'll be so happy when he leaves."

"Mother! Ko says he is a great master from the Western Heaven, sent to visit the emperor."

"Nonsense! I have heard all about these magicians from India. They play tricks on the mind. Well I for one don't like it! What if he puts us all under a spell?"

"Oh don't be so rude, Wang," Grandmother Ao said. "And don't forget who sent him here. Your brother is no fool. If he trusts the man, you should too."

"Grandmother is right," Hua said, putting her hand on her mother's arm. "I think Master Da Mo is very wise. I have a feeling about him."

"Master Da Mo," Wang said, "what sort of a name is that anyway?"

"It's an Indian name. I think he is a very interesting man. In fact, I was thinking of inviting him to dine with us tomorrow evening."

"Out of the question," Wang said, putting her spoon down in protest.

"No, it's a good idea," Grandmother Ao said. "Invite the monks and I'll cook something special."

"I won't eat with them," Wang said. "I won't be able to stomach my food."

"You're under a lot of strain, mother," Hua said. "Running the business isn't easy. I understand, but please try to be polite."

"I will do no such thing. Invite them if you wish, but I'll eat alone in the study. I have a lot of paperwork to attend to anyway."

Hua sighed, but did not press the matter. Her mother had made up her mind, and once that had happened, Hua knew it would take more than a few words to change it.

Da Mo and Ko sat in the workshop and prepared to meditate. Ko waited for Da Mo to light a stick of incense, but Da Mo twirled the flint in his fingers without striking it. "How do you find it here?" he asked instead.

"It's quite enjoyable," Ko said, "I like looking after the grubs."

"Good. It seems they like you too."

"How much longer do we need to stay here, Master?"

"Until the season is over."

"Why so long?"

"Because the silkmakers have been kind, letting us stay here. They are taking a risk. We should repay them."

Da Mo paused, and Ko waited, bemused at his apparent struggle to find the right words.

"I have noticed several young women coming and going from the local town," Da Mo said at last.

"They come in to work on the looms," Ko explained.

"Some of them are quite pretty," Da Mo said.

"I noticed that too," Ko chuckled.

"Don't become entangled with any of them."

"I have done nothing improper," Ko said, reddening.

"I did not say you had, Ko. Just keep it that way."

"Is it part of The Way?" Ko asked, "to refrain from, well, you know..."

"Celibacy is an important part of The Way."

"Forever?"

"In some temples, yes."

"What about in your temple?"

"I have no temple and no strict rules," Da Mo said, "However, while we are here, you can practice celibacy."

"I will," Ko smiled, "but it must be difficult for a monk to live without a woman his entire life."

"A man can learn to live without many things."

"But why would he want to?"

"To bring his desires under control. Consider it part of your training."

"I'll try."

"Just think of your little grubs instead."

Da Mo lit the incense and Ko closed his eyes and set about clearing his mind and counting breaths, but the prettiest girl from the looms popped into his mind. He pushed her away. She disappeared, only to return a moment later, her legs parted to either side of her apparatus. He lost count of his breaths and started again; but now her robe had fallen open revealing a firm, flat belly and plump white breasts. The soft silk brushed against her thighs.

"Grubs!" Da Mo said loudly.

"Yes Master!" he said unhappily, and returned once more to the elusive task of clearing his mind.

The Silent Forest

The sun shone brightly in the azure sky and the temperature climbed with it, reminding Da Mo of the searing heat of his homeland. He smiled as he walked through the mulberry grove and into the virgin forest beyond, remembering how he had once walked to Prajnatara's temple all those years ago. He continued until he came to the clearing he used for exercise and meditation. The beautiful little glade was sheltered from the sun by a bamboo grove that whispered in the gentle breeze. He stripped to the waist and inhaled deeply, taking the warm air down to the bottom of his lungs, then squatted low on powerful legs. His arms snaked this way and that, replaying the attack and defense drills from his youth against unseen opponents in his mind. He repeated the exercise over and over, until a fine sheen of sweat covered his body. Then taking his weight on his hands, he began to press his bodyweight in a relentless rhythm before twisting onto his side, then his back, working every muscle and tendon of his giant frame.

After an hour, he stood before an ancient tree and began to

strike at the soft bark, first with his hands, then with his forearms, elbows and feet. The power of his blows made the bark crumble to dust. The sound echoed around the forest like the beat of a giant drum, pounding out its relentless rhythm for the other instruments to follow. In between each strike he could hear the hum of the forest, the subtle music of birds and cicadas, snakes and lizards, rats and monkeys, making themselves known to the dark figure in their midst.

Then his ears picked up a change. The music of the forest had stopped.

He scanned the trees for the cause of the silence. He had only heard such a silence twice before, in the jungles of India, when a big cat had been close by. Nothing else could affect the forest so. Both times, he had seen a tiger from a distance, a flash of black and gold in the undergrowth, but now he felt its presence close by. He reached for his walking staff, though he knew it would be of little use if he were forced to use it.

The air crackled around him. Every hair on his body stood up. A low growl shook the ground beneath his feet, though it was little more than a breath, a distant peal of thunder. Not a leaf moved. Not a creature stirred. Not a breath of wind played in the foliage. Then it appeared, a long tawny form no more than ten paces away emerging from a thicket of bamboo. He took in the giant expanses of muscle and sinew that moved so smoothly across the ground, the enormous paw that could break the neck of an ox with a single blow. But it was the fathomless amber eyes that held his gaze, examined him, unblinking, for an endless moment. He felt himself lost in their savage beauty. If the tiger were to tear him limb from limb, it would be worth it to see those eyes so close before he died.

The tiger blinked once, then turned slowly and disappeared through a gap in the thicket. The noises of the forest returned, but he remained where he was for a long time, humbled by the brutal grace of the beast.

Later, when he sat to meditate in the glade, the tawny shape returned to his mind, stalking through his thoughts. He was unable to remove it. The tiger was too powerful. He gave up trying and welcomed the beautiful creature instead. It was then that he realized the tiger was a messenger, and its message was clear. Death had come close, only to pass him by once again. It was a reminder of what he had lost at the tragic events of Tiger Leaping Gorge, and all of a sudden, he was filled with an unutterable joy. He had forgotten how beautiful it was to be alive.

Grandmother Cooks

Hua was lighting a lamp on the porch when the monks emerged from the dusk. She welcomed her guests for the evening and ushered them inside with a smile.

The house was filled with delicious smells from the kitchen, where Grandmother Ao had been working hard for most of the day. Her forehead was damp from the steam that rose all around her, but she stopped and beamed at the monks when she noticed their arrival.

Hua led them through to a spacious dining room. Exquisite tapestries hung from the walls and they stopped to admire the fine workmanship.

"Look Master, the Yangtze," Ko said, "here are the gorges where we sailed." He leaned closer, "It's uncanny, but this scene could have been us. Look, there's a junk that looks like the Goddess Yao Chi."

"That is the Yao Chi," Hua smiled. "The captain is my uncle, after all."

Ko peered closer. His happy smile vanished and a frown crossed his forehead. "Impossible," he muttered.

"What is it?" Da Mo asked, looking closer himself.

"It's me, sitting in meditation!"

"You're right, it could be you," Da Mo laughed.

"And look, this figure here. It's you!"

He pointed to a dark figure larger than the other sailors. It was impossible to make out a face, but the body was crouched in an unmistakable posture from Da Mo's exercise routine.

"It's the eighteenth position from the exercises!" Ko said in astonishment. "How could anyone have known?"

Da Mo looked closer and saw that it was true.

"When was this tapestry created?" he asked.

"Many years ago," Hua replied, "you can see how old it is by looking at the cloth." She stepped closer and examined the figures on the junk. "But you're right, those figures could be the two of you."

"Uncanny," Da Mo said.

"It was created by my Grandmother," she explained. "Her designs often come to her from dreams and visions. More than once her visions have proved true.

Ko inspected the other tapestries and saw scenes of snow-capped mountains, deserts, lakes, and forests. In each of them a dark figure mingled among the others, unnoticeable unless one was searching for him.

"You are in all these scenes!" he said to Da Mo, unable to believe what he was seeing. "These are scenes from all over China. All except this one. It looks like a jungle, perhaps it's in the far South."

"No," Da Mo whispered, staring at the scene in disbelief. "That is not China. It's India. I recognize my homeland of Pallava. He peered closer, pouring over the details of the scene, scarcely able to believe his eyes. "This purple tree is a jacaranda in bloom. These blue hills in the background are covered in the kurinji, which blooms only once in twelve years." He moved along the tapestry, examining each detail. "By The Buddha's bones! There's even a temple by a river that could be Prajnatara's."

"And this is you," Ko said, pointing to a dark figure on the riverbank standing beside a jetty.

"I crossed at just such a place," Da Mo said softly, transported back to the warm embrace of his homeland so far away.

"Has Grandmother Ao ever been to India?" Ko asked.

"India?" laughed Hua. "Grandmother has rarely left this farm since she was a child. She has never been farther than Wuhan."

"Then how does she know?" Ko demanded.

"She is a seer," Da Mo said.

Ko examined the other tapestries. "Maybe our future is here too," he said, stopping before a new scene. "Look, here is a great city. It could be Nanjing! Let's see if we are there."

"No," Da Mo said seriously, taking him by the arm and drawing him away. "It is best not to look too closely at the future, since it is never certain."

Ko was about to protest, but just then Grandmother Ao appeared from the kitchen and greeted them warmly. He turned to the old woman. "Grandmother," he smiled, "we have been admiring your tapestries."

"Speak up, she is a little deaf," Hua advised under her breath.

"Your tapestries," Ko shouted, "they're very beautiful."

"Oh, they're not really mine," she smiled, "they come from the Heavens."

"We noticed some interesting figures in them."

"I'm sure you did," she said, "I was beginning to think the dark monk would never appear, but he is here at last."

"These other scenes, where are they?"

She looked at him blankly, and he was about to repeat the question, when she finally spoke. "I have no idea, young man. They are places from my dreams."

"Ko," Da Mo said, placing a hand on Ko's shoulder, "go and help Grandmother Ao to bring the food in from the kitchen. Those pots look heavy."

Ko obeyed with a frown and soon the table was filled with pots of rice and thick vegetable broth, dumplings, steamed buns, finely carved fruit, and aromatic soup.

"My mother sends her apologies," Hua said as they sat down to eat, "she is very busy and unable to join us."

"But I cooked enough for everyone," Grandmother Ao said, frowning in disapproval.

"I'll take some up to her in the study," Hua said.

"No! Wait until after we have eaten. Your food will get cold and she should know better. The study is no place to eat dinner."

Hua blanched and sat back down.

Tien, who had driven the ox cart, appeared and took a seat beside Hua.

"It was kind of you to invite us," Da Mo said lightly.

"It is nice to have company," Hua said.

Tien poured a little wine for the guests and himself. He had hardly spoken to them since he had brought them in the cart from Wuhan, but now he joined in the conversation as they enjoyed the delights of Grandmother Ao's cooking. When there was a brief silence, Hua turned to Da Mo with a smile. "Master Da Mo, there is something we would like to ask of you."

"Then please ask it," he replied.

She turned to Tien expectantly, who waited a moment before speaking. "I need to go and pick up supplies tomorrow," Tien explained. "It's a day's journey from here, so I won't be back until the day after tomorrow. I usually pay someone to guard the warehouse overnight, but I was hoping you might keep an eye on the place."

"We will happily guard the warehouse," Da Mo smiled. "I will watch it during the day while Ko is nursing his worms, and we can meditate there overnight."

"Good," Tien said, shifting uneasily in his chair, "there's just one thing. The silk is very valuable. If anyone should try to steal it, well …"

"You're worried that monks are supposed to refrain from violence," Ko said.

"It crossed my mind," Tien said apologetically.

"Don't worry on that score," Ko grinned. "I'll make sure the silk is safe, and as for Master Da Mo, well he's not afraid to use his stick when it's called for."

"Really?" asked Hua.

"Oh yes, you should see him …" Ko began, but Da Mo silenced him with a look.

"The silk will be safe with us," Da Mo assured her, then turned to Grandmother Ao. "What is the name of this soup? It's very tasty."

"It's Grandmother's own recipe," Hua said, turning to her Grandmother and raising her voice so she would be heard. "They like your soup, Grandmother!"

"Of course, it's Monk's Soup," Grandmother Ao beamed.

"That's not what she usually calls it," Hua whispered.

They laughed together and Grandmother Ao laughed too, though she had not heard a word of what had been said. She was simply delighted that the dark monk had arrived safely in her country. She knew how much farther he had to go and the dangers he would have to face, but for the moment, he was here, eating soup and enjoying her family's hospitality, and that was reason enough to be happy.

The Mulberry Grove

It should have been a morning like any other for Ko, filling his basket with leaves and taking them to the feeding sheds for the silkworms, but when he leaned his ladder against a tree at the far end of the mulberry grove, he found it swarming with black flies. He checked the next tree, and all the surrounding trees, and found the same flies everywhere. The flies were eating the mulberry leaves at an alarming rate.

He hurried back to the silkmaker's house to inform Hua, but when he knocked on the door there was no answer. He went inside and called out until Madam Wang appeared at the top of the stairs.

"Hua and Tien are making a delivery this morning. What is the matter?" she asked.

He told her about the infestation and she ordered him to show her the affected trees. They walked to the grove together in silence. One look at the trees told her all she needed to know.

"Take some rope and mark out the infested area," she ordered. "I'll be back in two hours. We can deal with it then."

She reappeared in the mulberry grove at midday with a bulging sack over her shoulder. Ko hurried to help her carry it, but when she handed it to him, he found it surprisingly light.

"What's inside?" he asked.

"You'll see soon enough. I trust you have marked out the infested area, as I asked?"

"Yes, Ma'am."

She stopped at the first infested tree and opened the sack. Inside was a bundle of thin cloth bags with a looped handle. She took one of the bags and hung it on a branch.

"How will a bag stop the flies?" Ko asked, bemused.

"It's not the bag that stops the flies," she said, prodding the bag gently, "it's what's inside."

To Ko's amazement, a black line of ants began to emerge and make its way up the handle and along the branch of the tree. He watched, wide-eyed, as they marched onto the leaves and began to attack the flies.

"Incredible," he shouted, so excited that Wang could not resist a faint smile.

"They eat the flies, but not the leaves," she explained. "Just put one bag on each tree."

Ko took a handful of bags and set about hanging them up. He waited by each one until the ants began to emerge, and if none appeared, he prodded the bag gently until they marched out. Wang took more bags and set off in the other direction. She had reached the outer edge of the grove and almost finished hanging the bags, when a movement in the bamboo forest caught her eye. A dark shape was moving stealthily. A panther! She froze in fear, then relaxed when she realized it was the Indian, stripped to the waist, his hair falling around his shoulders, performing a strange tribal dance. She watched as he swayed and flexed, his limbs moving slowly and then in a blinding flash, his eyes intent, boring into an unseen enemy. She shuddered. He frightened her. His body was too big for a man. His muscles rippled, like some beast's from the forest.

A movement from behind startled her. It was Ko. She reddened, embarrassed to be caught watching the monk.

"What black magic is he performing now?" she demanded angrily.

"It's not magic, Ma'am. He is exercising."

"It looks like he is training for war. It's not the way of a monk!"

"It is his way of training."

"Who is he fighting, anyway?" she demanded.

"I think he's battling unseen demons," Ko replied.

"That's not the same as fighting real people."

"He is a skilful warrior, Madam Wang. I can assure you of that."

"Pah! So he says, but have you seen him in battle?"

"I have," Ko said.

Wang eyed him suspiciously, but Ko held her gaze. "A monk is supposed to be a man of peace," she said finally, "not a warrior! I don't know why my mother is so excited by his arrival. The figures in her tapestries are too small to be clear. They could be anyone. He doesn't look like much of a Buddhist to me at all."

"He has come all the way from India to visit the emperor," Ko told her.

"You pay him too much respect, Brother Ko. He leaves you to do all the work while he wastes time sitting in a trance or battling invisible spirits. How did you end up following him?"

"I wanted him to teach me to fight."

"And did he?"

"No."

"Why not?"

Ko thought for a moment before answering. "Before I was a monk, I was involved in too much violence already."

"So what does he teach you instead?"

"Meditation."

"Day-dreaming, I call it."

"I wish it was as simple as daydreaming, Madam Wang," he smiled.

"You are Chinese, Ko. What's wrong with Chinese wisdom? Why do you have to learn from a barbarian?"

"He's no barbarian!" Ko spoke with a sharpness that surprised even himself. He continued more gently, "I have learned more from him in a few weeks than from any Chinese teacher."

"Then you are not acquainted with the great sages," she retorted quickly.

"The sages are long dead. Master Da Mo is alive and willing to teach me."

"No good will come of it," she said, turning to watch Da Mo's dance once again. It was strangely captivating. When she turned back to speak to Ko again, he had gone.

She hung up the last of the ant-bags and made her way back to the house. The sky had changed from blue to grey and there was a new chill in the air. By the time she had reached the porch, she could feel the first spots of rain on her skin.

The Warehouse

The sound of the rain muffled the snap of the lock and the first of the thieves was inside the warehouse seconds later. He squatted inside the doorway, peering into the darkness, cars alert for the sound of an alarm being raised or footsteps approaching, but there was none. He sheathed the dagger that had been clenched in his fist and lit a candle. Its flame revealed rows of shelves piled high with silk.

Outside, the second thief saw the faint light coming from inside. It was his signal to leave the shadows and join his friend. He brought his wheelbarrow into the warehouse and closed the door behind him. They worked quickly, leaving the embroidered robes, which were too easily traced, taking only plain garments and rolls of material. Soon the wheelbarrow was filled with precious silk and they were ready to leave. They made their way to the exit and snuffed out the candle before opening the door.

It took a moment for their eyes to readjust to the darkness outside. When they did, they shrank back in terror. A giant shadow was blocking their exit, a demon etched in the faint moonlight.

"Leave the silk and you can leave with your lives," it said.

The voice was rich and deep, the words were spoken by an unearthly tongue.

The thieves stepped out of the doorway slowly, taking a better look at the dark figure before them. They exchanged a glance. The demon held only a gnarled stick by his side.

"You won't escape with the silk," he told them.

"What if we kill you first?" the first of the thieves said, growing bolder. There were two of them and it was not a demon, just a foreigner, a barbarian with a stick.

"You can't kill me," he smiled, "but see, there is room to pass by. Leave the cart and you can go free."

The first of the thieves fingered the hilt of the knife in his belt.

"I see what you're thinking," the dark man said. "It's a mistake."

"It's you who should be afraid," sneered the first of the thieves. "You won't be the first to die for the sake of a few rolls of silk." With that he drew his knife and his companion did the same.

"And you won't be the first thieves to be shot for stealing," another voice said.

A Chinese guard appeared from the shadows carrying a loaded crossbow that was aimed directly at them. "Throw down the knives," he ordered.

"Let us pass as you promised," the first thief said.

"Things changed when you decided to try to kill my master," the guard said.

"Let us go," the second thief said, throwing down his blade. "We're unarmed."

"We're leaving the silk, so let us pass now," the first said, throwing down his knife too.

"You're going nowhere," the guard sneered. "You need a permanent reminder of what happens when you try to steal from the Wang warehouse."

He lowered the crossbow, aiming at the groin of the first of the thieves.

"What are you doing?" the thief cried.

"You tried to run. We had to stop you from escaping with our silk."

"We're not running!"

The guard turned the crossbow on the other thief. "What do you think, Master? Shall we shoot one or both of them?"

"One would be unfair," the dark man said.

"Then both it is, but who should be first?"

"This one seems to be the leader," the dark man said, pointing to the first thief.

The guard aimed the crossbow at him. "Then he will be first, but where should I shoot him? Legs or groin?"

"I leave it up to you."

"I can't decide."

The guard moved the crossbow from one to the other.

"For pity's sake," the first thief begged, weeping with fear, a hot stream of urine running down his legs.

"Please," the second cried, kneeling before him, his arms outstretched to protect himself.

The first thief fell to his knees too. "Please, we're begging you …"

"Shut up!" the guard shouted. "You're ruining my concentration. I really can't decide now. The next person to move or make a sound will be first."

The thieves knelt on the ground in terrified silence.

"Close your eyes," the guard ordered, pacing before them.

They complied, every nerve straining at the sound of his slow footsteps on the dirt before them.

Then the dark man came behind them and bound them with a length of rope. They were hauled into the warehouse and locked in a room to await the return of Tien and his ox cart, which would take them to the magistrate's in the morning.

Woman Serves Tea

Da Mo stopped at the well to fill his flask before making his way to the bamboo forest. When he turned, he noticed Madam Wang on the porch and gave her a polite nod before setting off.

"Master Da Mo," she called out, her voice barely audible above the breeze. He stopped and waited for her to continue. She hesitated and brushed a stray lock of hair from her forehead. "I heard about what happened last night in the warehouse. Nothing was taken, I understand."

"No, but you will need a new lock for the door," he smiled.

"Tien is going to get one from the town this afternoon."

Da Mo regarded her patiently, waiting for her to say more.

"They drew knives on you?" she asked finally.

"Yes."

"You would have been within your rights to kill them."

"Perhaps," he shrugged, "but there was no need."

"They would have killed you. Now they'll get a light punishment and steal again," she said bitterly.

"You would have preferred us to kill them?"

"Yes I would!" Her eyes bored into his, defying him to contradict her.

"That is not our way," he said evenly.

"Those scavengers steal our livelihood! It's not the first time they've been here," her voice cracked with emotion.

"There would have been bloodshed without reason."

"Our silk is not a good reason?"

"Not good enough to risk Ko's life, or mine. Or even to take the life of a thief," he said with a certainty that she did not have the strength to challenge.

She sighed. "I don't want to seem ungrateful, Master Da Mo. I came out to thank you. We are all grateful to you and Ko."

"You're most welcome, Madam Wang."

She regarded him for another moment. "Perhaps you're right," she said finally. "There has been enough blood spilled over silk already."

The wind blew the stray lock of hair over her face once more. She left it where it was, her limbs clutching her body, as if warming herself against a chill. There was a sadness in her pale face that touched him.

"Your husband?" he asked.

"Yes, he died four years ago, protecting a shipment on its way to Changan. The silk was very precious, but not worth his life."

Da Mo said nothing. Wang examined his face once more, wondered what those piercing eyes were thinking. There was no superiority in his gaze, and certainly no condescension or pity, which would have been intolerable.

"I understand you enjoy tea?" she said finally.

"I do," he replied.

"I was about to make a pot. Perhaps you would like to join me?"

"That would be most agreeable," he smiled.

"Good, please come inside."

Da Mo followed her into the house and stood beside the screen that divided the kitchen and the dining area. He watched as Wang prepared the tea, knowing she was aware of his eyes on her—a gaze that would have made most woman uncomfortable—but Wang's expression remained serene. She moved with the grace of a classical dancer, and he admired her performance. His eyes took in the curves of her silk robe, embroidered with a simple pattern of falling leaves, the long hair piled high and fastened with a silver pin, the jade bracelet. She wore no other jewelry or adornments; there was no need to mask her beauty with trinkets.

"We have several varieties of tea," she said without turning to look at him. "Which do you prefer?"

"Which do you recommend?"

She took several packets from the shelf and brought them to him.

"Green tea is refreshing," she said, offering him the packet to smell.

He put his nose to it and sniffed gently. "I am familiar with green tea," he said.

"It is very common."

"It is a little bitter to my taste."

She closed the packet without a word and opened another. "This is a very strong tea from Fujian province. It is roasted over wood-smoke. We call it caravan tea."

He sniffed and raised his eyebrows appreciatively. "A powerful flavor. I think it would need plenty of sugar."

"That would be an aberration," she said stiffly, folding the packet away and opening another, "but caravan tea is best taken after a meal, so perhaps this variety is better."

He put his nose to the third packet and sniffed cautiously. The tea was delicate and fragrant.

"Jasmine tea," she said, "light and refreshing. Probably the best choice for this time of day."

"Then let us have Jasmine tea," he smiled.

She put a handful of leaves into the boiling water and whisked them around in the pot. When the color was to her satisfaction, she poured two cups and handed one to him with a bow. He accepted with a bow. He opened his mouth to speak, but she held up her hand.

"This tea is very light. It does not require sugar."

He took a sip of the scalding liquid and pursed his lips.

"You are quite right," he said. "It is perfect as it is."

She inclined her head a fraction.

"You have tea in India?" she asked.

"Many varieties, but they grow wild. It is not cultivated as it is here in China."

"I am told you like to add spices and sugars to your tea."

"And honey! Honey is especially good in tea."

"A quality tea requires no additional flavor, Master Da Mo. It simply masks its natural perfection."

"Ah, but the world is a place of infinite variety, Madam Wang. In Tibet, for example, they add not only sugar but rancid yak's butter, and dip pellets of barley into their brew to soften them up."

"Then I shall remember never to venture to Tibet," she said with a thin smile.

"I must admit their tea is not to my taste either," he chuckled, "but I have found that each nation's tea seems to suit the land where it is drunk."

"Tea originates in China. The rest of the world should learn to drink it the proper way."

"Which way is that?"

"The Chinese way, of course."

"Well I'm afraid you're mistaken, Madam Wang. Tea originates from India. Everyone knows that."

"Nonsense! Tea was discovered in China, by the Emperor Shen Nung, many thousands of years ago. It is common knowledge, and written by Confucius himself."

"Ah, Confucius! Apparently, he was a sage."

"The greatest of all sages, and he never lies."

"Well, please continue with your theory."

"It's not a theory," she glowered. "It is the truth."

"There are as many truths as there are people in the universe." He smiled.

"Perhaps in India, but in China, there is only one truth. Now, shall I continue?"

"Please do."

"Emperor Shen Nung was very wise. He ordered all drinking water to be boiled, to remove impurities. One day, while traveling in the countryside, a servant brought a cup of hot water to slake the emperor's thirst. Just as the emperor was about to take a sip, a gust of wind blew a leaf into his cup. This leaf infused the hot water with a warm glow and when the emperor tasted it, he noticed a pleasing flavor. By the time he had finished the cup, he felt much revived, and that is how tea was discovered."

"That is remarkable, because I heard a different story," he said.

"And what is your story?"

"Well, there was a monk who was on a long journey ..."

"And where was this monk?" she demanded.

"In India, of course."

Her eyes narrowed.

"Shall I go on?" he asked.

She nodded reluctantly.

"This monk had been traveling for many days and he was very tired. When dusk fell, he collapsed, too weak to prepare food for himself. In desperation, he reached out and plucked a few leaves from a nearby bush and ate them. Immediately, he noticed a pleasing flavor and felt much revived."

"Is that your story?"

"That is the true story of tea."

"He ate the leaves?" she asked, her lips curling in disgust.

"That's how it was discovered. Perhaps he added hot water later."

"Then he did not discover tea. He simply chewed a leaf, like a goat."

Da Mo looked down his long nose at this strange, beautiful woman and laughed out loud. His rich laugh was infectious, and Wang could not help laughing too.

"And did you Indians discover silk too?" she demanded.

"No. That much I concede. It was the Chinese who discovered silk."

"I'm delighted to hear it. Do you know how?"

"I don't. Perhaps you would enlighten me."

"Silk was discovered many centuries ago by Lady Hsi Ling Shih, the wife of the Yellow Emperor. She was drinking tea beneath a mulberry tree when something fell into her cup, a cocoon, with an insect inside. The cocoon began to come apart in the hot liquid. The lady fished it out and noticed it was made of a single filament which, when she unraveled it, stretched for over a li. She twisted the filaments together to create the first silk thread."

"A beautiful story," Da Mo sighed, "and remarkably similar to the way tea was discovered."

"It is true," she assured him.

"A true legend," he offered.

She placed her teacup down firmly.

"Our country is very fond of legends, Master Da Mo. You must understand this if you are to understand China."

"I will try," he promised.

They sat together in enjoyed silence.

"Would you like some more tea?" she asked.

"No, thank you. I must go. I have work to do with Ko this afternoon."

"You are going to teach him to fight?" she asked.

"Yes," he answered, surprised by her insight.

"I find it curious that you spare the lives of thieves who try to kill you, but teach a monk how to fight."

"It was Ko who spared the thieves, not me. Now his self-restraint will be rewarded," Da Mo explained.

"I'm sure he'll be pleased," she said, "He's desperate to learn your Way."

"He told you that?"

"We spoke about it recently."

"Once his training begins, he won't be so keen," Da Mo said gravely.

"Don't be too hard on him!" she said so earnestly that Da Mo could not help laughing.

"Don't worry, Madam Wang, he will still have a little strength left to take care of his grubs."

"That's not what I meant, Master Da Mo."

"I know, and you're very kind to consider his well-being, but Ko is a tough young man, and I think the training will do him good."

"If you're sure," she said, unconvinced.

"I am."

He rose to leave, and their eyes met. "I have enjoyed taking tea with you very much," he said, stepping out onto the porch, "and learning about China, of course."

"I'm glad. Join me again, if you wish," she said, following him outside, "I often take tea at this time."

"I would like that very much, and perhaps we can try another variety of tea?"

"I'm sure we can," she said with a small smile.

"Wonderful," Da Mo said with a happy grin, then turned and made his way toward the mulberry grove with a determined stride.

Monks Fight

Ko punched softly to avoid hurting his master. Da Mo parried and struck Ko in the chest with such force that it sent him staggering backward, gasping for air. He called Ko forward to punch again. Ko struck harder. His fist was deflected as before, but this time, he copied Da Mo and parried the returning punch.

His delight was short-lived. They continued for over an hour, until he could no longer raise his arms. The muscles in his back and shoulders burned. His chest ached where he had been struck countless times. Hot stabs of pain shot through his body whenever he moved, and just when he thought he could bear no more, Da Mo would strike him again.

Tien appeared at early evening and watched in silence for a few minutes before announcing that dinner was served at the house. They went to the well to wash and Ko struggled to remove his sweat-soaked tunic. He examined his chest and arms. They were covered in ugly welts and bruises. When Da Mo removed his tunic and washed beside him, Ko noticed he had hardly broken a sweat. His broad chest was unmarked, though Ko was sure he had struck him hard on many occasions.

When they entered the house, Ko was surprised to find Madam Wang at the table.

"How are you this evening, Brother Ko?" she enquired as he took his seat.

"Brother Ko is just fine," Da Mo answered cheerfully.

"Some broth?" she asked, ignoring Da Mo, "I know you have been working hard today."

"Yes please," Ko said, surprised by Wang's new civility.

She passed a steaming bowl of broth to him, and he was forced to raise his arms to accept it. He grimaced as hot needles ran through his aching limbs.

"Ah, soup! Thank you, Brother Ko," Da Mo said, holding out his hands for the bowl. Ko passed the bowl on to Da Mo, then raised his aching arms once again to accept another.

Wang shot Da Mo an accusing look, but he gazed straight ahead and sipped his broth contentedly. Tien poured a little wine and soon the conversation flowed. Only Ko ate in silence, lost in his own thoughts.

"You're very quiet Brother Ko," Wang said with concern, "is everything alright?"

"I have a lot on my mind," he answered quietly.

"You're not unwell?" Grandmother Ao asked with a worried frown.

"No, but thank you for asking," he said, forcing a smile.

"Perhaps you're working too hard," Hua said, turning to her husband. "Have you been giving him too many tasks, Tien? The young man is clearly exhausted."

"Nothing more than usual," Tien shrugged, "I think it was Master Da Mo who exerted the boy."

All eyes turned to Da Mo. "The Way can be demanding," he said piously.

"The Way is very demanding," Grandmother Ao nodded, echoing his words.

Wang served the rest of the soup tight-lipped while Da Mo sipped his soup without a care.

When Ko finished eating, he made his excuses and retired early to his bed. Da Mo remained for another hour, enjoying the relaxed atmosphere around the table. When he retired to the warehouse himself, he discovered Ko was not asleep there. He searched around but Ko was nowhere to be seen. Concerned, he looked outside and caught movement in the mulberry grove, barely perceptible in the faint moonlight. When he drew nearer he saw it was Ko, practicing the movements he had learned that afternoon. He watched from the shadows, unseen, and to his satisfaction, he saw that his new student had not forgotten a single one.

A Warm Day in the Mulberry Grove

Wang checked the infested trees at the far end of the grove and found the flies had all but disappeared. In the bamboo forest beyond, she noticed Da Mo training as he did each morning. A sheen of sweat glistened on his body, but with his hair tied back and his beard neatly trimmed, he no longer seemed quite so wild.

He saw her and smiled.

"I think the ants have won the war," she shouted to him.

"That is good news," he shouted back.

"I have some cold tea if you're thirsty."

"Cold tea?" he asked, stopping his practice.

"It's refreshing on a hot day like this."

He joined her in the shade of the mulberry tree. "I thought we'd tried all the different varieties of tea," he said, intrigued.

"There are still plenty that you haven't sampled, Master Da Mo," she said with a smile, offering the flask.

He took a long drink. "It's sweet."

"There's pear juice in it which adds a little natural sweetness."

"I thought you didn't approve of such things?"

"Cold tea is different," she said.

"Well, it's very good," he beamed, "thank you."

"I'm sorry if I'm disturbing your practice."

"You are not disturbing me at all. It is good to see you. You are most thoughtful."

"I'll leave you to it. I feel guilty, distracting you."

"That much is true," he smiled, "you do distract me."

"I'm so sorry," she said, preparing to leave, "I'll go."

He put his hand on her shoulder and held her gently. "No, stay. It is a welcome distraction. You're difficult to ignore, Madam Wang." He touched her face, gently brushing away the lock of stray hair that had fallen across her forehead. "You are a very beautiful woman."

She did not look at him, nor did she pull away. He put his hand under her chin and turned her head gently until he could see her face. He offered her the flask of tea. "Drink some yourself. It's hot today."

She put it to her lips and drank deeply, then handed it back to him.

"You need it more. Please finish it."

He drank the rest and a droplet fell into his beard. She smiled and wiped it away with her thumb. Her hand lingered near his face. His hand covered hers. He bent and kissed her. She responded for a moment, her lips soft on his, then pulled away.

"This is very difficult for me," she began, "ever since my husband died, there has been …"

He stopped her. "There's no need to speak of such things to me. We are here, now, that is all there is to it."

She reached up and ran her fingers through his long hair, before pulling his lips onto hers with surprising strength. He held her gently as they kissed again, this time they took their leisure, exploring each other. He pulled away slowly.

"There's a glade, deep in the forest, beautiful and quiet."

"Show me," she whispered.

He led the way. "I saw a tiger there once," he said as they walked among the swaying bamboo.

"There are no tigers around here," she said.

He shrugged.

"Are you sure? You really saw a tiger?"

"Quite sure."

"What if it's still nearby?"

"It is not."

"How do you know?"

"I can hear it."

"You can hear a tiger?"

"No, I can hear the forest. It's noisy. There is no tiger around here today."

They came to the shaded glade and stood for a moment, uncertain, searching each other's eyes. Da Mo reached out, touched her cheek and stooped to kiss her. She responded, running her fingers through his long hair. Ignited by the sweetness of her lips, he lifted her effortlessly into his arms. Wang clasped her hands behind his powerful neck and wrapped her legs around his waist, her lips still on his. Her fingers found his hair once more and pulled hard. Shocked by the intensity of his desire, he slammed her into the trunk of tree and pressed his weight against her. She broke free of his kiss and loosened her robe urgently, her lip curled in a lustful snarl, then pressed his mouth to her breasts. Her sighs quickly grew into insistent moans, and Da Mo could wait no longer. Reaching beneath himself with one hand, he tugged aside his loincloth and her undergarments. They made love where they stood, against the tree, her hot breath in his ear urging him on to a swift and violent climax.

"Are you alright?" he asked afterward, replacing her gently on her feet.

"Why wouldn't I be?" she asked with a frown.

He shrugged apologetically.

"You flatter yourself, Master Da Mo," she said with a smile. "I am more robust than I look."

"I got a little carried away."

"You did? I didn't notice. I was a little distracted myself."

They sat and spoke in the forest for some time, then removed their robes completely and made love once again, this time more slowly, until their hunger was finally sated. Da Mo draped his robe over her naked body and she lay in his arms listening to the sound of the forest.

"It's still noisy," she said.

"Then we're quite safe."

She took his hand and pressed it between her palms. "Are you really going to see the emperor?"

"Yes, it's my mission."

"When will you go?"

"At the end of the season."

"Your decision is made?"

"It was made long ago. I cannot unmake it now."

He stroked her neck, savoring its smoothness with his fingertips. "Why do you ask?"

"I'd like to know how long you will be here."

"Not as long as I would like."

"No matter," she said lightly, "I will enjoy your company while you are."

"I'm sorry."

"Don't be!" she said seriously, turning to kiss him. His arm pulled her to him but she resisted and rose to her feet. He propped himself onto an elbow and watched her putting on her robe, admiring her slender body, the soft perfection of her skin. She turned her back. "Don't look at me," she said.

"How do you know I'm looking at you?"

"I can feel your eyes on me."

"I'm simply admiring the beauty of the forest," he chuckled.

She retied her hair quickly into a neat bundle and fixed it with a pin. "For a wise man you are full of nonsense, Master Da Mo," she sighed, turning back to face him.

"Will you bring more tea tomorrow?" he asked with a grin.

"If you like it so much."

"I do. I like it very much, and I think tomorrow is going to be another very warm day."

A New Monk is Ordained

The long days of summer gave way to autumn and the time of the monks' departure drew near.

Ko's grubs had grown fat under his care. He had taken them carefully from their trays and placed them on mulberry branches to begin spinning their precious cocoons. When the cocoons had formed, he had helped the local women to steam them open and unwind the precious filament. Some of the grubs had been allowed to mature into moths, and he had watched in fascination as they emerged from their cocoons and laid eggs of their own to continue the next season.

Meanwhile Da Mo had helped Tien to trim back the mulberry trees and repair the factory buildings, and Hua had gathered supplies for the monks to take on their journey to Nanjing, including a bundle of silk for barter, since silk of such quality was a currency as good as gold or silver in China.

On the day before their departure, Da Mo found Ko in the feeding shed stacking the trays in preparation for the next season.

"I think you'll miss your grubs," he said.

"I will. I have enjoyed looking after them."

"And, you did it well."

Ko felt a surge of pride. It was the first time Da Mo had ever praised him. He was about to speak, but Da Mo's expression turned grave and Ko waited to hear what else he had to say.

"I am going to the emperor's palace in Nanjing, as you know. It was the task given to me by my Master in India and I vowed to fulfill it. But it is my mission, not yours. This is your chance to go home to Hubei. You must have family or friends who can help you?"

"I want to travel with you," Ko said.

"That's impossible. Besides, we're more likely to be recognized together. We should split up. It is safer that way."

"There's something I should tell you," Ko said, swallowing hard, "something I should have told you a long time ago, but I have not wished to think about it. I committed a sin—an act of violence. That is why the army was hunting me. Whether I'm guilty or innocent, I can't decide myself now, but the army will find me guilty, that much is certain." He stopped for a moment and searched Da Mo's eyes for a clue to his reaction, but Da Mo merely nodded for him to continue.

"My hometown is not far from here. I could disappear into the hills, I have family who can help me, but there's nothing for me there."

"You should go home, Ko."

"This is the first time in my life that I have known what I want. I want to study with you. I want to follow The Way. Let me travel with you to Nanjing. You can instruct me as we go. I can help you. I'm Chinese. I can be your guide. I'll go wherever you go and I swear I will never let you down."

Da Mo shook his head and Ko's face crumbled.

"There is something else," Ko said quickly, "please hear me out. Your disciples died because of me. I know that. I admit it. I wish to make amends and this is the only way I know how. I will become your disciple. I'll ..." But he did not know how to continue.

Da Mo snarled. "Don't be a fool, Ko. You're just a few days' journey away from freedom, and you want to ignore it and put your life at risk instead."

"I wish to make amends," Ko said weakly.

"You can never replace my disciples," Da Mo said, startled at the strength of his anger.

"I know," Ko said hoarsely.

"Go home."

"I want to follow you."

"No!"

"And what of The Way," Ko pleaded, "are my studies complete?"

"You can continue your studies elsewhere."

"Do you think it will be easy to find a place that teaches The Way as you do?"

Da Mo turned away angrily.

"Is it common for a master to abandon his student so easily?"

Da Mo turned back in fury and grabbed Ko by the robe, dragging him in close. His eyes pierced Ko with the same coldness Ko had seen in the monastery in Tiger Leaping Gorge when Da Mo had held the knife to his throat, but this time, Ko stared back into the black eyes.

Then it was Da Mo's turn to be transported, and he was back in Prajnatara's study, his face dripping from the water that Prajnatara had thrown in his face. His master had never given up on him. He could do no less to Ko.

He released Ko's robe and paced around the feeding shed. When he spoke again, his words were barely audible.

"You'll wish you went home when you had the chance."

"No."

"You'll beg to be released, and I will refuse."

"I won't, Master!"

"You'll pray for the army to find you and take you away."

"I can become your disciple?" he asked hopefully, ignoring Da Mo's threats.

"A soldier can't become a disciple," Da Mo cut back, "Only a monk can become a disciple!"

"Then ordain me," Ko demanded, then his voice softened. "Just tell me what I have to do and I'll do it."

Da Mo paced around the feeding shed once again. Moving helped him think. He considered the ceremonies and vows required for a young man to become a monk in India. It would be impossible to recreate such ceremonies or even demand Ko should make such vows. He stopped his pacing and stood before Ko with a frown.

"You must shave your head."

Ko's hair had grown back since he'd shaved his head before, but he did not mind being bald again. It did not seem like much to ask. He nodded his agreement solemnly.

Da Mo held his head in a vice-like grip and shaved the last remnants of his hair away. Then quickly, before Ko could object, shaved his eyebrows too.

"What was the purpose of that?" Ko demanded, but Da Mo silenced him.

"Hui Ko," he said solemnly, "your ordination as a monk is unique, because our situation is unique. I do not ask you to make vows that you cannot keep. There are no rituals to perform, no witnesses to your ordination but yourself. You can do all of these things at another time. Today, the loss of your hair is the only requirement of your ordination into the Sangha, the sacred brotherhood. It is a symbol of what I offer you—a new beginning. Do you accept?"

"I do," Ko said quietly.

"Good, then arise, Brother Hui Ko, and make sure you have everything packed and ready for the morning. We leave at dawn."

"Yes, Master!"

"Now there is something else I must attend to," Da Mo said quietly. Sadness crossed his face and Ko knew he was going to the house to say farewell to Madam Wang.

"Just one thing, before you go Master," he said, hurrying from the room and reappearing a moment later, "this is for you, for the journey." He held a walking staff in his hands and presented it to Da Mo with a bow.

Da Mo took it and turned it over in his hands. It was made

from mulberry and finely polished. He put the end on the ground. The carved handle came to the height of his shoulder and fitted neatly in his grip. He raised it and spun it in a dazzling arc above his head. It had a pleasing weight and feel. He examined the handle more closely and saw a mulberry leaf carved into the wood.

"It is quite beautiful," he said, touched by Ko's gift. He placed it by his pack in readiness for the next day's journey, and as he did, he noticed a similar staff beside Ko's pack.

"What's this?" he asked, lifting the other staff to inspect it.

"That is my own staff," Ko said happily. "I made two."

Da Mo examined Ko's staff and saw a silkworm carved into the handle. Ko waited, worried he might be scolded for his presumption, but Da Mo replaced the staff without comment.

Ko felt a pang of sympathy for his master. Though Da Mo had tried hard to conceal it, it was clear his feelings for Wang ran deep. Ko knew all too well how heavy his heart would be in the morning, how easy it would be to stay at the silkmakers, and how hard it would be to venture out again on the long and perilous road to Nanjing.

沃野

Part 4
PLAINS

The Emperor's Maid

Mistress Yu opened her desk drawer and took out the list that was written in her own meticulous hand. It contained all the names, dates, and prices that she had paid for the servants and slaves she had bought over the years. It went on for several pages, but even as she scanned it, she knew it was pointless. She remembered every name and price perfectly and even recalled the exact date of most transactions.

Mistress Yu was the head of the household service in the imperial palace of Nanjing, a position which made her, as far as she knew, the most powerful servant in the world. She was known by courtiers, monks, eunuchs, soldiers, guards, servants, and slaves. Even the emperor knew her name and had spoken with her on several occasions regarding the care of antique furniture and art treasures. Her efficiency was legendary. It had become a standing joke in the palace that if the imperial army were run with the same discipline as the imperial maid-service, the empire would have little to fear from the barbarians at its borders.

The secret of Mistress Yu's success was very simple. She was always vigilant. Heaven help any maid who made even the smallest mistake. Mistress Yu had a sharp tongue that could reduce a girl to tears in seconds and a bamboo cane that she used without hesitation. The bamboo was only used twice at the most. A third offense and the offending maid would be sold on the slave market, where Mistress Yu always got a good price. Former palace maids had become something of a status symbol among the noble houses of Nanjing.

It had been over a year since Mistress Yu had had any problems beyond the usual complaints, petty squabbles, and illnesses that were the daily business of her position. Recently, however, a new issue had arisen. One of her best maids, a woman called Yang who had served her diligently for many years, had begun to show the first signs of her advanced age. The floor beneath a heavy chair had not been polished. A fine layer of dust on a cabinet had not been lifted. A teacup had not been removed from the royal chamber. Few would have noticed, but Mistress Yu had spotted it immediately. Moreover, since Yang worked in the emperor's private quarters, Mistress Yu had been forced to reassign her immediately to less demanding duties.

The correct choice of replacement had been obvious: a young maid called Liang, whose work was exemplary. Mistress Yu had gone as far as summoning Liang to tell her of her promotion, but on seeing her waiting outside her office, she hesitated and reviewed her list of names for alternatives. She could not decide on the cause of her trepidation. She looked out at the waiting girl. Liang was wearing the same robe that she had worn when they first met five years earlier, though she filled it out a little better now. Her expression was serious, almost dour, and with her hair tied in a severe knot and no hint of make-up, she could almost be mistaken for a plain girl. Almost.

Mistress Yu remembered how she had arrived at the palace, a girl of thirteen, with a woman called Feng. Feng claimed to be the girl's adopted mother, but she had brought her with the intention of selling her, though the girl had not known it at the time. After a brief inspection and a few sharp questions, Mistress Yu had decided that Liang would indeed make an excellent maid, and, after long negotiations with Feng, she had paid the highest price ever paid for a junior maid.

Her instincts had proved correct and Liang had turned out to be the perfect young maid: hard-working, quiet, diligent, obedient; and though she had grown into a beautiful young woman, even if a little sinewy in Mistress Yu's opinion, she did not flirt with the guards or flutter her eyelids at the courtiers. She was friendly with one or two maids, but kept herself to herself. Some of the others called her conceited, but Mistress Yu did not care what those silly girls thought. They were jealous of Liang, whose austere beauty made her seem remote to those who did not know her.

She sighed. Liang was clearly the correct choice for the promotion. She would have to trust her instincts, which, when it came to servants and slaves, were rarely wrong.

"Come inside Liang," she called to the girl, and Liang entered with a low bow and knelt before her.

"I have rearranged some of the cleaning duties and your responsibilities will change. You will take over Maid Yang's duties in the royal quarters and the temple. That means you'll be cleaning in the royal bedchambers, the study, the library, the dining-room, the theatre, the royal court, and the auditorium."

"Yes, Mistress Yu," Liang said seriously.

"This is a position of great responsibility, Liang. These are the rooms of the most important people in the world. They are full of priceless artifacts and antiques. You'll have to be extremely careful. I will instruct you personally in the correct methods of care for these pieces tomorrow. Naturally, your conduct in the presence of the royal family and the senior monks must be impeccable and beyond reproach."

"Yes, Mistress."

"You must redouble your efforts!"

"Yes, Mistress."

She stared down at the girl coldly, waiting for her to say more, but Liang was silent, her face a mask.

"Is that all you have to say, girl?" Mistress Yu demanded.

"I won't let you down, Mistress Yu."

Mistress Yu pursed her lips in annoyance.

"I'm sorry Mistress Yu," Liang said, seeing the mistress's displeasure, "please forgive me."

"Forgive you, for what?"

Liang hung her head in shame.

"Liang," Mistress Yu said with a sigh, "this is a promotion for you. Your hard work has not gone unnoticed. You are being rewarded. It's a great honor to serve the emperor so closely. I expected you to be a little more pleased, that is all."

Liang met her eye for the first time, and Mistress Yu gave her a nod of approval. "You have done well, girl."

Liang smiled, and Mistress Yu realized she had never seen her smile before. The transformation was quite astonishing. "You are quite a beauty, when you smile," she said gently.

"Thank you, Mistress," Liang said, blushing.

"Keep it well hidden in your new role. It will bring nothing but trouble. Now, certain privileges come with your new position. A room has become available, nothing fancy you understand, just a small place under the staircase by the kitchens. It is barely enough room for one person, but it is private. It would mean leaving the dormitory of course..."

"I know the room you mean," Liang said, her voice barely able to contain her excitement now.

"Well it's yours, if you want it."

"Oh yes, please, Mistress Yu, I would like it very much! Thank you so much."

"Good. Then fetch your things and I will take you there myself."

Liang collected her possessions into the small wooden chest that she had arrived with as a child. Though it contained everything she owned in the world, it was light enough to be carried easily and she hurried down the dark corridors of the palace to her new room. When she arrived, Mistress Yu was waiting and the door was unlocked. Mistress Yu opened it and handed her the key.

"It's yours now. Arrange it as you please. Put some of your personal things out and it will feel more like home."

Liang turned around in the tiny room, trying to take it all in. It was bare, except for a roll of bedding in the corner. The ceiling sloped beneath the staircase, so she couldn't stand upright at one end and the walls had been built at an angle. Together with the sloping ceiling, the effect made her quite giddy. The only source of natural light came from a window on the staircase outside, so when the door was shut, the room would be dark. In truth, the room was little more than a cupboard, but that did not matter. She had never had a room of her own, a place where she could be herself, and she was thrilled beyond words.

She became aware that Mistress Yu was waiting for her to unpack her things as she had suggested, so she opened her chest and took out a comb, some hairpins, a vial of oil, soap, and a sheet of calligraphy.

"You have calligraphy?" Mistress Yu said in surprise.

"It belonged to my mother."

"To Madam Feng?"

"No, to my real mother. It was one of the few things that was with me when Auntie Feng took me in. These things are all I have of my real parents."

"Do you know what the writing says?"

"It's a poem." Liang wondered whether Mistress Yu would ask her to recite it, but she did not.

"How do you know?" was all Mistress Yu asked.

"Someone was kind enough to read it for me once."

"Someone in the palace?" Mistress Yu asked suspiciously.

"No, a monk in a temple in Dongshan, where I used to clean with Auntie Feng."

"Such things are best left to monks and scribes," Mistress Yu said sharply.

"As you say, Mistress," Liang said quietly, and began laying out her possession as Mistress Yu had suggested.

When Liang looked up again, Mistress Yu had gone. She jumped up and locked the door, then turned to survey her new room once again. Her room. She breathed in the air—her air—a little stuffy, perhaps, but hers nonetheless.

She snatched up the poem that lay on the chest. She hadn't looked at it for years, but still she could remember every word easily. She rolled out her bedding and lay on it, looking up at the sloping ceiling above her, and recited it to herself quietly, so no one outside would hear.

What would Mistress Yu say, she wondered, if she found out that she herself had copied the characters from a book she had found on Auntie Feng's shelf. Or if she discovered the many other sheets, painstakingly copied from the same book, hidden in the bottom of her chest.

Liang had shown her copies to an elderly monk at the temple in Dongshan and he had read them without difficulty. He had even commented on the elegance of the calligraphy, never suspecting that the girl who cleaned his temple had penned the sheets herself. She had begged the kind old monk to repeat one of the poems several times, so that she might commit it to memory. That way, she had come to know what she'd written on at least one of the sheets; for while she could copy with uncanny flair, she had no idea what the words meant. She had never learned to read.

Monks Walk

Da Mo and Ko followed the road east, through a flat landscape of rivers and lakes, and fertile plains where patchwork rice paddies stretched across the horizon. As they walked, Ko learned of The Buddha's life and his doctrine. Da Mo spoke at length of karma and nirvana, until Ko could no longer hold his tongue.

"This place called nirvana, where is it?" he asked, exasperated.

"In your mind."

"Then why can't I find it?"

"It is not a destination. It reveals itself when the time is right."

"What is it like?"

"You will feel awakened to reality."

"Are you telling me this is all an illusion?" Ko demanded, pointing at the surrounding rice fields.

"No, it is real enough, but our senses deceive us. Haven't you noticed how people only see what they want to see? They look at the world through colored veils, instead of gazing directly at the truth."

"Who puts these veils there?"

"We do."

"Then how can we get rid of them?"

"By following The Way."

They walked in silence for another li, passing a farmer ploughing his field with a buffalo. The beast was plodding slowly under the yoke, never quite stopping.

"When we were on the river, you spoke of escaping the wheel of birth and death," Ko said. "Is it possible to avoid death?"

"Everybody dies," Da Mo grinned, "even The Buddha died. But it is not flesh and bone that fears death. Only the mind fears death, and the mind can be freed from this fear."

"Everyone fears death," Ko said with certainty, "except a

madman."

"That's because people view themselves as existing."

"Now you're telling me I don't exist!" Ko said incredulously.

"Tell me this," Da Mo laughed, "are you the same person as you were when you were a baby, or a young boy?"

"Inside I am. I have simply grown up, that's all."

"And changed."

"Only my body has changed."

"Your mind has changed, too."

"I have learned new things," Ko admitted, "but I'm still the same person."

"You cling to the idea of yourself," Da Mo laughed, enjoying himself immensely now that he had such an eager opponent to argue with, "but what are you clinging to? Someone in the past who has already gone? Someone in the future who does not yet exist? You exist only now," he said, clapping his hands in Ko's face.

"And that moment has already passed. Now, you only exist now!" he clapped his hands once more.

Ko looked away in frustration.

Da Mo felt sympathy for the young man. He had wrestled with the same questions himself for many years. When he continued, it was more gently.

"Nothing about us is constant. Our mind changes. Our body changes. Our spirit changes. The only thing that is constant is the idea that we exist at all."

"It's a strange way of looking at the world."

"To view things this way is to use the Buddha-mind and see the truth. When you do, you will see there's nothing to fear. Neither birth nor death can touch you. That is bliss. That is nirvana."

"How can I reach this Buddha mind?"

"It can take a lifetime, or a moment. For many, it never appears. Others are born with it and never know."

He saw the disappointment on Ko's face and his tone softened. "Let us not dwell on imponderables for too long, and forget our basic training. Things often look different when you leave them and come back to them later. Let us train, instead."

And so they ran, until all thoughts of birth and death left Ko's mind and he gasped for air and willed his weary limbs on for another li, and another li, and still another.

The air turned cold with the onset of winter. They wore light tunics and ran on that desolate highway to stay warm, stopping only to perform exercises before continuing on the long east road.

As Ko grew stronger, Da Mo added his own pack to Ko's shoulders. When they came to a steep hill he would climb onto Ko's back, and when the road was flat he would hold Ko's feet and have him walk on his hands for one li. When they passed through the forest he would wrap a length of twine around a sapling, or fill a sack with sand and hang it from a tree. Ko would strike it relentlessly with his hands, fists, forearms, elbows, knees, feet, while Da Mo mixed an ointment to mend the cuts and temper the skin.

At the end of each day they would bathe in icy rivers and streams, or in the still waters of the region's many lakes, washing their clothes on the stones by the lake shore. Then they would light a fire, and as it burned Da Mo would massage his student's exhausted body, happily ignoring the howls of protest as his iron fingers sunk deep into his flesh. As he worked each muscle, tendon, and bone, he would name it, so his student might know his own body. His fingers would probe each vital organ and he would describe its function before tracing the pathways of life forces with his fingertips: the breath, blood, and nerve signals that flowed through the body of his hapless victim.

When Ko awoke each morning, he found himself remarkably

recovered from the exertions of the previous day, which was fortunate, since they would be repeated as soon as he and Da Mo had drunk a cup of hot, sweet tea.

As the weeks passed, Ko felt his body responding to the training. His muscles grew strong and supple. His breath became inexhaustible. Then Da Mo pushed him to new limits. He squatted one hundred times with a heavy log across his shoulders and lifted giant stones above his head. He pulled himself up on tree branches and pressed boulders from his chest, until he could do no more and lay helpless beneath the stone until Da Mo deigned to remove it.

When they came to a swamp, he stood knee-deep in the mud as Da Mo tested his condition by striking at his body and limbs. A powerful strike to his stomach had him bent double and vomiting, until Da Mo taught him to control his breath and his muscles to protect his body. When snow fell, he walked in the deep, pristine snow, kicking it into the air from morning until evening. On the days when the snow was too severe to continue, they would find shelter in a cave or a farm building and perform exercises to keep warm.

This continued until, after countless weeks of training, Ko had become so strong that Da Mo could not tire him, no matter what new torment he devised, and Da Mo knew that he had taught his student well.

Professor Reads Poetry

The study was Liang's favorite room in the entire palace. Its walls were hung with delicate ink paintings and beautiful calligraphy. Its bookcases were filled with scrolls and manuscripts containing the wisdom of centuries on their yellowing pages, and in the center stood two antique desks, where Professor Lin and his pupil, Prince Wu, worked each morning.

Liang had quickly grown to love the atmosphere created by the old man and the young boy; studious, but never too solemn. She listened as she cleaned while they read from classic poems and texts, and glanced over their shoulders as they painted famous Chinese landscapes. When the prince began to study calligraphy she could barely contain her excitement and lavished extra care on the room just to remain inside a little longer.

The professor wrote out a new poem for his young pupil to copy, reciting it as he did:

On still water the moon shines clear,
Grasp it and the moon departs,
Waiting to reappear.

"What do you think it means?" he asked.

The prince studied the words for several minutes while the professor waited patiently. There was no need to hurry the boy. It was good for him to think.

"The moon on the water is a reflection," the prince answered tentatively.

"Good," the professor smiled encouragingly. "Now let us move onto the second line, which is far more interesting. Tell me what you think about it?"

"When you put your hand in the water to grasp the moon, it makes waves, so the moon disappears."

"Exactly," the professor said. "And the last line?"

"If you wait long enough, the water becomes still again, and the moon returns."

"Yes, Highness."

The prince looked puzzled. "But what does it mean?"

"That is a very good question," the professor smiled, scratching his thin beard for a moment, "it is what we must investigate."

Liang realized she had stopped working to hear the answer and busied herself once again as the professor searched for the right words.

"The moon is often used as a symbol for wisdom," he began. "Wisdom and truth are unchanging. Like the moon, they exist for all to see. Yet these things cannot be defined in words—they are too big and too beautiful—it would be like trying to pluck the moon from the water and hold it in your hands. As soon as we try to own it, it slips from our grasp. Yet if we leave it undisturbed, it remains clear and easy to see."

"I don't understand," the prince said sadly.

"These things take time," the professor said with a kindly smile. "Now read the poem aloud for us, if you please Highness, so we may enjoy it once again."

As the prince read in a small, clear voice, Liang stopped working to listen. Suddenly she noticed the professor's watery eye on her and feared she had been caught day-dreaming instead of cleaning. The professor had every right to scold her.

"Young lady, you are new here, are you not?"

"Yes Professor," she nodded, her cheeks scarlet with embarrassment.

"You appear to enjoy poetry."

"I apologize, Professor Lin. I was moved by the beauty of the poem. I will attend to the cleaning immediately. Please forgive me."

"All in good time, young lady. First, please be so kind as to fetch some paper from the chest. The prince is about to copy out his first poem. You appear to know your way around the study well enough by now, so I am sure you will find it."

"Of course, right away," she bowed and went to get the paper.

"Thank you, Miss …?"

"Liang, Professor."

"Thank you, Miss Liang," he smiled.

She returned quickly and he laid the roll of paper on the desk and smoothed it down carefully. Next, he showed the prince how to prepare the ink and then, selecting a fine brush, he dipped it into the ink. He pressed the brush against the ink stone to drain the excess and smooth the brush hairs, and when he was ready, he wrote out the words of the poem in big, bold characters for the prince to copy, saying each one aloud as he did.

"Watch how the letters are formed," he ordered. Liang remained by the table, standing beside the prince, admiring the firmness and vigor of the old man's strokes. She tried to keep her face expressionless, hoping to hide her joy at being part of the prince's lesson, though she felt she would burst with the thrill of it.

When he had finished, the professor handed the brush to the prince, who practiced writing each character until the professor was satisfied. "Good, Highness," he said finally. "That is plenty for today. We will continue tomorrow."

Liang gathered up the prince's scrap papers into her rubbish bag and replaced the inks and brushes in the desk drawer. As she did, a thought occurred to her. She knew the poem by heart. If she could make a copy of the professor's sheet, she would know the form and meaning of a whole new set of words.

But the professor's sheet was not a piece of scrap that she could salvage from her bag later. It would remain in his desk drawer for use in tomorrow's lesson. She wondered about keeping one of the prince's sheets instead, but the characters were too crude. She needed the professor's original. A quick glance around the study saw the little prince disappearing out of the door and the professor with his back to her, saying good-bye to the prince. She slipped the professor's sheet into her bag and closed it, then hurried past the professor with a short bow. As she made her way down the corridor toward her room, the danger of what she was doing rang loud in her head and she struggled to draw breath.

She slipped into her room and locked the door behind her. Taking the professor's sheet from her rubbish bag, she held it at arm's length to admire it. It was so beautiful, she wanted to stay and copy it there and then, but she had many more chores to finish before the end of the day. Instead, she hid the paper in the bottom of her chest and rushed out to complete her shift, spurred on by the anticipation of what lay ahead that evening.

Monks Hunt

The trail led them higher up the mountain. The snow fell so deep that it came in over the rim of their boots, and their toes became numb. Soon the simple act of walking became a test of strength and even Da Mo began to struggle. All training came to an end. Instead, their energy was channeled into moving forward, one li at a time. Their aim was to reach the pass before the weather became too severe, but the snow was relentless, and the wind screamed louder with each turn of the steep road. In the end, they were forced to accept defeat and seek shelter or risk losing their battle with the winter.

They stopped by a lone cabin set back from the road and Ko shouted a greeting from outside. A dog barked furiously nearby, but there was no reply from inside. No one appeared. He tried the door and finding it unlocked, pushed it open and went inside, followed by Da Mo. It was a rough, single-room cabin. The walls had been smeared with clay for extra warmth and insulation. Thick furs had been stretched across the floor and windows to keep out the wind. In the center of the room was a stove and a handful of embers still glowed a faint red. Thin wisps of smoke rose and curled away slowly through a vent in the roof.

The dog continued to bark. They followed the sound through a second door at the back of the cabin and found an old man seated on a log outside. He was dressed from head to foot in leather and fur, and working on a deerskin with a knife. Many more skins had been stretched out on a bamboo frame beside him, lynx, sable, deer, bear, wolverine. A pile of deer-horns and wild boar tusks lay in a pile at his feet and bamboo traps were neatly stacked against the side of the cabin. A fishing net hung from a nearby tree.

The trapper's watery eyes assessed them coolly. He seemed unruffled by their unlikely appearance, and unconcerned, but the monks noticed a loaded crossbow lay within arm's reach, and he held his razor-sharp skinning knife loosely by his side. Beside him, a dog lay on its side on a rough straw mat, its legs firmly tied with leather bonds. The fur on its side had been cut away and there was a bandage around its body. The furious barking had opened the wound beneath the bandage and spots of fresh blood had begun to seep into the cloth. The trapper muttered angrily at the dog, but the dog continued to bark and struggled in vain to get to its feet.

"Greetings sir," Ko said, "I apologize if we startled you."

"No startle," the old man said, "we hear you coming long time."

"You did?"

The old man ignored the question and continued working on the deerskin.

"The road has become impassable up ahead. We were hoping to wait out the thaw here, if we may? We can offer you a few coppers, or perhaps a roll of silk, if you prefer?"

"Traders?" the old man asked.

"We are monks."

"Don't look like monks."

"We have been on the road for a long time," Ko said lamely.

"Who is dark man?" the trapper demanded.

"He is Master Da Mo from India. My name is Brother Ko. May we know yours?"

"Tai Chu," came the answer.

The trapper resumed his work on the skin. He seemed to feel enough had been said, and it appeared he had accepted their offer.

Da Mo knelt beside the dog, which stopped barking and growled menacingly. It was a typical mountain dog, not big, but tough and powerful, with a red-brown coat, spiked ears and a tail curling over its back.

"What happened to your dog?" hc asked.

"She unlucky. She chase a big man after I hit him with an arrow. He hurt her bad."

"You shot a man?" Ko asked, wondering if he had heard correctly.

"A man didn't do this," Da Mo said, examining the wound. "It looks like tusks from a boar."

"She's a brave dog if she chased a wounded boar," Ko said.

"No, shc vcry foolish woman," the trapper said, "I tell her not chase a wounded man. She never listen. Her only job to find. My job to kill."

Da Mo put his hand on the dog's neck. She tried to bite his hand, but when he scratched her, she began to writhe in ecstasy and yelp with delight.

"What's her name?" Ko asked.

"Lailao."

The dog's ears pricked up at the sound of her name, and the monks laughed. Tai Chu finished working on the deerskin and hung it beside the other skins, then set about butchering the meat with an axe. When it was done, he opened a chest that had been sunk into the frozen earth and placed the neat cuts inside with other meat that had already frozen, then closed the heavy lid and bolted it shut. Lastly, he covered the chest with heavy stones and shoveled snow over the top.

"The animals must be very persistent," Ko said.

"Wild dog very bad," he spat, treading the snow down above the chest, "bear worst of all. Open lock with claw."

Ko helped him to tread down the snow until it was packed solid beneath their feet.

"We go inside," Tai Chu said, lifting the dog on her straw mat and carrying her into the cabin. With the doors shut and bolted, he pulled furs across the doorways to keep out the draft and lit an old lamp. Soon the fire in the stove was burning again and the atmosphere grew smoky and warm. He took three chunks of meat from a box in the cabin and set about roasting them over the fire.

"Monks eat meat?" he asked.

"Not by choice," Da Mo said.

"No choice, unless you eat snow," the old man laughed.

They had survived almost exclusively on rice and vegetables since they had left the silkmakers and the roasted pork, when it was ready, tasted delicious. But their bodies had forgotten how to deal with the rich meat and their stomachs growled in complaint. The trapper fed scraps of meat to the dog and boiled up a bitter-tasting tea from local herbs, which the monks accepted gratefully, hoping it would help their digestion.

When they had finished he passed around a flask of liquor and the fiery liquid sent warmth into their bellies and made them drowsy. The trapper prepared two extra beds of sackcloth and furs and the monks wrapped their blankets around themselves tightly and listened to the wind howling outside.

"It sounds like a storm," Ko said.

"Big storm."

"How long do you think it will last?"

"Long time."

"All night?"

"Young man is impatient," scoffed the trapper. "Storm stay for many days. You will see."

The storm raged for five days. During that time, Tai Chu busied himself mending clothes and boots, sharpening tools and repairing traps. Each morning, he went outside with the monks to clear the snowdrifts around the cabin and fetch fresh supplies of meat and firewood into the cabin.

Back in the warmth of the cabin, there was little to do while the snow fell outside. Ko fed strips of meat to Lailao and watched her grow a little stronger each day. When her wound had developed a good scar, Tai Chu bound it tightly so she could not scratch it and cut the leather bonds from her paws. She tried to stand too quickly and collapsed, her legs flailing beneath her. With help from Ko, she rose and stood shakily, whining softly, and walked a few faltering steps. When the blood came back to her legs, she began to circle madly, hoping to reach the bandage. Frustrated, she sat and scratched at it, yelping in pain as she did. By the evening, she had grown used to it and dozed by the stove, growling and barking in her sleep, her legs twitching as she chased unknown creatures across her dreamy wilderness.

Finally the blizzard blew itself out. They emerged from the cabin to find the deep snow glistening in the bright sunshine. Shallow puddles had already formed on the snow's surface and shone like mirrors. A fine spider's web of sparkling streams plotted their courses down the mountainside.

"Road clear in a few days," Tai Chu said. "You go then. Take meat, if you like."

"How much do we owe you?" Ko asked.

"Nothing," the old trapper said.

"We must give you something. Money or silk perhaps?"

"Nothing," he repeated waving his hand dismissively, "No need money or silk."

It was true. The trapper had no need of either.

"There must be some way we can repay you?" he insisted.

"Ko is right," Da Mo said. "Tell us, what will you do now that the storm is over?"

"Hunt," Tai Chu replied, as if it were a stupid question.

"Then we will hunt with you," Da Mo said.

Tai Chu laughed. "What do monks know of hunting?"

They looked at each other.

"I know very little," Ko admitted, looking to Da Mo, "how about you?"

"I hunted in India as a boy, but the jungle is very different from the mountains, and besides, we follow a different path now. Monks cannot kill animals. Nevertheless, I know the weight of a carcass. We will help you carry whatever you kill."

Tai Chu scratched his beard and regarded the monks thoughtfully. Earlier that winter he had been forced to leave a valuable boar carcass because it had been too heavy—one he would have managed a few years earlier. He had buried it and returned later with an axe to bring it back in pieces, but it had already been dug up and devoured by wild dogs.

"All right," he agreed reluctantly, "but stay close. Outside is dangerous, specially for monks."

They woke at first light. Lailao knew what was happening and rushed around the cabin yelping in a frenzy of excitement. Tai Chu opened the door and she rushed out, only to return seconds later, circle the cabin once and rush out again.

The monks had packed warm clothes, furs, and food as Tai Chu had instructed. Tai Chu checked his arrows and sharpened his already razor-sharp knife once more before sliding it into the worn leather sheath on his belt. They were ready to go.

"What are we looking for?" Ko asked as they set off into the wilderness.

"Animals," Tai Chu said.

"Which ones?"

"All," the trapper grunted. "No more talk now. Animals hear you, smell your breath."

Ko was about to answer, but thought better of it. Instead, he looked around at the vista before him. Snow still clung to the higher ground but grass and flowers had begun to sprout on the lower slopes where snow had lain just a day earlier. They followed a narrow track that wound its way among birch trees, tall pines, and scattered oaks, descending into a shallow valley. When they rounded a bend, they came to a scene so picturesque that it might have been painted on a silk canvas: a pristine lake of dazzling green, surrounded by a sweep of evergreen forest and set against a background of white-tipped mountains.

"Jade Lake," Tai Chu announced. The lake appeared so sharp and green in the thin mountain air that it might indeed have been carved from a precious stone.

He stopped at a stream that emptied into the lake and they collected rocks and fallen branches from nearby. Soon they had built a dam with a small gap in its center, just wide enough for fish to swim through. Then Tai Chu hooked his net across the gap.

"We stop here on the way back. Net full of fish. You see."

How long do you plan to stay out?" Ko asked.

"Till you can carry no more," Tai Chu grinned, clapping him on the shoulder, "and you look like strong young man!"

As they approached the Jade Lake, they discovered animal tracks crossing in the snow.

"Stay close," Tai Chu warned, "many dangerous people visit

lake to drink."

"What type of dangerous people?" Ko asked, unable to stop himself talking like the hunter.

"Tiger, leopard, wolf, dog, boar. The pig is very fierce man, never underestimate him."

"You mentioned every dangerous animal in China," Ko said, looking about in alarm.

"No, bear still sleeping, usually ..." he added with a grin.

Lailao ran around in great arcs, sniffing in the undergrowth with relentless energy. She flushed out birds: grouse, crow, goose, and snow partridge, which Tai Chu shot down with his crossbow.

At the lake shore, the monks were amazed to see ducks nesting in the trees. Tai Chu's arrow downed a plump drake just as it left a branch and Ko collected its carcass in his sack. Lailao flushed out a bamboo rat from a bush. Ko had seen some big rats at Yulong Fort, but this was the biggest he had ever seen. The rat faced the dog, knowing if it turned to run, the dog's jaws would clamp over its spine, killing it instantly. It bared its razor-sharp teeth. Lailao circled close, avoiding the dangerous teeth until the rat moved and then, with expert timing, knocked it over with a swipe of her paw. The rat twisted to get up but it was too late. The dog's powerful jaws closed over it. She snapped them shut and shook hard until the rat was dead.

Soon she picked up another scent and hurried into the nearby trees. Ko followed and saw she had found a creature unlike any he had seen before. It was the same size as Lailao and resembled a fat lizard with scales and a long snout, yet walked on straight legs. It seemed unafraid of Lailao and ambled by without paying her the slightest attention. Lailao barked and growled, but kept her distance. Ko looked to Tai Chu, expecting him to fire his crossbow, but the trapper called the dog away and Lailao, for once, obeyed.

"What is it?" he asked.

"Him name Pangolin. Eat ants. Him flesh is big delicacy. Scales is big medicine, but Tai Chu does not kill him. Bad luck. Many years ago my uncle kill Pangolin. Make a chant to ask forgiveness, but not enough. Two months later all hair fall out. One month after, dead." The Pangolin entered its burrow and even Lailao waited patiently until it had disappeared before running off in search of new scents.

She spotted a group of tall wading birds in the shallows of the lake and streaked across the beach toward them. She was upon one of the cranes before it could take flight. There was a flutter of white feathers as the crane beat its powerful wings in her face. Lailao surged forward to bite. The crane stepped backward lightly, as if floating on the surface of the lake. She lunged again. The crane pecked ferociously at her face until she stopped in the shallows, panting and staring in disbelief at the thin bird, poised and ready, daring her to come forward.

"Who would have thought such a delicate-looking bird could be so dangerous?" Ko said.

"Watch and learn," Da Mo said. "See how gracefully it moves, without wasting energy. And how it strikes hard at delicate spots."

Lailao lunged once more and the crane pecked ferociously at her eyes. Lailao was blinded for an instant and yelped in pain. The crane seized its chance to flee and began a slow run that would launch it into flight. Lailao saw what was happening and gave chase. The crane's wings began to beat. The dog was closing the gap, fast. The bird swerved toward the center of the lake, knowing the deeper water would slow down its pursuer. Its feet hit the surface while Lailao ploughed through the chest-deep water, barking and snapping madly at the tail feathers. Suddenly there was an explosion of water and white feathers. The monks could not make out what was happening, until the white form of the crane emerged from the fray and took off across the water, the beat of its powerful wings muffled by the sound of furious barking.

Lailao, defeated, would not even look at her master. She turned to continue the hunt and the trio followed, skirting the lake, until they came to new tracks in the snow. Tai Chu stopped to examine them more closely. "Wolverine come this way earlier," he explained. "Climb tree. Wait for deer, but no deer come. He go away. Yesterday, lynx pass by. Old and sick. Maybe find his body today, if dogs not eat it. Porcupine was here too, but him far now."

"How do you know all this?" Ko asked.

"It is plain," Tai Chu said, as if no further explanation was necessary.

As they walked, a flock of geese appeared overhead, so high that they were little more than black specks against the blue sky. Tai Chu fired two shots from his crossbow. Both arrows went close to one of the geese, but both missed, and the old man cursed angrily to himself.

"The geese were very far," Da Mo said, impressed with Tai Chu's marksmanship, regardless of the miss.

"Eyes no good now," Tai Chu said with disgust. "Before, never miss. Now happen, too much."

At closer range, his arrows still found their targets. In the course of the afternoon, he succeeded in killing two long-haired monkeys, a civet, and a young takin, which restored his spirits somewhat. They ventured beyond the lake where Tai Chu had laid a series of traps before the snows, and collected the carcasses of rabbit, sable, fox, and marten, all of which were added to Ko's sack.

As evening fell, the temperature plummeted. Tai Chu lost no time in chopping down branches and creating a frame, hammering it in the ground, and stretching a canvas across it. Ko and Da Mo gathered ferns and leaves, which they laid on the ground beneath the canvas and Tai Chu covered these with thick goatskins. The shelter was complete.

"Snow tonight," he muttered.

"How do you know?" Ko asked.

"The birds."

Ko listened, but there was no sound. "I don't hear anything," he said.

"They quiet, they know," Tai Chu said pointing into a tree. "Look, see crow?"

Ko took some time to spot the crow in the highest branches.

"He know the air. He face east."

"But the wind is coming from the west," Ko said.

"Soon change. East wind cold."

"So he faces into the wind?"

"Of course. Otherwise wind blow up his feathers. He be very cold."

Ko scoffed, but Tai Chu nodded his head seriously. "Soon see."

An hour later the snow was piling up on their shelter, driven by an icy easterly wind, just as Tai Chu had predicted. A fire spluttered in the mouth of the shelter, giving off just enough heat to cook meat and boil water for tea. Small, dry snowflakes flew in gusts around them. When they had finished and the fire was put out, Tai Chu pulled the canvas flap shut and they wrapped themselves tightly in furs, lying side by side, the dog with them, and slept fitfully as the weather raged outside.

In the morning, they emerged to find the storm had left a thin layer of fresh snow covering the landscape around them.

"Yesterday we hunt little people. Today big men," Tai Chu smiled as they dismantled the shelter.

They continued into a new valley of pristine snow and shimmering pines. When they came across the fresh tracks of a musk deer, Tai Chu set off in a steady loping run. The monks followed, marveling at how swiftly he moved despite his advanced years. Lailao ran alongside joyfully, the pain of her injury forgotten. She was in her element once more.

After an hour, Tai Chu stopped abruptly and raised his hand for silence. Through a gap in the trees, they spotted a great stag sniffing the air. The monks held their breath as the old hunter raised his crossbow with infinite patience. Lailao watched beside them, still as stone, her bright eyes fixed on the great beast, waiting for the kill. Even with the animal in his sights Tai Chu hesitated, as if waiting for an auspicious moment to release his arrow. They were downwind, and the stag did not pick up their scent. Yet, it had not survived so many winters without knowing when danger lurked close by, and it scanned the surrounding trees steadily for the source of the threat that it felt in its bones.

It spotted the old hunter just as the arrow struck.

The shot was good, close to the heart. The stag ran a few paces before falling heavily. Tai Chu approached the dying beast slowly, ordering Lailao back with a flick of his hand. She obeyed, lying patiently in the snow. He knelt beside the deer, his head bowed, and waited in silence until it had breathed its last.

They heaved the carcass onto Da Mo's broad shoulders and began the long walk back to the cabin, the old hunter walking briskly ahead while Ko and Da Mo labored side by side under the weight of his many kills.

"The trapper is a strange man," Ko said, breathlessly. "He talks as if animals are people."

"Is that so strange?" Da Mo asked.

"It is a very primitive way of looking at things, don't you agree?"

"It is a common belief among those who live close to nature."

What does The Way say about such things?" Ko asked, barely able to speak from the exertion of carrying the carcasses up the hill.

"Animals are beings, with feelings."

"But they're not the same as people."

"No. But people are part of nature, no matter how much they

run from it. A monk must learn to see this, learn to love nature and appreciate its beauty."

"But we have developed beyond animals, haven't we?"

"Yes, and much suffering it has brought us."

"But it has brought good things, too."

"Yes."

They came to the top of the rise and Da Mo stopped. Ko stood beside him expectantly, but Da Mo gazed ahead at the white trail that dipped down toward the Jade Lake. Tai Chu was far ahead now, nearing the lake shore, while Lailao darted from bush to bush, following new scents that only she could perceive.

"Monks who follow The Way seek the ultimate truth," he said. "They seek it everywhere, high and low, here and there. If only they would look straight ahead, they would see it. Here the world is natural, unmarred by human hands. Beautiful, but harsh. Noble, but cruel. The animals live without affectation and artifice, from the greatest to the humblest. Do you think they worry about such trifles as good or evil? The tigress is deadly to her prey, but caring to her offspring. Is she good or evil?"

"It's easy for the tigress," Ko said, "What about for her prey?"

"Do you think the pig lives in fear of being eaten by the tigress?" Da Mo asked.

"Maybe he's too stupid to think about it, unless he's in danger."

"Or too clever," Da Mo smiled. "Why worry about something unless it's happening? That is an illness of the human mind. The pig doesn't waste time thinking about things that are not important."

"But it is important! The tigress is dangerous!"

"Don't be mistaken. He is aware of the threat of the tigress and doesn't forage near her lair. But neither does he worry constantly about being eaten. Fear of the tigress does not consume him."

"So why are people different?"

"We have too much on our minds, too many fears for the future, too many desires that distract us from the simple joy of being alive."

Ko walked on in silence considering his reply. "What you're saying is I should try to be more like a pig?" he asked at last, with grin.

"You can try," Da Mo laughed. "It shouldn't be too difficult. I noticed your potential when we first met."

They followed Tai Chu along the shoreline of the lake until the ground rose again, back in the direction of the cabin.

"It's the same in combat," Da Mo said as they walked. "You can learn a lot by observing how animals fight, their strategies, tactics, and how they think."

"But animals fight differently than humans," Ko protested.

"Accepted," Da Mo said, "but they fight naturally, which is the best way. A way you should study. They use the weapons given to them by nature. The tiger is enormous and powerful, with deadly teeth and claws. It pounces on its prey and overwhelms it with ferocity. The wolf is less powerful. Its strength is its endurance. It wears its prey down by chasing it until the prey is too exhausted to resist. Yesterday by the lake, we watched the crane evade and strike at weak points against a dog. Each animal employs its own strategy quite naturally. The python wraps its prey ever tighter, until the life force ebbs away. The viper uses stealth and poison..."

"What should a man use?" Ko asked.

"None and all, depending on the circumstances. A man's greatest weapon is his mind."

"Then why observe animals?"

"To see strategy at work. You can never master combat until you understand strategy."

They arrived at the stream where Tai Chu had built the dam. The old trapper was standing beside a net filled with fish that he had hauled out onto the snow. He slung it over his shoulder and fell in with their slow progress up the hill toward his cabin.

"What strategy should a man use?" Ko asked, his warm breath

forming silver in the crisp air.

"The right one," Do Mo said.

"How will I know which is right?"

"We will examine this question in our next practice," Da Mo answered.

Though it was spoken lightly, Ko detected an ominous undertone in Da Mo's words, and they walked in silence as the Jade Lake disappeared behind them into the fine evening mist.

The Palace at Night

Liang finished copying the final character of the professor's poem and held her paper beside the original. In the flickering candlelight it was difficult to make a clear comparison, but she was pleased. It was her best attempt. Her previous efforts lay all around her and the hour was late. The professor's sheet had to be returned to the study before morning.

She tidied everything away and put the professor's sheet inside her robe, smoothing the paper against her skin so it could not be seen, then blew out the candle and waited for her eyes to adjust to the dark. She opened her door a crack and put her ear to it. The corridor outside was silent. She made her way toward the study. The servant's quarters were in complete darkness, but as she mounted the staircase, a faint torchlight came from inside the kitchens and she could hear the head chef berating his staff.

In the royal quarters, torches burned day and night in the passages between the royal chambers and the senior courtiers. Armed eunuchs stood guard and no one passed without being seen, but they rarely asked questions unless there was cause for suspicion. Liang knew it was not uncommon for a young maid to pass through the royal quarters at night. She summoned the nonchalance of a serving girl just doing her job and passed the eunuch, avoiding his eye, and continued to the passage that led to the study. Inside she lit a small candle and replaced the professor's poem in the desk drawer in readiness for tomorrow's lesson. She was in the room no longer than a minute, and when she left, there was no trace she had ever been inside.

But the eunuch was not the only person who had seen Liang pass by. Prince Wu often padded around the corridors of the royal chambers when most adults were in their beds, and the rest were usually in someone else's. He enjoyed keeping track of the nighttime liaisons that were so different from those of the day. High officials met with humble servant-girls. Royal ladies entertained guards and even foreign slaves. Men welcomed other men to their chambers and women slept with women, and in the morning, not a word was spoken about any of it.

He had been intrigued to see which chamber the new maid would visit, and followed her. He had been surprised to see her going into the study room. He had seen the faint light of a candle inside; and had watched from the shadows as she emerged moments later and made her way back the way she had come. He had followed her, unseen, as far as the kitchens and watched her slender form disappear down the stairwell to the servants' quarters. Intrigued, he had returned to his own chamber and fallen asleep wondering what use he could make of this new information.

Monks Train in the Snow

The carcasses from the hunt had been stacked neatly outside the cabin. Tai Chu sharpened his knives and cleaver methodically, working each to a razor-sharp edge in preparation for the long task that lay ahead. The work of skinning and butchering the meat was reserved for Tai Chu himself and he would not allow the monks to help him in any way.

"Very well," Da Mo said, when he was certain that the old man would accept no further assistance, "we will keep you entertained, instead." He motioned to Ko, calling him to stand before him in the snow. "It has been some time since we last sparred, Brother Ko. You have grown fitter and stronger. Perhaps this time, you will beat me? Ko obeyed, the beginnings of a smile on his lips. It was true that he was feeling strong, and it would be good to repay Da Mo, even in some small way, for all the punishment he had received in the past.

As soon as they began, Ko grasped the hopelessness of his situation. Da Mo evaded his attacks and seemed to strike him out of nowhere. Tai Chu watched in amusement and Lailao barked and growled, but did nothing to help Da Mo's hapless victim. As his frustration mounted, Ko's limbs seized up and he struggled to launch a single strike. Meanwhile, Da Mo seemed to have warmed up and now the blows were landing faster than ever.

"Why can't I hit you?" Ko said finally, his mouth bloodied and hanging open, red droplets falling into the churned snow beneath their feet.

"You're trying to strike too hard."

"There's no point in hitting softly."

"You draw your hand too far back."

"Is that wrong?"

"It's predictable. It allows me to read your intention."

"I should strike softly?"

"Strike with no thought of soft or hard. Only think of hitting your target. A fast strike opens the way for a harder strike."

He peppered Ko with a barrage of lightning fast strikes until Ko did not know where he was. "And remember, when you're striking, you're not being struck," Da Mo laughed.

"Young man needs to learn," Tai Chu chuckled loudly.

Ko turned to speak to the old trapper but Da Mo slapped him hard across the jaw and Ko's legs gave way beneath him. He sat heavily in the wet snow.

"One more thing," Da Mo said seriously. "Never look away."

Ko struggled to right himself on unsteady legs and raised his hands to fight, but Da Mo ignored him. "In fighting, which animal is the most powerful?" he asked instead.

"The tiger," Ko answered.

"How does the tiger fight?"

"It overwhelms its victim with teeth and claws," Ko said, remembering their earlier conversation.

"Yes, and that is easy if you are more powerful than your opponent. But if you can't overwhelm him, you need a different strategy."

"Which one?"

"The strategy of another animal."

"Maybe a bear can defeat a tiger?"

"You think fighting me like a bear is the answer?" Da Mo asked.

"No," Ko said miserably, "but what can defeat a tiger?"

"Consider the animal's fighting methods, not its size. A cat uses the same methods as a tiger, but only against a mouse."

"I can't think."

"Think of the Jade Lake."

Ko replayed the events of their recent hunting trip in his mind. "We saw Lailao attack a crane," he said, "but the crane fought her off and escaped."

"How?" Da Mo probed.

"The crane beat its wings and stepped to the side while pecking at the dog's eyes."

"The crane used classic methods of warfare: distraction, evasion, and striking at weak points."

"That should be my strategy against you?"

"Try it and see."

"I'm not sure if it will work," Ko started to say, but Da Mo's fist was already flying toward him. He jumped aside, blocking hard. Another strike came and he ducked, but Da Mo's hand rolled over and whipped back toward his temple. He blocked with his forearm and aimed a punch at Da Mo's side. Da Mo evaded and swept his leg. Ko staggered, stamping his weight down hard into the ground to prevent his balance being taken.

"You block too hard," Da Mo said without ceasing his attacks. "This time, go with the sweep and see where it takes you."

Ko nodded. Da Mo swept the leg again and Ko allowed his foot to be taken. The force spun him around and he found himself at Da Mo's side. He lashed out with the edge of his hand. Da Mo covered up but Ko's kick was already following in a high crescent. Da Mo stepped in and took his leg, lifted him and dumped him in the snow.

"Stay calm," Da Mo warned, as Ko sprang to his feet. "Remember, today you're a crane, not a tiger."

Ko took a deep breath. Da Mo attacked again. He tried to block and evade, but could not land a strike. Finally he stopped.

"I still can't strike you," he said, forlornly.

"Your movement is better, but you're still blocking too hard. By the time you have finished, my next strike is on the way. Such powerful blocks are unnecessary. Do just enough to avoid being hit and pay it no more attention. Look instead for your own strike."

"I don't understand."

"My attacks are not a problem once you see them coming. They are opportunities. Each one presents you with a target. Try to observe where the opening occurs and accept what is offered. These targets are a gift. Do not ignore them."

Da Mo attacked slowly, giving him time to react, and Ko began to find his openings. His strikes hit their mark. Da Mo went faster, and Ko's hands and feet continued to catch him. Finally, Da Mo attacked at full speed and still Ko's strikes found their way through.

"The young man is learning," the old trapper laughed. Then he winced, as Ko struck Da Mo on the jaw and a trickle of blood ran from the Indian's lip.

"I apologize, Master," Ko offered, wondering if Da Mo would get angry, but Da Mo appeared perfectly calm.

"No need to apologize," he smiled. "Do you wish to continue?"

Ko hesitated. Would Da Mo punish him for the strike? He decided Da Mo probably would, but his sparring had reached a new level. Perhaps he was finally a match for the Master? Excitement and hope coursed through his body. He nodded and they bowed once more.

Da Mo threw a punch, which Ko parried easily, but his lightning fast counter did not find its mark. Instead it was deflected as Da Mo's hand struck him on the forehead, his palm so rigid that Ko felt he had been struck with a shovel. White light turned to red and then black, flickering inside his head. Dazed, he waited dully for more strikes, but they did not come. When his sight returned, he swung his elbow at Da Mo, who trapped it and drove a knee hard into his thigh, crushing his muscle. He threw a punch. His fist struck the point of Da Mo's elbow. His hand was in agony and useless now. He held it limply against his ribs. He struck with his other hand, but Da Mo, in one motion, brushed it aside and caught him hard in the gut, knocking the air from his body. Ko gasped, and threw another wild swing. Da Mo moved inside the arc of the punch with both arms raised, blocking the swinging punch and striking him across the neck at the same time. The back of his hand passed across Ko's face in a blur. It was a slap, but it had whipped through fast and heavy. Ko's head spun around, teeth rattling in his jaw. The effects of the force barely reached him before Da Mo's hand returned in a second blur, cupping the back of his neck hard enough to send a shock-wave down his spine.

His legs gave way and he collapsed forward. He felt his arm twisted behind his back, a wrenching pain in his shoulder, his head pressed down in a vice-like grip. Then he was spinning, falling. He was on his back, looking up at the dark outline above him. Da Mo had control of his arm and twisted it against his own knee until Ko's elbow joint was extended to breaking point.

The old trapper clapped in delight.

Da Mo eased the pressure slightly so Ko could sit up. He was about to speak when Da Mo twisted his arm the other way. The pain forced him onto his front and he found himself face down in the snow.

"You did well today," Da Mo said.

"Until you changed the game," Ko said through a mouthful of snow.

"How did I change it?"

"You didn't block and strike."

"What did I do?"

"You did both at once."

"At least you noticed," Da Mo said cheerfully. "That is promising."

"How do you do that?"

"First you must learn to see."

"I can see," Ko grunted, lifting his head from the wet ground.

"No you can't," Da Mo laughed, pushing his face back down into the dirty snow.

Maid's New Assignment

"You look tired, Liang," Mistress Yu said, watching her work from the doorway. Liang guessed her face was pale and drawn from her late night copying the professor's scroll. "Heaven only knows what you have been up to girl," Mistress Yu continued, "but make sure you get a proper sleep tonight, and don't slack today. I'll be watching you."

"I won't disappoint you Mistress Yu," Liang assured her, scrubbing the floor with renewed vigor.

When she glanced up again, Mistress Yu had gone. She forced herself to keep going. The excitement in the pit of her stomach made up for the lack of sleep, giving her an energy she had never felt before. She was learning to read and write! It was more than she had ever thought possible. Perhaps one day, she might even escape the life set out for her since birth and do something else. Something wonderful. She stopped scrubbing for a moment and knelt upright, charged with possibility.

There were footsteps in the doorway. Fearing Mistress Yu had returned, she threw herself forward and resumed her scrubbing, but it was Prince Wu on his way to his morning lesson. He stopped and watched her at work. She bowed, pressing her forehead to the wet floor.

"Good morning Maid Liang," he said.

Liang looked up from her kowtow, surprised that the prince knew her name. Her surprise grew to astonishment when he entered the room and stood before her. "Are you tired this morning, by chance?"

"If I appear to be working slowly please forgive me prince," she said quickly, pressing her forehead to the floor once more to hide her face. "Please rest assured that this room will be spotless very soon."

"You are tired," he continued evenly, "because you have been busy doing other things. Last night, I happened to be going to the study when I saw you in there. I want to know what were you doing."

Liang sat up and felt the blood rush from her head. The room spun and she felt sick with dread. "Oh, Prince Wu," she stuttered, trying to laugh but failing, "I was merely tidying things away to make the study immaculate for your lesson this morning."

"You don't tidy the study in the middle of the night," he said quickly. "Tell me what you were doing!"

A maid was not allowed to look directly into the face of royalty, but Liang stole a glance into his brown eyes to see how much he really knew. She saw a little boy, full of himself and his own power, but a boy nonetheless. She drew herself up a little higher on her knees, until she was taller than him. "May one enquire what Your Highness was doing near the study so late at night?" she asked, knowing it was a huge gamble, but trusting to her instincts.

"I went to read the professor's poem," he answered, caught off guard.

"Is that so?" she asked pointedly.

Their eyes locked and she held his gaze. The prince had rarely been spoken to so sharply, and never by a maid. His mouth opened to a perfect circle but no words came out. Despite the danger of her situation, Liang could not help smiling.

The prince had not seen her smile before. She looked nice when she smiled, not so aloof any more. "Tell me what were you doing?" he ordered again.

"Very well," she sighed, "but can you keep a secret?"

"Tell me first," he demanded.

"When I was cleaning in the study, I overheard Professor Lin reading the poem with you. It was so beautiful that I wanted to learn it. I borrowed it—that is all. You watched me return it yourself."

"What use is a poem when you can't read?" he asked suspiciously.

"I dream of learning to read," she blurted out. "I wanted to learn to copy out the poem, like you do."

The prince could have her killed for her insolence, but she prayed he would rather keep a secret.

"Why do you want to learn if you don't have to?" he demanded.

"Sometimes it's good to use your head as well as your hands," she said, holding her raw hands to the prince, water droplets falling from her red fingertips. "I hope it will be our secret, Highness?"

The prince considered it silently for a moment. He was about to speak when Professor Lin passed by the doorway. "Ah, there you are Prince Wu," the old man said. "Are you ready to join me for our lesson?"

"In a moment," the prince answered without taking his eyes off Liang.

"Very well," the professor said happily, "I shall await you in the study."

The prince stepped forward and leaned close to Liang.

"It will be our secret," he said seriously, leaning over her.

"Oh thank you, Majesty!" Liang said with relief.

"And if you like writing so much, you can do more. I will leave my exercises under your door to complete each evening. They had better be done by the morning or there will be trouble."

With that, he turned on his heel and trotted away before Liang could protest.

All day as she worked, Liang could think of only one thing, that the prince would change his mind or forget to put the papers under her door, but when she opened the door to her room that evening, they were there on the floor as he'd said they would be.

The first sheet contained eight characters that the prince had been practicing in class with Professor Lin and there were three more blank sheets. She guessed his assignment was to repeat the eight characters on the other three sheets.

She would have to reproduce the boy's style of writing. Could she do it? A creeping dread came over her. She realized she could not. She put the scrolls on the floor and stood for a long time, wondering what to do. It would only be a matter of time before she was found out. The boy had already discovered her secret, and children could not keep secrets for long. If others found out, her life at the palace would be over. But if the boy's assignment was not done by the morning, she would be discovered anyway.

She forced herself to breathe slowly, to steady her nerves and her hands. She knelt down and placed the first scroll in front of her. She traced over the characters twice with a dry brush, hoping to capture the boy's childish strokes. She dipped the brush in ink and rendered a character. It was too thin. She had been too hesitant. She went over it again to thicken the line, but there was too much ink on the paper. It ran and made a mess. She stopped, her hand trembling uncontrollably. She felt her throat tighten and sharp tears pricked her eyes.

You stupid fool! She chided herself. What are you doing? You'll get caught and everything will go wrong. She was finished. Her life was over.

She did not care any more and scratched another character on the scroll. And another. She drew the lines angrily without a care, until she had covered the entire sheet and cast it aside and stood, sobbing silently.

For the first time her tiny room was no longer a safe haven from the rest of the world. It was a prison cell, so small that it felt as if she'd breathed all the air and there was none left. She struggled to control herself. She could not open the door with the papers strewn across the floor. After several minutes, her composure returned. Her mind had retreated to that place where no one could reach her, and only an outer shell remained. This was the shell that she used in everyday life, to deal with the disappointment and emptiness that she had known ever since she could remember. Whatever happened, only her shell would suffer, not her.

She dried her tears and reached for the prince's sheet, but for a moment she was not sure which one was his. The characters were remarkably similar. She picked up the sheets in astonishment and held them together, turning them to the dim candlelight, barely able to believe what she was seeing. The characters written in anger bore an uncanny resembled to the prince's! She had been trying too hard to be careful. She needed to draw more freely, like the boy.

Replacing the sheets on the floor, she dipped her brush in the ink once more and formed another character with a fast, smooth stroke. It was a little rough, but passable. By the time she had reached the bottom of the paper, her renderings looked remarkably like the prince's. Laughing silently, trembling with emotion, she copied line after line, until all three sheets were filled with characters. Then she placed them together on the floor and compared each new sheet to the boy's original. Hers were a little neater than his, so she added a few more mistakes and splashes, then sat back and waited for the ink to dry. Shortly before dawn, she stole back to the study to put the scrolls out, ready for the prince and the professor in the morning.

Back in her room, she lay on her narrow bed and willed herself to sleep, but sleep would not come and instead her mind spun, forming endless characters against a white sky. She tried to stop the images, but found herself powerless to rid her mind of the calligraphy. An hour later, the morning bell rang and she jerked awake, not sure how long she had slept, a matter of minutes at the most, she suspected. She splashed cold water on her face. Her eyes felt tight and small. She peered into the water, hoping to see her reflection. It was hard to tell, but she was sure she looked terrible. She tidied her hair and rushed to the kitchen where the other servants were already eating.

She finished her breakfast quickly and disappeared from the kitchen before any of the other maids could speak to her. Soon she was scrubbing the floor in the library, as she did each day, and keeping one eye on the entrance to watch for Prince Wu. Finally she saw him pass, accompanied by Professor Lin, heading toward the study for their morning lesson. The prince glanced at her and she nodded imperceptibly.

She did not want to be in the study when the professor saw her work, fearing she would give herself away, and lingered in the library until the lesson was finished. She was packing up her things to move to the next room when a voice stopped her in her tracks.

"Liang!" It was Mistress Yu, she had not heard her enter.

"Mistress?" She turned with an obedient smile.

"You still look terrible, girl. What is the matter with you? Are you ill? Is there something you wish to tell me?"

"Thank you for your concern, Mistress Yu. I must admit, I have been feeling a little unwell. It is that time of the month and I am having difficulty sleeping."

Mistress Yu's ran her eyes over Liang's face, examining her closely, as if searching for the cause of her illness in the features of her face. "I'll get Doctor Ang to prepare a remedy for you," she said sternly. "A young maid like you has no business getting sick."

"Thank you, Mistress, you are too kind," she answered sincerely, touched by Mistress Yu's concern.

Mistress Yu opened her mouth to speak but the sound of little feet stopped her and she turned to find Prince Wu standing beside her. The prince pulled up quickly and composed himself, but it was clear he was in a rare state of excitement.

"Prince Wu," Mistress Yu smiled, "you seem very excited."

"I'm not excited," he corrected the senior housemaid with all the dignity he could muster, "just pleased, Mistress Yu."

"May we know why?" she asked with a smile.

"Professor Lin said my assignment was excellent today."

"That's wonderful, Highness," Yu said, "you must have worked extra hard."

"No, I did not. I simply found a better way to complete my assignments."

"Well, that is good too. I imagine you will use this new method for all your assignment from now on?"

"Yes I will," the prince said imperiously, turning on his heel and walking from the room.

Mistress Yu watched him leave in silence, curious to know the reason for his sudden eagerness to confide in her. She glanced at Liang, searching for an explanation, but Liang was busy collecting her things and Mistress Yu could not catch her eye.

Monks Plant Rice

The winter snows had retreated and the first buds of fruit had already appeared in the trees. Newborn animals walked on unsteady legs in lush pastures, and rice-planters trod up their waterlogged fields in preparation for their precious crop.

Da Mo and Ko followed the road eastward as it descended into rolling hills of fruit orchards and rice paddies. They had finished the old trapper's provisions several days earlier and traded the coppers from the last roll of their silk for food. It had been more than a day since they had eaten, and Ko's stomach began to complain bitterly. Da Mo seemed oblivious to their plight and walked happily in silence, until Ko could bear it no longer.

"We're still far from Nanjing," Ko said finally. "We need to stop and get food."

"Food?" Da Mo asked. He had not considered it until that moment.

"Yes, and we have no money left," Ko said seriously.

"Having no money is not a problem," Da Mo smiled. "It is a blessing."

"How is it a blessing?"

"It means we must beg."

They continued in silence and Da Mo sensed Ko's reluctance. "You don't want to beg?"

"It's humiliating."

"When I first met you, you were quite happy begging."

"I was not happy, I was desperate."

"And now?"

"We Chinese don't like beggars. Perhaps it is different in India."

"In India it is quite normal to beg."

"For the poor and destitute, maybe, but why should monks have to beg?"

"To see a beautiful side of life, Brother Ko."

"What side is that?" Ko asked skeptically.

"That those who have the least also have the most because they are not captive to their possessions."

"You were from a rich family yourself, were you not, Master?"

"Yes, our family is wealthy."

"So you were a rich man, begging from poor folk?"

"It all depends how you measure riches. I was poor in spirit. I was shown a better way by those far richer than me."

"Why are Indian people so happy to give to beggars?"

"They believe they will be rewarded with good karma."

"Maybe things are different in India, but here in China good deeds are ignored and evil goes unpunished."

"It all depends on what you expect of karma. If you want it to act like a legal system, you're searching in the wrong place. It is only in a person's innermost spirit that karma brings a sense of balance."

Da Mo glanced across at Ko and saw the doubt etched on his brow. "Some people do good deeds to earn merit, but a buddha acts with compassion expecting nothing in return. That way he is always happy, even if good fortune does not come his way. That is true freedom. That is nirvana."

"Is there more than one buddha?

"A person who is enlightened is called a buddha. The Buddha was simply one of many."

"Well, can being a buddha put food in my belly," Ko asked, "because I'm starving?"

"Being a buddha can only nourish your spirit," Da Mo laughed.

"Is there no other way apart from begging?" Ko asked miserably.

"What do you suggest?"

"How about working? Hard work is good for the spirit too, is it not? And we can keep our pride at the same time."

"Pride is a sin, Brother Ko."

"You would rather take food from a poor farmer and give nothing in return?"

Da Mo laughed long and hard, then clapped Ko on the back. "Very well, Brother Ko, but what work would you have us do?"

Ko looked around them. "Maybe in the rice fields?" he suggested.

"Have you ever worked in rice fields?" Da Mo asked seriously.

"No," Ko admitted, "but how difficult can it be?"

"I worked in temples in India where they grew rice," Da Mo said dourly. "By the time you have finished one day's work, you'll wish you had agreed to beg."

They found work on a small plantation. The owner, a keen Buddhist himself, allowed them to sleep in one of the barns near the main house and sent a little rice from the kitchens to welcome them. For the first in several nights Ko slept soundly, without the gnawing pangs of hunger in his belly.

At dawn the next day, he rolled up his leggings and waded into the paddy fields with the other workers. Working beside Da Mo, he spent hours treading up the wet ground that sucked at his feet and sapped his strength, until it was time to plant the rice seeds in neat clusters. Following Da Mo's example, he bent double and pushed the rice seeds into the waterlogged earth by hand. The back-breaking work continued until dusk finally fell over the sweltering fields and he was able to return to the shade of the barn.

He fell exhausted onto his mattress of straw, but his rest was short-lived. Da Mo had been inspecting the rows of tools and farm implements that hung on the wall of the barn, and summoned him to his side.

"Choose one," he ordered.

"For what purpose?" Ko asked, though even as the question left his lips, he knew the answer.

"To defend yourself with," Da Mo said, seizing a wooden millstone handle that had been leaning against the wall. All Ko could see was the blurring arc before his eyes, forming a dazzling pattern that threatened to draw him into its deadly path. Just in time he snatched up a hoe as Da Mo's handle descended to split his skull. The impact sent shocking pain down his wrists, but he had no time to dwell on it. Da Mo had directed another strike up between his legs. Ko lowered his hoe to cover his groin. Too late he realized his left hand was in the path of the handle. He heard a loud crack and waited for the agony, but to his relief, he felt nothing but the hoe buzzing in his hands with the force of the impact. Da Mo had redirected the handle at the last moment and it had struck a finger's width from his hand.

Raising the hoe, Ko flipped it and cut toward Da Mo's head with the metal end. Da Mo stepped inside the arc of his attack and trapped Ko's hand on the hoe. Ko felt two rushes of air pass his head in quick succession as the handle flew out and back from Da Mo's grip. Da Mo had missed by a hair's breadth. Ko pulled away hard and Da Mo released him. He staggered back, giving Da Mo time to seize another handle from the wall. Ko surged forward again, determined to land a blow of his own. Looking high, he swung low toward Da Mo's knee. Da Mo spun his new handle down to block, then stepped in and thrust the butt of the other handle into Ko's solar plexus. Ko gasped for air, but could take none in and mouthed only silent words as the handles created new and deadly patterns around him.

"You have something to say?" Da Mo asked at last.

Ko choked out his question, nodding at the handles fearfully. "Those are weapons in India?"

"No, they are used as millstone handles."

"Then where did you learn to wield them like that?" he asked.

"Nowhere," Da Mo replied.

"You have never used them before?" Ko asked in disbelief.

"No, but once you understand the nature of movement, any implement can be used as a weapon."

"And what is the nature of movement?"

"A good question," Da Mo chuckled, "but unfortunately, the answer cannot be conveyed in words."

"Then how can I know it?"

"You must learn to appreciate it." Da Mo saw the frustration on Ko's face and attempted to explain further. He replaced the handles against the wall and took up a set of rice flails. "An object does not wield itself, only a man can turn it into a weapon." The flails spun in dazzling spirals around his body as he spoke. "Even a sword is useless without a hand to wield it and an eye to guide it. Body and weapon must work as one. The more natural the union, the more deadly the weapon. To appreciate the effectiveness of an object you must become sensitive to its nature. Learn to feel how it wishes to move in your hand. If you compel it to move unnaturally, it will resist and make you slow. Practice until you can guide it naturally, until your intention can be transferred through whatever object you touch."

Da Mo flipped the flails into his palm and the savage flight of the hardwood came to an abrupt halt. He set them aside and took up a stick, which he spun in a simple arc before handing it to Ko.

"Start with a stick. It's safer," he said with a smile. "There will be plenty of time for the flails in due course."

Maid Learns a Lesson

"You have done well today Prince Wu," Professor Lin said, putting a hand on the boy's shoulder. "We can complete the rest tomorrow."

The prince dipped his brush in the water to clean it, as the professor had shown him, but Professor Lin stopped him. "Don't worry about that, Highness, Maid Liang will take care of it today."

Liang stopped what she was doing when she heard her name mentioned, impressed that the professor remembered it, since he was renowned for his forgetfulness. The little prince left the room without a backward glance and she hurried over to take care of his brushes. As she rinsed them and dried them on white silk cloth, she had the feeling the professor was watching her. Once the brushes had been neatly replaced in the desk, she checked the prince's papers to make sure the ink was dry before moving them.

"Be careful Liang," Professor Lin said quietly, "a lot of work has gone into those scrolls."

A red glow flamed on her cheeks. "Of course, professor. I will take the utmost care."

"If you move them too soon the ink will run, though I'm sure you know that," he sighed, reaching for one of the scrolls and holding it at arm's length. "The prince writes with great confidence for one so young. Sometimes it's easier for children. They have no fear of making a mistake, no hesitation. Look, see how his strokes end briskly, with no lingering of the brush."

"I fear I am no judge, professor."

"Oh, there is no need to be so humble," he smiled. "Everyone can appreciate the beauty of calligraphy, wouldn't you agree?"

"I wouldn't know," she answered, hoping her face was not betraying her.

"Well, let me show you," he said patiently, turning the scroll so she could see it more easily. "See here, this scroll is the prince's work from this morning, bold and daring…" He went to the cabinet and withdrew another scroll, "and this is the one he did last night as an assignment. It is also bold and daring, yet the strokes end with a tapering elegance that this morning's work lacks. Strange, don't you think?"

His gaze turned to her for the first time and looking into his eyes, she knew she had been caught.

"Perhaps His Highness was in a different mood this morning," she offered hopelessly.

Ignoring her answer, the professor took more scrolls from the cabinet and laid them out on the desk. "Here are more examples of work from some of my other pupils. Do you see how each one has a different stroke? They are as recognizable to me as their faces, often more so, if I am honest."

She looked into the professor's face but he continued to study the scrolls and did not return her gaze. "See how the brush leaves the paper," he continued, "and returns in a different way for each pupil? See the unusual form of the curve on this scroll, the cautious up-stroke on this one, the wide down-stroke here and here. No two hands are ever identical. Some even say that calligraphy is a window into the writer's soul, since the characters come from deep within the artist himself, or herself."

Liang had no idea what to say.

The professor's eye fixed hers. "The only thing that is true of all these writers is they all require further practice. Do you not agree?"

"As you say, Professor," she whispered.

He looked away, addressing his comments to the wall, "Nevertheless, if another artist were to borrow papers and brushes from time to time, and place their work in my private desk, I should be happy to comment on his or her penmanship."

Liang struggled to find words but the professor continued before she could speak. "However, let there be no doubt that the prince must complete his tasks himself, and this is my final word on the matter. Do you think that is fair?"

"Yes, Professor," she said, blinking back a tear at his kindness.

"That artist would learn much," he smiled, "for they display an ability and sincerity that is lacking in many of my other pupils, and that is something I treasure most highly."

With that, Professor Lin left her to finish clearing the desk. Once she heard the study door close behind him, she dried her eyes on her sleeve. Her mind swam with the implications of what just happened, the excitement, the danger. Then all thoughts of the professor were forgotten and her mind filled with dread at the prospect of telling Prince Wu that she could no longer complete his assignments.

She made her way slowly to the prince's private quarters. The guard outside his chamber heard her footsteps and his hand moved to his sword. A maid had no business in the royal quarters at this hour. He was about to order her to leave when he saw it was Liang and hesitated. She smiled and put her hand on his, seemingly oblivious that it still gripped the hilt of his sword.

"Oh, I'm glad it's you," she smiled, "I have been a silly girl. There's a small matter I need to take care of in the prince's chamber. I need to go inside, just for a moment."

"The prince is in his chamber," he answered, "you'll need to come back tomorrow."

"Oh, that doesn't matter. I often clean while he's in there, and this won't take a moment, I promise."

"It's against regulations."

"It's a small matter that need concern no one, although the prince will certainly want me to take care of it."

She gave the guard a knowing look and he relented, knocking softly on the prince's door before ushering her inside. She entered and shut the door before the guard could change his mind, and hurried forward to kneel before Prince Wu.

"I have bad news Highness," she whispered hurriedly, before he could say a word, "I'm afraid I can't do your assignments for you any longer. You must understand, it's not because I don't want to. It's just that, well, Professor Lin suspects, and if we're discovered, we will both be in trouble. I beg your forgiveness."

A frown crossed the prince's smooth forehead. He was unused to being told what to do by anyone except his father, and certainly not by a maid.

"No," he said coldly, "the professor knows nothing about it. You're making it up and I won't allow it. You will continue."

"But Highness," she whispered urgently, "Professor Lin has been comparing scrolls, looking at your old work and comparing it to the new work. I saw him this morning, when you left to go to the ceremony. Please believe me. There will be trouble if I am caught. They'll send me back to my village in disgrace, perhaps even worse. And if your father finds out, he will be displeased with you, too," and her eyes filled with tears at the thought of the emperor's fury.

She saw in his face that he was troubled. He was too young to understand the severity of her situation, and when he was older, he would be too important to care. But now, still a little boy, he hesitated for a moment and it touched her, despite her fears.

"I'm sorry Highness, it is all my fault," she said softly, "I should never have copied the calligraphy in the first place. You should not get into trouble over it. "Don't worry, I will speak to the professor tomorrow and tell him it was all my doing."

He stared at her, thinking about what to do. She kowtowed to the floor. "Please forgive me."

"No, you will not mention anything to Professor Lin," he said imperiously. "A maid has no business doing calligraphy anyway. It is not her place. You will stop immediately. That is my order."

She looked up gratefully. "Your order?"

"Yes. Do you question it?"

"No, Highness," she smiled through her tears, "I would never do that."

She leaned forward impulsively and kissed his forehead lightly before he could react, then rose and hurried to the door before he could change his mind. As she emerged, the guard tried to speak to her, but she brushed past him with little more than a nod of thanks and disappeared into the gloom as quickly as she had appeared.

The Monsoon

The monks remained at the plantation throughout the rice-growing season, and during that time Ko discovered the nature of the stick, the scythe, the pitchfork, the axe, and the sickle. He practiced for hours every evening, until each object moved easily in his hands. Then, he took up the millstone handles that Da Mo had used against him, and finally, when he had learned to wield them strongly, he reached for the rice flails that waited for him on the barn wall.

The flails swung in unfamiliar arcs around him and his head and limbs were soon covered in bumps and bruises, but eventually even the troublesome flails were tamed, and—he believed—he had mastered all the weapons of the barn.

It was then that Da Mo produced a length of chain with a heavy iron lock on the end. Ko watched grimly as Da Mo bound the lock tightly in a thick layer of cloth, having already guessed why the lock was being padded. Once the chain was swung, the path of the lock could not be corrected, and Ko knew that any mistake would be met with punishment from his own weapon.

During the long summer evenings, he practiced behind the barn, turning the chain, slowly at first, then faster, until it flashed around him at blinding speed, following the path that his will commanded without question. Finally, he removed the padding from the lock and continued to spin the deadly chain. The lock hissed through the air in fierce circles around him as the chain described its beautiful, deadly arcs, flowing first downward, then, with a step and turn, upward, above his head, behind and around his back. The lock passed close to his skull but he did not flinch. He knew its path and knew he was safe.

When the gathering monsoon clouds released their deluge over the land, there was little work to be done on the plantation.

During those days, he fought with Da Mo, pitting one weapon against another until he began to see the patterns that ran through everything. When the rains broke and it was time to return to the fields and pick the rice, he rose before dawn to practice with his weapons, and after each long day in the fields, he swung his chain long into the night.

Once the rice had been harvested and the other workers had all returned to their villages, Da Mo and Ko prepared to continue their journey to Nanjing. On their final evening at the plantation, Da Mo made his way to the owner's house to collect the money that was owed to them. The owner welcomed him warmly and offered him a cup of rice wine as he handed over the pouch of coppers. Soon they were talking and another cup of rice wine was served, and then another.

When Da Mo returned to the barn late that night, he had to find his way by a thin moonlight. As he approached, he noticed light flickering inside. He stopped in the entrance and watched in silence as Ko tethered and released the power of his chain, his movements illuminated by a single candle. Da Mo noticed the chain was moving in patterns he did not recognize, patterns he would not have considered himself, and had certainly never taught to Ko. Yet seeing them now, he could easily imagine their effectiveness. Ko paused and Da Mo watched in appreciation as Ko added a second lock to the other end of the chain and began to create a pattern in which both ends of the chain moved independently. Time after time, Ko struck himself with the heavy locks that he had not bothered to pad, but he would not be defeated and eventually the chain spun evenly around him once again.

"The chain is a good teacher," Da Mo said, stepping from the shadows.

"Yes," Ko said without turning.

"Strict, but fair."

Ko smiled grimly and continued his practice.

"We have a long journey ahead of us tomorrow," Da Mo said.

"I'll turn in in a moment. There's something more I want to try."

Da Mo went to his bed at the far side of the barn, where the combination of rice wine and the rhythmic whirring of the chain lulled him to sleep quickly.

He woke with a start several hours later to find the bed beside him empty. He wondered where Ko was. Perhaps he had gone outside to relieve himself? Then he heard the familiar chink of the chain and the whirring of the iron lock, and he realized Ko was still training.

In that moment he saw that Ko was not like the other students he had known. Many had spoken of their dedication to The Way, but Ko pursued it with a restless hunger he had only come across once before, and for a moment, he could not recall where. It had not been in the young monks he had taught in India, nor even in his beloved disciples Vanya and Yin Chiang—they had both been too mature to throw themselves into his training methods in such a way. Yet that desire, that obsession, that gnawing pain in the belly, it all was deeply familiar to him. When he finally figured out where he had seen it before, he laughed out loud.

It had been in himself.

The Grandmaster's Robe

Liang removed her shoes, knelt down and bowed at the entrance of the monastery. The attendant monk returned her bow with a smile. The monks appreciated Liang for the care she lavished on their home. For her part, she enjoyed being there in the open space and serenity of the temple—so different from the politics and scheming in the dark corridors of the palace.

Liang began her work in the meditation hall, then moved to the study rooms and the library before climbing the stairs to the upper levels of the monastery and the living quarters of the resident monks. The junior monks kept their own cells clean, but some of the older monks were too sick or feeble to clean their own rooms so she did it for them, and the most senior monks were too busy with important matters such as the translation of the great sutras of India.

One such monk was Brother Jung, whose room was more like a study than a bedroom. His mattress was barely visible beneath the piles of scrolls, books, and manuscripts that littered his room.

When Liang entered to clean his cell, he was hunched over a tiny desk, engrossed in his work. He looked up when he heard her.

"Brother Jung, I hope I'm not disturbing you."

"Not at all. I'm grateful for your help."

"It looks like you need it."

Brother Jung's eyes widened at her audacity but then he relented. It was not the tidy dwelling a monk was supposed to keep.

"I guess I do," he sighed.

She set to work cleaning and tidying quickly. Brother Jung wanted to admire her pleasing figure as she did, but that was not the way of a monk. He turned back to his scrolls and did his best to concentrate as the young woman worked around him.

"Shall I tidy these scrolls for you too?" she asked when she had finished.

"There's no need, I need to file them."

"Poetry, history, scriptures..." she said lightly, leafing through them "...and another group that I can't identify."

"You can read?" he asked, turning in astonishment.

"I'm just guessing. It's not difficult."

"Well you guessed correctly," he said, rising to stand next to her. "So maybe you can tidy them, after all. This last pile is royal decrees. I often draft the wording before they are passed on to the imperial calligraphers to be written down officially."

"No wonder you're so busy," she smiled.

"There is no shortage of official decrees," he said ruefully.

When she had sorted the scrolls into neat piles she went to the door to go. "I'll leave you to your work, Brother Jung."

"Thank you, Maid Liang."

A wisp of a smile touched her lips and Brother Jung realized what he had said.

"Oh, I didn't mean to thank you for leaving, I meant, you know, for your hard work, you understand…" he said, his cheeks reddening.

"Of course, Brother Jung," she said, suppressing a laugh, not wishing to embarrass him further.

She turned into the corridor that led to the private chambers of Grandmaster Tzu to complete her final job for the day. Grandmaster Tzu was the head of the palace temple, which made him the most powerful monk in all of China. He was renowned as a powerful sorcerer. His height and bearing, together with his cold eyes, unsettled her. She tried to make sure he was engaged on business elsewhere when she cleaned his rooms. A little while earlier, she had seen him talking with a group of senior monks in a nearby meeting room and took the opportunity to go in and begin her tasks, working quickly until the chamber was spotless. She finished by removing the writing implements from his lacquered writing desk and polishing it until it gleamed, before replacing everything exactly as she had found it. Mistress Yu had told her Grandmaster Tzu was very particular about such matters.

She was about to leave the room when she saw a robe folded across a chair and picked it up to replace it in Grandmaster Tzu's ornate wardrobe. Most of the monks in the temple kept only three plain robes of orange cloth, but Grandmaster Tzu had many more and they were all made of the finest silk. She brushed her hand along the line of exquisite robes hanging inside until she noticed one of pure gold that was intricately embroidered with entwining dragons. It was easily the most beautiful of all his robes and she lifted it from the wardrobe to take a closer look. The silk shimmered in the daylight. She took it to the window and held it up to the light, and it was if the sun itself was shining out of the cloth in her hands.

"I see you admire fine workmanship," a voice behind her said. It was Grandmaster Tzu.

"Oh, yes," she answered turning quickly and wondering how she had not heard him enter the room or get so close, since he was standing at her shoulder, "it's very beautiful."

"You like this particular robe?" he smiled.

"I think it's the most beautiful of all."

"You have good taste. It's my favorite too."

He stepped close and took the edge of the robe, holding it out so they could both admire the embroidery. "It's a very special piece, created over a hundred years ago by an ancient family of silkmakers in Hubei."

She felt his breath on her neck and wanted to move away, but it would be impolite.

"It is exquisite," she murmured.

"Quite," he said, the thin smile still playing on his lips. "I have seen you around the temple a few times recently. Are you new here?"

"Yes, Grandmaster."

"Well good, Mistress Yu is very kind to us, always sending us the most diligent maids to help us maintain our monastery, and for that we are most grateful."

"Please forgive me for taking up your time," she said hurriedly, hoping to bring the conversation to a close. "Your chamber is finished, Grandmaster Tzu, so I will leave you in peace."

"What is your name?" he asked, ignoring her attempt to leave.

"Liang, Grandmaster."

"Liang—a pretty name for a pretty girl."

"You are too kind," she muttered, turning to go, but he held her by the arm. "Wait a moment Maid Liang, there's no rush. It's nice to talk with a pretty housemaid once in a while, instead of those ugly old monks with no teeth and bad breath."

"I really must go," she said more firmly. "There are duties that await me at the palace."

"Those duties can wait," he said coldly, his smile vanishing. He let go of her arm, but Liang knew she could not leave and stood frozen before him.

"There's something interesting about you, Liang," he began slowly, as if trying to remember what that might be. "You admire fine workmanship, you have taste, and this morning, I saw you coming to the temple from my window. Imagine my surprise when I saw you dancing in the palace gardens, when you thought no one was looking."

"I'm sorry, Grandmaster Tzu," she said quietly.

"There is no need to apologize for dancing, is there Liang? It's quite understandable. You are a young girl, full of exuberance. But your interests in things other than your duties could get you into trouble, if they became known."

She kept her eyes down, furious with herself for being so careless and stupid.

"Still, you have nothing to fear from me Liang," he continued. "It will be our secret." She was quiet, not knowing what to say. "Don't look so worried, Liang," he continued, "how about a smile instead? I'm sure you're even prettier when you smile."

"I must go," she grimaced.

"Stay where you are," he ordered, stepping to block her exit. His hands closed on her shoulders and he bent to press his lips to hers. She was horrified and turned away in disgust.

"Come now, don't be stubborn, Liang," he warned, turning her face back toward his and pressing his thin lips onto hers, one hand circling her waist while the other felt for her breast.

For an instant she had no idea what to do. Should she allow him to do as he pleased with her? If he criticized her to Mistress Yu she would be punished and dismissed from the palace. But even as she considered it, she couldn't bear his touch any longer and twisted away, prying his hands off her body. He reached for her again, holding his mouth to hers until she shook her head violently. Her forehead caught him hard on the mouth and a spot of blood appeared on his lip. He dabbed at it with his fingers and stared at her in fury.

She darted past him and ran, fleeing headlong down the dark corridor outside his room, praying that no one would see her, that no scandal would be created, and the matter could be quietly forgotten, though in her heart she knew that it never would be. She fought desperately to suppress the sobs of anguish that gathered in her chest and threatened to overwhelm her. First she would get to her room. Then she would lock the door. Then she would lie on her bed, on her side, and clutch her knees to her chest. And only then would she weep.

Monks Enter Nanjing

The flat landscape outside Nanjing was crossed with countless canals and waterways that converged on the Yangtze, filled with vessels from every corner of the empire. Giant barges laden with rice and grain floated slowly toward the main port while bamboo rafts carried barrels of wine and animals for slaughter. Local fishing boats unloaded their catch from the river while competitors brought specialities from the great lakes or the coastal waters. Merchant junks sat low in the water with their cargoes from around the empire, while sampans ferried passengers, traders, dock-workers, soldiers, and monks across the waters.

The air was filled with the sound of life on the water: a captain shouting orders to his crew, a merchant calling out the price of his wares, a docker urging his companions to help him with a heavy load. On the giant houseboats where five generations lived together, the tinkling of the tiny bells could be heard, worn by children to tell their parents they were still safely aboard; and from beneath the coverings of the brightly-painted wupans, the sweet songs of flower girls could be heard as they entertained their visiting guests.

Da Mo and Ko crossed the river at a busy ferry station and made for the smoke that rose from enormous ramparts in the distance. At first, it seemed the city was ablaze, but these were simply the fires of industry that burned night and day in the greatest city on earth. When they arrived at the great Eastern Gate, they found it guarded by soldiers, but men and women from all over the world were passing in and out unchallenged, along with their donkeys, horses, camels, oxen, porters, and slaves, and for once, even Da Mo aroused no special interest.

Inside the city gate, they found themselves on a broad avenue of beaten earth. The ground had become soft in the recent rains and neat drainage ditches had been dug along its edges to prevent it from becoming a bog. They followed the crowds, taking in the sights of the city as they went: a donkey pen offering animals for hire, a wine merchant who also sold medicine, a peddler selling oil and firewood, a furniture maker displaying his tables and chairs, an instrument-maker working on a zither, a potter turning a jug on his wheel.

The town was laid out in a neat grid, and the main avenue was crossed by many smaller streets. On the next block, Da Mo and Ko found themselves outside an army barracks where soldiers drilled in tight formation and archers hit the centers of their targets with every arrow. These were the cream of the imperial troops and the emperor's personal bodyguards.

They passed brightly-painted Buddhist shrines, grand Taoist temples, gated monasteries and nunneries, even a Persian church standing on a crossroads. Above the rooftops, a giant pagoda towered over the other buildings and reminded Da Mo of the stupas of his homeland. They continued through the bustling streets until they came to a square where a sizeable crowd had gathered to watch a wrestling bout. They stopped to watch, impressed with the quality of the contestants, before moving on to a street of tea shops and restaurants.

At the end of this street was a square where a carnival was in full swing. High above the crowd, a young girl balanced upside-down on a pole, which in turn was balanced on the forehead of a stout woman who was weaving among the crowd. It seemed the girl was about to fall at any moment. The woman shook with the effort of holding up the girl and the crowd watched, bewitched, waiting to see the fall that never came.

A little farther, they watched in amusement as a hunchback placed a blanket over a giant horse and held it steady while a dwarf announced he would perform an incredible feat. When enough people had gathered, the dwarf raised the end of the blanket and, it appeared, launched himself head-first into the horse's backside. The hunchback removed the blanket and there was no sign of the dwarf.

"How on earth…" Ko began.

"Don't ask," Da Mo smiled.

After much waiting and speculation, the hunchback covered the horse's head and the dwarf reappeared in the blanket.

A new crowd gathered around an Indian fakir who began his show by swallowing a razor sharp knife. The people in the crowd were unimpressed. "We have seen magicians who can swallow entire swords," they jeered. The fakir withdrew the blade from his mouth, his eyes flashing angrily.

"You want blood?" he demanded.

They did. Suddenly he pulled out his tongue with all his strength, the sinewy mass extending an obscene distance, and severed it with the knife. Crimson spewed from his mouth, splashing his bare stomach and splattering the ground at their feet. The crowd gasped in horror. He opened his mouth to reveal the bloody stub of his tongue, grunting furiously, unable to speak now, and the crowd shrank back from the crazed Indian. He bent down and hunted among his possessions until found what he was looking for, a bowl to put his tongue in. He held out the bloody offering to the crowd for inspection. Most shrank back appalled, but one or two came forward, prodding and poking at the strip of human meat that had been butchered before their very eyes. Finally the fakir rinsed the tongue in water and replaced it in his mouth. After much sucking and chewing, he parted his lips wide to reveal the tongue, reattached.

Ko clapped his hands in delight, and even Da Mo could not resist a smile. As they turned to go, the fakir took a sword and stabbed himself through the heart.

"Wait, I must see this, Master," Ko said.

"Don't worry, he'll be fine," Da Mo assured him.

"How do you know?"

Da Mo did not answer but walked on and Ko was forced to follow him, looking back to see the fakir staggering a few steps before collapsing on the ground.

At a crossroads, they came to a small Buddhist temple where a monk was sweeping the steps of the entrance. Da Mo stopped to admire the temple's roof. The monk smiled at the strange visitor outside.

"A beautiful temple," Da Mo said, "it reminds me of my homeland."

"You have traveled from India?" the monk asked.

"I have," Da Mo smiled.

"Then you have made quite a journey," the monk replied. "Are you a monk yourself, sir?"

"This is Master Da Mo," Ko said, stepping forward, "sent from the Western Heaven to instruct the emperor himself."

"Da Mo, you say?" the monk asked with a frown.

"The name is Bodhidharma," Da Mo answered, "but it is a little difficult for Chinese tongues."

"Bodhidharma?" the monk said without difficulty. "With such a name, you must bring great enlightenment to our city."

"Your knowledge of the holy language is most commendable Brother," Da Mo said, impressed.

"Won't you come inside?" the monk asked with a smile. "We are about to eat. You are welcome to join us. My name is Brother Chuang," he said, opening the gate so they could enter. "I am the head monk here. It is a very small temple. We run an orphanage for the lost children of the city. I'm afraid our facilities are very basic, but you are most welcome."

They accepted gratefully and followed him into a hall where two monks served rice and broth and a group of young children sat on rough tables, chatting noisily.

"We have sixteen orphans at the moment," Brother Chuang explained, "I'm afraid it's not as quiet as a monastery should be."

"It is a happy noise," Da Mo said cheerfully, taking a seat on a table beside the children. Bowls of the steaming broth were quickly served to them and Brother Chuang pressed him for information on India while they ate.

Da Mo spoke at length of his pilgrimage in Magadha, and of the giant monastery of Nalanda. The monks and orphans listened rapt, until the hour grew late and the senior monks ushered the children to their dormitory. Afterward, Da Mo sat with Brother Chuang late into the night seeking information on the emperor.

"The emperor embraces all the religions of the world—Buddhist, Taoist, even Persian and Zoroastrian churches are allowed in the capital," Chuang told him. "He is a deeply spiritual man and very open-minded compared to his predecessors. However, he favors Buddhism above all else. The palace temple is the largest Buddhist temple in all of China, and it's reported that he's building an even bigger one outside the city, a monastery to rival Nalanda in size, if not in learning."

"That is good news," Ko said.

"Perhaps, but don't be too hasty," Chuang warned. "The competition for the emperor's favor is intense. The power wielded by the senior Buddhist masters is enormous. I fear you'll find many have strayed far from the ideals of The Way."

"How so," Da Mo asked.

"The larger monasteries have become centers of commerce rather than enlightenment," Brother Chuang said bitterly. "They act as moneylenders and pawnbrokers. They own vast holdings of land and grow rich from charging rent and paying no taxes. They own the mills that supply the city with grain and the presses that supply oil for the city lamps. They receive gifts and donations from wealthy patrons hoping to avoid punishment in the next life or seeking to help their ancestors suffering in the afterlife. The head of the palace temple is Grandmaster Tzu, a powerful sorcerer who, from what I know of him, will do everything he can to prevent you from gaining favor with the emperor."

"We will be careful," Ko assured him.

"How do you plan to get inside the palace?" Chuang asked.

"The emperor will invite us inside," Da Mo said confidently.

"I can take you as far as the gate," Chuang said doubtfully. "Hopefully, The Buddha will open it for you."

The next morning, Brother Chuang led them toward the center of Nanjing. The narrowing streets were filled with the shops and offices of Turkish merchants, Arab craftsmen, Persian traders, and Uighur moneylenders. At the busy meeting point of three roads, a face-reader was telling the fortune of a rich merchant, who was sitting at the table of a local tavern. The tavern had set its tables in the streets and a woman with golden hair and blue eyes entertained its patrons with a mournful song in an unknown language. Though the meaning of the words was unclear, the sentiment was obvious and the emotion in her voice held her audience spellbound.

"Come along Brother Ko. It is time to move on," Da Mo said putting his hand on the young man's shoulder, but Ko stood, bewitched.

"Just a moment, the song, it's so beautiful."

"Are you sure it's the song you find beautiful?"

"Where is she from?" Ko asked, enchanted by the golden woman.

"From the far West," Chuang answered with a smile.

"India?" Ko mused without diverting his gaze.

"There are many lands west of India," Chuang said, "but come, we are close now."

At the end of the street, they came to a holding pen filled with men, women, and children of all ages. The men sat listlessly, their heads bowed, while the women held the younger children, and the older children played in the dirt, oblivious of their miserable existence.

"These people are prisoners," Chuang explained, "taken in military campaigns in the North. They are waiting to be sold as slaves."

"Not all of them look as if they are from the North," Ko said.

"Some were sent to the emperor as tribute from other kingdoms. They are artists, craftsmen, horse-trainers."

"Those women and children look Chinese," Da Mo said.

"They are the relatives of men condemned for treason," Chuang explained. "They are unlucky. A new emperor might free them as an act of clemency to mark his new reign, but Emperor Wu is strong. He is here to stay. There will be no mercy for them."

They continued on to a new market selling clothes and hats, leather goods, furs and blankets, gold and silver jewelry, copper ornaments, tools and weapons. Old men sat at tables outside taverns drinking tea or wine and playing the strategy game of weiqi with black and white stones on a board. The traditional market gave way to a Persian bazaar where traders sold precious metals and gems, strings of pearls, antique furniture, paintings, pottery, and ivory carvings.

They turned into a large square and saw a sight that stopped them in their tracks. A roof of pure gold rose high above massive outer walls. The building dwarfed everything around it. Archers patrolled the ramparts and guards waited at attention beside the enormous iron gate that stood between the city and its emperor.

"The palace of Emperor Wu Di," Chuang announced formally and waited a moment while Da Mo and Ko took it in. "I wish you good fortune in your quest to meet the emperor," he resumed, "but

I must return to the orphanage."

They said farewell to Chuang and he disappeared quickly into the streets from where they had come. Da Mo and Ko stood in silence for another minute, awed by the forbidding splendor of the place.

"How will we get in?" Ko asked.

"We will wait to be invited," Da Mo answered, striding into the middle of the square and laying his blanket on the ground, "and in the meantime, we will meditate." A crowd quickly gathered, expecting to see some exotic magic from the wild-looking Indian. Ko rose to address them. "This is Master Da Mo. He is not a magician. He is a Buddhist master from India who has come to meet with the emperor."

"Then why is he waiting outside the gate like a hermit?" the crowd demanded.

Ko was about to answer when Da Mo tugged on his sleeve and told him to begin his meditation. Ko obeyed reluctantly and closed his eyes, though he could not shut out the presence of the crowd. He opened his eyes and glanced at Da Mo, who seemed unaffected, as if his mind was far from the dusty square outside the palace.

The crowd waited, hoping the Indian would float in the air, or move objects with his mind. When nothing happened, people began to grumble and leave. Some of the children grew bold and came forward to tug at his robe, but when he did not react, they tired of their game and drifted away in search of new entertainment. Though most of the crowd dispersed, some remained and sat beside him.

A troop of soldiers crossed the square. The palace gate swung open to allow them to enter, and closed again quickly behind them. Next, a merchant appeared at the gate and spoke at length to the guard before being allowed to enter through a small side gate.

A group of monks emerged from the same door shortly afterward and crossed the square, passing close to Da Mo and Ko, but none stopped to investigate the strangers. It seemed monks from other temples were of no interest to those in the palace.

By evening, more people had joined Da Mo in his meditation. As the hour grew late some left, but others came, drawn by the stillness and serenity of the seated mass in the center of the busy capital. The crowd grew so big that the palace guard was finally compelled to march over and investigate. Some of the crowd were ordered to move since they were blocking access to the palace, but the Indian monk and his disciple were allowed to remain.

The guard returned to his duty by the gate and shortly afterward a maid appeared before him, returning from an errand.

"What's going on?" she asked, "I could barely get past all those people."

"Just some madman from India," the guard told her. "He's been sitting in the square all day hoping to see the emperor."

"Are you going to let him in?" she asked.

"Not unless he has an official invitation."

"He's come all the way from India, you say?"

"Yes," he smirked. "All that way for nothing."

"How long do you think he'll wait?" she asked.

"Who knows with foreigners."

"Is he a magician?"

"They say he's a monk."

"He doesn't look much like a monk," she said with a frown. "How long do you think he'll sit there?"

"No idea," the guard shrugged, "but I imagine he's going to need a good long rest before he heads off home. It's a long way back to India."

Maids Gossip

"It's a long way back to India…"

Maid Ai laughed as she recounted her conversation with the guard to the other maids, who giggled and pressed her for more information.

"The Indian was a monk," she told them, "a Buddhist master, they say, and there was quite a crowd around him."

Liang had been trying to eat her breakfast in peace, but she had no appetite and her rice gruel sat untouched before her. The other maids were huddled nearby and chattering urgently before their morning shift. She rarely joined in, but she overheard Ai and it peaked her interest.

"Who are you talking about?" she asked, moving over to join them.

The others were startled. Liang seldom spoke to them. "Why are you so interested?" Ai demanded with mock severity. She was Liang's friend, but liked to tease her in front of the other maids.

"No special reason," Liang answered casually, "but tell me, what else do you know about this monk?"

Ai raised her eyebrows, as if considering whether to share the information with Liang, but Liang didn't look in the mood for jokes. She relented. "They say he's been sitting in a trance outside the palace for hours, waiting to see the emperor. He has come to show him the true way of The Buddha. They say he is a descendant of The Buddha himself."

"I've heard Indian masters have incredible powers," one of the other maids said. "They can walk through fire and make themselves invisible. Tame wild beasts and read your mind. Even make you do their will."

"Did you see him do any of these things?" Liang asked eagerly.

"No," Ai said, "but he was a giant, as big as two men, with

black skin and hair all over his body."

The other maids gasped in horror.

"Has anyone informed Grandmaster Tzu?" Liang asked.

"No, and I pity the person who does," Ai said.

"Why?" Liang demanded, leaning forward now, her mind racing.

"He'll be furious," whispered Ai.

"But why?" one of the younger maids asked. "Grandmaster Tzu is a Buddhist too?"

Maid Ai's voice was little more than a whisper. "Grandmaster Tzu doesn't want to share his power with another master."

"Especially not a barbarian," Liang said, almost to herself. The maids continued gossiping, but Liang's mind was elsewhere and she slipped from the table without another word.

All day she hurried to complete her tasks, unable to shake the image of the monk from her mind. She could see his face quite clearly from Maid Ai's description, and the form of another smaller monk beside him, though this young man's face was less clear. By evening, she knew exactly what to do. When she finished her chores, she did not return to her room as she usually did, but went instead to the kitchen, where she found the head chef arranging his spices on a shelf. She waited in the doorway until he noticed her.

"Liang! How lovely to see you," he beamed. "What brings you to the kitchen? Are you hungry? Here, eat. You're far too skinny." He held out a tray of freshly steamed delicacies that he had been preparing for the emperor. Liang hesitated. No servant was ever allowed to eat the same food as the royal family.

"Take one," he urged, "I need to know what you think. Go ahead, no one's looking."

The other cooks were all busy working, and in the kitchen, the head chef was king. He often gave out morsels of his mastery to the servants he favored, and Liang received more delicacies than most. She took a piece and ate it slowly, savoring the taste for an exquisite moment.

"Do you know what's inside?" he asked.

"Swan?"

"Correct! You have a good palate, my dear girl."

"It's delicious," she sighed. "How do you create such flavors?"

The head chef laughed and waved away the question. He could not even begin to describe how he achieved such perfection. "Never mind that," he smiled. "What brings a lovely creature like you to my hellish kitchen?"

"I was wondering whether you needed any ingredients from the night market, that was all," she said lightly.

He searched her face trying to discern a hidden motive, then shrugged and turned to check his shelves. "As a matter of fact, there are a few things we need, if you wouldn't mind fetching them for me?"

"It would be no trouble at all," she smiled.

He reeled off a long list of ingredients, which she repeated back to him exactly.

"A good palate and an orderly mind! You would make a good cook," he said with a smile.

"I would love to be a cook," she said sadly.

"If you worked in my kitchen, I would make you into a great chef."

"Unfortunately, I'm just a maid, and always will be. It is my destiny."

"In this life," he said, "but perhaps in the next? The Buddhists tell us we live countless new lives in an endless cycle."

"Then there is hope," she smiled.

"But the next life depends on your deeds in this one."

"Then I will try to be good, and perhaps The Buddha will allow me to be a cook."

"Let's hope so," he said.

"What do you think you will become?" she asked.

"Probably a dog or a toad," he chuckled.

"Then I might have to cook you and eat you," she smiled mischievously.

"You would do that?"

"Do you know any good recipes?"

"Get out," he ordered, reaching for his cleaver and spinning it expertly in his hand, but by then she had already gone.

The Indian monk was as strange as Maid Ai had described, with black hair that fell to his shoulders in wild curls and a beard that grew down to his chest. His enormous body seemed to have the power of a great beast, but his face was serene. Beside him was a young Chinese monk with an earnest expression and Liang wondered how he came to be with the Indian.

Several offerings of food and drink had been set before them but remained untouched. She squatted down and set out the rice cakes and tea that she had brought from the night market. As she did, she stole a closer look at the black monk. Though his dark eyes were open, they appeared to be gazing at distant wonders unseen. She was about to rise when suddenly he shuddered, coming out of his trance, and fixed her with one round eye. She held her breath in fright. Then he winked. She fell onto her rump in surprise, blushing furiously. The Chinese monk beside him was watching her now, doing his best to look straight ahead and fighting to keep a smile from his lips.

"We can abandon our meditation for a moment, Brother Ko," the Indian said in perfect Chinese. "This young lady has been kind enough to bring tea, and I have developed quite a thirst in this dusty city."

"It's nothing," she murmured, rising to leave.

"Wait a moment, good lady," he ordered. "Sit with us while we eat and drink tea. You came just in time. Brother Ko's stomach has been rumbling so loudly it was disturbing my meditation."

It was Ko's turn to redden, but he did not protest.

"What do you do in this city, Miss?" Da Mo continued happily.

"I am a maid in the palace, Master," she answered.

Ko turned to look incredulously at Da Mo, who seemed unsurprised. "How fortunate, because we are seeking an audience with the emperor. Perhaps you could inform him we are here?"

"I'm afraid I'm just a servant, Master. I never speak to the emperor," she said.

"I've always found servants are one of the best ways to pass information around any household," Da Mo smiled. "Is it not true of the palace?"

"That much is true," she admitted with the beginnings of a smile.

Then his laughing eyes held hers for a moment and she realized he was serious. Though his request was impossible and absurd, she found she could not refuse.

"May I know your name, Master?" she asked.

"Bodhidharma," he answered.

She hesitated, unable to repeat it.

"You can say Da Mo," he offered. "You will not be the only one."

"I will see what I can do," she promised.

"That is all we ask. I think you will find a way," he nodded reassuringly, and Liang rose to do his bidding.

Maid Ai was helping the young prince to dress when Liang entered the chamber. She was earlier than usual and went about her tasks with such brisk efficiency that Maid Ai could see she was in rare state of excitement.

"How are you this morning, Liang?" she asked in a whisper. They were not allowed to speak in front of the prince, though the rule was rarely enforced.

"A little tired," Liang replied.

"Did you have trouble sleeping?"

"I couldn't stop thinking about the man I met last night."

"Was he very handsome?"

"Not that sort of man!"

"Is there any other sort?"

"Really Ai! It was the Indian magician you were telling me about."

"You saw him? Is he still outside the palace?"

"Oh yes, and you were not exaggerating. He's like no man I have ever seen—the size of two men, with black skin and long hair all over his body. They say he has incredible powers. He can control objects with his mind. He was seated, but I swear he was floating above the ground. They say he can read your thoughts too. I think I felt him inside my mind!"

Maid Ai gasped. Liang held her fingers to her lips to stop her saying more. She did not want to discuss it further in front of the prince.

"Oh, you're right," Ai whispered. "Such frightful things are not for young ears." She patted the prince on his shoulder. "Besides, you're dressed and ready for your morning lesson with Professor Lin," she said, summoning the guard who was waiting outside to escort the boy to his studies.

Professor Lin noticed his pupil's mind was not on his writing that day and when their lesson came to an end, the little prince insisted on seeing his father. The professor informed the prince's personal bodyguard, who took him directly to the emperor's quarters where he was ushered in without delay.

The emperor listened dispassionately to his son's request, his eyebrows raising only once at the boy's description of the Indian's powers. When the prince had finished, the emperor ordered an attending eunuch to find out more about the curious visitor outside the palace.

Soon the entire palace was alight with rumors of the dark monk with incredible powers; he was a magician, a sorcerer, a wizard sent by the patriarch of the Western Heaven to China. Finally the news reached Grandmaster Tzu, and Brother Jung was summoned to his chambers.

"You speak Sanskrit, Brother Jung," Tzu said as soon as he entered.

Brother Jung was unsure whether it was a question or a statement and stammered out a cautious reply, "Well, it might be more correct to say that I am able to read the sacred language, and even write it, to a certain degree..."

"You cannot speak it?" Tzu said incredulously. "Then is there anyone else who can?"

"In the palace?" Jung asked.

"Of course, in the palace!" roared Grandmaster Tzu. He saw the fear in Brother Jung's eyes and realized he was getting nowhere. He took a deep breath and softened his tone.

"Brother Jung, there is an Indian monk at the palace gate. I would like you to go and visit him. Speak to him. Find out what you can about him. Try to ascertain his intentions. Do you think you can do that?"

Brother Jung considered the request silently. He was fluent in Sanskrit, but he had never spoken to an Indian before. He wondered if he would be able to make himself understood.

"Is there anyone better qualified than you to speak to this

so-called master?" Tzu demanded impatiently.

"No," Brother Jung replied truthfully.

"Then go, and hurry. Report back to me immediately."

Brother Jung hurried out of the palace, but even as he emerged onto the busy square, he saw he was too late. An imperial messenger had arrived moments earlier to summon the Indian into the palace. The master and his disciple were collecting their possessions and preparing to follow him. The Indian was huge and wild-looking. Jung examined his face, searching for signs of his intention, but could detect nothing. Then for a second, those piercing eyes were fixed on his and he felt the Indian looking into his very soul.

He turned away to collect himself. When he looked back, the Indian was standing before him with an expectant smile. Suddenly all eyes were on him. Brother Jung cleared his throat. "Welcome to Nanjing and the Imperial Palace," he said in his best Sanskrit.

"Thank you, Brother," the Indian replied, "you are very kind and please accept my compliments on your ability in the sacred language. You speak it most eloquently."

Brother Jung lost himself in the Indian's praise and the warmth of his smile, and fell quickly into conversation as the messenger led them into the palace. The conversation flowed freely as they passed through ornate halls and grand function rooms, and stopping only when they reached an anteroom in the royal quarters. Here Da Mo and his disciple were seated and told to await their audience with the emperor, and Brother Jung took his leave.

He hurried across the palace grounds to the temple to report his findings to Grandmaster Tzu, filled with excitement at the arrival of a great Indian master and dread at the prospect of informing Grandmaster Tzu.

Da Mo and the Emperor

The chamber door swung open and an usher led them inside. The room was filled with courtiers, and all heads turned to see the barbarian monk. The walls of the chamber were lined with guards who stood with their spears, exactly three paces apart, as was the custom. On a platform at the far side of the chamber, a slight man was seated on an ornate chair. He wore a wide headpiece with strings of pearls that hung before his face. His robe was decorated with a dragon of pure gold that coiled around silver mountains, but it was his expression that left no doubt of who he was. It was the face of a man in his middle years, narrow and finely boned, unremarkable except for the eyes that bore the unmistakable signs of power, a lifetime of intoxicating power that came with leading the mightiest nation on earth. This was the emperor of China, Wu Di.

Beside him sat a woman with black hair piled high on her head. Her face was painted with white make-up, as Da Mo had seen on other women in the streets of the capital, but this woman's face was serene and immaculate. Beauty marks had been drawn on her cheeks and forehead. As he came closer, he could see that her eyebrows had been removed and repainted like the wings of a butterfly. She watched impassively as he approached. Beside her sat a young boy with a round face and almond eyes, who stared wide-eyed at Da Mo as if seeing a mythical beast in the flesh.

Behind the royal family were gathered mandarins in fine robes, eunuch guards, and senior monks. Among them Da Mo recognized Brother Jung. Beside Brother Jung stood a tall thin monk with a white beard, whose eyes assessed them with a sinister glare behind a welcoming smile. Da Mo guessed it was Grandmaster Tzu.

The emperor's face, like his wife's, was impassive, but Da Mo was pleased to see compassion and intelligence behind the steady gaze. The usher bowed deeply before the emperor, and Da Mo and Ko did the same. "Master Da Mo from the Western Heaven," the usher announced.

There was a brief silence, then the emperor turned to his advisers. "What sort of name is that?" he murmured.

"I'm not sure I heard it correctly," Grandmaster Tzu said, a sly smile playing on his lips.

The usher stood dumb, unsure what to do next. Da Mo waited in silence. Finally Ko took a step forward.

"The master's name is Bo Di Da Mo," he said, loud enough for all to hear.

"I imagine you mean Bodhidharma," Grandmaster Tzu said with exaggerated slowness.

"Yes, that is his name," Ko answered.

"A formidable title," Grandmaster Tzu said, turning to the emperor to explain, "It means 'Teacher of Enlightenment.'"

A murmur went around the courtiers until the emperor raised his hand and the room fell silent once more. With a flick of his finger, his aides hurried forward with gifts for the visiting master, silk robes, ivory carvings, jade statues, beautiful scrolls of poetry, and paintings by the finest artists in China. When the emperor's aides had finished, Grandmaster Tzu motioned to two novices who brought more exquisite gifts: boxes of fine scents and oils, cups and pots of the finest porcelain, silk paper, bottles of ink, and fine brushes of sable with handles of ebony.

Then Brother Jung stepped forward, cleared his throat, and addressed Da Mo in Sanskrit. "The emperor welcomes Master Da Mo to the Middle Kingdom. He is an honored guest in the palace, and Grandmaster Tzu wishes to extend a sincere greeting to his brother from the Western Heaven."

He repeated the message in Chinese for the emperor and the

courtiers to hear. Then all eyes turned to Da Mo as he stepped forward to respond.

"I thank the emperor and Grandmaster Tzu most sincerely for their welcome and their magnificent gifts. They have both been more than generous."

A stunned silence fell in the chamber. No one was more surprised than Brother Jung, who stood open-mouthed, wondering how to respond. Had the Indian really spoken Chinese? Da Mo waited for those around him to regain their composure before continuing. "Unfortunately, I have no gifts to give in return."

The silence grew uncomfortably long. Finally Tzu stepped forward with a smile. "There is no reason that you should understand the customs of the Chinese people, Master Da Mo."

Prince Wu rose from his seat and whispered in his father's ear. The emperor nodded and the boy disappeared through a door behind the throne, accompanied by a eunuch guard.

"My son also wishes to give a gift," the emperor said.

"There is no need, Highness," Da Mo smiled. "The court has already been too kind."

"Nevertheless, the prince insists," the emperor replied.

"If the prince insists ..." Da Mo spread his hands.

"He is expecting to see a great miracle."

"Then I fear the boy will be disappointed," Da Mo said. "I bring only the teachings of The Way. No miracles or magic."

"Then you offer no proof of your divine ability, Master Da Mo?" Grandmaster Tzu asked.

"I cannot perform illusions and then ask the emperor to see the truth," Da Mo retorted.

"The truth?" Tzu said. "Well, then perhaps you will live up to your name and enlighten us all as to its nature?"

"I can only point the way," Da Mo said curtly.

"Then please do so," the emperor said sharply, "because after many years of study, it still remains a mystery to me. What is this ultimate reality that can only be seen with the buddha-mind? Where is this place called nirvana? I read endless words about its sublime beauty, yet find myself no closer to it. Perhaps you can tell us where to find it?"

"Sadly, the truth cannot be found in words, Highness," Bodhidharma answered. "Words are the problem. They are not the same as reality. They confine and restrict the truth. One might as well try to put air into a box."

"Now you speak in riddles," Grandmaster Tzu sneered.

"Then let me make it more simple," Da Mo said, stepping forward with his staff in hand. He stopped to examine it for a moment, running his palms along the smooth mulberry wood before continuing. "When I say the word "staff" the idea of a staff appears in your mind. But what do you know about this staff? Is it the one I'm holding now, or a different one? Is it long or short? Old or new? From which tree is it carved?"

Suddenly his staff was spinning in a blur above his head. He covered the ground between himself and the emperor in two swift strides and the wood whistled through the air before reappearing in his hands. He held out the staff to the emperor.

"No words can describe it better than your own eyes can see it or your own hands can feel it. So here, I give you the staff in its entirety."

There were gasps from the courtiers. The guards were shaken. They had allowed a foreigner with a weapon to get within striking distance of the emperor. They sprang forward and held their spear-points on Da Mo.

"Take it, Highness," Da Mo urged, ignoring the razor-sharp points on his throat and body. The emperor never lost his calm exterior but his eyes danced with interest. He reached out and took the staff. He ran his hand along its length and examined the workmanship of the handle slowly while the guards focused their spears on Da Mo.

All of a sudden, the prolonged silence was broken by the sound of running footsteps in the chamber. The little prince had reappeared with his gift for the Indian. He almost ran into the guards that had surrounded Da Mo, and stopped in mid-step, unsure what to do next.

"What do you have for me, Little Prince?" Da Mo asked politely.

The boy hesitated, then held out his hand to the dark monk. Da Mo reached out, pushing against the spears, and the prince dropped a smooth lilac stone into his palm.

Da Mo looked at it, then held it up for all to see. "How wonderful, thank you! It is quite beautiful. Where does it come from?"

"From the garden," the prince replied.

"It is a gift which I will treasure always," Da Mo said, placing the stone carefully into the folds of his robe. The spears tightened on him as his hand disappeared, but he ignored them. "I only wish I could give you something in return, but alas, we traveled light on our journey from ..." he stopped and began to cough, "... we did not bring ..." his cough grew worse and he could not stop, "there is something in my throat ..." he gasped, his face growing a deep shade of purple.

He coughed harder, until his eyes bulged and he gripped his stomach as if he had eaten poison. The guards looked to their captain for orders, but before he could speak the Indian gave a final retch and the prince's lilac stone popped out of his mouth. It fell to the floor and came to rest by the prince's feet.

There was another stunned silence in the chamber.

Then the emperor gave a bark of amusement.

One of the courtiers clapped his hands in delight, and all at once the room burst into laughter and applause. The guards were too nervous to share in the amusement, but they relaxed their spears just enough for Da Mo to retrieve the stone and clean it on his sleeve. He returned it to his pocket and held up his hand to assure the prince it was empty. Then he hawked again, and the stone reappeared in his mouth.

This time, the prince laughed too and clapped his hands in glee. Da Mo replaced the stone in his robe and coughed it up a third time, until the boy squealed with delight and the courtiers applauded noisily. Finally, Da Mo reached for the boy. The guards closed ranks so he could not touch the prince, but the emperor gave the faintest nod and they eased their spears enough for Da Mo to reach the boy's ear.

"What's this?" he asked, his fingers working frantically. "Ha, here it is," he said, pulling the pebble from the prince's ear. The boy giggled loudly, holding his ear, then ran to his father, who drew him close and inspected his ear with mock concern.

"Please excuse my guards, Master Da Mo," the emperor said courteously. "They are a little overzealous at times."

"A guard can never be overzealous in protecting his master," Da Mo replied.

"I am glad you understand. I have examined your staff and find it to be a pleasing piece of workmanship. A little crude in places perhaps, but sturdy and well suited to its purpose. Where did you obtain it?"

"It was a gift from my disciple, Brother Ko."

"A good deal of care has certainly gone into it."

"I believe so," Da Mo said. "Please accept it as a gift, if it pleases you."

"If the young man does not object?" the emperor said, turning to look at Ko for the first time.

"It would be an honor," Ko stammered, unable to believe that the staff he had carved at the silkmakers would now belong to the emperor himself.

"Then I accept. Perhaps Brother Ko can make a new one for his master when he has the inclination. Now, Master Da Mo, I often walk in the gardens at this time of day. Perhaps you would care to join me? I have matters that I would like to discuss with you at our leisure."

"With pleasure," Da Mo said.

The guards withdrew their spears and the two men left the chamber together as Grandmaster Tzu looked on with ill-concealed fury.

They walked among fragrant spice trees and apricots in blossom, past ornate rock gardens, and sparkling pools filled with fish of red, yellow, and gold, until they came to a group of mulberry trees that reminded Da Mo of a place he had come to know so well.

"How delightful," he smiled. "The gardens capture the natural beauty of China so perfectly: the mountains and rivers, lakes and trees …"

"It is one of my greatest joys, walking in these grounds," the emperor said. "Have you had a chance to travel in our land? I presume you came by sea to Canton?"

"No Highness, we came through Tibet."

"Then you have truly seen China!" the emperor exclaimed. "You traveled on the Yangtze?"

"For over a thousand li," Da Mo replied. "These gardens remind me of my journey. They are truly magical."

"We have rare plants and flowers from every corner of the kingdom and the world," the emperor said, pointing them out as they went, "magnolia, azalea, peony, white and pink lotus, and the rare blue lotus of India."

They followed the path as it meandered through dazzling flowerbeds and crossed painted bridges spanning bubbling streams.

White deer roamed freely among the conifers and bamboo and the soft scented air was filled with the melody of songbirds. They passed bright pavilions where birds of prey perched in gilded cages. In giant pens, lions and tigers roamed among fallen trees. Panthers lazed in the sunshine. Elephants and rhinoceros wallowed in deep pools. Great apes from the southern jungles watched impassively as they strolled by.

The emperor turned to Da Mo. "I have a question for you, something that has been troubling me for many years, and I can find no real answer to it."

"Then ask it, Highness," Da Mo said.

"I am, as you are no doubt aware, a strong supporter of Buddhism," he began, stroking his thin moustache as he spoke. "I build great temples and fill them with fabulous treasures dedicated to the glory of The Buddha. I support whole cities of monks who do good work, caring for the poor and sick, teaching people to read and write, helping to keep the peace and maintain order. That is right and proper, is it not?"

"It is very noble, Highness," Da Mo said.

"And the scriptures speak of acquiring merit, do they not?"

"They do," Da Mo nodded slowly.

"Then I ask you how much merit have I acquired for the innumerable benefits I have bestowed on the followers of Buddha?"

Da Mo laughed.

"Why do you laugh?" the emperor asked with a frown.

"Because the answer is: no merit," Da Mo answered with a smile.

"Explain yourself!"

"You have earned no merit for your good deeds. None whatsoever. However, I commend you most highly on your choice of question, Highness."

"And why is that?" the emperor asked testily.

"Because the answer is one that nobody wants to hear. And so it presents you with a rare opportunity."

"And what is that?"

"To accept the truth, Highness." Da Mo beamed at the emperor, his eyes sparkling with mirth. "There is only one truth. There is no other truth. To accept the truth, no matter how unpalatable it may be, is the mark of a truly enlightened being."

"You speak very plainly, Master Da Mo."

"Forgive me Highness, I have no wish to cause offense, but the idea of earning merit is for novices who are just starting out on The Way. Those who truly seek enlightenment must look beyond such paltry concerns. The teachings are stepping stones to the truth, not the truth itself."

"Then what is the truth?"

"The enlightened man does not act in order to receive merit. He does not seek to cultivate good karma, nor does he fear bad karma. The man who has realized his true nature is beyond worrying about such trivial things."

"My priests tell me I have acquired merit beyond measure," the emperor retorted.

"I'm sure they do."

"Then how shall I find The Buddha, Master Da Mo?"

"Give up your search, Highness. There is no need to seek him. Simply know your own mind and you will know The Buddha. Do not revere him. Do not fear him. Trust that your own mind is basically pure. The man who sees his own true nature is a Buddha."

"Then what is the point of doing good?"

"No point. A buddha does not seek to do good or evil. He acts with no thought for reward, and enjoys freedom in good fortune and bad."

"Does not The Buddha say to do good?"

"A buddha acts with infinite compassion, but that is not the same as seeking to do good. Who are we to decide what is good or evil? What is good for one person is usually bad for another."

"Then how shall a buddha make a decision, or know how to act at all?"

"A Buddha does not worry about such things. He simply acts in accordance with nature, which is always correct."

"It sounds rather easy, being a Buddha," the emperor smiled.

"Sometimes it is the simplest thing in the world," Da Mo laughed.

"If only the same could be said of being an emperor," the emperor said lightly.

"Let me ask you this," Da Mo said as the walked. "When you have a difficult decision to make, do you ever wonder what another would do in your place?"

"I often wonder what my father would have done," the emperor said.

"He was wise?"

"Yes."

"And does the answer come to you?" Da Mo asked.

"Usually it does," the emperor replied.

"Is it always the answer you hoped for?"

"Not always."

"Nevertheless, it is correct, yes?"

"Yes," the emperor conceded.

"Then it is neither good nor bad. It is simply the answer. To define it any more is unnecessary."

"A bold approach, Master Da Mo. What if the answer proves incorrect?"

"You consulted with your ancestors, your conscience, and your intellect. You acted in accordance with The Way. There can be no cause for regret if the decision proves wrong, nor self-congratulation if it proves right. These are trivial emotions compared to the joy of acting in accordance with The Way."

"A fascinating perspective, but you speak of the spiritual well-being of the individual. I must consider the needs of my subjects, who number in the millions. They are simple people, living off the land. How can I tell them good and evil are not important? They won't understand. Order will break down."

"Certainly these ideas can only be introduced under the correct guidance," Da Mo said.

"The guidance of a strong and caring master."

"Most definitely," Da Mo smiled, "The Way is both long and arduous."

They stopped to admire a collection of flowers where butterflies and bees swarmed around the brightly colored petals. "Chrysanthemum," the emperor said, "the symbol of long life in China."

Da Mo, held out his hand to allow a butterfly to land on it. They remained by the flowers in comfortable silence for a long while, until the emperor felt it was time to speak again.

"I have found our conversation most stimulating, Master Da Mo, most stimulating … I will consider what you have told me, and what I have learned today. I want our land to benefit from the wisdom you bring. I shall decide on how best that can be achieved in due course. In the meantime, please make yourself at home. If there is anything you require, simply ask and it shall be yours." He signaled to one of his aides and ordered him to show Da Mo to the special guest quarters. Then he turned back to Da Mo with a smile.

"No merit, you say?"

"None whatsoever," Da Mo shrugged apologetically.

The emperor shook his head in amusement. "That explains rather a lot. Thank you."

With that, the emperor went back into the palace and his aide guided Da Mo to his new room.

Behind the Lattice Screen

When Liang heard that Master Da Mo had entered the palace, she went to look for him in the special guests' quarters. A guard informed her that the Indian and his disciple had gone into the palace grounds to perform their daily rituals. She went in search of them but the gardens were vast and the monks were nowhere to be seen. She was about to give up and return to her duties when she noticed a movement behind a lattice screen in a distant corner of the grounds. She guessed the monks might have chosen this quiet spot for the purposes of meditation, but as she drew nearer, the rapid movement behind the screen told her that whatever they were doing, it was not meditation.

She peered through a gap in the lattice and saw the huge Indian beating his disciple unmercifully. Brother Ko was doing his best to defend himself, but he was no match for Da Mo, who grinned as he beat him. She gasped in horror and her heart went out to the little Chinese monk.

"Stop!" she shouted, and before she knew it, she had run around the screen to stand beside them. Ko turned to look at Liang, a trickle of blood coming from his nose. At that moment Da Mo swiped him hard across the jaw with the flat of his hand and Ko fell, his eyes rolling in his head.

Liang leapt forward and stood between them, glowering at Da Mo. "Enough," she said angrily, "what are you doing to this man?"

"I'm afraid it is you who did that to him," Da Mo said.

"Me?"

"You stole his concentration."

Ko groaned, and rolled slowly onto his knees, his face flushed.

"Are you alright, Brother Ko?" she asked.

"He's fine," Da Mo said.

"He does not look fine," she said, peering closer into Ko's eyes.

"Master Da Mo is right," Ko said, working his jaw to click it back into place. "We were training in combat. There was no need to interfere."

"Combat? What sort of training is that for monks?"

"Ko was exercising his mind," Da Mo said.

She looked at him in disbelief.

"It's true," Da Mo smiled, "I told him to keep his mind alert and think only of fighting. Not to break his concentration, not even for a moment, not for anything! In fact, he was doing quite well, until you came along."

Liang turned to Ko for confirmation but he avoided her eye. "I was fine," he said lamely. "There was no need to worry." She continued staring at him as if he were mad. Ko looked at her with a frown, "Although I suppose I should thank you for your concern."

"Either way your intervention taught him a valuable lesson," Da Mo said. "Next time he won't be so easily distracted, not even by someone as pretty as you."

It was Liang's turn to blush. She had made a fool of herself and they were laughing at her. She turned to leave.

"Wait a moment, Miss Liang."

She turned back, surprised that Da Mo knew her name. She did not remember telling him. His eyes twinkled in amusement, but there was no mockery in them. "Perhaps you would like to practice with us?" he offered.

"You want me to fight?"

"No, at least not yet. First, we will teach you. Come, practice with us."

"My duties," she said lamely.

"Tell your mistress that Master Da Mo required your presence. You could not very well offend a guest of the emperor."

Liang knew Mistress Yu would never believe her, but she was

intrigued by the Indian master and his offer. She could not resist.

"Just do as I do," he said without waiting for a reply.

She stood between Da Mo and Ko, wondering what manner of training the powerful monk had in store for her. He stepped forward and sank low, and Ko did the same. She followed. Da Mo raised his arms and turned, first to the left, then to the right, his limbs working in fluid lines, shooting forward, snaking in arcs and turning in tight circles, creating beautiful patterns in the air. It looked like a dance, of sorts. She copied, turning as he turned. When she could no longer see Da Mo, she followed Ko instead. Ko moved well enough but he was a little stiff compared to the giant Indian who flowed like the waters of a powerful river.

The three moved in unison through a brief sequence, which they repeated many times until Da Mo was satisfied. Then he stood apart and watched as Liang performed alongside Ko. She had learned with remarkable speed, just as he had suspected she might.

When he was satisfied that they had done enough, he raised his hand to stop them. "You have just studied the principles of combat," he told her with a smile. "Now you can study the practice."

"How shall I do that, Master?" she asked.

"Ko will attack you," he said.

"What should I do?"

"Defend yourself."

"But I don't know how!" she protested.

"You have just learned. Watch!" he smiled, nodding to Ko, who stepped forward and aimed a punch at Da Mo's head. Da Mo parried the punch and countered with one of his own which he pulled a fraction before impact."

Do you recognize this defense?" he asked.

"I have never seen it before," she answered, puzzled.

"Are you sure?"

Da Mo's eyes bored into hers. She searched her memory hopelessly; she had never seen it before. She was about to say so when the truth dawned on her with sudden clarity, "It's the beginning of the sequence!"

Da Mo nodded once, then ordered Ko to repeat the attack, this time on Liang. There was no time for self-congratulation. There was no time for anything. Ko lunged forward and threw his punch. She had seen how hard the monks fought and countered quickly, deflecting his arm and striking him full in the mouth. Ko's head spun with the force of her unchecked blow and he staggered drunkenly, struggling to stay on his feet.

"Oh dear, I'm so sorry, Brother Ko," she said, covering her mouth in shame. Ko touched his lip and saw fresh blood on his fingers. She looked from Ko to Da Mo, "I'm so sorry!"

"Again," Da Mo ordered.

This time Ko launched a hard strike with full intent. Liang's parry was too weak and Ko's punch got through, striking her on the forehead. She flinched, but refused to cry out or rub her forehead, though her eyes watered and her cheeks reddened.

"Once more," Da Mo said.

This time Ko struck hard and Liang parried with a sharp slap that deflected his blow safely past her ear. Her own punch stopped a hair's breadth from Ko's chin, just as Da Mo's had done. Ko felt the latent power in the strike and looked straight into her face. He saw the same controlled ferocity in her that he saw in Da Mo's eyes. How had she learned Da Mo's methods so quickly?

"Again," Da Mo said, and they repeated the attack and counter many more times. Next Da Mo had Ko seize his wrist and showed Liang how to reverse the grip and place Ko in an excruciating lock. It was the second movement from the sequence they had learned. Da Mo did not mention it, and Liang, though she realized it, did not say. Instead she simply practiced it many times with Ko, until they moved onto the defense against a strangle hold, which was the third part of the sequence.

Liang was dimly aware of time slipping by, time when she should have been working in the palace, but she could not bring herself to stop. In the end, it was Da Mo who ordered her to return to her duties. "Perform the sequence each day to remind yourself of these teachings," he urged.

"I will," she promised.

"Thank you for training with us, Miss Liang. You did well." A brilliant smile flashed across her face. He took her hand and leaned down, putting his mouth to her ear as if sharing a confidence with her, though he spoke loud enough for Ko to hear, "And I hope that now you can appreciate that Brother Ko requires a firm hand at all times?"

She glanced at Ko who scowled in annoyance.

"I should never have doubted you Master Da Mo," she replied innocently. "And now, I really must go."

She hurried back to the palace to catch up on her duties, but she had only got as far as the entrance when an imposing form emerged from the shadows.

"Liang!" She froze. It was Grandmaster Tzu. There was no way to avoid him. Tzu's expression filled her with dread.

"You have surpassed yourself this time Liang, cavorting with so-called monks in the gardens. What were you thinking?"

"I'm sorry, Grandmaster Tzu," she said, bowing low before him, cursing her own stupidity for staying out so long.

"Sorry for what, girl?" he said icily.

"Master Da Mo invited me to take part in his practice. I did not wish to cause offense by refusing."

"You abandon your duties to the emperor in favor of a wandering hermit from India?"

"Not abandoned, Grandmaster, I am going to attend to them now."

"You contradict me?" he hissed.

"I was trying to please the emperor's guests."

"You're not here to entertain the emperor's visitors, Liang."

"I'm so sorry Grandmaster Tzu," she said, her eyes pricking with tears.

"Your recent conduct has been inexcusable."

She did not dare look up, but could feel his cold gaze boring into her.

"I shall speak to Mistress Yu on the subject." He stared at her, waiting for her to speak, but she said nothing. He sighed, his voice dropping to a murmur, "It gives me no pleasure to see a young woman disgraced, Liang. If you wish to discuss the matter further, I am open to exploring a more amicable solution. This evening I will be performing a short ceremony for the emperor. After that, you will find me in my chamber. I suggest you attend me there before I meet with Mistress Yu in the morning." He waited for her to reply but she said nothing. "Do I make myself clear?" he demanded, the sharp edge back in his voice.

"Yes, Grandmaster," she whispered.

"Then I leave the matter in your hands," he said, leaving her where she stood, too stunned to move.

The Buddha's Finger

The great ceremonial hall of the palace had been closed throughout the day in preparation for Grandmaster Tzu's special event. Its purpose had remained a closely guarded secret and expectation permeated the air. All that was known was that hundreds of oil lamps had been hung in the great room, and seating had been arranged for the royal family and over a thousand courtiers.

That evening, Da Mo and Ko joined the courtiers in taking their seats and the hall echoed with the sound of excited chatter. After a long wait, Grandmaster Tzu entered and walked with great dignity onto the dais at the front of the hall. The emperor was the last to appear, and the audience fell silent as he took his place beside Grandmaster Tzu.

The court musicians had been playing softly in the background, but now their music took on new purpose, the rhythm faster. It filled the senses of the onlookers. The music ended abruptly and the chamber doors flew open. A procession of monks entered and at the end of the line, four monks carried an ornate palanquin. The procession stopped before the emperor and one of the senior monks drew back the palanquin's curtain to reveal a small box. The wizened monk withdrew the box with great reverence and offered it to Grandmaster Tzu.

Grandmaster Tzu descended from the dais to take it, his hands trembling visibly. As his hands touched the box, a gust of wind blew around the hall and the oil lamps flickered amid the anxious sounds of the crowd.

"What is happening?" Ko murmured to Da Mo.

"This is common practice among those who do not teach the true Way," Da Mo said.

"Magic?"

"Illusion."

"This cannot be illusion," Ko said seriously.

"A few days ago you watched a man cut out his own tongue."

"That was magic," Ko said defiantly.

Grandmaster Tzu walked up the steps of the dais to rejoin the emperor and, with great care, opened the box. The oil lamps spluttered and died and the hall was plunged into darkness. Candles were quickly lit and the hall was bathed in an unearthly glow.

Attendants hurried to fetch the ladders and flints needed to relight the oil in the lamps.

There was a cry from the crowd, and the courtiers began to point and murmur. A weak light was coming from the box.

"What is this, Grandmaster Tzu?" the emperor asked.

"Please, see for yourself, Highness," Tzu said.

The hall fell silent as the emperor rose and peered into the box, his face was lit by the strange glow.

"A sacred relic?"

"A bone, Highness … from the hand of The Buddha himself."

Grandmaster Tzu offered the box to the emperor, who accepted it and held it out before him. Grandmaster Tzu reached inside and removed a silk pillow with a small fragment of bone nestled in its center. He raised the pillow before the audience, his expression changing as he did, from reverence to awe and then wonder. Slowly the bone fragment began to levitate. The audience gasped. There were cries of joy. The monks gave praise and many wept openly.

The relic descended onto the cushion and Tzu replaced it in the box. Once the lid was closed, the oil lamps flickered and came on again of their own accord. Tzu raised his hand to address the stunned audience, taking a moment to compose himself before speaking.

"The relic comes from the Western Holy Land," he said, his voice quavering with emotion. "Its power will bring great fortune to the city and the empire."

The crowd applauded wildly. Suddenly Tzu's strength failed him and his legs gave way beneath him. Monks rushed onto the dais to assist him, and worked urgently to revive him. The Grandmaster's eyes fluttered into consciousness and the hovering monks helped him to his seat beside the emperor.

"Incredible," Ko whispered.

"The weak-minded are easily fooled," Da Mo grunted, as the relic was returned to the palanquin and the crowd slowly dispersed.

The Emperor's Decision

Grandmaster Tzu watched in silence as the emperor took the tiny teacup and turned it slowly in his fingers, admiring the delicate workmanship of the porcelain. He picked up his own cup and did the same, hoping to hide his anxiety as he waited for the emperor to speak.

"I trust you have recovered from your episode at the ceremony earlier this week?" the emperor inquired.

"I am much improved, thank you Highness," Grandmaster Tzu said graciously.

"Excellent. You must beware of overdoing things these days. We are none of us as young as we once were."

"Indeed, Highness."

"The sacred relic is a most valuable gift. We thank you once again for bringing such a treasure to the Middle Kingdom."

"It is an artifact of great power, Highness."

"Quite, as you so ably demonstrated in your performance."

Grandmaster Tzu was about to protest at the word "performance," but the emperor continued before he could object. "A piece of such importance requires a setting of great dignity, don't you agree?"

"Of course, Highness."

"Good, because I have decided it will be displayed in the Great Temple that we are constructing outside the city."

"A perfect setting and a perfect choice, Highness."

"We have also been giving the matter of the Indian monk some thought of late," the emperor said, and Tzu's smile froze.

"We believe Master Da Mo has much to offer our nation. His is a deep insight into The Way. However, his methods are not suited to the palace or the Great Temple."

Tzu inclined his head in agreement and waited for the emperor to continue.

"You have served the palace and the empire for many years Grandmaster Tzu, and the appointment of Grandmaster of the Great Temple will be yours."

"Thank you, Highness," Tzu said with a low bow of his head.

"However, we do not want Master Da Mo's skills to go to waste. If we recall correctly, there is a temple in Song Shan that is in need of a new leader. The head monk died recently, an Indian too, if I'm not mistaken?"

"Yes Highness, his name was Batuo."

"Has a successor been appointment yet?"

"No, not yet. I believe one of the senior monks has taken charge until the successor is announced."

"Then let us send Master Da Mo to Song Shan and see what becomes of it."

"An excellent choice, Highness."

"You will make the arrangements?"

"I will attend to it at once and inform Master Da Mo of the decision. I am sure he will be most satisfied."

"We believe he will, too," the emperor smiled. "Then it is settled. We leave it in your hands, Grandmaster Tzu."

The emperor took a sip from his teacup and Tzu did the same, but when he said nothing more, Tzu understood the meeting was over. He replaced his cup gently on the lacquered table and bowed deeply before leaving the emperor's presence.

Back in his own quarters, Grandmaster Tzu summoned Brother

Jung and told him to inform Master Da Mo of the decision.

When Brother Jung had departed, Tzu sent for a second monk who came to his chamber after midnight to discuss the fate of Master Da Mo in more detail.

Brother Jung found Da Mo meditating in the gardens with his disciple and waited nearby, unsure whether to disturb them or return when they had finished their contemplation.

"Brother Jung," Da Mo called without looking round, "come and sit with us."

Jung hurried over. "I bring word from the emperor," he said breathlessly as he sat before them, "but it is not the news you might have hoped for."

"Why so, Brother Jung?"

"The emperor has decreed that you should go to a monastery in Song Shan that is in need of a new leader."

"That is good news," Da Mo said with a smile.

"But Song Shan is in the wilderness, Master!" Ko said.

"Brother Ko is right," Jung said sadly. "The monastery is small and very remote. There's just a handful of monks. I fear your knowledge will be wasted there, Master."

"The Way does not require a large temple," Da Mo said. "It does not care where it appears. Please convey my sincere thanks to the emperor. We will leave at once."

"So soon?" Ko asked.

"I think you have been enjoying the luxuries of the palace a little too much," Da Mo said, turning to Brother Jung with a smile. "He seems reluctant to return to a life of austerity just yet."

"It's understandable," Brother Jung said before Ko could object. "The palace is filled with easy temptation. Nevertheless, Brother Ko might have his wish, at least for a time. There is a strict protocol in these matters. An Imperial Decree of Appointment must be sent to the temple before your arrival."

"Then it appears we will stay a little longer after all," Da Mo said.

"There's something else I should tell you," Jung said, checking to make sure he could not be overheard. Leaning closer and lowering his voice to a whisper, he said, "A word of warning: take care on your journey. There are many dangers on the road north."

"We have traveled through wilderness before," Ko said.

"I'm sure you have," Brother Jung said, "but beware of more than bandits this time, Brother Ko."

"I don't understand," Ko said, bewildered.

"The emperor's favor comes at a high price," Da Mo said.

"Quite," Jung said, "and those who possess it will go to great lengths to ensure they don't lose it."

"Politics, even in religion?" Ko asked.

"In all things," Jung said, "and especially here in the palace."

"It's good of you to warn us," Ko said.

"I only wish I could do more to help," Jung said wistfully. "Master Da Mo's approach to The Way is deeply inspiring. I would gladly accompany you to Song Shan, but my duties lie here in the palace, one of which includes preparing the imperial decree. I will draft it as soon as possible. However, it will be more than a week before it is ready and you can leave."

"A week is not so long," Ko smiled.

"Tell us a little more about this monastery in Song Shan," Da Mo said, ignoring Ko's comment. "Have you been there yourself?"

"Unfortunately, I have only heard of it from visiting monks. It is said to be small but very beautiful, set in green woodlands on the slopes of a mountain. It is an area of great natural beauty, a land of pointed peaks shrouded in delicate mists and beloved of our Chinese poets. The monastery takes its name from the young forest that surrounds it. It is called the Shaolin Temple."

Maid Listens

Liang lay awake long into the night, searching for a way out of her dilemma, though in her heart she knew there was none. One word from Grandmaster Tzu would be the end of her. Mistress Yu would be forced to act. She would not dare to cross him, even if she did not trust his motives.

Liang wondered about confiding in Mistress Yu, but with no witnesses, Yu would be powerless to help; and besides, the mistress had been displeased with her conduct recently. There was no way out, and Liang knew her punishment would be swift and severe if she did not obey. She would be flogged with the bamboo cane and sold as a slave. She could not return to Madam Feng; the shame would be too much to bear. There was no escaping it, to refuse Grandmaster Tzu would be the end of her life as she knew it.

She began to wonder if she could do as he wanted? Perhaps she could. She would shut it out of her mind. Exist only in a tiny quiet space deep inside herself. No more dreaming. No reading, no calligraphy, and no training with foreign monks. She would listen to Mistress Yu's advice and keep her mind on the job. Grandmaster Tzu would tire of her eventually and turn his attentions to another young maid, and she would be left in peace.

She got up from her bed and lit a candle, examining her face in her tiny mirror. It was wet with tears. She had not known she had been crying. She dried her cheeks and tied back her hair, breathing steadily until she was calm, pushing all cares from her mind as she had learned to do as a child. She would visit his chambers. She would go to him now, tonight. A touch of make-up around the eyes was all she needed. A little rouge on her pale cheeks. A splash of the scent that she rarely used. Her hand trembled as she removed the lid and applied a little to her neck and breast. Then she made her way down the dark corridors of the palace and out into the dimly lit courtyard that led to the palace gardens. Twice she was stopped by guards, but they recognized the young maid and let her on her way. When she arrived at the monastery, she found it deserted except for an attendant monk in the entrance hall who looked at her sleepily but said nothing.

She climbed the stairs slowly and stood at the end of the passage that led to Tzu's private chambers. She wanted to continue, but her feet would go no farther. She put her hand against the wall for support as she cried silent tears. Then she grew angry with herself. This was justice, after all. This was her punishment for her own foolish pride, for believing she could read and write and practice with monks. She deserved to suffer for such vanity. She had to go forward and accept her punishment.

Yet she could not take another step. Her anger turned to fury. How could a man, especially a man who called himself a monk, impose such indignity upon her. She would not give into his demands. She would rather face any shame. Rather die. She would leave the palace and begin a new life. She had no idea what it would be or where to go. All she knew was that she was a resourceful young woman, and she would be free. She would leave Nanjing and go far away, where no one would find her. She would escape tonight.

As she turned to go back down the stairs, she heard footsteps approaching. A shiver of dread went through her. She slipped into a dark doorway and pressed herself into the shadows. A figure passed by. It was not Grandmaster Tzu. It was a grey-haired monk whom she had seen in the monastery several times before. She did not know his name, or anything about him, yet she sensed he was a man of malevolent power.

Sensing someone, he paused as he neared her and looked around. Liang held her breath and tried to make herself small and insignificant. Seeing nothing he proceeded to Tzu's quarters. She heard him knock lightly before entering and could make out the murmur of Tzu's voice in the stillness. She knew this late-night meeting with the sinister grey monk would not be about everyday temple business, but that was no concern of hers. Relieved she had escaped notice, she turned to go, but as she did, it struck her with complete certainty, what they would be plotting.

All thoughts of escape deserted her. They were planning to kill Da Mo. She had to stop them, to help the Indian monk. She could not explain how or why she knew, but her future, her life, was linked to his. She fought the urge to flee and instead, turned her ear to the corridor. Tzu's conversation with the grey monk was too low to be heard. She needed to get closer. There was a private meeting room beside Tzu's chamber that would be empty at that time of night. She slipped inside and waited for her eyes to adjust to the blackness. She had cleaned the room enough to know its layout and made her way silently between the furniture to the door that connected it to Tzu's chamber. The voices were audible, but the words were obscured by the pumping of her own heart. She forced herself to breathe deeply, softly. It took a minute to slow her heartbeat so she could hear.

"You will take care of everything?" Tzu asked.

"As always," the grey monk answered, "Goodnight, Excellency." The grey monk was leaving. She had missed it.

"Just out of interest, where exactly will it take place?" Tzu enquired.

"It is best for some things to remain unknown, Excellency," the grey monk answered.

"Always so cautious. That is why you serve me so well."

"Thank you, Excellency. Rest assured, it will not be near the palace. Once they are north of the Yangtze, the road goes through notorious bandit country. No traveler is safe there. I simply need a few days to make the arrangements."

"That is no problem," Tzu said. "They will remain in the palace for another week at least. An imperial decree takes time to prepare."

"Perfect."

Liang heard the door slide open and close. The grey monk had left. She waited for several minutes before slipping out of the office and hurrying away from the temple, her mind reeling. By the time she was back in her bed, a plan had begun to form in her mind. The audacity of her decision filled her with excitement and terror in equal measure.

Da Mo noticed the young maid waiting impatiently by the lattice screen and smiled.

"Have you come to practice with us again, Miss Liang?" he called out to her.

"No," she said, a little too abruptly, then smiled apologetically, "I'm sorry Master Da Mo, but I must speak to you about something important."

"Then come and sit with us," he smiled.

She sat beside them, looking from one to the other hesitantly before beginning. "It may seem a strange request, but could you tell me your plans for the future?"

"It is not strange," Da Mo reassured her. "We will be leaving shortly to go to a temple in Song Shan."

"It's as I feared," she began, looking around to make sure they could not be overheard. "I have heard rumors. I fear you will be in danger on your journey."

"You're not the first to say so," Ko said, "but don't worry, we will be careful."

"How soon do you leave?" she asked, ignoring Ko and addressing her question to Da Mo.

"We are awaiting an imperial decree which needs to be sent in advance. Once the monks of Song Shan have received it, we will make our way there."

"Perhaps you could take the decree and present it yourself. That way you could leave sooner," she said.

"You are in a hurry to see us leave?" Ko asked.

"No," she said tersely, "it would be safer, that's all."

"It's a good idea," Da Mo said, "but Brother Jung tells us an imperial decree takes over a week to prepare."

"It can be done faster than that," she assured him.

"How quickly?"

"By tonight."

"If it's ready tonight, then we will leave in the morning," Da Mo said cheerfully.

"Good," she smiled, then rose and with a quick bow hurried away without another word.

"A remarkable young woman, don't you think?" Da Mo said, watching her go. "A pity she did not train with us again."

"Perhaps she didn't enjoy it the last time," Ko said.

"She enjoyed it," Da Mo assured him.

"You think so?"

"I know it."

He saw Ko looking after her retreating figure hungrily and laughed. "Take a break and go after her if you wish."

Ko looked at Da Mo quizzically. He did not need to be told twice. He jumped up and ran after her, catching her when she was almost at the palace door.

"You did not want to train with us today?" It was all he could manage to ask.

"I'm a little busy," she answered, "and besides, you don't need me for your practice."

"You make a welcome change from training with the master," he said lightly.

"Because I don't hit as hard?"

"I wasn't thinking of that."

"Then what were you thinking of, Brother Ko?"

"You're far easier on the eye," he laughed.

"Is that so? I didn't think a follower of The Way was so easily distracted."

"I guess I'm just an apprentice," he shrugged.

Liang smiled, despite herself. "You haven't mastered your art?"

"Not yet," he chuckled, "I just can't help noticing a pretty face, even when it's intent on hurting me. Anyway, where are you going now?"

"I have duties, and matters to arrange."

"Then perhaps we could meet up tonight?"

Liang's smile vanished.

"You think I'll spend the night with a passing monk and wave good-bye to him in the morning, wiping a tear from my eye? You are very much mistaken."

"There's no need to get so angry," he said quickly, chastened by her vehemence. "I meant no offense."

"I'm not offended, just disappointed. But don't worry, we'll see each other again, soon enough."

"I doubt it ..." he began, but she entered the palace and shut the door in his face before he could follow.

Ko sat down with a sigh and Da Mo put his hand on the young man's shoulder.

"You like her?" Da Mo asked.

Ko shrugged. "She doesn't like me."

"She's far too troubled to be interested in any man, even a fine fellow like you Ko," Da Mo laughed.

"You think so?"

"I know it."

"Can you read her mind?"

"I can see her suffering."

"How can you see it?"

"How can you not see it? This life was not meant for her. Her fate lies in another direction. That's why I reached out to her."

"You did?"

Da Mo shook his head in despair. "I invited her to train with us. Didn't you see how eager she was to accept?"

"Yes, but we're leaving tomorrow. What was the point?"

"There is always a point. We just may not see it right away." Da Mo squeezed his shoulder affectionately. "Now come, let's continue our practice. We have wasted enough time."

They stood, and Ko raised his hand just in time to deflect a vicious punch aimed at his throat.

The Imperial Decree

Liang had no need of a lamp or candle, she knew the monastery well and hurried along the dark passages until she came to Brother Jung's door. It would be unusual for a monk to receive a visitor at this late hour, especially a female visitor. She hoped Brother Jung would understand.

The door opened a crack and Brother Jung's face appeared in the gap.

"Forgive me, Brother Jung, but I must speak with you," she whispered.

Jung heard the note of urgency in her voice and ushered her

inside. "Is something the matter, Miss Liang?"

"It is Master Da Mo," she said breathlessly, then stopped and examined Jung's face for any sign of disapproval. It was not a maid's place to concern herself with a visiting master, but Jung's eyes were open and honest. She had to trust him. "I heard they will be leaving soon to go to a monastery in Song Shan," she said.

"Yes, the Shaolin Temple. It was the emperor's decision," Brother Jung said, "but what is the problem?"

"I fear they will not reach it safely."

"What makes you say that?" he asked quickly, though he harbored the same fears himself.

"I overheard plotting. I believe an attack is being planned for their journey to Song Shan."

"Who was plotting?"

"I cannot say, Brother Jung."

"You must!"

"It is best if you do not know."

Jung thought for a moment and sighed in resignation. "Have you warned Master Da Mo?"

"I told him of the danger, yes."

"Then there is nothing more to be done."

"I believe there is," she persisted.

"Go on," Jung urged with a frown.

"The attack will take time to organize. Master Da Mo is waiting for an imperial decree to be sent to the temple before he sets off."

"Yes, and I am drafting that decree myself."

"But if we can create it quickly, he can leave now and take it with him. He'll be on the road before the ambush can be organized. He can present the decree when he arrives, and once inside the monastery, he will be a lot safer than on the open road."

Brother Jung chewed his lip as he considered the suggestion.

"It's a good idea, if a little unorthodox, but I'm afraid it will be impossible to execute. Once I draft the decree it has to be rewritten by a royal calligrapher and submitted to the Office of the High Commission for the royal seal. The process takes several days at the very least."

"Can't you write the document yourself?"

"I do not have the official paper, nor a good enough hand."

"I can get you the paper," she said.

"You can?" Brother Jung regarded the young maid doubtfully.

"It is not a problem," she assured him

"I won't ask how," Brother Jung said with a smile.

She picked up one of the scrolls from his desk. The writing was neat and elegant, with a surprising flourish for so orderly a man. "Your hand looks rather good to me too, Brother Jung," she said, "indistinguishable from a royal calligrapher's, in fact."

"You flatter me," Brother Jung said, though he could not resist another smile at the compliment, "but what about the royal seal?"

"I can arrange that too."

"Are you serious?"

"It is amazing what you can do when you are invisible."

Brother Jung looked at the humble maid with a new eye and saw her for the first time. It's possible, he thought for one fleeting moment. Then his face fell. "There is one more problem. The royal calligrapher signs the decree in his own hand. I cannot fake his signature."

"Leave that to me too," she said.

Brother Jung shook his head. "When they find out that the monks have gone early, there will be trouble."

"I will be gone by then," she said. "You can tell them I stole a draft from your office when I was cleaning."

"They will hunt you down."

"I will be far beyond their reach," she said, her gaze steady.

"Why are you doing this, Miss Liang?" he asked.

"Because it is right."

She opened the door to leave. "Why are you doing it, Brother Jung?"

"To act in accordance with The Way."

She regarded him blankly and he realized she knew absolutely nothing of The Way.

"For the same reason as you," he explained with a smile.

She smiled too and he was filled with admiration for the beautiful young girl. "Be careful, Miss Liang," he called to her, but it was too late. She had already gone.

She returned an hour later with several sheets of the finest silk paper for him.

The following morning, Brother Jung presented her with an immaculate imperial decree. Next, she went to the office of the High Commission where three calligraphers were at work hunched over their desks. They took no notice of the maid who tidied around them. No one saw her slip a recently signed paper into her bag, or take one of the imperial seals from the shelf before she left.

Back in her room, she stared at the calligrapher's signature, examining each part in detail, noting the elegance of the strokes, the firmness of the down-stroke, the lightness of the brush as it left the paper, until she felt she knew the hand that had signed the paper as well as her own.

She took her own scrap paper and rendered the signature countless times until she was satisfied. The copy was so good that only Professor Lin would be able to see the subtle differences, and even then, only if he had been looking for them. Now she was ready to write the signature directly onto Brother Jung's decree. Her brush hovered above the paper, but her arm began to tremble.

She stood up, breathing deeply to bring herself under control. She walked around her room until she was calm and knelt once more beside the paper, her brush poised.

"Liang!"

It was Mistress Yu's voice outside her door. She scrambled to hide the paper. "Yes Mistress, I'm coming."

Had Grandmaster Tzu spoken to Mistress Yu already?

"Hurry up girl and open this door!"

There was no time, she unlocked the door and peered out. Mistress Yu glared at her from the corridor. "I have seen you going back and forth between the temple and the palace for no reason I can fathom. What is going on?"

"I was running an errand, Mistress Yu."

"An errand, for whom?"

"Master Da Mo."

"The Indian monk? What business do you have with that foreigner?"

"He wanted information, from the temple, Mistress, nothing of great importance."

Mistress Yu's eyes bore into hers and it took all of Liang's will not to look away.

"Let me in," she commanded, and Liang stood aside.

Mistress Yu looked around the room while Liang held her breath. Even the most cursory search would reveal where she had hidden her papers.

"You have no business running errands for foreign monks, girl. There are servants for that."

"Yes Mistress."

"Besides, how could you bear to be near him? He is not even Chinese. He looks more like a wild beast than a man, and smells disgusting."

"I didn't notice any smell," Liang said quietly.

Mistress Yu glared at her. "They say he speaks Chinese, although I can't believe it."

"It's true, Mistress."

"It must be sorcery. He has you under his spell."

"Even the emperor spoke with him," Liang said.

Mistress Yu slapped her hard across the face and Liang cried out.

"Just remember your duties, girl. No good will come of trying to better your station in life. Only misery and disaster. This is your final warning. Next time it will be the bamboo."

"Yes Mistress Yu."

"After that, I'll sell you back to your so-called mother in disgrace, or take you to the slave market. Would you like that?"

"No, Mistress."

Mistress Yu left without another word. Liang's eyes glistened and her lip trembled as she closed the door behind her. She was sorry to have angered Mistress Yu, who had been kind to her, in her own way. The mistress's warning rang in her head and she wondered if she was making a terrible mistake? She sank onto her bedding and cried until there were no tears left, only a slow, dull anger that she could not shake. It was the same anger she had felt outside Grandmaster Tzu's chamber, an anger so powerful that she no longer cared what happened to her, as long as her life was hers, and not ruled by someone else.

She took the decree from where she had hidden it beneath her bedding. An icy calm flowed through her limbs as she dipped her brush in the ink. At last, she was sure of what she wanted. She rendered a perfect signature and finished the document with the stamp of the imperial seal. It was ready to go.

The hour was past midnight when Brother Jung delivered the decree to Da Mo, who held it up to the lamplight to examine it.

"It looks splendid," Da Mo smiled.

"Yes it does," Brother Jung said proudly.

"How was it produced so quickly?" Ko asked.

"We had help from a rather unexpected source," Jung said.

"You must know some important people in the palace, Brother Jung," Ko said with a grin.

"Actually it was just one person, and someone quite unimportant," Jung answered seriously. "I will have another decree drawn up through the proper channels and sent to the temple independently, but you can present this one on arrival. It will suffice until the official document arrives."

"You have been a good friend to us, Brother Jung," Da Mo said.

"I fear I have done very little," Jung said sadly. "It has been an honor to meet you, Master Da Mo. I wish you well on your journey. Take good care when you are north of the Yangtze."

"We will," Da Mo said gripping his arm in thanks.

"You will leave soon?" Brother Jung asked, concerned for their safety.

"Very soon," Da Mo assured him. "We leave at dawn."

The Road to Loyang

They avoided the busy ferry stations near the city and followed the southern bank of the Yangtze, seeking a more secluded place to cross before traveling north to Loyang. By late afternoon, the deserted track led them into a patch of sparse woodland. As they entered the trees, Da Mo noticed a shadow that did not belong. He whispered instructions to Ko before vanishing into the trees. Ko continued on the forest track as Da Mo had ordered, gripping his staff firmly, breathing lightly so he could hear the slightest noise. His right hand felt in the back of his waistband for the knife and his fingers curled reassuringly around the hilt.

The trees came alive with creaks and groans. The rustling of the leaves in the undergrowth was deafening. Dark shapes appeared suddenly in the shadows, only to vanish equally as quickly in the dim light. He surveyed the gnarled trees behind him. He had not see the figure that Da Mo had spotted and wondered if he had been mistaken. But when he turned back again there was a figure in his path.

It was no illusion. His grip tightened on his staff as he approached, ready to react in an instant if need be.

"Ko!" the figure called.

He stopped in his tracks. He did not recognize the man.

"Who wants to know?" he demanded. Had the army finally caught up with him?

The figure did not look like a soldier. Perhaps it was a bounty hunter. The man's hand went up, reaching for a sword that was strapped to his back. "Stop!" Ko shouted, leaping forward and pointing his staff at the stranger's throat. "What do you want?"

The stranger's hand moved slowly to his hood and drew it back, but in the dim light, Ko still did not recognize the face. The man's long hair was tied back, his skin smooth. He was little more than a boy.

"It's me Ko, you fool," a familiar voice said.

"Liang?" he said, incredulously, "what are you doing here?"

"Where is Master Da Mo?" She asked, ignoring his question.

"Right here."

Da Mo was standing one step behind her. It was Liang's turn to be startled. "And you are a long way from the palace, Miss Liang," he continued.

"Yes Master," she stammered. "Please forgive me, but I had to come, to warn you."

"I believe you warned us already," he said.

"Yes, but I have more details now. It was Grandmaster Tzu who I overheard plotting with another monk. He is planning an ambush for you once you cross the Yangtze. They are sending assassins to kill you."

"We are aware of that," Da Mo said, "and Brother Jung kindly helped us to leave the palace early."

"You have your decree?" she asked.

"We do, and I believe we have you to thank for that," Da Mo smiled, "now, please tell us why you are here?"

Liang looked into his eyes but could discern nothing from his steady gaze. She glanced at Ko and then back to Da Mo. "I have a request," she said hesitantly.

"Then make it."

Liang sank to her knees and bowed before Da Mo.

"I wish to travel with you to Shaolin."

"You want to become a nun?"

"I want to study with you."

"You have permission from the palace?"

She was quiet, wondering whether to tell the truth. Looking into his eyes, she saw he would know if she lied.

"No. Mistress Yu would never agree."

"Then you should return."

"I can't stay in the palace. It is not safe for me now."

"Then return to your home, your family."

"I have nowhere to go."

"We are not a refuge for runaways, Miss Liang."

"I wish to follow in The Way."

"What do you know of The Way?"

She looked up to Ko for assistance, but Ko's face was impassive. "Nothing," she admitted forlornly.

"The Way is not for women," Ko said gently.

"As I understood it, The Way is open to all," she replied.

"I'm only telling you the truth," Ko continued. "You have seen how hard we train. Master Da Mo's Way is not for someone like you."

"Someone like me? What type of person is that?"

"Perhaps a different order would suit you better?" he offered.

"Let me tell you who I am," she said, her anger mounting with each word, "I am called a servant, but I was born a slave, and live as a slave. Perhaps you think it ungrateful of me to wish for more, but all the time I keep wondering if I could be something else. Is my fate fixed until I grow old and die? Is it wrong to hope for something more?" She turned to Da Mo and her voice softened. "When you invited me to practice with you, I felt myself come alive, as if the whole of nature was coursing through my body and my mind ..." she stopped and her eyes filled with tears. It sounded so foolish.

Da Mo regarded her silently.

"If you will take me as your student, I will devote my life to The Way, I swear it."

He stood close to her, speaking barely above a whisper. "Be careful what you promise, Liang. To give up one life for another is never without a price."

"I will pay it," she said firmly.

"Ko is right to warn you. The Way is long and arduous. Nevertheless, it is open to all—rich and poor, Indian and Chinese, men and women. There are few enough who can follow its path without making exclusions."

"Then I may join you?" she asked in a small voice.

"Yes."

Da Mo picked up his belongings and set off through the trees. Liang dried her eyes and went after him, but Ko caught up with her before she could reach him. She glared at him angrily.

"There's no need to be angry," he said. "I was only trying to warn you, like the master said."

"What's the matter, Ko? Do you fear the presence of a serving maid?"

"It's not that. It's just that you might find the hardships of palace life are nothing compared to life with Da Mo."

"Don't judge everyone by your own standards, Brother Ko. And besides, what sort of monk are you? Not like any I have met before."

"You have only met palace monks."

"There are many good monks in the palace. Didn't Brother Jung risk much to help you?"

"Yes, but things are different with Da Mo. He's not like other monks."

"Don't compare yourself to him."

"I'm not," Ko said, struggling to keep up with her, "but his Way is not conventional, that's what I was trying to tell you."

"If it's unconventional, then why do you object if a woman follows it?"

"I was only trying to help," Ko said, throwing his hands up in defeat.

"Help someone else," she snapped, and increased her stride to get away from him and catch up with Da Mo.

The sun dipped low on the broad horizon. They made camp in a clearing and gathered around the fire. Ko cooked rice and handed her a bowl. She accepted without a word. The air had turned cool and stars appeared above them. It was the first time she had ever spent the night in the open, beneath the vastness of the night sky. The familiar walls and sloping ceiling of her lop-sided room in the palace seemed far away and she drew her blanket more tightly around her shoulders.

Da Mo made tea with sugar and spices and held out a cup to her. She did not know what to do.

"You wish me to add something to it?" she asked uncertainly.

"No, it is for you."

Unused to being served by a master, she took the tea gratefully. It was horribly sweet but she sipped it dutifully, relishing the warmth of the frothing liquid that spread from her core to her limbs and revived her senses.

"I have been thinking about the safest way to reach Shaolin," Da Mo said abruptly. "We must split up."

"Why?" Liang asked in dismay.

"If there are assassins on the road to Loyang, they will be looking for two monks," he explained, "one Indian and one Chinese. So we will change things. You and Ko will travel together. A young Chinese couple on the road will not arouse suspicion. There is a ferry crossing half a day from here. Take it and make your way to Loyang. I will find a different way across the river and take a different road. We will meet in Shaolin."

"But won't we all be safer together?" Ko asked.

"Being together is not as good as being invisible."

"How will we be invisible?" she asked.

"You of all people should know that," Da Mo answered.

Liang looked to Ko for an explanation.

"People only see what they think they see," he said, "a soldier, a monk, a maid." He turned to her and smiled, but she stared into the flames without catching his eye.

When the fire finally began to splutter and die, she laid her bedding a modest distance from the men and settled down to sleep. The night was not cold, but she shivered beneath her blanket and sleep would not come. She looked at the silver moon so clear above her against the blackness and thought of Professor Lin's poem. It was still so far from her grasp. She was free from her life of bondage, but freedom came hand-in-hand with uncertainty. She closed her eyes and willed sleep to come, without success.

Ferry Across The Yangtze

The ancient junk came toward the quayside where Ko and Liang waited. It had been stripped down to a bare deck to allow more cargo aboard and sat perilously low in the water. Two enormous ox carts had been loaded onto the same side and the boat listed badly as it approached the shore. It steered haphazardly into the quayside and before the mooring had been secured, people jumped off and forced their way through the crowds waiting to get on.

Ko and Liang clambered aboard and the ferry quickly filled with farmer's carts and barrows, workers bringing supply wagons and tools, mules laden with bags and boxes. An army sergeant shouted at his troops to get aboard. A party of novice monks was ushered on by a senior monk, who was forced to pay the ferryman like everyone else. No one traveled free across the Yangtze.

When the last of the wagons was aboard, its rear wheels teetering on the edge of the deck, its back hanging out over the brown water, a crewman hammered a wedge behind one of the wheels to secure it and slipped the moorings. The ferry drifted from the quay and soon they had left behind the quiet waters of the banks and entered the midstream current.

Near the end of its journey across China, the Yangtze was a vast expanse of water, a brown sea with waves. Ko looked out over the water, wondering whether this really was the same river whose savage rapids had pummeled them through the gorges a thousand li to the west. Liang came and stood beside him, watching the waves rolling on toward the eastern ocean.

"They say the Long River divides the world in two," she said quietly.

"I believe it," Ko said.

"I have seen it many times, but never crossed it."

"I've had my fill of this river."

"You have traveled on it?"

"Yes, with Master Da Mo. We were on it through Yunnan and Sichuan."

"You have seen the gorges?"

"Yes."

"Were they as beautiful as the poets describe?"

"I suppose they were. I didn't notice at the time."

"How could you not notice? They say that heaven and earth meet in the gorges."

"The poets should try swimming in Tiger Leaping Gorge before they compare it to heaven," Ko laughed.

"You swam in Tiger Leaping Gorge!"

"Not by choice."

"Tell me," she urged, her eyes sparkling with excitement.

"I will, but keep your voice down," he said, checking around to make sure they could not be overheard.

"Sorry," she whispered, coming closer and turning her ear to him. Ko looked at the line of her neck, the way her hair fell over her ear, and fought the desire to run his fingers over her immaculate skin.

He told her how they had been set upon by bandits and how they had escaped by jumping into the gorge, and how they had paddled a sampan through water so fierce that it seemed their little boat was being attacked by an angry dragon.

"Maybe it was a different river," she said, looking out over the mellow brown waves that rolled away from the ferry.

"It is the same river," he assured her.

The waves subsided and the ferry entered the calm waters by the opposite shore. They disembarked and squeezed through the waiting crowds at the quayside. A small local road led them through the township that had sprung up around the ferry crossing and they followed it for several li until they reached the main highway to Loyang. The road cut through a flat area of rice paddies and fields of wheat and barley. When they entered the first area of woodland, they scrambled behind a thicket and waited in silence to make sure no one was following them.

A farmer went by with two mules. An ox cart passed by a few minutes later. The novice monks from the ferry went by with their master, and then the road was quiet for a long time. They were about to leave their hiding place when an old woman appeared under an enormous bundle of sticks. She moved so slowly that at times she appeared not to be moving at all. They waited what seemed like an age for her to pass, not wanting to arouse suspicion by appearing suddenly from the bushes. As she passed by, Ko drew Liang close and put his lips to her ear.

"I think we have found our assassin," he whispered.

Liang struggled to stifle a giggle. They waited until the old woman was out of sight and the road was empty in both directions before clambering out of the undergrowth.

It did not take long for them to catch up with the old woman.

"A good monk would carry her burden," Liang said.

"We're in a hurry," Ko answered.

Liang shook her head in disapproval.

He ignored the old woman as they passed her and continued for several minutes, then reluctantly returned to take her bundle from her. The old woman walked no faster without her sticks and Ko was forced to stop and wait every few minutes, glaring at Liang as he did.

It was evening before the old woman finally took her sticks back and turned off the road without a word of thanks. They continued into the dusk until they found a quiet place by a brook to camp for the night. Liang sat down on a fallen tree and removed her shoes. Ko noticed her feet were blistered and swollen.

"Put your feet in the cold water," he suggested. "It will help."

She hobbled to the brook and sat on a rock, resting her feet in the bubbling water.

Ko lit a fire, then handed her a cloth to dry her feet. "I have some ointment if you want it."

"I don't need it, thank you," she said.

"Da Mo made it for me when we first began walking. My feet were in a bad way. You'll be surprised how good it is."

She regarded him warily.

"Come," he said patiently, kneeling beside her and holding out his hand. She put her foot in his hand and he placed it in his lap. It was white and slender, the skin soft and perfect except for the angry sores on her heel and sole. He scooped a little ointment onto his finger and massaged it into the sores and around her entire foot, kneading the tired muscles until he felt her foot loosen and relax.

"You have blisters. We need to remove the broken skin. It might hurt a little. Try not to flinch."

He took the knife from his waistband and cut away the blistered skin carefully. She watched him at work, ignoring the pain, and wondering instead what to make of Da Mo's disciple. His hands were dry and warm, his touch surprisingly gentle. She noticed the smooth bulge of muscle on his forearms that tapered to narrow wrists. She examined the brown neck and strong jawline. He was handsome, there was no denying it, and he knew it, too.

"I hope you're not expecting anything in return?" she said coolly.

"What are you suggesting, Sister Liang?" he said, turning indignantly.

"You know what I mean."

"No I don't. Please tell me."

"Sometimes you are very fresh for a monk."

Ko was about to protest but could not find the right words. She laughed despite herself as he turned away, tight-lipped, to continue tending her foot.

Later they ate sparingly from their rations. As darkness descended, Ko put out the fire and prepared a bed for himself on the soft ground. Liang did the same, placing her blanket on the other side of the fire embers and well away from his. They lay in silence, but despite her exhaustion, Liang could not sleep. She was too excited, too afraid, and too cold.

"It's so cold," she said, her teeth chattering. "I can't stop shivering."

"Sometimes, when Da Mo and I were in the mountains, it was terribly cold, much worse than this."

"What did you do?"

"You won't like it."

"Tell me."

"Master Da Mo and I would sleep together—back to back, you understand."

Liang did not answer.

"It's a lot warmer with two bodies together," he said.

Still there was no reply.

"And two blankets to cover you."

She said nothing.

"But there was also a drawback," he continued lightly, "Da

Mo did snore, quite loudly. I hope you don't snore, Sister Liang. If you do, I'll have to withdraw my offer."

She rose with a sigh and laid her bedding next to his, then threw her blanket over him and crawled in beside him. She turned her back, careful not to touch him. Slowly, he moved until his back touched hers. She felt the extra warmth immediately and did not move away.

"There's something digging into me," she complained.

Ko removed the knife from his waistband, and put it beneath the knapsack that he used as a pillow. Soon after, he felt her relax and heard her breathing deepen. She was asleep. It was good. She needed to rest.

Later in the night he turned over and put his arm over her sleeping form. She sighed but did not wake. He had never slept with a woman like this before and found it strangely exciting.

"There's still something digging into me," she grumbled, sleepily.

"Sorry," he murmured, "I can't do anything about that."

The River Spirit

The river had been good to the fisherman. His basket was so full that the last of the fish jumped out and flapped about in the bottom of his canoe. He returned it to the basket, but it flipped out once again. The little fish was so determined to be alive that he threw it back into the river. It was good to keep the river happy. An angry river was a terrible thing.

The sun was setting over the plains and the sky had turned red and grey. A storm was gathering in the west, still several hours away, but it was time to go home.

He had only gone a short distance upriver when a giant sturgeon came close to the boat and circled lazily near the surface. It was far too big to catch, and besides, the sturgeon was a river spirit. It would bring bad luck to kill it.

The fish swam upriver, leading him home, and he followed it. When it swam too far ahead it stopped and circled, as if waiting for him, and he paddled hard to keep up. Soon his village came into view through the trees and he made for the jetty. The great fish darted toward the riverbank, leaving a fleck of white foam on the surface. He lost sight of it and searched the murky waters in vain. All at once a gnarled shape on the riverbank caught his eye. It was a giant, etched black against the angry sky.

The giant held out his hand, drawing him in. He found himself gazing into fierce black eyes, hardly human. He could not resist. His canoe touched the shore and the stranger stepped aboard without a sound.

The fisherman paddled to the opposite bank while the spirit stood, gazing at the far shore, his weight causing the boat to sit low in the water. In the middle of the river, larger waves began to rock the tiny craft, but the spirit did not move until they had reached the opposite bank. Then it stepped out and disappeared into the night without a word.

The lights of his village twinkled in the dusk, beckoning the fisherman home. He turned and paddled toward their welcoming glow. He was almost at the jetty when the sturgeon reappeared and circled once around him. He had obeyed the river's wishes and it had allowed him to return home safely, as it had so many times before.

By the time he reached the jetty, the wind had picked up. The waves were already breaking hard against the old wooden beams. He lifted his boat from the water and carried it to a sheltered spot in a thicket of bamboo where he lashed it down firmly against the coming storm. When the boat was secure, he felt spots of warm rain on his face, and as he lifted his basket of fish onto his shoulder, the first crackles of thunder rumbled in the distance.

森林

Part 5
FOREST

The Novice Gate

Novice Lao left the temple from the side gate. It was the same gate he had used to enter the temple two years earlier, and as he passed through it he thought back to that day.

He had come to Shaolin with his mother and father on a misty morning in early autumn and they had waited by the side gate, known as the Novice Gate, as was the custom. They had brought blankets and provisions, since it was not uncommon to wait several days for an audience with one of the senior monks.

"Patience and determination are treasured in Shaolin," his mother had told him as they waited on the mountainside.

On the third day, an elderly monk had appeared and spoken with his father. When the monk had left, his father had knelt beside him and told him they were leaving. He was to remain and continue to wait alone. If he showed patience, determination, and good manners, he would be allowed to enter the temple and become a monk.

"But when will that be?" he had asked, holding back the tears.

"Soon," his father had smiled.

"How soon?"

His father had hugged him briefly and turned away. His mother had knelt before him and held him, stroking his hair. He had whispered to her, so his father would not hear, begging her not to leave him.

"You will get food and shelter and a wonderful education at the monastery," she had said through her own tears, "a better life than you could ever have in the village. You are a clever boy Lao, and I know you will do well here."

"But I don't want to be a monk," he had sobbed quietly.

"You will love it here very soon, I promise. Please try. It will make me very happy if you turn out to be a fine young monk."

He had held her tight, wanting to stay with her, with his father, wanting to go home with them.

"Speak politely to the master," she had whispered, "and to all the other monks. Study hard and be humble. You will be allowed to come and visit us very soon."

"Is father angry with me?"

"No, he is sad. He will miss you very much. Please make him proud."

He had nodded through new tears, and she had held him, unable to let go, until his father had taken her by the arm and led her away.

Lao remembered how much he had wanted to run after them, but he had not. Instead, he had waited by the Novice Gate for another day and night, until the old monk had finally reappeared with food and water. The old monk had sat before him and shared out a little rice onto two plates. He had waited for the old monk to eat first, as his parents had instructed. Good manners were highly prized in Shaolin.

"What is your name, young man?" the old monk asked at last.

"Lao, Master."

"Lao? A fine name. The name of a great sage. Did you know that?"

"Yes, Lao Tzu, Master."

"And what do you know of Lao Tzu?"

"He wrote about The Way, Master."

"He did, but his Way is different to our Way. He was a Taoist and we are Buddhists. We follow a different path. Do you know the difference, young man?"

Lao knew his future depended on his answer. If the master did not like his response, he would be sent home. Part of him would be glad to go, but part of him would be ashamed, and he had no wish to disappoint his parents.

"I don't know Master," he answered honestly.

The master looked away, studying the trees. He sensed the old man's disappointment.

"Then why did you come to Shaolin, Lao? Do you believe wisdom can be found here, there, and everywhere?"

"It was my parents' choice, Master."

"You blame your parents for your own ignorance?"

"No, Master," he said quickly.

"Perhaps they should have taken you to a Taoist temple," the old monk said, "since it makes no difference to you."

He did not know what to say. He felt his chances of entering the temple slipping away. The master watched him expectantly. He looked at the ground helplessly. "What do you say, Lao?" the old monk prompted.

He felt the master toying with him, able to defeat him with any argument he might put forward. Yet since he was already defeated, it no longer mattered.

"Wisdom is wisdom, how can there be two different Ways?"

He looked into the old man's eyes defiantly.

"There is a difference," the master said sternly, "a very big difference."

Lao knew he had failed and looked at the ground in despair, tears pricking at his eyes.

"However," the master continued lightly, "the difference is in the path, and not the final destination."

Lao glanced up and saw the faintest smile playing on the old man's lips.

"The destination, as you rightly say, is the same."

Lao stared dumbly at the old master.

"Now please, have some more rice," the master said, serving another small portion into a bowl for him. "You must be hungry."

"Thank you," Lao said, accepting the bowl with both hands. He waited until the master had eaten his first mouthful before taking a small amount, and chewing slowly, determined not to appear greedy, despite his raging hunger.

The master had waited quietly while he ate and when he had

finished his bowl, the old man encouraged him to have more. Too hungry to refuse, he ate the second bowl of rice, still chewing slowly. Again the old monk waited patiently until he had finished, then rose and walked to the Novice Gate without another word.

Lao had noticed the cups and plates left on the ground and called out after him. "Master, the cups and plates ..."

"Please take them to the kitchen," the master had said as he disappeared through the gate. He had collected the cups and plates and hurried after him. Once through the gate he looked around but the master was nowhere to be seen. He had searched in dismay.

A group of young monks crossed the courtyard far away, but took no notice of him. He had turned around, wondering where to go. Finally, he had opened the nearest door and found himself in a hall full of women. He had entered a nunnery, and blushed crimson. Amid suppressed giggles, one of the nuns had told him where he could find the kitchens and told him to ask for Brother Tan. He had followed her directions and come to the kitchens, where he found a young man cleaning pots.

"Excuse me, I'm looking for Master Tan."

The monk had taken the cups and plates from him with a sigh.

"I'm Tan, and there's no need to call me "master." Brother is fine. You must be Lao?"

Lao was astonished.

"Don't look so surprised, Lao. Master Chui was here a moment ago. He told me to expect you." Brother Tan had handed him a scrubbing brush. "Your education starts here. Oh, and by the way, welcome to Shaolin."

Lao had worked hard, washing hundreds of cups and plates each day. Soon he was helping to prepare food, collecting vegetables from the garden and bringing rice from the storeroom. He chopped the vegetables and washed the rice, while Tan stood over the giant pots that bubbled on the stove. He had worked tirelessly and without complaint. Soon Brother Tan had begun to trust him with more important tasks, like delivering tea to the senior monks, or taking broth to those who were old or sick.

One day, Tan had taken him onto the mountainside and showed him the places where the herbs and grasses grew in the forest, explaining how each was used for cooking or medicine. Together they had filled their basket with new supplies. A few weeks later, Tan had sent him out alone and Lao had returned with a full basket. When Tan inspected it, he found Lao had not missed a single thing, and since then, it had become his regular task.

At first Lao had felt lonely wandering in the wilderness on his own, but soon he learned to enjoy the tranquil beauty of Song Shan. He came to know the animals that lived there, the deer, the wild pigs, the ducks, and the geese. He knew the flowers, the trees and bushes, and how they changed with the seasons. He stopped dreaming of returning home, though he thought about his parents often and looked forward to their visits. He grew to love his life at the monastery, just as his mother had promised.

On this morning, he was wandering high on the wooded slopes, collecting herbs and roots that even Tan did not know about. Lao knew every path, every animal trail, every cave and den. Familiar trees and bushes pointed the way like signposts. He was never lost. The rocks had the gnarled faces of old men and women and they kept him company as he went. High above Shaolin, he had discovered a cave that offered a cool resting place from the midday heat.

He was about to enter the cave and take a sip from his flask of water when he noticed that an unfamiliar rock had appeared inside. He waited for his eyes to adjust to the gloom and saw it was not a rock but a man, sitting, staring at the cave wall. His posture was that of a monk in meditation—his back straight and knees braced on the floor—but that was where the resemblance ended. This man was like no monk Lao had ever seen, and he was certainly not from Shaolin. His skin was black, his nose long and hooked. His hair fell in wild curls.

Lao guessed he was Indian, like the former grandmaster of Shaolin Master Batuo, who had died shortly after Lao joined the monastery. Batuo had had the same dark skin and curious features, but Batuo had been a small, portly man with a gentle smile. This stranger's face was fierce, even in meditation, and Lao was not entirely sure it wasn't a bodhisattva.

He decided to leave him to his contemplation and returned to the temple, telling no one about the dark monk in the cave. However, by evening his curiosity got the better of him and he returned. The stranger was still in the cave, seated like a rock, gazing at the wall, and Lao was convinced he had not moved a muscle since the morning. This time he summoned his courage and called out to the stranger, "Sir, I apologize if I disturb your meditation, but there is food and shelter in the monastery nearby, if you need it."

The stranger did not reply. Lao returned to the monastery. He had done his best.

As he lay in his bed at night, he could not get the vision out of his mind. Just before he fell asleep, a new thought struck him. Perhaps Buddha had appeared to him in the cave? He had seen paintings of Buddha, a dark man with a long nose, just like the stranger in the cave! He wondered whether to inform Brother Tan or Master Chui that Buddha had arrived on Song Shan. They would not believe him, and somehow he knew that if he took them up to the cave, Buddha would not be there. He decided to check on him again in the morning. He would bring an offering of food and if Buddha ate it, then he would be real and he would tell someone. With this decided, he fell into a satisfied sleep.

The Young Forest

After traveling together for many days, Ko and Liang had fallen into an easy routine, speaking occasionally or walking in comfortable silence, collecting firewood, cooking, and sleeping side by side at night.

But now, as they turned off the main road to Loyang and followed the path among the saplings of Song Shan, they were both gripped by a nervous excitement, and the unspoken fear that Da Mo might not meet them at the Shaolin Temple. Liang was also filled with trepidation at the prospect of a new life that she knew so little about.

"Tell me what you know of The Way," she asked, hoping to ease the mounting tension.

"It leads to a place called nirvana," Ko answered, "where the only feeling is bliss."

"Where is this place?"

"Da Mo says it is in the mind."

"Have you been there?"

"I can't find it," he answered truthfully, "although I've searched many times."

"Master Da Mo can find it?" she asked.

"Yes, he visits it often."

"Why doesn't he stay there?"

"I asked him the same thing," Ko said with a smile, happy that he was not the only one who struggled to understand, "and he told me the world is suffering and needs his help."

"How noble," she said, her voice filled with admiration, "to give up nirvana to save others from suffering."

"I never thought of it like that," Ko laughed. "It must be annoying, not being able to enjoy your bliss in peace."

Liang did not laugh.

"Does he really think he can save the world from suffering?" she asked seriously.

"Not the world," Ko said. "He told me once that he would be happy to save even one person."

"Did he mean you?"

"Maybe, but I don't think I'll ever reach nirvana."

"Why not?"

"Da Mo says it can only be found when I stop seeking it."

"How can you find something without looking for it?"

"Exactly!" Ko said, clapping his hands in delight, "That's what I said too."

"What do you think the monks of Shaolin will make of his methods?"

"They will do as they are told," Ko shrugged.

"You think so?" she asked. "I have yet to meet a monk who is interested in fighting."

"Da Mo says that what is good for a warrior is also good for a monk."

"We will see," she said doubtfully.

But by the time they had reached a clearing and stopped for water, she had changed her mind and stood before Ko eagerly.

"I think I can still remember what you taught me in the palace gardens," she smiled, "so maybe we can practice together?"

"I should not teach you," Ko replied hesitantly.

"You won't be teaching me," she assured him. "We will just be practicing what I already know."

Ko considered her request. It would be good to practice with someone other than Da Mo. He was tired of getting hurt every time he trained. He bowed ceremoniously to Liang, who returned his bow with equal dignity.

"Are you sure you can remember what to do?" he asked.

She answered by lunging forward and striking at his face. He had not expected her to attack so fiercely and her fist smashed his chin before he could parry. He stumbled backward, stunned. She rushed forward to apologize, but before she could say a word he had swept her feet from under her. She flew high into the air and landed heavily on the ground, knocking the air out of her.

Now they were even, he bent down to help her up and her foot lashed out and hit him in the face. She tried to kick him a second time but he trapped her leg and twisted her ankle until she was forced over onto her front. He stepped over her and began to sink his weight into a painful leg-lock, but she twisted like a snake and he lost his grip. Still on the ground, she kicked at his groin, then spun around and struck his face with clawed fingers.

He leapt out of range and she sprung to her feet, breathing heavily.

"Relax a little," he said between breaths. "We're only playing, not fighting."

She glared at him, her blood up, but she knew he was right. She could not go on like this for much longer; she was already exhausted. He stepped forward and struck slowly. She parried his hand and caught his arm, attempting a sweep. Ko's balance was not broken, and he remained standing.

"Pull my arm as you sweep," he advised. She ignored him and kicked the back of his knee instead. His leg collapsed and his knee twisted painfully as he went down.

"Perhaps this is not such a good idea," he said, tight-lipped. She ignored him and waited until he got up, her fists raised. He considered calling a halt to the practice, but he knew she would be insulted if he did.

He lunged forward instead. She parried his punch and moved aside. This time she gripped his shoulder and pulled him off balance, just as he had suggested. He felt his leg being swept. As he landed on his back, her foot slammed into his stomach. She had not controlled her kick and he rolled onto his knees and elbows, fighting for breath.

She stood aside, allowing him to get to his feet. He felt his anger rising uncontrollably, and kicked hard to her stomach. She parried and struck. He checked her punch and slammed his fist into her chest. She moved behind him, her hand snaking around his neck. He took it and leaned forward, twisting to throw her. She flipped in the air and landed on her feet. Keeping her wrist, he pulled her forward and struck out with his forearm. It caught her on the neck and dazed her. He took her hand behind her back and wrapped it up high, hoping for a shoulder lock, but she was too supple. The lock did not hold. She threw herself into a forward roll to escape and landed back on her feet.

Ko was momentarily stunned by her agility. It was as if she had trained for many years already. He wondered how a simple palace maid could know so much about fighting. Her foot lashed out toward his groin. He blocked with his knee just in time. It caught her hard on the shin. She hid the pain well, but it had hurt her badly. She kicked again, this time to his stomach. His hand came down to parry. Her kick switched in mid-flight and landed on his jaw. Clusters of white light popped in the blackness. His legs buckled under him.

She watched, waiting for him to fall. In an instant he recovered enough to grab her arm and pull her onto a roundhouse kick. His shin slammed hard into her ribs. This time she gasped in pain. Still gripping her arm, he smashed a hard punch into her solar plexus. She doubled over, unable to draw breath, feeling herself choking. She fought the panic, and forced herself upright, fighting for air. He kicked high into the side of her head, then swept her legs from under her and dumped her hard on her back.

He stood over her and watched as she writhed on the ground, her eyes rolling in her head. Finally, her stomach moved and she took in great gulps of air. She glared up at him, her eyes filled with hatred.

He went to get a drink of water from his pack. There would be no more pleasant discussions about nirvana when they continued on the road. It was going to be a long, silent day.

Da Mo Enters Shaolin

Inside the cave, Buddha had still not moved a muscle. Lao left rice and tea by the entrance and hurried back to the temple before he was missed.

When he returned in the afternoon, the food and drink had been consumed. The cup and plate had been cleaned and left outside the cave, but the stranger was still gazing motionless at the wall. Lao collected up the utensils and set off happily down the slope. The real Buddha did not eat rice and drink tea. It was just a man, after all.

He wondered whether to tell Brother Tan of the monk or report the matter directly to Master Chui when he noticed two more strangers on the mountain. The woman beckoned to him.

"Young man, we are seeking the Shaolin Monastery."

"It's nearby," he answered, "I will take you, if you wish."

"Thank you," she said. "I am Liang, and this is Brother Ko. We are also looking for our master. His name is Da Mo. He may be here already?"

"I don't know his name," Lao answered, "but there is a stranger in a nearby cave who I have not seen before and I think he is a monk."

"He is not Chinese?" she asked.

"No," Lao said.

"Covered in hair, terribly ugly?" Ko said with a grin.

Lao did not know what to say.

"I think you have met Master Da Mo," Liang said gently. "He is from India."

"I have not met him," Lao corrected her. "He has been meditating very deeply for two days. But if you follow me, I will show you where he is."

As they approached the mouth of the cave, Lao was astonished to see the dark monk emerge with a beaming smile. Standing up, he was even taller than Lao had imagined, taller than any man he had ever seen. The eyes that had gazed at the cave wall so fiercely now sparkled with delight at the sight of his disciples, and he embraced them warmly. Lao waited as they spoke of their journeys to Song Shan, then the dark monk turned to him.

"Thank-you for the food and tea, Novice Lao. We will make a fine monk of you one day, I'm sure, though I can't say the same for your chef. What is his name?"

"Brother Tan," Lao said quietly.

"His food is disgusting. I think we'd better go and meet with Brother Tan without delay," Da Mo grinned.

Lao led them down the slope, puzzling to himself. He did not recall mentioning his name to Master Da Mo at any time, and Liang and Ko had not introduced him. He was still wondering uncomfortably what Master Chui and Brother Tan would make of the Indian when the red and gold roof of Shaolin appeared between the saplings. The tiles gleamed bright in the afternoon sun.

"It's beautiful," Liang whispered excitedly.

"Do you know when it was built, Lao?" Da Mo asked.

"A long time ago," he answered, "twenty years ago, I think."

"Then it is quite new," Da Mo said.

Lao blushed but then he felt the master's huge hand squeeze his shoulder gently. It was highly unusual for a senior monk to touch a novice, but Lao felt himself drawn to the warmth of the stranger.

"And tell me," Da Mo continued, "who is in charge of the monastery?"

"Master Chui," he answered.

"Then I would also like to speak with Master Chui."

"I will request an audience at once," he promised.

He led them past the round windows of the gatehouse and through the main gate that was reserved for important visitors.

Inside the temple's ornamental garden, Da Mo stopped to admire the fish pond. Giant carp darted in the crystal water in flashes of gold, silver, and red. They continued, passing beneath the bell tower and entering the courtyard. Four gnarled trees grew from the hard earth and giant stones had been placed in a pleasing array and painted with calligraphy. Finally, they came to the entrance of the main hall, guarded by two fierce stone lions. Here Lao asked them to wait while he went to speak to Master Chui.

It had been a long time since Lao's first meeting with Master Chui by the Novice Gate. Master Chui had become his teacher, instructing him in reading, writing, and Sanskrit, and Lao had quickly grown to love their lessons together. But when Grandmaster Batuo had fallen ill, Master Chui had taken over his duties in running the temple. Another senior monk had become Lao's teacher. Master Hui was both learned and thorough, but he lacked Master Chui's infectious enthusiasm and Lao missed their hours spent together.

Now he found Master Chui seated at his desk with paperwork piled up before him. It was not the scriptures that Master Chui enjoyed translating so painstakingly, but rather lists of supplies and columns of figures. The task of running the temple had taken its toll on the old master. His cheeks had grown hollow, his skin sallow, his eyes lacked the liveliness that Lao had enjoyed during their lessons.

"Lao, it is good to see you," Master Chui said. "You look concerned."

"There is a visitor wishing to speak with you, Master," he said, "his name is Master Da Mo."

"Da Mo? What sort of name is this?"

"He is from India. There are two disciples with him."

"There are no Indian monks around here," Master Chui sighed, "I think you must be mistaken. And sadly I do not have time for an audience with every stranger who visits Shaolin. Perhaps I might find time to meet with him tomorrow. Please pass on my regrets and ensure he is shown the customary hospitality."

Master Chui returned to his paperwork, but Lao remained where he was.

"Is there something else?" Chui asked patiently.

"I believe Master Da Mo is a very important man, Master."

Master Chui leaned forward. "What makes you say that, Lao?"

"His meditation is very deep."

"How do you know how deep his meditation is?" Chui demanded.

"I saw him. He gazed at a cave wall for two days and two nights without blinking," Lao answered seriously.

Master Chui stared at him for a moment, and Lao wondered if he'd made the master angry. Then Chui sighed and rubbed his eyes.

"Very well, Lao. Since you appear to insist, I will see him. But first, please show him around the temple and take him to the guest quarters and offer him refreshments. I'll see this Master Da Mo as soon as these affairs are in order. Would that be acceptable to you?"

"Thank you Master," Lao smiled, feeling a rush of warmth for his old master.

"Good, now tell me how your studies are going. Have you finished the text I gave you, the one written by your namesake?"

"Not yet, Master. It is hard to understand. I have to read each page several times."

"You must persevere, Lao. You wrote a book of great wisdom in a previous life. I'm sure it will come back to you in due course."

"I will," Lao promised, pleased to see the twinkle had returned to his master's eye, if only for a moment.

Lao led the newcomers on a tour of the temple that began in

the busy translation hall. Rows of monks and nuns sat hunched over scrolls and manuscripts, their faces pale in the weak lamplight. He continued through an empty ceremonial hall decorated with murals of The Buddha's life to the study rooms around the edge of the courtyard where monks were free to read and practice calligraphy. When they came to the meditation hall, they found a handful of monks seated in meditation. The incense had only just begun to burn, but already several were slumped over on their cushions. Ko wondered uneasily what Da Mo would do, but Da Mo simply nodded to Lao to continue the tour and Lao led them on.

They came to a building raised on pillars and Lao went inside, emerging a short time later with an elderly nun, who waited for her eyes to adjust to the light before scrutinizing the strangers before her.

"Well Lao," she began, her head shaking as she spoke, as if finding each word an effort, "before I show our guests inside, let me ask them a question. Why do they think this building has been placed on pillars?"

Ko looked to Da Mo and Liang to see if one of them would answer, but both stared resolutely at him. "To protect it from flooding?" he ventured.

"Precisely," she said, making her way slowly down the steps until she was eye to eye with him. "But what are we protecting that is so valuable?"

"A sacred relic?" he suggested.

"No," she scoffed, "something far more valuable than an old piece of bone. Perhaps the girl can guess?" she said, turning to Liang.

"Historical artifacts?"

"If you mean little golden statues of The Buddha, then the answer is no."

Neither Ko nor Liang dared venture another guess, so the old woman turned her watery eye to Da Mo.

"Perhaps the barbarian will enlighten you?"

"Come now, Grandmother," Da Mo said lightly "hurry up and show us your books."

She glared at Da Mo. He smiled and took her arm to help her back up the steps.

"You are very rude, even for a barbarian," she muttered as they entered the dim rooms of the library and breathed in the heavy air of ancient paper, lamp oil, and dust.

"Tell me how an old woman like you can see well enough to keep a library?" Da Mo said, ignoring the barb.

"Simple, I am the only person in the whole of Shaolin who knows where everything is filed."

"Ah, then you wield great power," he said knowingly.

"They give me extra oil for lamps, though I don't even need it," she chuckled. "Now tell me, have you come from Magadha?"

"Yes, I was at Nalanda."

"Ah, Nalanda … you must tell me all about it in due course. But first, tell me your name."

"My name is Bodhidharma, but my disciples call me Da Mo."

"Bodhidharma? Quite a mouthful for Chinese tongues. My name is Fan. Nice and simple. Why do you Indians always have such long names, almost an entire sentence for one name? We Chinese are much more pragmatic, as you will discover. Though Da Mo is a good compromise, I suppose."

"I have grown used to it," he said.

"Good." She said patting his hand like an old friend. "We have waited quite some time for you to appear, Master Da Mo. What took you so long?"

He was about to reply but she continued without waiting. "Have you met Master Chui yet?"

"Not yet."

"Chui is a fine master," she whispered, "but not cut out to run a temple. Be patient with him. Now please light a lamp so I can show you the treasures we hold here." She handed him an oil lamp and turned to Ko and Liang.

"You were both right," she told them. "The library does indeed contain sacred relics and artifacts, for any monk who treasures wisdom. It contains books!"

Da Mo walked beside her with the lamp as she led them down a row of bookshelves. She stopped at the end of the row and took down a bundle of cloth. "We keep the most precious of them wrapped up, to protect them from the light, which causes the ink to fade. Some were written over a thousand years ago and you can still read them today. Is that not a miracle? This is how wisdom is passed down from the ancients. Imagine if you didn't know how to do the simplest things, to make fire, weave cloth, build a wheel for a cart ... would you be able to invent it yourself?" She stared at Ko, awaiting a response.

"I doubt it," he admitted reluctantly.

"In that case, it's good that we aren't relying on you. Someone has already done it for you! The wisdom of the Great Sages is passed down in the same way."

She unwrapped the most precious of her manuscripts with great reverence, revealing scrolls of Chinese philosophy and poetry, sutras from India, histories from Central Asia and Korea, and proceeded to read some of her favorite passages aloud. Liang was barely able to contain her excitement.

"May we come and see these pieces again?" she asked hopefully.

"Of course," Fan said, "that is why they are here. Most of the young monks only read what their masters tell them to read, but that is not the way to enlightenment. Come to the library whenever you wish. I will show you some beautiful writings."

"My reading is not good," Liang admitted.

"Then it will soon improve. I will help you, and in return you can help me keep the place tidy."

"That is something I can do," Liang said happily.

"And the boy?" asked Fan, pointing to Ko.

"He will learn too," Liang answered for him.

"They will both learn," Da Mo said with a smile. "In fact, I think we will all spend some time in the library."

Masters Meet

Lao introduced Master Chui to Master Da Mo and stood still, waiting to see if he could be of any further assistance.

"Thank you, Lao," Master Chui said with a nod and a smile. Lao bowed to the two masters in turn and hurried from the room, closing the door silently behind him.

"Welcome to Shaolin, Master Da Mo," Master Chui said, his smile still fixed.

"Thank you," Da Mo replied, "I am most grateful that you have agreed to meet with me at such short notice."

Chui waited for him to say more, but Da Mo was silent. "You are far from home," Chui said at last. "Have you been traveling around China?"

"I have been until now," Da Mo said, leaning forward and shifting in his seat. "Please forgive me Master Chui, this will come as something of a surprise to you, but I have come here at the request of the imperial palace."

"From Grandmaster Tzu?

"From the emperor himself."

"The emperor?" Chui said, taken aback.

"Yes," Da Mo said, allowing Chui a few moments to collect himself before continuing, "I believe the former grandmaster of Shaolin passed away recently, a Master Batuo?"

"That is correct," Chui answered, "you are acquainted with him?"

"Not personally, but I offer my condolences."

"Thank you. It has been a time of great sadness for everyone. Master Batuo was my teacher and mentor for many years. We are awaiting word from the palace on the appointment of his replacement."

"That is why I am here," Da Mo said gently.

"You bring word?"

"I have been invited to take that position," Da Mo said.

Master Chui's eyes widened. "I have received no official notice of this."

"We were forced to travel before a messenger could be sent, but I carry an imperial decree with me," Da Mo said, handing the paper to Chui.

"This is all highly irregular," Chui said, scanning the paper quickly and then putting it aside on his desk. "Normally a messenger would arrive with the decree in advance."

"We were told of danger on the journey," Da Mo explained, "and were forced to leave ahead of schedule for safety's sake. However, an official messenger will arrive independently in a few days time."

Master Chui said nothing for a long time, and Da Mo waited patiently for him to speak.

"Novice Lao says you are from India," Chui continued.

"Yes, I was born in Pallava," Da Mo smiled.

"A kingdom in the South East of India," Chui said.

"Indeed, though few in China have ever heard of it," Da Mo said.

"I am a keen student of The Buddha's history and homeland," Chui said modestly. "You studied in Pallava?"

"I did," Da Mo said.

"Then perhaps you can refresh my memory. There is a famous master in Pallava, his name escapes me..."

"Perhaps you are thinking of Master Prajnatara," Da Mo said with fond remembrance.

"Prajnatara, yes, that was it!"

"Prajnatara was my master. It was he who ordained me and sent me to China." Da Mo felt a pang of regret that the little master could not see how far he had come. "It seems like a long time ago now," he said half to himself.

"I imagine it was," Chui said.

"You are very well informed about India, Master Chui. Have you been there yourself?"

"Sadly no, though I have always dreamed of visiting the Western Heaven. You know Magadha, I presume?"

Da Mo nodded. "I made a pilgrimage to the holy sites and stayed at Nalanda before coming here."

"I have heard that the library of Nalanda is the size of an entire monastery and contains over a million scrolls?"

"It's true, the library is immense."

"I have heard they need ladders to reach the scrolls on the highest shelves," Master Chui said, his eyes shining with excitement. Da Mo was reminded of someone he once knew and tears pricked his eyes. He could not speak for a moment.

"Something is the matter, Master Da Mo?" Chui asked.

"Nothing of great importance," Da Mo said. "I was visited suddenly, by the ghost of a friend. Someone you would have enjoyed meeting."

"May I know who?" Chui asked, intrigued.

"A Chinese monk named Yin Chiang whom I met in Nalanda.

A learned scholar who translated many of the sutras. He was returning to China with me, but died on the journey, and his translations were lost on the way."

"A tragedy," Chui said earnestly.

"Yes."

"His translations would have been most useful here." Chui continued, "Shaolin is renowned as a place of study. We have dedicated ourselves to the translation of scriptures, to show the wisdom of The Way to the Chinese people."

"A noble sentiment," Da Mo said.

Master Chui detected the note of uncertainty in his voice. "Naturally, we engage in meditation too," he added quickly, "Novice Lao showed you the meditation hall, I presume?"

"He did, though I did not see any meditation," Da Mo smiled.

"Really? What did you see?" asked Chui, astonished.

"Just a few tired monks, sitting on cushions."

Chui stared at Da Mo, uncertain what to make of such frankness, then spread his hands and sighed. "Sometimes I think we demand too much of them. They spend so many hours translating the sacred texts."

"Exercise would make them more robust," Da Mo said.

"We have no time for such pursuits," Chui said stiffly.

"I have found that what strengthens the body also strengthens the mind," Da Mo persisted.

Master Chui pursed his lips in silent protest, and Da Mo decided it was not the time to press the matter.

"My own disciples have probably done too much exercise of late," he said instead. "They both need to attend to their studies. I was hoping you could find room for them in one of the classes?"

"Of course," Chui said graciously.

He rearranged the papers on his desk and studied Da Mo for a moment before continuing. "I will hold a meeting with the senior council this evening and inform them of your appointment. However, I must delay the announcement to the temple as a whole until we receive official confirmation. I hope you understand."

"Perfectly," Da Mo said.

"In the meantime, may I suggest we continue as normal, so as not to disturb the smooth running of the temple?

Da Mo nodded his agreement.

"Thank you," Chui said with a short bow, "we prize peace and tranquility most highly at Shaolin."

Liang sat forlornly in the bare cubicle that was her new home in Shaolin. After the freedom of the open road, she felt confined in the tiny room, living by strict rules, and wondered whether she had simply exchanged one life of servitude for another. She inspected the roll of bedding that was in the room and found it lice-ridden. Tossing it aside, she laid out the blanket that she had used on her journey. Despite the shelter of the four bare walls, she knew the night would be cold without Ko beside her.

There was a knock and Da Mo appeared at her door.

"Come!" he ordered.

She followed him through a maze of dark corridors. To her surprise, he seemed to know his way around the temple perfectly and they arrived at the meditation hall moments later. Inside, a handful of monks were seated in meditation. Several more were snoring softly.

Da Mo picked up a cushion and put it by his feet. "Sit," he said quietly. She sat cross-legged before him and placed her feet on her thighs, as she had seen him do. He leaned over her, his mouth by her ear, and pushed slowly on her knees until they touched the floor. "Brace yourself against the earth, like this. Then you can sit firm," he whispered. She felt his hands on her head, pulling her up gently, until her back was straight. The warmth of his touch felt good. His fingers cupped her chin and he lowered it. His hands moved to her shoulders where they rested heavily until she relaxed. "Good," he said finally. "Now your mind can be free."

Several monks had turned to watch the strange pair who had entered the meditation hall. "What are you looking at?" he asked, his deep voice shattering the silence of the quiet hall. More eyes opened and several slumbering monks woke in surprise.

"Is this how you meditate? Don't look at me, fix your gaze, and fix your minds!"

Another sleeping monk woke to find himself staring into the eyes of a fearsome giant and shrank back in fear.

"Wake up, boy," Da Mo ordered. "A monk with a strong mind is not seduced by sleep, nor distracted by comings and goings. He comes to the meditation hall to work, not rest. Are you such a monk?" The young man blinked beneath the stranger's piercing gaze, and turned his eyes to the floor.

Da Mo walked among them, stopping here and there to correct their postures and breathing, speaking softly to each of them, until he was satisfied that their meditation was being performed correctly. He returned to Liang and tapped her shoulder. She screwed her eyes shut, not wishing to anger him by opening them. He knelt behind her and put his mouth to her ear.

"You have a question."

She nodded, her eyes still shut.

"Then ask it."

She waited, unwilling to break the silence.

"Go ahead," he said gently, "there will be plenty of time for you to sit in silence later. Ask your questions now."

"What should I think about when I am meditating?"

"You want to think?"

"Isn't that the purpose of meditation?"

"No," he said curtly, "the purpose of sitting is to sit."

She resisted the urge to fidget on her cushion. "My mind can go where it will?" she asked.

"No, the opposite! It must be still. Clear of all thoughts. If one appears, wait for it to pass like a cloud. When all thoughts disappear, then your mind is pure, like The Buddha's."

He placed a cushion beside her and sat down. She measured her breaths with his and it made her feel calm and safe.

She realized that she had been thinking. She tried to banish all thoughts from her mind—to clear the sky of clouds. This too was a thought. She began to despair. And that too was a thought. The clouds were building up instead of going away. Only the wind could chase away clouds. But even that was a thought, which had to be chased away. And try as she might, she could think of nothing that could chase away the wind.

Monks Eat

The monks of Shaolin waited until Master Chui and the High Council had taken their seats before filing into the dining hall. Once all the monks were seated, four novices brought food from the kitchen, serving the most senior monks first, as was the custom.

When Da Mo appeared in the doorway, Master Chui beckoned to him to join him on the high table and introduced him to the members of the High Council: Master Tung, Master Pei, and Master Nieh.

"This is Master Da Mo, who I mentioned earlier," Chui told the council members. Each senior monk greeted Da Mo formally and Da Mo thanked them all for welcoming him to Shaolin. After this, he simply sat and a long silence descended on the table, which was finally broken by Master Tung.

"I understand you have already toured the monastery," he said cordially.

"Yes, Novice Lao showed us around. He was an excellent tour guide."

"And what do you make of our temple, Master Da Mo?" Master Tung enquired.

"It is beautiful, and the setting is delightful—more lovely than I ever imagined."

"The Shaolin temple is renowned for its beauty throughout China," Master Pei said.

"And more importantly, as a center of learning and education," Master Tung added.

"We place great importance on the translation of the sutras," Master Pei said, "so The Buddha's wisdom may be passed on to all."

"Apparently so," Da Mo said.

"Master Chui tells us you believe in the importance of exercise," Master Nieh said.

"I hope you will not expect us all to perform exercises," Master Tung laughed. "Some of us are not so young any more."

"Exercise benefits monks of all ages," Da Mo said. "In India, the practitioners of yoga often live to be one hundred and fifty years old.

"We favor exercise of the mind," Master Pei said.

"Master Da Mo contends that mind and body are one," Master Chui said. "An interesting premise, I'm sure you will all agree."

The masters exchanged glances and there was another brief silence. "On more specific matters," Master Tung began, "we heard there was a disturbance in the meditation hall this afternoon..."

"I may have disturbed a few sleeping monks," Da Mo chuckled.

"We operate a strict policy of silence in the meditation hall,"

Master Tung said, "perhaps you did not know."

"No one mentioned it while I was there," Da Mo said mischievously.

Master Tung stiffened. "Forgive us if we appear to take our traditions a little seriously, Master Da Mo. They have served us well for many years."

"Meditation is the tradition, not silence," Da Mo replied. "That is why it must be taught properly."

Novice Lao appeared at the table and began to serve Master Chui a bowl of thick grey broth. Chui raised his hand to stop the young monk. "Please, serve our guest, Master Da Mo, first," he ordered.

Lao placed the bowl before Da Mo, who raised the tepid broth to his nostrils and sniffed. His nose wrinkled in distaste. He took a spoonful of the broth and his mouth turned down in disapproval. The High Council watched in horror as Da Mo spat the gruel back into his bowl.

Lao did not know where to look. The monks seated nearby noticed what was happening, and soon a hush fell over the entire dining hall.

Master Pei whispered urgently to him, "Master Da Mo, you may not know it, but that is considered exceedingly rude in China."

"Serving food like this is considered rude in India," he said, loud enough for all to hear him. Then he turned to Lao, who was gazing red-faced at the floor. "Novice Lao, who is responsible for this food?"

"Brother Tan," he answered miserably.

"The same Brother Tan who made the rice-gruel that you brought to the cave?"

Lao nodded.

"He is in the kitchen now?"

"Yes."

"Then let us pay him a visit, with your permission Master Chui," Da Mo said, rising and heading into the kitchen, followed closely by Lao.

The monks at the head table were mortified and rose to intervene, but Master Chui stopped them with a wave of his hand. Certain disciplines had slipped at the temple of late, and the quality of the food was one of them. Master Chui had not had the heart to confront Brother Tan about it, but it seemed Da Mo had no such qualms. The masters returned to their seats with similar thoughts. Brother Tan was a terrible cook, but he was also a big monk with a bad temper. If the Indian wished to challenge him about his cooking, then who were they to stop him?

Da Mo discovered a tall young monk sitting on a stool in the kitchen, his forehead streaked with grease, his orange robe stained to a drab grey.

"Brother Tan," Da Mo said warmly, "I am delighted to meet you at last!"

"Can I help you?" Tan asked, looking from Da Mo to Lao, the beginning of a frown on his brow.

Da Mo ignored him and walked around the kitchen, examining the surfaces, cupboards, and shelves. A pot of gruel was still simmering on the stove and he stirred it with the iron ladle. Tan's face turned from a mild frown to real annoyance. "Is there a problem?" he asked, rising from his stool.

"Yes, I believe there is," Da Mo smiled.

Brother Tan stepped forward angrily but something in Da Mo's eyes stopped him in his tracks and instead, he turned to Lao questioningly.

"This is Master Da Mo from India," Lao said, finding his voice at last.

"I notice you do not wear an orange robe," Da Mo said.

"This is an orange robe," Tan said.

"No, it is grey."

Tan's face began to redden in fury, but Da Mo continued regardless. "It is grey like your soup, your rice, and your vegetables," he chuckled, "and I came to ask why."

"What do you want exactly, Master Da Mo?" Tan said angrily.

"I want to know why your robe is grey."

"My robe is grey because it is impossible to keep a robe clean in a busy kitchen."

"Is that because your kitchen is filthy?"

"There are over eighty monks to feed!"

Da Mo walked around the kitchen, examining the piles of dirty pots and utensils. He bent down to inspect the food on the floor and leant close to the walls, rubbing his fingers into the grime that had built up over the years.

"You appear unhappy with your lot in Shaolin, Brother Tan," he said at last.

"I didn't come here to cook," Tan said.

"Then why did you come?"

"To follow The Way, like the other monks."

"You believe The Way is found only in books and meditation?" Da Mo asked, his eyes wide in surprise. "It exists in all things, Brother Tan."

"In cooking rice?" Tan scoffed.

"Most certainly in cooking rice. You have simply not seen it, that is all."

Suddenly Tan was treated to a beaming smile. "So don't despair, Brother Tan, I will instruct you personally in The Way, and you will be pleased to know it manifests itself far more clearly in the kitchen than it does in books and meditation. We will begin afresh tomorrow."

Monks Go to Market

They met in the kitchen two hours before sun-up and scrubbed until it was spotless. Ko and Liang helped out while Da Mo supervised the cooking of the rice-gruel for the monks' breakfast. Later, as the plates were collected and washed, Da Mo sorted through the storeroom, throwing out anything that was not fresh. By the time he had finished, there was little left for dinner. "We must go to the market," he ordered.

"It's twenty li from here in Yangcheng," Tan told him.

"Then we had better leave at once."

On the way, he demanded to know which ingredients Tan intended to buy. Tan recited a long list and when he had finished, Lao added a few more that he had forgotten.

"Good," Da Mo said cheerily, "and which dishes will you make?

"Dishes?" Tan said, scratching his head.

"Which recipes will you follow," Da Mo asked patiently.

Tan shrugged. "I don't follow recipes."

"Then how do you cook?"

"I mix ingredients in the pot."

"You need recipes," Da Mo snorted.

"Do you know any?" Lao asked hopefully.

"I know plenty but they are all Indian recipes. The ingredients are different in China. The cooking is different. We need some expert help."

They had come to the edge of a crowded market in the center of the village. The first row of stalls sold fruit, a colorful array from all over China and Da Mo insisted on learning the name of each one: lychee, longan, kumquat, persimmon, and pomegranate. Next they came to a row of butchers' stalls with specialities of wildcat, owl, magpie, and camel hump. The fish stalls sold catches from the Yellow River and Dongping, including delicacies of oyster, crab, and turtle. Salt vendors called out their prices and spice merchants displayed their wares from all over the world: pepper, cardamom, ginger, fish-paste and pungent bean mash, mushrooms and cassia.

At the end of the market, they came to a row of stalls serving hot meals. One in particular had a large crowd waiting for service and Da Mo made his way there to join the throng. When he reached the front, he ordered Tan to find out what was available. The old man behind the counter reeled off a list of specialities, "Pork and beans, noodles in soup, mutton broth, steamed buns and dumplings, deep-fried fish, pickled egg with ginger …"

"Splendid," Da Mo said loudly, "please serve us with a little of each." He leaned close to Tan and whispered, "Do we have enough money to pay for it?"

"Not if we want to buy supplies," Tan answered.

"Then ask him if he will feed three monks in exchange for a blessing. Tell him it will bring him good fortune, and truthfully, who can afford to offend the Heavens?"

Tan colored with embarrassment, but repeated what Da Mo had said to the old man, while Da Mo and Lao took a seat at a nearby table.

Some time later, the old man arrived with plates of steaming rice, noodles, meat, vegetables and beans. It seemed Da Mo's offer had been accepted, and the three of them ate until they could eat no more. When they had finished, Da Mo leaned back on his seat and massaged his stomach contentedly. "I have not eaten so well since I left the emperor's palace," he told Tan and Lao. "Please go to the kitchen and pass on my compliments to the chef."

Tan went to the back of the stall and delivered his master's compliments to the old woman cooking at the stove. She waved her hand dismissively at him, but Tan could see she was delighted.

When he returned to the table, Da Mo grew serious.

"Now think about what we ate," he said, laying the empty

plates and bowls out in a line before them, "and consider the simple magic of each dish. The old woman combines only one or two flavors, but they go together perfectly. She cooks quickly. The ingredients are not expensive, yet the food is delicious. How did she do it?"

Tan and Lao sat in silence, looking to Da Mo for an answer.

"I don't have the answer," Da Mo said, "so go and find out!"

"What shall we say?" Tan asked.

"Whatever is required," Da Mo said curtly.

He rose from the table and went to the front of the stall, where he closed his eyes and raised his arms to heaven. The crowd made space around him. They had heard of the power of Indian monks and waited to see what miracles he would perform. A low keening sound came from his lips, and mysterious words and sounds emerged. His eyes flicked open and focused intently at the sky above the stall. His words slowly took form and he began to chant in a tongue they had never heard before. He walked around the stall three times, chanting in the language of his homeland. By the time he had finished, the crowd had grown. People had come came from all over the market to watch the spectacle and many stayed to eat at the stall blessed by the Indian.

Meanwhile, Tan and Lao chopped vegetables and ran errands for the old woman in the kitchen, which had suddenly become busier than ever, thanks to Da Mo's blessing. When they had served all those waiting for their food, Tan asked the old woman for some ideas to feed the monks of Shaolin.

"Why not simply follow the Quimin Yaoshu?" she asked.

"What is that?"

"A book, of course. You can read, can't you?"

"Yes," Tan said indignantly, "but I have never heard of this book."

"It is filled with the recipes of the ancients," she said, as if explaining to a child.

"I don't think we have it in our library," he said.

"Then perhaps you should get a copy instead of filling your heads with all that mumbo jumbo you learn," she said curtly. "The Quimin Yaoshu will teach you how to combine the five flavors and fill your bellies with tasty food."

Tan and Lao exchanged a vacant glance.

"You don't know of the five flavors?" she shook her head in despair. "I thought you said you were cooks! Heaven knows what those poor monks at the temple must be eating. Let me show you," she said, laying out the ingredients as she spoke. "Honey and sweet fruits create sweetness. Vinegar and sour fruits create sourness. Bitterness comes from smartweed, beer, or bitter herbs. Saltiness is from salt, naturally, but also fish paste and seaweed. The fifth flavor is the food itself, which should never be masked, but simply enhanced by other flavors."

She offered them a ladle of broth and they took a sip. "Balance the flavors evenly. Don't use too many or you will confuse the tastebuds. It's really quite simple, once you get a feel for it."

They spent another hour with the old woman, who noted down simple recipes for the monks of Shaolin, and then they hurried to find Da Mo and buy the ingredients they needed.

Later, as they labored to push their wheelbarrow of supplies back up the slope to Shaolin, Da Mo strolled ahead with only his walking staff in his hand. "I can't believe we ate for free," Tan said, his voice cheerful, despite the effort of pushing the cart.

"Nothing is free," Da Mo said.

"But the old man gave us food and we didn't pay," Lao said.

"Yes, and his wife gave you her knowledge, which is even more valuable, but they also received something in return."

"A blessing?" Tan asked dubiously.

"The old man fed three monks and the old woman passed

on her skills to two willing apprentices. What could be more rewarding?"

"And now that you have blessed their stall, it will be more popular than ever," Lao said between breaths.

"That is a better reason, I suppose," Tan said.

"You think so?" Da Mo scoffed. "They are both old! Now they will have to work harder than ever. You consider that a blessing?"

"What is it then?" Lao asked.

"What is what?"

"Is it a good thing or a bad thing?" Lao persisted.

"It is neither. There's no need to call it one or the other. It is simply the way things turned out. Just remember, if you seek a blessing, it often comes with a curse."

They walked in silence as the slope grew steeper, and Da Mo left them to go on alone, lost in his own reverie. When they reached the gates of Shaolin, he was waiting for them.

"There is something you must do for me, Lao," he said.

"What is it, Master?" Lao asked, concerned by the unexpected severity of the master's tone.

"Men will be seeking me at the temple gate. Watch for them and direct them to the cave. I will be waiting there."

"Who are these men?" Tan asked with a frown.

"They are of no concern," Da Mo said, "but I am counting on you, Lao, not to waiver in your task, whatever you may think. Do not let them enter the monastery. You must direct them to the cave."

"I will," Lao promised.

Tan picked up the handle of the wheelbarrow to go inside, but Lao remained where he was.

"What is the matter, Lao?" Da Mo demanded gently.

"How do you know men are coming?" he asked.

"I know."

"Did you see it on the cave wall?"

Da Mo smiled. "It is easy to see the future when you know what to expect."

"Can I learn to do it too?" Lao asked.

"If you study the past and observe the present most carefully, the future is usually clear," he smiled. "Now go, wait for the men, and tell no one what I have told you."

The Shadow in the Cave

Lao woke with a start. He was not in his room. He looked around, confused. Through a round window, he saw the flickering light of a torch.

He was in the gatehouse. There were voices outside, footsteps on the stony path. He hurried to the window and peered out. Four figures were approaching and as they came into view, a creeping dread filled his heart. One was tall, lean, with white hair, older than the others. He carried a club that he spun as he walked. Beside him a stout man held the torch, his short hair and flat nose made him look like an angry bull. The third was thin and pale. In the flickering light, Lao saw him smile. His teeth were black and rotting, giving him a cruel sneer. The fourth had a black hat made of felt and a long moustache in the style of the northern tribes, a Turk, with a short sword on his hip.

Lao wondered what to do. The men were bandits. He could not lead them to Master Da Mo, nor allow them inside the temple. They stopped at the gate. One rang the temple bell. He knew he had to act quickly before another monk arrived. He ran from the gatehouse, still unsure what to do, and stood at the gate.

"Hey little monk, open up," the Turk said.

"May I ask your business at Shaolin, Sir?" he asked, noticing that the Turk had hidden his short sword from view. He glanced at the tall man, and saw that he too had concealed his club behind his back.

"We are visiting a friend," the Turk smiled.

"May I know who?" Lao asked politely.

"First open the gate."

"Some monks are away from the temple at present. If you could tell me who you seek …"

"We have come for the Indian monk."

"Master Da Mo? Then it is as I said. He is not in here."

"Where is he?" the Turk demanded.

Lao swallowed hard and fought to retain his composure. "He is meditating in a cave nearby. If you follow the path up the hill for half a li, you will find it."

"He had better be there, or we'll be back," the Turk said.

"He is there," Lao assured him, holding his gaze despite the churning in his stomach.

As soon as they had gone, Lao rushed out to find Tan but Tan was already approaching, "I heard the bell. What's happening?"

"Four men were here. They had weapons and looked like bandits. They're going to the cave to see Master Da Mo. We have to help him!"

"Get Ko and anyone else who's prepared to come. Tell them to meet me here," Tan said, hurrying into the guardroom.

"Where are you going?" Lao asked.

To get weapons. Hurry, go now!"

Lao raced to the dormitory where Ko was sleeping, but even as he did, he knew they would be too late to save Da Mo.

The bull-like torchbearer thrust his flame into the cave entrance and the others peered inside. The cave was empty. They went in, weapons drawn, eager to find the monk. There was a cushion on the ground near the cave wall, dented where someone had been sitting on it, but no sign of the sitter. The black-toothed man touched the cushion. "It's still warm. Someone was here a moment ago. And what's this on the wall?" The Bull brought the torch closer. Two neat holes had been bored into the rock, as if drilled by hard metal. It took the bandits a moment to realize their significance. They were at the same level as the monk's eyes.

"What sort of monk could do this?" Blacktooth asked with an involuntary shudder.

"No monk can do that! Search the back of the cave," the tall man ordered.

The Bull went forward slowly with his torch, stopping with each step, afraid now.

"Hurry up, it's just an old monk," the tall man urged, but he too trod slowly now, his club at the ready as they moved deeper into the darkness.

The air was dank and still. The crackling of the torch was the only sound apart from the scratching of rodents and the shuffling of bats overhead. The cave bent and narrowed into a tunnel, which they followed farther into the mountain.

"He's not in here," the Turk said. They could all hear the relief in his voice. "Let's search outside."

"Finish searching here first," the leader insisted. "It can't be much farther."

They went on, every muscle alert in case the monk should appear, but when they reached the end of the tunnel there was nothing but stale air and water trickling down the granite walls.

"Perhaps the novice was lying," the Bull said. "We should go back to the temple and search there."

"Then why was the cushion still warm? I don't like it," the Turk said. "Perhaps someone warned him. They could be waiting outside."

"Don't be ridiculous," the leader said. "Nobody knew we were coming."

"From the description we were given, the Indian sounds more like a demon than a monk. Let's get out of this stinking cave," the Bull said, leading the way with his torch. The others followed close behind. Near the entrance, he stopped short. There, silhouetted against the moonlight at the cave mouth, was a man, seated and staring at the wall.

For a moment, the monk's slow rhythmic breathing hypnotized the men into stillness. Breaking the spell, the tall man stepped forward and raised his club. "On him, you fools!"

He stepped past the Bull's torch to reach the monk, and as he did, his body cast a shadow that plunged the area into darkness. By the time his eyes had adjusted, the monk had vanished.

He stepped into the shadows, lashing out with his club, slicing thin air. A blinding pain exploded in his head. He fell. Iron hands flung him around and propelled him into the torchbearer. He crashed into the flame. The fire scorched his face. He screamed, flailing at the torch until it fell to the ground. The Bull darted forward to retrieve it but too late, the shadow moved first. A sharp crack resounded off the walls of the cave. The monk's staff landed with a sickening thud on his skull. As he fell, he felt the heavy staff guiding him onto the flaming torch. He screamed until his mind spared him from the pain and released him into oblivion.

The cave returned to darkness. Black-tooth lashed out blindly, striking left and right, crazed with fear, but unwilling to move forward in case the monk was there. The Turk made a dash for the entrance, running past him, his sword cutting into the blackness. He almost made it, when his foot hit something hard. His legs were clamped together tightly, tripping him. He threw his arms out to break his fall, dropping his sword as he did. An inhuman strength lifted him, spun him around, and before he could think which side was up, he felt both arms pinned behind his back.

Black-tooth saw the rising shadow in the mouth of the cave, black against the faint moonlight outside.

"You're the last one," an unearthly voice hissed. Black-tooth swung his axe toward the shadow that blocked his exit.

"No!" screamed the Turk. The monk thrust him forward into Black-tooth's path and the axe buried itself deep in his chest. Black-tooth tried in vain to pull it free, but the blade was lodged in his companion's shattered collarbone. He fumbled for his dagger, but before he could grasp its hilt, the monk's foot came high and struck him on the temple. His fingers lost their function. Iron hands controlled him. His legs were kicked from beneath him. He landed hard on his back and the monk's heel crashed down on his head.

The tall man woke on the floor, his head bursting with pain, his hands and face in agony from the torch burns. There was an acrid smell in his nostril, the stench of his own seared flesh. He could see the monk clearly now in the moonlit entrance. He leaped with a guttural roar and clawed at the monk's eyes. His arm was twisted savagely and he felt a searing pain in his shoulder. He leaned forward to ease the tearing muscles. His neck was seized in a vice-like grip and his head cannoned into the cave wall.

Later, he did not know how much later, he floated in a vivid dream. He had died, and a demon had come to carry him to the underworld. He felt himself descending into the unknown, aware of others nearby, but they could not help him. He was strangely calm, and only dully aware of the torment that awaited him.

Ko and Brother Tan arrived, each with a ceremonial spear from the guardroom, just as Da Mo was bringing the last of the four bandits from the cave. Lao stood behind them, horrified that he had directed four assassins to his Master. Liang appeared a moment later with a small group of monks who had been roused from their sleep by the commotion.

"You are all just in time," Da Mo smiled. "Help me get these men back to the temple. They need medical attention, urgently."

In the doorway to the infirmary, Master Chui stared in disbelief at the scene that greeted him. Bloodstained bandages were piled up on the floor and Da Mo worked furiously to stem the flow of blood from a gaping wound in one man's chest. Another was having herb-soaked bandages placed on his burns, while yet another lay unconscious nearby and a fourth stared around, glassy-eyed, unaware of where he was.

"Master Chui?" a voice said at his side.

"Yes" Chui said absently, unable to take his eyes off the havoc before him.

"There is a messenger to see you."

"Not now," he told the young monk.

"He is from the imperial palace," the monk persisted.

Master Chui turned, blinking slowly, struggling to decide what to do. "Very well," he said finally, "show him to my office, I will meet him there."

The messenger was clearly exhausted, but walked briskly into the office and bowed deeply before Master Chui.

"Thank you for seeing me so quickly," he said smartly, "I have come with all haste from the palace. I bear an imperial decree, which must be placed directly in your hands. Will you accept it now, Master Chui?"

"I will," Chui said.

The messenger placed the scroll in his outstretched hand and Chui broke the seal and read it slowly. It looked exactly like the previous document that Master Da Mo had shown him. He rolled it up solemnly and placed it in his drawer.

"Is everything in order, Master Chui?" the messenger asked, concerned at his appearance.

"Apparently so," the old master said wearily. He looked at the messenger and rubbed his eyes with his fingers. "You have come a long way. I will have someone give you a bed for the night, food and fodder for your horse. Please remain as long as you wish."

"Thank you, Master," the messenger said, "one night will suffice, and I am grateful."

Chui smiled.

"There is one more thing," the messenger said. "I require your official stamp to acknowledge safe receipt of the document, if that is possible."

Chui stared at him for a moment, still in shock. He drew a deep breath to collect himself. "Of course," he said quietly, reopening his drawer and reaching for his seal.

Da Mo Meets the High Council

Lao served tea to Da Mo and the members of the High Council carefully, determined not to rush and spill the hot liquid despite his wish to be gone from the room as soon as possible. The tension was palpable. Of the five masters present, only Da Mo noticed him and smiled as he poured the tea. The other four stared at the table, and Master Chui's kind face looked troubled and drawn. Lao bowed and hurried from the chamber.

Master Chui cleared his throat before speaking. "Yesterday we received official confirmation of your appointment as the new grandmaster of Shaolin, Master Da Mo."

Da Mo waited for Chui to continue, but Chui was silent, his lips pressed tensely.

"I trust the paperwork was in order?" Da Mo prompted.

"Yes, it was in perfect order. Nevertheless, before we announce your appointment to the Brotherhood of Shaolin, there is something we must discuss."

"What is that, Master Chui?"

"The High Council is deeply troubled by the terrible incident that took place in the cave outside Shaolin."

"What troubles the High Council exactly?" Da Mo asked.

"This is a peaceful temple, Master Da Mo!" Chui said sharply, struggling not to raise his voice. "Not only is violence of all kinds abhorrent to us, but now we face the prospect of reprisals and further violence!"

"I share your concerns," Da Mo said.

"Do you, Master Da Mo?" Chui glared at him.

"Of course."

Chui held his eyes for a long moment. "It appears you are highly skilled in warfare. Would that be a correct assumption?"

"Yes, I believe it would."

"I also understand you instruct your disciple Ko in the art of war. Is that correct?"

"It is."

"Well, this is intolerable to us, as it should be to all Buddhists."

"Violence is as abhorrent to me as it is to you," Da Mo said.

"I wish I could believe that," Chui said. "Yet you teach violence, Master Da Mo, and already in the short time you have been here, our infirmary is filled with seriously injured men. Tell me, do you consider that a mere coincidence?"

"I do not teach violence. The violence arrived with the four assassins, not with me or my students, Master Chui."

"There was violence on both sides, Master Da Mo."

"You do not distinguish between the two?"

"I do not."

"And does the High Council share your view?"

"It does."

"Perhaps you would allow its members to speak for themselves?" Da Mo said evenly.

Chui was about to claim it was unnecessary, but changed his mind. "Of course," he said testily.

Master Tung was the first to speak. "The causes of violence may differ, Master Da Mo, but the effects are the same. Violence breeds violence, as Master Chui rightly says."

"Quite," Master Pei said, "our concern is that training in violence will only lead to more violence in the future.

"Do you accept that a man is entitled to defend his own life?" Da Mo asked.

Master Pei did not answer.

It was Master Nieh's turn to speak. "I accept that the violence on your part was not performed in the same spirit as that of the assassins, Master Da Mo. They would have killed you, yet you spared them and even brought them to the infirmary."

"The incident put the entire temple in danger!" Master Tung cut in.

Master Nieh raised a finger to silence him. "Master Da Mo did everything in his power to protect the temple from those violent men. He dealt with them alone without putting any other monks at risk."

"But Master Da Mo is an expert warrior," Master Tung said. "He was able to protect himself. Some of the younger monks went to his aid. They could have been harmed. They took up weapons! We are Buddhists, it is against our laws to bear arms. Ours is a way of peace."

"There is no such thing as a peaceful way," Da Mo said. "There is only The Way."

"The Buddha would never countenance violence," Master Chui protested.

"The Buddha told us to see the truth. We live in a violent world, Master Chui."

"Then we must do everything we can to bring peace to it."

"The Buddha spoke of a middle way."

"Not this way," Chui said, placing his palm firmly on the table as he spoke.

A heavy silence entombed the room and Da Mo assessed the faces of the High Council, until Master Nieh spoke again.

"Rumor has it that the men who attacked Master Da Mo were well-known bandits. They have been terrorizing this area for many years. Some of the younger monks are saying that they deserved what they got, and more. They are saying it was karma at work."

"And what do you say?" Chui asked.

"I confess to having some sympathy with their view," Master Nieh said carefully.

"It is not our place to dispense justice," Chui said tersely, "much less to mete out punishment!"

"But neither can we hide away from the outside world entirely, however much we may wish. Several monks from Shaolin have been attacked in recent years. The temple has been robbed countless times. We are vulnerable, out here in this wilderness."

"Violence only breeds more violence."

"Knowledge of how to handle violence can also prevent violence," Da Mo said.

"Master Da Mo, I accept you did nothing to provoke the attack," Master Chui said. "Moreover, the assassins got better treatment than they would have given. I even accept that a man may use violence to defend himself, though personally I find the notion abhorrent. I fail, however, to see your reason for wishing to teach warfare in a temple."

"The Way is not concerned with judging what is right or wrong, but with seeing things as they truly are. If we look clearly, we see that on occasion, the only way to keep the peace is through the use of force. This is distasteful to those who love peace, as all true Buddhists do. However, it is not our way to bend reality to fit our wishes. We must appreciate the truth in its entirety."

"Just because violence exists in the world does not mean we should embrace it," Master Pei said.

"I agree," Da Mo nodded.

"Then why do you teach your student the art of war?"

"For a different reason entirely, Master Pei. One that has nothing to do with violence. For a young man like Ko, martial arts are a path to self discovery. The warrior's training requires the same discipline and dedication required for a monk to achieve enlightenment. And the conditioning of the body enhances the ability to sustain the rigors of monastic life. A stronger body creates a clearer mind. A clearer mind sees the truth more easily."

"But it is not the path of The Buddha!"

"There are many paths. Who are we to insist on a single one?"

Master Chui could not argue with that, since he had said the same thing himself many times in the past.

"I have a question," Master Pei said, filling the brief silence, "Did you learn the art of war as part of your Buddhist training in India, Master Da Mo?"

"No," Da Mo smiled, "although my master encouraged wrestling to build health and character in young students."

"That is hardly the same. May I ask where you did learn it?"

"In a previous life."

"And you still practice these deadly methods?"

"I do."

"You really find no contradiction?"

"None whatsoever, Master Pei. Skill in battle is simply one more way of acting in harmony with nature. This harmony can be achieved through many art forms but for me, it is achieved through the martial arts. In his innermost self, the warrior and the monk face similar battles against common enemies. To hone a skill requires sacrifice and determination. Submission is easy, but victory requires courage. The outcome of our life is governed by our willingness to face these battles."

"To fight or surrender, to kill or be killed," Master Pei said, "these are weighty questions."

"They are," Da Mo said, "and whatever our decision, we must accept the consequences. That is karma, and to hope for anything else is folly."

"Then you accept that your actions last week may bring further violence to Shaolin?" Chui asked.

"They may," Da Mo conceded.

There was another long silence, then Master Nieh spoke again.

"And they may not. We should also remember that a clear message has gone out. When people see what happened to the bandits, they will think twice before attacking a Shaolin monk again."

"Master Nieh has a point," Master Pei said, warming to the argument. "We live in a wild country where it is dangerous to walk outside the temple. Unarmed monks are at the mercy of any criminals they come across."

"I am surprised to hear such views," Master Chui said sadly. "We are men of peace. I understand the desire to defend oneself, but I simply cannot agree to training in battle-craft. This is, after all, a monastery."

The others were silent, conflict evident in their faces.

"Master Chui, Members of the High Council," Da Mo said finally, "I am deeply grateful that you have raised these important concerns. I wish to make clear that I have no wish to turn a peace-loving monastery into a military training camp. I propose only physical exercises to strengthen the bodies and minds of our young monks. Nothing more."

"And what of your martial training with Brother Ko and Sister Liang?" Master Chui asked.

"I would like to continue it," Da Mo replied, "since I feel it is important for them. However I propose to conduct their lessons in private, away from the monastery."

Master Chui gave the monks time to consider Da Mo's statement. After a few moments he looked around the table at the other masters, "May I have the opinion of the High Council regarding the teaching of physical exercise in the temple?"

"I do not object," Master Nieh said seriously.

Master Pei nodded his agreement and finally Master Tung added his reluctant consent. "So be it," Chui said gravely. "The High Council has decreed that non-violent exercise may be permitted in Shaolin. I will announce it when we announce your appointment, tomorrow morning, if you are agreeable Master Da Mo?"

"I am," Da Mo said, "and may I say how honored I am that we had this honest discussion. If we had not, I should have been most concerned."

"Why do you say that?" Master Tung asked.

"It is the role of a High Council to take the safety of its brotherhood most seriously," Da Mo smiled warmly. "I commend you all for your diligence in these matters, especially you, Master Chui."

"You do?" Chui asked, astonished.

"Most certainly. With such a dedicated High Council, Shaolin cannot fail to be a great success."

Grandmaster Tzu Receives News

Grandmaster Tzu opened his door a crack and saw the grey figure waiting in the darkness. He stepped aside to allow the monk to enter and closed the door behind him.

"I have news from Shaolin," the grey monk said quietly, "and it is not good. The men we sent failed in their task. The Indian defeated them."

"Then tell them to go and finish the job," Tzu said angrily.

"That will be impossible. They say the Indian is a demon with supernatural powers. He took their weapons as if they were children and used them against them. They are terrified."

"Then get someone else. There are plenty more bandits in that area."

The Indian's reputation has already spread as a holy man of mystical power. No one will dare face him."

"Idiots and superstitious fools!" Tzu raged.

"I fear we have underestimated him," the grey monk said evenly, ignoring his master's outburst. "However, I have a new suggestion."

"Then let's hear it," Tzu said, breathing hard to control his fury.

"There have been rumors of a skirmish on the upper reaches of the Yangtze at Tiger Leaping Gorge."

"What does this have to do with that cursed Indian?"

"An Indian monk and a runaway conscript were involved in a fight with a troop of soldiers. Several people were killed, including three monks and one soldier. Now they are both wanted for murder." He took a paper from his robe and read out the description of the Indian monk and the Chinese fugitive.

"It can only be them," Tzu said. "What do you suggest now?"

The grey monk smiled. "The army has abandoned its search for the two men, believing them drowned in the rapids at Tiger

Leaping Gorge. But no bodies were ever found, and clearly they did not drown."

"Then we will simply inform the army and let the army take care of it. Who is the officer in charge?"

"Captain Fu Sheng in Yulong Fort on the western frontier."

"Fu Sheng? The name is familiar," Tzu said, tugging at his beard gently. "Is he not the cavalryman who quelled the barbarians on the northern plains?"

"The very same," the grey monk said.

"They say he won his last battle almost single-handedly and with unbridled savagery."

"Yes, and I understand that for once, the stories have not been exaggerated."

"Then we should send a message to the captain. Tell him the men he was seeking are hiding out in Shaolin."

The grey monk looked doubtful. "He may simply arrest them and put them on trial. The emperor might intervene and pardon the Indian."

"Then we must bring the captain here first," Grandmaster Tzu said, "and persuade him to avoid the embarrassment of a trial."

The grey monk gave a thin smile. "All we need is a reason to summon the captain to the palace."

"Leave that to me," Grandmaster Tzu said, opening the door to signal the end of the meeting. "Have a messenger prepare to ride to Yulong Fort right away. It's a long way to the frontier."

Monks Exercise

The morning wind whipped fine clouds of dust in tight circles around the courtyard. Ko paced impatiently, watching the doorway, waiting for someone to appear. No one came.

Da Mo sat beneath the bell tower and Liang waited dutifully by his side. Like Ko, she could not help glancing to the doorway from time in the hope that someone might appear.

"No one is coming," Ko said, the frustration clear in his voice, "I told everyone of the time and place for morning exercise. They have ignored it."

"They will come," Da Mo said, rising from his seat. "Let us begin."

He led them through the exercises that Ko already knew so well, drawing his hands to his chest and lowering his weight slowly so that Liang could follow. Ko pushed away with his palms, then squatted low and stretched his arms, first left, then right, high then low, until he had covered all directions. Then he placed his hands on the ground to bend and stretch. Da Mo counted out loud as they went and each time he reached the eighteenth movement, they began again. Once they had repeated the eighteen movements for an hour, Da Mo stopped and watched Ko and Liang.

From the corner of his eye, Ko noticed a handful of novice monks gathered in the doorway, but when Da Mo turned to look at them, they hurried away.

"Continue," Da Mo ordered as he left the courtyard.

Ko counted as he moved and Liang followed, tracking his every movement. They turned and Ko caught a glimpse of her face. Her expression was so intense that it made him smile. He wondered if she knew how beautiful she was. They turned again. Now her back was to him. Her body was graceful and supple, elegant, like a cat's, her steps natural and balanced. When she performed Da

Mo's exercises, she brought them alive. They turned again. Now they were side by side. He rose onto one leg. She followed. His hands pushed out slowly, then circled and straightened. Liang's did the same. They were moving in perfect unison. He stopped for a moment and Liang copied him, watching expectantly. He turned to her and smiled, and for a moment she forgot herself and beamed at him.

"You're doing well," he said.

Her smile vanished quickly. "You are not my teacher, Ko."

"No, but I am your senior. You should listen to me."

"You're a fool."

He was about to answer when he noticed a figure in the shadow of the doorway. For a moment he thought it might be Da Mo, returning to watch them, or even Master Chui come to show his disapproval, but the figure was too small to be either.

It was Novice Lao.

Ko beckoned to him. Lao hesitated, then stepped into the courtyard.

"Master Da Mo calls this The Eighteen Movements," Ko smiled. "You're welcome to join us, if you wish. It will make you strong."

"I don't know what to do," Lao said.

"That's easy," Liang said, "just follow Ko. He can be your teacher."

Lao looked unsure.

"Stand between us," Ko said. "You can follow us both."

They began again and Lao followed, slowly at first, but later with more confidence. The three of them continued until a bell rang to signal the end of the period.

"You did well Lao," Ko told him. "Will you practice with us again tomorrow?"

"Yes," Lao promised.

Another figure was waiting in the doorway. It was Tan.

"Oh Heavens, the food!" Lao cried, remembering his duties, and ran to help Tan in the kitchen.

Ko and Liang left the courtyard and made their way to the bathing pool.

"Are you enjoying the lessons?" he asked, hoping to break the strained silence.

"Which lessons? Your lessons, or those of Master Da Mo?" she asked.

"Neither. I meant the reading and writing lessons, here in the temple."

"I love them. I always dreamed of studying like this. How about you?"

Ko shrugged.

"You don't enjoy learning?" she asked, turning to look at him in surprise.

"The scriptures don't make sense. They're nothing like real life."

"I think they show a better way, an ideal."

"One that's impossible to follow," he said sourly.

"Why do you say that?"

They reached the bathing pool and Ko stooped to rinse his face with the cool water. "Because things always go wrong. Life is imperfect. There's evil in the world. People are cruel."

"Have you never done wrong?"

"I have, I admit it."

"Then we're all to blame," she said, "now turn around, so I can wash."

He turned his back as Liang washed herself quickly in the icy water. "Do you think Master Da Mo has ever done wrong?" he asked.

"Who knows? But I believe his intentions are good. It's a feeling I get. You must feel it too?"

"I do, although it took me a while to see it."

"Do you want to be like him?" she asked quietly.

He turned to see if she was mocking him, and saw her naked back, the line of her neck and shoulders, the side of her breast. She looked over her shoulder, holding his gaze, waiting for an answer.

"I don't think I'll ever be like him," he said.

"But you want to be?"

"Yes."

"Then you can be," she said, her face serious. "Now turn away. I'm getting out."

He turned his eyes away and swallowed hard, deeply moved by her faith in him. He heard her step from the pool, heard the water trickling off her body onto the hard ground.

"I would like to be wise and powerful like Da Mo too," she said, "so we'll both have to practice hard. You can get in now. I'm decent."

He removed his robe, acutely aware of the damp robe clinging to her breast, the twist of wet hair caressing her shoulder, the water droplets rolling down her slender thighs. He forced himself to look straight ahead as he passed her and plunged himself thankfully into the icy water.

The next morning Brother Tan was waiting with Lao in the courtyard and Ko led them all in Da Mo's eighteen exercises. The following day three more monks joined in, and each day the numbers grew, until the courtyard was filled with monks performing their dawn exercises. Soon it became too crowded for all to practice together and they moved to a clearing in the forest. The mountainside was filled with rows of figures, moving as one. Each morning, Da Mo watched from the cave high above them as the spray of orange robes moved against the vivid green of Song Shan.

Once the morning exercise had finished, Ko and Liang spent the day in study and meditation. When evening came, they hurried to the cave where Da Mo taught them new exercises, each more demanding than the last. When this training was over, Da Mo would teach them combat drills, which they practiced for several more hours. When it got dark, he would hang an oil lamp on a nearby tree so they could continue long into the night.

Messenger Arrives in Yulong Fort

Lieutenant Pai made his way to Fu Sheng's office, feeling uneasy about what might have brought an imperial messenger all the way to Yulong. He reached the captain's office just as the messenger and the captain emerged. Fu Sheng called for an orderly to take care of the rider and his horse, then ushered Lieutenant Pai into his office with a wave of his hand.

"It seems I am to be honored," he said with no trace of a smile.

"Sir?"

"I have been summoned to Nanjing to receive a medal in recognition of our victory against the Uighurs in the black valley."

"That's splendid news, Captain!" Pai said, relieved that it was nothing more serious.

"I believe the emperor may even present the honor personally," Fu Sheng said.

"It is high time your success was recognized, Sir."

"Our success," Fu Sheng corrected him.

"You are too kind," Pai said.

Fu Sheng walked to the window and stared out. Pai waited patiently for him to speak but Fu Sheng was lost in thought, gazing beyond the fort's outer wall to the barren peaks in the distance.

"Forgive me for speaking plainly Captain," Pai said interrupting the captain's reverie, "but you seem unsure about it?"

Fu Sheng turned with a rare smile. "No, I'm delighted. It's just a little irregular, that's all."

"In what way, Sir?"

"Why me? Why now? There are many other soldiers whose victories are never recognized."

"China needs her heroes, Captain."

Fu Sheng examined Pai's face for any trace of irony, but Pai hid his feelings well. "I'll leave in the morning. Have a horse and provisions prepared for the journey."

"Yes Sir. Shall I draw up a troop to accompany you?"

"No. I will travel alone. It will be faster and less tiresome."

"As you wish, Captain."

Pai felt his spirits lift as he left the captain's office. Fu Sheng would be gone for many weeks, which meant he would be able to relax. Though the captain treated him well enough, Pai hated him with a passion he found difficult to contain. Fu Sheng was easily the finest soldier he had ever served with, but Pai had seen the captain's eyes on the battlefield, the thirst for blood and slaughter, the ecstasy of the kill. He had seen the face of the demon that dwelt inside the quiet young man, and it was the face of nightmares.

The Use of Swords

It was spring on Song Shan and flowers and tree-blossoms had erupted on the slopes. The soft air was filled with the delicate scents of the forest and the sun shone late into the evening in cloudless skies.

On one such evening, Ko and Liang waited outside the cave for Da Mo to begin their lessons. He emerged carrying a long bag on his shoulder and set off wordlessly across the mountainside. They followed as he led them along a trail through the trees until they came to a thicket of bamboo. Hidden behind it was a clearing with a stream. Clear spring water tumbled over smooth rocks to create a waterfall in miniature. The water was cold and sweet, sparkling as it fell, with a sound as sweet as the tinkling of a tiny bell. Da Mo knelt on the soft grass and untied the fastenings on his bag. Slowly, he withdrew a wooden sword and handed it to Ko, and another, which he gave to Liang.

They spent the next hours learning to draw the sword and strike, cutting and thrusting, parrying high and low, to the left and to the right. Each evening for many weeks they returned to the same clearing and Da Mo supervised their practice. At the end of each day, he would take his own practice sword and test them. In Da Mo's hands the heavy wooden sword seemed as light as a cane, disappearing and reappearing in a blur, the only clue to its motion the sound of slicing air. His sword tip found their every weakness, the exposed wrist, the elbow, the throat, the groin. His blade sliced across a thigh, a flank, an artery in the neck, until they despaired of ever finishing one practice without being cut to ribbons.

When Ko attacked harder, Da Mo redirected his attack with a movement so small that he appeared to be still, yet Ko's strike was sent wide. He lost his footing and the hard wooden edge tapped his throat before he could right himself.

When Liang hesitated, searching for a way past Da Mo's defenses, he flew at her and overwhelmed her with fierce cuts and thrusts that brought her to her knees.

And late at night, when their tormentor had returned to his cave, Ko and Liang made their way slowly back to the monastery, exchanging barely a word, their arms limp by their sides, their heads bowed.

After countless hours, their constant practice began to pay off and their swordplay gained a graceful rhythm. When Da Mo was satisfied that their power matched their control, he sent them to the clearing alone, saying he would come along later.

"Why is Da Mo not with us tonight?" Liang asked as they walked to the clearing.

"Perhaps it's a test," Ko answered.

"Do you think he's watching us?"

"Sometimes I feel he's watching me, even when I know he's somewhere else."

"How does he do that?"

"With his mind."

They stepped into the clearing and stood beside the little waterfall.

"You think it possible?" she asked, taking a handful of sweet water and holding it to her lips to drink.

"With him? Yes."

"Then we had better be diligent," she said lightly.

"We will be," Ko said, bowing formally and raising his sword.

She saluted him with her sword, as Da Mo had shown them.

Ko attacked. A short vertical cut. She evaded and side-stepped, striking as she did. He checked her arm and the edge of his wooden blade drew across her side.

He grinned.

She pushed his sword away and struck low toward his thigh. He moved just in time, tripping as he avoided her cut. For an instant his sword was loose in his hand. She smashed it with hers and he lost his grip. His sword fell to the ground. She drew her arm back to strike at his head but his hand snaked out to her wrist and gripped it firmly. Then they heard laughter, and turned to see Da

Mo chuckling at Ko's situation.

Ko began to protest, and as he did, Liang slapped his hand from her wrist and struck. Her blade caught Ko on the temple.

She watched in agony as he crumpled to the floor. "Oh no, I've done it again!" she cried, but Ko did not hear her.

He woke a short time later to find Da Mo kneeling over him, and Liang looking over the master's shoulder. He tried to rise but Da Mo pushed him back down. "Lie still for a moment longer, until your head clears. And don't be angry with Liang. Be angry with yourself. What do I always tell you about concentrating?"

Ko looked away angrily.

"Calm yourself, Ko. You have had a valuable lesson today, the same lesson we tried to teach you in the palace garden, but it appears you still haven't grasped it. Never mind. Sit up now because I have something to show you, although perhaps I should wait a little longer ..."

"What is it?" Ko asked, eager to divert attention from his humiliation. Liang knelt beside Ko and reached out to examine his head. He brushed her hand away angrily. "Let me see," she insisted, taking his head and turning it to herself. There was a cut on his temple and a drop of blood trickled onto his cheek. A red lump was beginning to form. Her fingertips pressed down gently.

"I'm sorry," she whispered.

"Don't be," he said, ignoring her and watching as Da Mo untied a leather bag and withdrew a steel sword in its scabbard. He handed it to Ko, who drew the sword slowly. The blade was old and tarnished, but it had been sharpened to a fine edge and highly polished. He ran his thumb lightly over the edge, knowing that any more pressure would break the skin.

"It looks like a fine weapon," Ko said.

"Your father was an ironmonger, if I recall," Da Mo said.

"He was, and I know enough to recognize good workmanship.

Where did you get it, Master?"

Da Mo ignored the question and took another sword from his bag, which he handed to Liang.

She held it in both hands, staring dumbly at it.

"Go on, draw it," Da Mo urged. "It won't harm you. Just make sure your thumb is not in the way."

She drew the blade and held it out in wonder. "I have never held a real sword," she said, marveling at the weight and balance. "It fits so naturally in the hand."

Ko raised his sword and executed the cuts and thrusts and coils that Da Mo had taught him. The metal sliced effortlessly through the air, a sharp sound accompanying each movement.

"It feels very different from a wooden sword."

"Why?" Da Mo asked.

"Tauter, stronger, more balanced."

"Of course, wood is for furniture. Metal is for weapons. What other differences can you feel?"

Ko searched for the answer. "It feels dangerous. It can cut you, if you're not careful."

"Yes, you must treat it with respect, especially after what happened earlier. What about you, Liang?"

"It can kill," Liang said.

"A wooden sword can kill. A stone can kill," Da Mo said.

"But the sword is made for killing."

"Correct," Da Mo said, "and that is the truth of the matter. Never forget that the sword was created with one purpose in mind. Death. Never draw your sword unless your intention is to kill. Let there be no doubt in your mind. Not a moment's hesitation. You must cut your opponent down without a thought, or die yourself."

"Then how can we practice?" Ko asked.

"With death in mind!" Da Mo roared, his voice echoing around the mountain like thunder, his face so fierce that they were both shocked into silence. "Return your sword to its scabbard," he ordered. They obeyed and he took Ko's sword. He walked slowly to the center of the clearing and turned to face them, his gaze fixed on an imaginary opponent.

The sword emerged from the scabbard in a flash, cutting in vicious arcs, shredding the air, the blade blurring around him. He lunged forward, cutting close to their faces. But it was not the danger of being struck that made them so still. It was Da Mo's eyes. Ko had seen these eyes once before when Da Mo had held a knife to his throat, black eyes, cold as death. But Liang held her breath in horror. She had never seen such a transformation and suddenly the dark monk terrified her.

Da Mo stepped back and held his blade down to the side. "Each strike is a death blow. Each cut is fatal. Each thrust is death," he said, taking a small piece of silk from his belt. "When you have finished, clean the blood from your blade to remind yourself what you have done." He wiped the blade with three ritual strokes on each side and returned it to its scabbard.

Liang was quiet, contemplating the possibility of ending someone's life, wondering if she could do it. Ko was silent, too well aware of the hell that could be unleashed by taking a life, and wondered whether he could ever do it again.

"Now you," Da Mo ordered.

They performed the cuts, thrusts and parries that they had learned with their wooden swords, and then cleaned their blades with silk as Da Mo had shown. When they had finished, they returned the swords to their scabbards and handed them back to Da Mo.

"We will continue tomorrow," he said, tying up his leather bag and setting off down the mountainside toward the temple. They gathered up their wooden swords and followed a short distance behind.

"Are you all right?" she asked.

"Fine," Ko said, tight-lipped.

"I saw your hand shaking when you cleaned your blade."

"It's nothing."

"And how is your head? I'm sorry about that. Wait, let me see it," she insisted, stepping in front of him to make him stop. She reached up and took his head in her hands, turning it slowly to see the injury. "There's still a little blood that needs to be cleaned."

She put her silk cloth to her lips to wet it. "I'm sure Master Da Mo won't mind a bit of real blood on his cloth," she smiled as she dabbed at his temple gently. Her other hand cupped the back of his neck, holding him still. Her body was close to his. Her breasts pressed lightly against his chest.

Ko breathed in slowly, deeply. He could smell her: her hair, her breath, her body. It was the same sweet smell he had come to know in the wilderness when they had slept side by side. How much he missed it. He wanted to put his arms around her waist and pull her close, press his lips to hers, run his hands over her body. What would she do, he wondered.

"There," she smiled, stepping away quickly, as if reading his thoughts, and before he could say a word she had set off after Da Mo on the path back to Shaolin.

Captain Enters the Palace

A camel train crossed the main square of Nanjing, heading for the busy night bazaar. The beasts that spent their days wandering in the Pamir mountains and the wastes of the Taklamakan desert were unused to the crowds and clamor of the city. They spat angrily at anyone who came too close, including each other, and their drivers struggled to control them. Suddenly two camels began to fight.

Outside the imperial palace, the guard watched in amusement. There was little to occupy his time during his long watch, and it made quite a spectacle. The crowds parted quickly to avoid the vicious kicks and bites of the huge beasts. A cloud of dust began to envelope the camels, swirling up into the evening sky.

Then through the dust, a rider emerged. The guard shook his head and blinked. The rider appeared to have passed directly between the fighting beasts, but that would be impossible. He watched the rider approach, the camels forgotten. The horseman was a soldier, that much was plain. As he came closer, the guard made out a captain's insignia on his uniform. He took a pace forward, as was the protocol, and reached for the horse's bridle to steady it. The animal was exhausted, yet the captain appeared fresh.

"May I know your name and business at the palace, please, Captain?" he said, taking in the soldier's features as he spoke. He was young for a captain, little more than a boy, but when the captain presented his credentials, the guard stiffened and stood to attention smartly.

"Welcome to Nanjing, Captain Fu Sheng."

The captain nodded curtly.

"And may I say, Sir," the guard continued, "that your victories on the frontier have brought great joy to the palace and the city."

"Thank you soldier," the captain said.

"Please come inside."

The guard, swung open the gate and barked an order into the guardhouse. Two young soldiers emerged on the run. The captain's horse was taken to the stables and he was escorted to a spacious apartment adjoining the barracks.

Two servants arrived immediately to take care of his uniform and offer refreshment. A meal arrived shortly afterward and an immaculate new uniform followed soon after that. The captain was impressed to discover it fitted perfectly. An adjutant arrived with a message. "Captain, General Shou has been informed of your arrival and is delighted that you have arrived safely. He is keen to meet you, but he has a pressing engagement this evening. He will see you tomorrow morning. In the meantime, please make yourself at home and relax after your journey. Perhaps you would care to visit the officers' dining room? And if you require anything, please summon me. We are at your service."

Fu Sheng dined in his room and was preparing to retire for the evening when there was another knock at his door. He opened it to find a grey-haired monk in a dark robe.

"Captain Fu Sheng?"

Fu Sheng ignored the question and waited for the monk to continue.

"There is someone who wishes to meet you," the grey monk said quietly.

Fu Sheng regarded him impassively. He had little time for monks.

"His name is Grandmaster Tzu," the monk added.

"I don't know him," Fu Sheng said.

"Grandmaster Tzu is the head of the Imperial Temple of the Golden Buddha here in the palace. He feels a brief talk might be mutually beneficial ..."

"I can think of nothing to discuss."

"Please Captain," the grey monk said with a pained expression, "let me assure you Grandmaster Tzu would not take up your time unnecessarily."

Fu Sheng regarded the monk with a trained eye and noticed something he had missed before, a hardness behind the bland features that was unusual in a monk.

"Very well," he agreed. It might be amusing to know what two monks could want with him at this hour of the night. He followed the grey monk through the dark corridors of the palace to Grandmaster Tzu private chamber.

Inside he found himself face to face with a tall, white-haired monk dressed in an exquisite silk robe. The old man smiled but there was no warmth in his eyes.

"It is good to meet you in person, Captain," Grandmaster Tzu said. "Your exploits on the frontier have become a favorite topic of conversation here in the palace. Your reputation is growing quickly. You are considerably younger than I expected, but the empire needs youth and strength to uphold its laws and keep the barbarians in check. I commend you, and welcome you to the palace. Please be seated."

"There was a matter you wished to discuss," Fu Sheng said without sitting.

"Indeed," Grandmaster Tzu said, who remained standing too, his face darkening ominously. "And since you must be tired from your journey, I will take up no more of your time with small talk. I understand you are seeking two men who are wanted for murder."

"The army is seeking many men," Fu Sheng said evenly.

"These two were involved in an incident, last year, in Tiger Leaping Gorge. I understand several people were killed, three monks and a soldier from your own troop. A terrible business. The fugitives in question were disguised as monks."

"The men responsible for those crimes drowned in the rapids while trying to escape," Fu Sheng said.

"I believe that is the official version, though I understand their bodies were never recovered?"

"The rapids are murderous at Tiger Leaping Gorge."

"I'm sure they are," Tzu smiled. "Nevertheless, two monks matching their descriptions were here at the palace just a few months ago."

"How can you be certain they are the same men?" Fu Sheng asked.

"Captain," the grey monk said, "the Chinese fugitive could be mistaken for any number of young men, but the Indian is quite unmistakable. His description matches exactly even down to his skill with the wooden staff. Assuming they are the same men, we are offering you the chance to bring them to justice before this information becomes widely known."

"Might I ask why?" Fu Sheng demanded, looking from the grey monk to Grandmaster Tzu.

Tzu smiled. "Of course, Captain, let me explain. I am sure you have good reason for hunting the Chinese fugitive, but it is the Indian who is the real danger. It is intolerable that he was here at the palace, seeking favor for the twisted teachings that he dares to call the true Way. Now he and his accomplice are spreading his lies in a monastery on Song Shan. He must be prevented from poisoning the minds of young Chinese monks at all costs."

Fu Sheng regarded him closely for a moment before answering. "I have affairs at the palace to conduct before I can leave for Song Shan."

"We are well aware of your forthcoming honors," Grandmaster Tzu said smugly. "Naturally, we were delighted when the emperor agreed to recognize your brilliance on the frontier."

Fu Sheng examined the grandmaster's eyes and saw that it was true; his honors had been arranged by Tzu. He fought down the rage at the impudence of this monk and considered his options with the icy cold he reserved for the battlefield.

"Naturally you will need supplies for your detour to Song Shan," Tzu continued lightly, "I will arrange a contribution from the temple to cover your costs."

Fu Sheng did not answer.

"Our coffers are large," Tzu continued, "the emperor has been most generous in his contributions in recent years."

Fu Sheng eyed him calculatingly, knowing the sum of the offer would be enormous. Grandmaster Tzu continued without awaiting a reply. "Your reputation is spreading fast, Captain. One day you will be a man of influence, a general. Such a man needs friends he can trust, especially in the palace. As for a monk like myself, it is always reassuring to have friends in the army. The army and the church are not as distant as people believe."

Fu Sheng looked at his pale face and felt nothing but loathing for the man, but the old monk was right. It would be useful to have an ally at the palace in years to come. "Very well. I will visit the monastery in Song Shan once my affairs at the palace are complete."

"A word of warning," the grey monk said, "when it is time to make your arrest, don't underestimate the Indian."

"A foreigner with a stick?" Fu Sheng smirked.

"This foreigner was attacked by four armed men and he defeated them with their own weapons," the grey monk said.

"He is no monk, Captain," Grandmaster Tzu said, "he is a criminal, a murderer, an insult to the name of The Buddha."

"Do you need men to ride with you?" the grey monk asked. "It can be arranged."

"No, I will go alone."

"There are two of them, Captain," Tzu said, "how will you manage alone?"

"Leave that to me," Fu Sheng smiled, and for the first time Tzu glimpsed the demon that dwelled inside the young captain and took an involuntary step back.

"One more question," the grey monk said. "It is an important one. Do you plan to arrest the fugitives?"

"Yes."

"We ask because we fear a trial would cause considerable embarrassment to the army, and indeed to the emperor who has shown the

Indian some misplaced favor."

"If they resist they will be killed," Fu Sheng said evenly.

"And will they resist?" the grey monk probed. "Please think carefully before answering."

"I believe they will," Fu Sheng said.

"Both of them?"

"Both of them," Fu Sheng assured him.

"Naturally, we pray they come peacefully, Buddha be praised," the grey monk smiled, as he showed the young captain to the door.

A Cloud Over the Moon

In the clearing by the waterfall, high on the slopes of Song Shan, Ko and Liang practiced relentlessly, continuing late into the night until their aching limbs could take no more. They trained to strengthen the muscles required for the intricate sword work, until they could wield their steel blades with a speed and dexterity that almost matched the astonishing swiftness of their master.

For the next part of their training, Da Mo placed stakes in the ground for them to strike, and each evening they made hundreds of cuts on ever-thicker pieces of bamboo. After an hour of striking with the sharp swords, they took their blunt practice swords and fought one another, the ringing of blade on blade echoing around the forest. After many days, they grew to know one another so completely that they fought as one, neither winning nor losing but simply flowing from one strike and counter to the next, as though they had sparred in endless lifetimes before.

When darkness fell, Da Mo would leave them to resharpen their swords and apply a fine oil to the blade in preparation for the next day's training.

On a night when the clearing was lit by moonlight so bright that no lamp was needed to see what they were doing, they worked side by side in silence, neither wishing to break the stillness of the night. Then suddenly a single cloud covered the moon and they found themselves in complete darkness.

"Where's the lamp?" Liang asked, feeling around for it.

"Wait, the cloud will pass," Ko said.

"How strange, the sky was empty a moment ago. I saw stars everywhere." She reached around in the pitch black, looking for the lamp, but couldn't find it.

"Don't be afraid," Ko said.

"I'm not," she said.

"I know," he laughed.

They waited for the cloud to pass, but the blackness remained.

"Are you there, Ko?" she asked at last.

"I'm right here." His hand reached for her. She caught it and held it. His other hand reached for her too and she took it.

Slowly, he pulled her close. She could feel a whisper of his breath on her cheek. He released her hands and she felt his fingertips on the back of her neck. Then his lips touched hers. In the darkness, it seemed like the most natural thing in the world. They kissed, and held each other as if they had always been lovers. When the cloud finally passed and the moonlight returned, Liang slipped her hands inside his robe and explored his smooth chest and shoulders, running her palms over his flat stomach and drawing her fingernails softly across his back. He loosened her robe, kissing her neck, her shoulder, her breasts, until she moaned softly and dug her nails into his flesh.

She shrugged off her robe and Ko drank in the sight of her outline against the night sky. He pulled off his own robe and laid it on hers, then knelt before her and kissed her stomach, stroking her hips and running his palms around the back of her thighs. She sighed softly and sank down to face him. Their lips found each other's and they kissed again, their passion warming the night air. They melded together, the robes on the forest floor the only bed they needed, and they made love wordlessly, their urgent breathing the only sound to punctuate the stillness of the night.

Each night, the new lovers sought haven in the forest. During the summer, they slept in only their robes despite the cool mountain air. At the first sign of autumn's chill, they huddled beneath two blankets, as they had done on the road to Shaolin, and made love before creeping back to their dormitories shortly before dawn.

On such a night, Ko draped his arm around her slender form and buried his nose in the nape of her neck. "What are you doing?" she laughed.

"I like your smell," he muttered in her ear.

"How can you be so disgusting? I haven't even washed after our training."

"That's why I like it."

"You're like a dog," she complained happily.

He growled and licked her neck, until she cried out and turned to stop him. He knelt and howled at the moon.

She knocked him onto his back and pinned him beneath her.

"I can't breathe," he choked.

"How dare you," she laughed, and made to strangle him. He did not resist. Instead, he reached behind her head and pulled her mouth to his. She resisted, forcing him to use all his strength to bring his lips to hers. Then they were making love again urgently, as they had so many times before.

Later, he cradled her in his arms once more and she stroked his hand gently. In the faint moonlight, she could just make out the gleam of his eyes and the strong jawline that was so beautiful to her.

"Do you love me, Ko?" she asked quietly.

Many minutes passed before he spoke. "Why do you ask?"

"Because I love you."

"You do?" he asked in surprise.

"Yes," she laughed, "I have never loved anyone before, but I love you."

She waited for him to speak, but the only sound was the rustle of the leaves in the wind. "You have nothing to say?" she asked gently.

"I'm not used to talking about these things," he said.

"Surely you have told a girl you loved her before?"

"Yes, but I never meant it."

She rose onto her elbow, trying to make out his face in the darkness.

"Should I take it as a good sign that you haven't lied to me?"

"That's not what I meant."

"A bad sign, then?"

"No."

"You would only say you loved me if you meant it?"

"That's right," he answered, shifting uncomfortably on the rough ground of the forest.

"So you have changed recently, is that it?"

"A lot has changed, Liang."

"You have become a serious young man, at long last."

"Why all these questions? Can't we just be together?" he asked.

"I'm trying to understand you, Ko."

"You're better off not knowing me."

"It's a little late for that now."

He retreated into silence.

"Why do you say that?" she persisted. "Why don't you want me to know you?"

"I have done things. It's best you don't know."

"You can tell me. I'll understand."

"Another time, maybe. Not now. Not tonight."

"I won't think worse of you, I promise."

"That's easy to say."

"As you wish," she sighed, rising to her feet.

"Where are you going?" he asked, bewildered.

"Back to the monastery."

"It's dark."

"I can find my way."

"Wait, I'll come with you," he said, reaching for her, but it was too late, she had already pulled on her robe and slipped away. He watched, dumbstruck, as her figure vanished quickly into the night.

The next morning when Ko taught the eighteen exercises, Liang was not present. She did not attend their classes in writing and Sanskrit. He searched for her in the library and the meditation hall, but she was nowhere to be found. He went to the nunnery and asked to see her, but an elderly nun insisted she was not there. He considered barging past the old woman and striding into Liang's room, but instead, returned to his room and lay miserably on his bed.

In the evening, he made his way up to the cave, wondering what Da Mo would say about her absence, but the cave was empty. He checked the glade by the waterfall, but there was no one there so he returned to the monastery alone.

Over the following days, he saw her once in the dining hall. He wanted to go to her, but she was surrounded by nuns and deep in conversation. He tried to get her alone several times, but she avoided him artfully. Each evening he went up to the glade, hoping she might be there, but she was not, and each night he lay in his room and wondered whether he would ever kiss her and hold her again.

On the morning of the fifth day, he woke earlier than usual. Knowing he would not be able to fall asleep again, he got up and paced the room. Dawn was still some way off. There was at least an hour before he would begin teaching the morning exercises. He had not touched a weapon for five days, and suddenly, he wanted to feel its lethal weight in his hands.

He hurried from the temple to the cave to get his sword. To his surprise, Da Mo was there, gazing at the wall. He waited in the entrance, unsure what to do.

"You have come for your sword," Da Mo said.

"Yes, I couldn't sleep."

"Take it."

Ko opened the leather bag and saw Liang's sword was missing.

"Liang has been here already?" he asked.

"Yes."

"Did she say anything?"

"What is there to say?"

"Actually, there is something to say," Ko said quietly.

"Then go and say it," Da Mo said knowingly.

Ko watched her lithe figure moving gracefully in the bamboo, her blade flashing in the weak light of the false dawn. She stepped, cut, withdrew, turned, and parried, performing the precise sequences that Da Mo had taught them over so many evenings. She turned toward him, parrying and thrusting. She did not see him. Her concentration was fixed on the unseen enemy before her. She spun and cut again, striking low. He admired her precision and power. She had learned quickly from Da Mo, even more quickly than he had. She had a gift. But even as he thought it, he noticed her falter and she stopped in the middle of her exercise, her sword still low, her head bowed.

He stepped out from the trees. She turned, startled. He drew his sword and stood beside her, his sword low and to the right, like hers, and waited in silence. She moved, and when she did, he moved with her. They stepped and turned together, swords moving as one. A cut, a parry, another cut, this time low, and then withdrawal.

"There's something you should know," he said, raising his sword above his head to strike. She did not answer. They continued in silence, a step, a cut, a sweep, a parry, another step.

"I killed a man."

She stopped.

"A soldier," he went on, "I am wanted by the army."

"What are you talking about?"

"I haven't always been a monk. In fact, I was not a monk until after I met Master Da Mo."

She stared at him.

"It's the truth, what you wanted to hear, remember? Only now you don't want to hear it."

"I want to hear everything," she said quietly.

"Alright, you will! We were soldiers together, stationed on the western frontier. There was a fight in the garrison town near the fort and I killed him."

"You must have had good reason, Ko."

"I thought I did. I thought I was protecting someone. But I hated him, and perhaps that was the real reason."

He had said it, and it felt good now that it had finally been spoken aloud.

Confession.

Release.

He looked into Liang's eyes. She had promised to understand, but she could not, he could see that now. She could never love a murderer.

"He was beating an old man half to death. I stopped him.

Killed him. But perhaps I took my revenge at the same time."

"Did you?"

"I denied it for a long time, even to myself. I told myself it was justified. Now I don't know."

He saw the color drain from her cheeks. He was losing her but he could not stop.

"I stood behind him, pulled his head back to expose his throat. Then I cut it with my knife."

He watched her eyes fill with tears, her trembling hand at her mouth. "The worst part was not the blood. It was his face. I see it every time I close my eyes. The disbelief in his eyes. He looked at me as if to say, "Ko, we've had our differences, but you just ended my life. A little harsh, don't you think?" Even as he fell, I was filled with remorse. I wanted to apologize to him, to help him, comfort him in his last moments. But in the end, I did nothing. He died at my feet, with that look on his face."

Liang stared, ashen faced. He looked away, unable to meet her eye. "Does the master know?" she asked in a small voice.

"He knows I'm wanted by the army, but I have never told him why. He has never asked."

"Maybe you should tell him? It would be good to share your burden."

"There's no need for anyone else to share my burden," he said, suddenly angry.

"Then why are you telling me this now?"

"You wanted to know."

"Not like this, Ko. Not like this."

"Is there any other way to say it?"

He saw the pain in her eyes, and felt a stab of remorse for inflicting his story on her so brutally. Tears ran down her cheeks and he had never wanted to hold her more, to comfort her, kiss her, tell her how much he loved her. But he was abhorrent to her now. She turned and hid her face from him. Would she ever forgive him, ever say she loved him again?

The only sound in the glade was the chuckling waterfall and the gentle rustle of the bamboo.

"His name was Tsun," she whispered.

"How do you know?" he asked, astonished.

"You say it in your sleep."

He looked up at the lightening sky. "I'm sorry I'm not the person you thought I was, Liang."

"We should be getting back," she said, her voice wavering, "It's time to teach morning exercises. The monks will be waiting for us."

You go," he said, "I'll follow in a moment."

He watched her go. There was a stiffness in her shoulders, but he could not tell whether she was still crying. She looked small beneath the overhanging trees. He wanted to run after her, beg forgiveness for the way he had spoken to her, for the way he had hurt and deceived her, but it was too late now. He waited in the quickening dawn wind, until her retreating form was out of sight.

Stranger at the Gate

Da Mo's gaze bore into the cave wall while his mind circled high above, looking down on Song Shan and the little monastery glinting red and gold in the morning sun. He saw monks waiting by the temple gate for exercises to begin. He saw lovers talking in a clearing by a waterfall and watched them part. All was as it should be. Monks, teacherless, would be taught. Lovers, parted, would come together again. This was the ebb and flow of the world. His mind moved higher, further, wider, leaving the world behind to join the great emptiness beyond, where he was free to exist in the farthest reaches of the cosmos or sit beside an insect on a leaf.

Then he found himself in a familiar place. The sweet scent of a mulberry grove filled his nostrils. Wang was by his side. She offered him chilled tea and he took a long drink of the cold, sweet liquid. It was refreshing in the heat of the day. Then she was gone, and he was in the bamboo forest beyond the grove. All was silent. Not a bird sang. Not an insect buzzed. Even the leaves sat breathless on their branches. The long form of the tiger appeared, slinking through the bamboo, stalking its prey. Death in motion. He saw a deer grazing in the nearby glade, unaware of the danger. Even as he saw it, he knew the trees were not trees but monks, and the tiger was not a tiger, but a soldier. A killer. And even as he ran from the cave, he knew he was too late.

Liang noticed a stranger at the temple gate, standing among the monks who were waiting for their morning exercises. As she drew nearer, she recognized the uniform of an army captain, though the boyish face seemed too young for such a rank. She wondered what business a captain might have at Shaolin, but whatever it was, it was no concern of hers. She rubbed her eyes to make sure no trace of her tears remained and was about to call the monks to order when a shadow in her mind made her look again at the soldier.

He was gazing beyond her, up the slope. She followed his gaze and saw Ko behind her on the path. She looked back at the soldier who was now walking through the monks and knew why he had come. He moved with effortless grace, his steps appeared slow, but he had already passed the monks and was approaching fast on the path.

"Wait a moment, please Captain," she ordered, putting her hand out to stop him. He passed her with a movement so effortless, she felt no more than a gust of air caress her outstretched arm.

Ko saw the soldier at that moment. He had seen Fu Sheng before in Yulong Fort and had often wondered whether such a boyish-looking man could really be such a fearsome warrior. Now, even from a distance, he saw the secret joy of killing in Fu Sheng's eyes, and he knew he was looking death in the face. A terrible cold drilled down his spine. His legs grew heavy beneath him. He fumbled for his sword, knowing there was no way he could ever defeat Fu Sheng.

Suddenly a figure appeared on the path between them. Liang was standing before Fu Sheng once again, this time with her sword drawn.

"No!" Ko cried, but it was too late. Even as he rushed forward, he knew he had lost her.

Liang's sword began its deadly arc to stop the captain, but did not finish it. There was a glimmer in the air and she fell; her throat a flash of red against the green of the mountain. Her face white, serene, still beautiful, though her body bore the mark of his guilt.

Fu Sheng's sword was drawn and scarlet dripped from its point. Death was close, so close its bitter stench filled Ko's nostrils, yet it held no fear for him now, only the promise of release. He drew his sword and hurled himself at Fu Sheng, who waited with a smile on his lips.

Ko struck furiously at the Fu Sheng's throat, but the captain vanished before his eyes and a burning pain exploded in his belly. He looked down and saw his robe hanging open, ragged and bloody. He struck again. His sword sliced only air and a new wound opened across his thigh. He stumbled away, struggling to stay on his feet. Fu Sheng did not press his advantage. Instead he waited, his eyebrows raised, as if curious to see what Ko would try next.

Ko paused, knowing his fury would kill him as certainly as

the captain's sword if he did not control it. He looked into Fu Sheng's eyes. Behind the mask of indifference, he saw the pleasure Fu Sheng took in the game he played so well, the game with the highest stakes of all, the game he never lost.

Ko thrust to draw Fu Sheng's sword, then turned his wrist to send his blade in a lighting arc toward his neck. Fu Sheng adjusted his parry at the last moment and blocked the cut, then struck to Ko's knee. Ko blocked and thrust for the heart. Fu Sheng's shoulders turned smoothly as the blade cut the air where he had stood moments earlier. His sword flashed toward Ko head. Ko parried but Fu Sheng's sword switched and sliced his forearm. He ignored the pain and cut low, striking Fu Sheng's leg and opening a cut above the knee, then smashed his clenched fist into Fu Sheng's face.

Fu Sheng floated away and smirked, fresh blood on his lip. "A pity you deserted," he smiled, his voice high and clear. You fight passably well. Some unusual ideas. Your trainer is to be commended, whoever he is."

"It was certainly not Corporal Chen," Ko said, coming forward, his sword slicing in deadly arcs.

Fu Sheng evaded, his sword flashing so quickly that Ko was dazzled by the speed. Yet his own sword matched it, seemingly of its own will. He raised his blade to parry a high cut, then dropped down to prevent a thrust to the groin. Lunging forward, he drove the point of his blade to the Fu Sheng's chest. Fu Sheng circled away, then came forward again. Their blades clashed in a new flurry, neither able to finish the deadly exchange. They stepped apart to recover.

"And who trained you to kill women so bravely?" Ko sneered.

"A woman suffers because of you," Fu Sheng smiled. "It would not be the first time."

"Weilin never suffered because of me," Ko leered into Fu

Sheng's face. "She loved every minute of it. She begged for more every night, so loud I had to cover her mouth to stop her waking the whole fort."

Fu Sheng's eyes flashed with hatred. He stepped forward with a furious explosion and swung his sword to crush Ko's skull. Ko side-stepped easily, but Fu Sheng's brutal attack had been a feint and he tripped Ko as he passed. Ko fought to regain his balance, his sword rising automatically to protect his head as Fu Sheng's blade searched for his neck. He twisted, catching Fu Sheng's blade and sending it wide, then drove the pommel of his sword into his face. Fu Sheng's left hand blocked a hand's width from his forehead. Ko pressed forward desperately but the captain twisted and shoved him away. They parted again, gasping for breath.

"How is Weilin?" Ko panted, fearing his attempt to antagonize Fu Sheng might have jeopardized her life.

"Don't concern yourself with her," Fu Sheng sneered.

"Weilin is a good woman," Ko said. "You shouldn't blame her for what happened."

"Shouldn't I?" Fu Sheng smiled. "Since you ask how she is, I will tell you. Sadly, her health has suffered somewhat since we were married."

"It wasn't her fault, what happened," Ko said seriously. "It was mine."

"What, you want mercy now?" Fu Sheng laughed incredulously.

"No, not mercy. I want to apologize for what I did. It was wrong."

The captain halted for a split second in disbelief. Then his demon spirit returned and he surged forward, his sword striking with renewed fury. Ko fell back under the dreadful onslaught. The loss of blood from his earlier cuts had caught up with him and drained him of his strength. Fu Sheng's attack was merciless and Ko battled grimly against its shocking power. Fu Sheng struck downward, and then switched at the last instant to drive a ferocious upward cut to his chin. Ko smashed the blade away but his sword went wide. His head was unguarded. Fu Sheng launched a sweeping backhand cut. Ko watched its deadly approach, powerless to prevent it. A spray of pain seared across his face and he could see no more. He lashed out blindly but his sword found no target. He dabbed furiously at his bloody eyes. It was no use. He could not see.

He lowered his sword and waited helplessly for the final stroke.

It did not come. Ko felt Fu Sheng moving beside him, felt Fu Sheng watching him, enjoying the spectacle of his final defeat and humiliation. His mind flashed back to the fort, lying on his bunk in the warm barracks, listening to Huo whispering from the bunk above. The hour was late and the other recruits were asleep, but Huo often spoke in the darkness, and though he pretended to be bored, he secretly enjoyed his idle chatter. Huo was talking about Captain Fu Sheng, a hero to many of the younger soldiers, recounting rumors that a demon possessed the captain during battle, fueling his bloodlust and delighting in the torment of his victims.

Kuang felt the demon standing beside him now, waiting for him to attack, eager to punish him further. He smiled. He had seen it, but the demon had not seen him. He swung his sword in a crude arc toward it, offering an irresistible target: his sword arm. He felt his wrist bump into something hard. He felt his sword fall from his hand, but it did not matter, the knife in his left hand had found its mark. He gripped the demon tightly and twisted the knife deeper into its flesh. He heard a gasp of pain, or was it surprise, then felt it stiffen and slump forward.

Then the demon was gone and Fu Sheng's head was resting on his shoulder. He cradled it in his blood-drenched hand until he heard the labored rasp of his final breath, and laid the body on the earth. He knelt beside it for a moment, exhausted. He was unsure how he got up. He only knew he was walking, stumbling, his head swimming in the darkness, when strong hands grasped him and wrestled him on the floor.

"Master?" he whispered.

"I didn't see the soldier until it was too late!" Da Mo cried in anguish.

"It was not your fight."

"I am so sorry Ko!"

"Go and tend to Liang," Ko insisted, pushing Da Mo away.

"I need to tend to you."

"Is she alright?" Ko asked, his voice rising to an urgent pitch.

Da Mo ignored him and worked silently on his arm, holding his wrist with bone-crushing pressure. The pain was coming. The agony. Ko began to convulse.

"How is Liang?" he roared. "How is she?"

"Lie still," Da Mo ordered.

He began to thrash and only Da Mo's great weight held him down.

"I'm blind!" he cried.

"Let me see your face," Da Mo said, wiping the blood from his eyes to examine him. "The cut missed your eyes by a fraction. It is only blood. You are not blind." Da Mo turned to the young monks who stood around them, looking on in shock. "Bring hot water, soap, cloth for bandages. Build a fire. Hurry!"

Ko groaned, his body trembling uncontrollably now. Da Mo held him tightly. "I was in the cave," Da Mo explained in torment. "The soldier disguised his approach so well I did not see him in time. I tried to reach you."

"It was not your concern," Ko said, struggling to explain. "He came for me. Liang tried to stop him. Is she alive?"

Da Mo did not answer.

"She's dead," Ko cried. "I know she is. I saw it happen!"

"Yes," Da Mo whispered, struggling to keep his voice even.

Ko's lay back and screamed. The pain was immeasurable. His wrist was agony. Suddenly he knew why. Bile rose in his throat. He vomited. Da Mo wiped his face tenderly.

"My hand?" Ko gasped.

"It is gone."

He convulsed again and muttered incoherently before slipping into merciful unconscious.

Monks arrived with water and bandages. Da Mo worked quickly to bind the stump of his wrist and the wounds on his limbs, his stomach and his face, then cradled Ko in his arms and carried him into the temple. Inside, he prepared to cauterize the bloody stump of Ko's wrist, but Ko woke, and seeing the burning iron, began to thrash.

"Hold him down," Da Mo snarled at the attending monks. Four of them pressed him down on the narrow bed. Da Mo seized the hot iron but Ko fought so hard that even four monks could not hold him still.

"Forgive me," Da Mo muttered and slammed his palm into Ko's neck. Ko's eyes rolled in his head and he went limp once more.

"Have you killed him?" one of the monks asked in dread.

"Not yet."

Da Mo took up the red-hot iron and pressed it to the stump of Ko's wrist. The stench of burning flesh filled the room and the attendant monks emptied their stomachs on the floor. When he had finished his grim work, he cleaned and stitched the remaining wounds on Ko's body before leaving to take care of the other two bodies that waited outside the temple gate.

The Twilight

Da Mo stayed by Ko's bedside night and day, feeling for his faint pulse, listening to his shallow breath, waiting for the demons that would try and take his last disciple away. While Ko slept, he prepared a powerful medicine for the pain that lay ahead, and when Ko woke in the night he hushed his screams and gave him the medicine that sent him back to a tormented sleep.

In the darkest hours of the night, Ko was taken by a fever and spoke of childhood names and places that Da Mo had never heard before. Da Mo poured water into his parched lips and fed him a little cooled broth, wrapped him in blankets, held him as he shivered uncontrollably. The fever raged for three days. On the fourth day, Ko woke, lucid once more.

"Kill me," he begged.

"Sleep a little longer," Da Mo soothed.

"It will be a just punishment for my sins."

"Sleep. We will speak of it later."

"You don't know what I did."

"I don't need to know."

"Yes, you do." He was about to say more but a paralyzing pain gripped him and he groaned instead, waiting for it to pass. "I killed a man, a soldier from my own troop. His name was Tsun. That is why the army was hunting me. That is the reason your disciples died in Tiger Leaping Gorge, and that young monk from the monastery whose name I don't even remember. And now Liang, and Captain Fu Sheng. I deserve to die. Kill me. It is only right."

"There has been enough killing."

He reached for the master's wrist, his grip surprisingly strong. "This life is over for me now. I don't want it any longer. Kill me, so I can be reborn and try again."

"You can try again now."

"Let me go," he pleaded, "Liang is dead. Let me join her."

"There is work to be done here."

"I can't help you."

"You can."

Ko lay back, exhausted. His eyes flickered and closed and he returned to his dreams.

In the morning, he woke and attempted to rise from his bed. Da Mo held him down. He thrashed in vain, furious with the master.

"Liang is dead!" he roared. "Don't you care? Don't you grieve? Aren't you angry? How can you be so cold?"

"Yes, she is dead," Da Mo said, his powerful fingers digging deep into Ko's chest as he held him down, "which makes you my only disciple. I won't let you go."

"I'll leave Shaolin and never practice again."

"You can't even leave your sick-bed."

Ko struggled but he was no match for Da Mo, and spent from his efforts, he fell back into a long and fitful sleep.

When he woke next, the fever had gone. It was replaced by pain in his wrist so great that he could not speak, but merely choked in agony until Da Mo gave him a draft that took away all sensation and sent him drifting into a happy delirium. Da Mo continued the medication for seven days, until his patient's senses could be allowed to return.

Ko woke to the sounds of monks in the courtyard outside his window, passing on their way to studies or meditation. Through the bandages on his eyes, he found he could tell the difference between day and night. It was a sunny day, and the room was bright. He could feel Da Mo's presence. He wondered how many days he had lain in the infirmary, but could not summon the strength to ask. The pain in his arm had dulled, but when he thought of Liang, he found the ache in his heart had not diminished, and he fell back into a blackness from which there would be no escape.

Da Mo's strong hands raised him from his pillow and he sat up obediently. Da Mo cut the bandages around his eyes and unwound them slowly. Ko felt tepid water on his eyelids, his cheeks, and he allowed the master to wash him carefully without complaint.

His eyes flickered open. "I can't see," he said without emotion.

"Be patient," Da Mo said, "your eyes are unused to the light. Rest a little longer."

He lay back, his eyes screwed shut, as Da Mo redressed his other wounds.

"Why do we exist?" he asked, a thin smile on his lips, "I can see no reason for it."

Da Mo leaned close to his ear, his voice little more than a hum. "Don't be so hasty to give up on life, Ko. We are not finished yet."

"What do you want of me?"

"I want repayment, for the teachings I have given you."

"How can I repay it?"

"Stay in Shaolin and follow The Way."

"But I don't know The Way. You must know that. I can never be a monk, never be a Buddha, like you."

"Ah, you want pity now?"

"No!"

"But you are filled with self pity."

Ko turned away, but Da Mo continued relentlessly, his voice unexpectedly harsh. "Do you really wish for death? How stupid of you. Your wish will be granted soon enough. In the blink of an eye we will all be dust. No flesh. No bones. No memories. What is your hurry?"

Ko groaned.

"Your hand is lost, but where did it go? Who took it from you? Was it the soldier, or did you give it in exchange for his life?"

"The loss of my hand is a just punishment, but Liang's death …" Ko cried.

"Liang is gone too, but who is responsible for her death? Was it the soldier who killed her? Was it you? Or did she give her own life?"

"I am to blame!" he cried.

"You seek to give names to actions and judge them guilty, innocent, right, wrong, good, bad. These are the shallow wishes of a child."

"What would you have me do?"

"Carry your actions like a man, seeking neither praise nor blame."

"Words, riddles …" Ko's face twisted in misery. "I am responsible for Liang's death. Nothing can change that."

"Liang did as she wished," Da Mo said, gripping Ko's robe, feeling the thinness of his flesh over his ribs. "She was brave. She faced death without fear, without wavering. Who are you to feel sorry for her? Who are you to feel guilty?"

"I didn't ask her to die for me!"

"Don't be angry with her. She chose to draw her sword against the soldier. She chose to face death. Don't condemn her for her bravery."

Da Mo sat on the bed beside him and put his hand on Ko's shoulder as he wept. "You miss her. I miss her. We will miss her together," he said gently.

When his tears were finished, Ko spoke calmly. "If there is no right or wrong, no good or evil, and life is over in the blink of an eye, then what reason is there to live? To care? Why can't you let me go?"

"Life is a gift, Ko. Life is sacred. And we are all human, with emotions. We can care, and grieve, and mourn. Love, and laugh, and rejoice. Just don't mistake these feelings for reality, or you will never see the beauty of the truth."

"That is a cold way to live."

"Not cold, simply clear."

"Who can avoid being governed by feelings? Would you have us live by reason alone?"

"Not reason, wisdom."

"How can a man not give way to emotions? They are too powerful."

"You are right. Even a mind that sees the truth can easily be swayed. To resist requires great strength. That is why we train to forge a strong will. We perform rituals to prepare our spirit for the true path. We read scriptures to inspire us. We build temples and create myths to attract young minds. We promise them miracles ... bliss ... nirvana. We strengthen their resolve for years, until finally they are ready to accept that there are no miracles, no bliss, no nirvana, only the simple beauty of what they have always known. Only the strongest minds can make this final leap."

"I don't think I can do it."

"You can," Da Mo said quietly. "I would not ask it otherwise."

Ko lay still for a minute or an hour, he did not know which, then spoke again. "What you ask is so simple, yet so difficult."

"Yes."

"I know what you want. I think I have always known."

"Then give it to me."

"I'm afraid."

"Afraid of what?" Da Mo asked.

"Of what I might see."

"There is nothing to fear," Da Mo said, his voice little more than a whisper, and yet it filled Ko's soul. "The world, seen this way, is breathtakingly beautiful. Come and see it with me. I have been waiting for you."

The Knife

In the never-ending twilight that stretched from day to night, Ko lay in numbness and despair. His love was gone, his hand lost, his eyes blind. He had no wish to live and only Da Mo's will kept him alive from one day to the next. Novice Lao left food and tea for him but he ignored it and grew dangerously thin. Da Mo visited, but they had little left to say and his visits became less and less frequent.

Ko remained in his room, his ruined eyes closed, his mind seeking a peace he could not find. One afternoon he woke to a feeling of lightness. The day was unseasonably hot, and he could almost smell the sunshine outside his window. It was the hour when he and Liang would go to the cave and exercise with Da Mo. He saw a vision of her standing before him, her sword drawn, and felt her presence so close that he could make out the scent of her that he knew so well.

He allowed himself to think of her, not pushing her from his mind as he had done for so long. He thought back to the first time he had seen her outside the emperor's palace in Nanjing, and how Da Mo had startled her by opening his eyes and speaking to her. She had fallen backward onto her rump. He laughed at the memory. He thought of how she had practiced with them in the palace gardens and fought with him on the way to Shaolin. He felt her warmth beside him on those cold nights on the road, and the glorious feel of her body when they had made love for the first time in the clearing by the waterfall.

Then he saw the red line on her throat, the same mark he had left on Tsun, the mark of his guilt. Suddenly Tsun's ghost was upon him, etched against a white sky. He felt its weight pressing hard on his chest, crushing the air from his body. Vicious blows rained down on his head, pounding him senseless. Then Tsun's throat turned red and blood poured down into his eyes.

He sat up with a start. Had he been dreaming? He could not be sure. He lay back and a great sadness washed over him. A cry rose in his throat and he let it go. Soon, great sobs wracked his body. He wept for Liang, and for Tsun. He wept for Da Mo's disciples and the young monk who had died in Tiger Leaping Gorge. He wept for the soldier he had killed there. And he wept for Fu Sheng.

He wept until the breath left his body and he swayed on the border between life and death. Here he remained, able to cross back and forth at will. Death was serenity, silence, stillness, a place with no sorrow or shame, only infinite peace. It beckoned to him. But even as he gazed longingly at the freedom of the void, a dark presence blocked his way, and he could not pass.

The young monks moved as one in their morning exercises as Da Mo counted out his exercises for them. Novice Lao stood in the front rank so the others could follow his movements. Da Mo watched him approvingly; Ko and Liang had taught him well.

The group turned in unison. They squatted low, their hands pressing outward. Da Mo noticed Lao hesitate and stop. Some of the other monks stopped too. Something by the temple gate had caught their attention. Da Mo followed their gaze and saw the gaunt, wasted figure standing by the gatehouse. It was the figure of a young man who had once been so strong. He approached them slowly with faltering steps, his hand shielding his face from the sunlight. Da Mo stepped forward and embraced him in case he should fall.

Ko's lips were dry and cracked, his eyes red from crying. He struggled to speak, he had been silent for so long.

"I have come to repay my debt," he whispered.

"You have chosen a fine day for it," Da Mo said.

"How shall I begin?"

"You can lead the eighteen exercises once more for us, before we return to the temple."

Ko led the monks on shaking legs, struggling to keep his balance, his eyes half-closed, moving by instinct alone, fighting to complete the exercises that he had done so easily once before. The monks moved patiently, willing him to the finish, then Da Mo called an end to exercises and they returned to the temple.

"Come with me," Da Mo said quietly.

They walked to the cave in silence. Inside, Da Mo took a small bundle of cloth and handed it to Ko. Ko recognized its contents immediately and unwrapped it slowly. It was his knife, still caked in dark blood on the blade and hilt.

"It must be cleaned," he said quietly.

"Yes."

He lit a fire, struggling with only his left hand, but Da Mo did not try to help him. He watched as Ko heated a pan of water and slowly cleaned all traces of blood from the knife. Then Ko resharpened the blade and polished it until it gleamed.

Finally they went to the place where the soldier had fallen and Ko dug a hole and buried his knife in the soft earth, treading it down firmly until there was no trace of where it lay. Then they walked side by side to the clearing beside the waterfall, where a simple arrangement of stones marked Liang's grave. On the other side was another grave, that of the soldier.

"Your hand is buried beside her," Da Mo said.

Ko stared at the stones that were now the last reminder of Liang on earth. Then he turned to Da Mo, who held him tight for a moment, before releasing him. He knelt beside the grave and Da Mo left him alone to make peace with the girl he had loved, and the soldier he had killed.

When Ko returned to the cave, they sat side by side and watched the sunset over Song Shan.

"I have a question," Ko said.

"Ask it," Da Mo said.

"Do you wish to continue our training in the battlefield arts?"

"Do you?"

"I wish to follow the path you set before me."

"The Way is not fixed, Ko," Da Mo said slowly. "It can be found in the battlefield arts and outside them. But you have an aptitude for combat, so The Way manifests itself clearly for you when we practice."

"Then I wish to continue."

Da Mo nodded.

"There is only one thing I will not do. I have buried my knife and my past. I will never take a life again."

"I will never ask you to."

Ko looked into his master's eyes and saw the love he had for him, a love he had done so little to deserve. "I know," he whispered, drawing strength from Da Mo's unshakable faith in him and vowing silently to serve him with all his strength until his final breath.

Da Mo put his arm around his shoulder. "You must regain your strength before we can begin again."

"Yes."

"You must eat properly."

Ko nodded obediently.

"And drink hot, sweet tea."

"If you say so."

"I do, with plenty of spices."

"Not too many spices."

"Spices are good for the blood," Da Mo insisted.

"That's no way to drink tea," Ko said, the faintest of smiles on his lips.

"What do you know of tea?" Da Mo said, relighting the fire and setting a new pot of water to boil.

"We Chinese invented tea. Everyone knows that."

"That shows how little you know," Da Mo chuckled, unwrapping his bundle of tea leaves, sugar, and spices, and laying it out before them. "It was an Indian monk who discovered tea. Have I never told you that before?"

"No," Ko said, "I don't believe you have."

"It must have been someone else," Da Mo smiled. "We have plenty of time, so listen carefully and learn."

EPILOGUE

Song Shan, A.D. 529

The Snowdrop

Nine winters passed. The saplings on Song Shan grew tall and strong, their yellow-green leaves changing to a deeper green, their branches reaching out to the sky and casting long shadows on the earth. And during this time the monks of Shaolin learned to sit firm in their meditation and came to see the subtle meaning of the scriptures. They grew strong and supple through their daily exercise under the watchful eye of Brother Ko. They learned to clean, and wash, and cook, and pay attention to the smallest details in all things, and so began their journey to discover the beauty of The Way that joined all things in one.

Brother Ko became Master Chui's finest student, studying with a discipline that the old master had never encountered before. Soon his knowledge of Sanskrit and the sacred texts rivaled that of the temple's foremost scholars. He spent countless hours in the library where Mistress Fan presented him with a never-ending supply of divine texts from the world's greatest sages. And when his studies were finished for the day, he would go to the cave to train with Da Mo, until, even with one hand, he was able to match Da Mo in every arena of combat, and the student had become the master.

Novice Lao grew into a tall young man and a fine monk. When

Brother Tan was promoted to a senior position in charge of temple supplies, Lao took over as chef and taught his own novices how to assist in the kitchen. He showed them the hidden places on the mountainside where they could find herbs and medicines, and how to tend the vegetable gardens behind the temple. There was one task they were not permitted to do. None was allowed to bring tea to Master Da Mo in the cave. That was Lao's duty alone, and he guarded the privilege jealously. Besides, he told them, only he knew exactly how the master liked his tea—with the rare spices that he obtained from the Persian traders in Yangcheng. In winter, the cave was icy cold and he worried about the master's health. Occasionally he would wrap a blanket around Da Mo's broad shoulders, but Da Mo seemed unaffected by the cold and his body was always warm to the touch. Nevertheless, Lao was always pleased when winter finally gave up its hold on the mountains and the snows retreated from all but the highest peaks.

It was on just such a morning, when the moon was still large in the clear dawn sky, that Ko left the temple and set off alone up the mountainside. He ran at a pace that none in the temple could match, driving himself relentlessly, as he always did, with no thought or care for the protest of his tired flesh. He saw that spring had arrived on Song Shan, and a new energy crackled in his limbs. He ran far higher than usual, unwilling to stop, until he had broken through the treeline and found himself on rough stone and shingle. The wind blew hard and cold over the barren ground where the last patches of snow refused to melt, and the views of the surrounding landscape were stunning. He pressed on, eager to reach the summit before stopping to admire the scene that would be his reward. Even here, high on the rocky track, the signs of spring were visible. Green shoots had pushed their way up through the last of the snow. Above him the distant cry of an eagle carried on the wind. A single snowdrop sheltered behind a rock.

He stopped abruptly and went back to admire the flower. How beautiful it was. How fragile. He knelt beside it and brushed its soft petals with his fingertips, all thoughts of reaching the summit forgotten. He sat beside the snowdrop, unaware of the hours that sped by, or the plummeting temperature as night began to fall.

Hours later he made his way to the entrance of the cave where Da Mo sat gazing at the wall.

"What brings you to visit your old master?" Da Mo asked without turning.

"Do I need a reason?" he replied.

"You act without one?" Da Mo demanded.

"And you think you can still toy with my mind?" Ko answered brusquely.

"Forgive me, Brother Ko," Da Mo laughed heartily, turning to him, "I sometimes forget you're not the same young man I met all those years ago, though it seems like only yesterday. Come, sit with me. We can meditate together, like we used to."

"Actually, there is a reason," Ko said with a smile.

"I knew it! What reason?"

"A flower—a snowdrop to be more precise."

"A snowdrop? How wonderful. Tell me about it."

"I was running near the summit of Song Shan when I saw it. It had pushed its way up through the last of the snow. It was so high up the mountain, I wondered what it was doing there. It was so beautiful, so fragile." His voice trailed off and they sat in silence, though Da Mo continued to listen, engrossed in the words that were still unspoken. "It made me think of Liang," Ko said quietly.

"You haven't spoken of her for many years," Da Mo said gently.

"No, but today, I realized something about her which made me very happy."

What was that?"

"She was a Buddha-child."

Da Mo stared at Ko intently. "That is a good description," he said at last.

"She didn't know it," Ko smiled.

"No."

"But that doesn't matter. You knew it the moment you saw her."

Da Mo nodded.

"How ironic, that she tried so hard to learn The Way when she already knew it. I remember you once told me that you had simply set her free, but I didn't understand. Yet I was always surprised how quickly she learned your methods. It was as if she had done it all before in a previous life."

"Some people are born to The Way without knowing it," Da Mo said, "while others spend a lifetime seeking it in vain. I simply helped her to shrug off the bonds that the world had put on her so she could follow it freely."

"She loved you for that," Ko said with a sad smile.

"It was you she loved," Da Mo corrected him gently.

Ko looked at the floor. "For a long time I could not forgive myself for that. I never told her how much I loved her. She never knew."

"She knew," Da Mo assured him.

"I hope so."

"The whole temple knew. You were like a love-sick dog," Da Mo chuckled.

"Then maybe she did," Ko said, laughing through the tears that stung his eyes. "I pray she did."

"She knew," Da Mo repeated, as Ko wept silent tears of joy.

They sat throughout the night, watching the changing shades of the darkness, watching as the first fingers of dawn found their way into the cave.

Da Mo sighed deeply. "You know what I am about to say."

"You are leaving," Ko answered, his voice heavy with sadness.

"I am."

"And I cannot persuade you to stay."

"No."

"Where will you go?"

"I have often dreamed of traveling the desert roads beyond the western frontier, where they say the land stretches wider than an ocean."

"And what of Shaolin?"

"You will lead Shaolin."

"Me? What about Master Chui?" Ko asked in surprise.

"Master Chui and I have already discussed the matter in depth and the High Council is in agreement. Master Chui has no wish to lead Shaolin. He is happiest teaching the scriptures, as you know. It is his talent and his greatest joy. Let us not deprive him of it. To lead Shaolin is your destiny. You must fulfill it now."

Ko sat still, trying to take it all in. "I will try," he said from the depths of his being.

"You will succeed," Da Mo said. "I have seen it in a vision, and such things cannot be ignored."

"What did you see?" Ko asked warily, knowing the power of Da Mo's visions.

"I saw a time far in the future, when the world is unlike anything you can imagine today. The Shaolin Temple is known in every land, and pilgrims travel from the farthest corners of the earth to learn its methods."

"That is quite a burden you saddle me with," Ko protested.

"You have broad shoulders," Da Mo laughed. "Come, let us return to the temple and tell Master Chui the happy news."

They rose and stood by the cave mouth watching the dawn sun rise over Song Shan. Da Mo saw the sadness on Ko's face and embraced him as a father holds a beloved son. Warm tears fell on his dark cheeks, and Ko wept silently into his master's robe.

"When are you leaving?" he whispered.

"I would leave now, but I expect the monks will require some sort of ceremony before I go."

"If it keeps you here a little longer, then I require a ceremony too," Ko said firmly.

"Very well," Da Mo sighed as they set off down the slope together, "we shall have a grand ceremony. I will conjure up the twenty-seven patriarchs of old and even The Buddha himself to bless you. You will become the greatest grandmaster of Shaolin and your name will be remembered throughout the ages."

"No," Ko said, seriously, "it's you who will be remembered for Shaolin, not I."

"Nonsense, I have no wish to be remembered," Da Mo said, waving his hand dismissively.

"To seek fame is the greatest folly of all," Ko said, repeating a phrase his master had told him many times in the course of their studies.

"Quite so, Master Ko," Da Mo nodded proudly.

"I believe you," Ko said as the roof of the temple came into view through the saplings. "Despite all you have achieved, you haven't the slightest wish to be remembered. But you know, Master, for that reason alone, I think you should be. And I believe you always will be."

And for once, the great Master Da Mo had no answer for his one-time student.

Historical Note

Countless Eastern martial arts trace their origins back to Bodhidharma and the Shaolin Temple. In China, he is more commonly known as Da Mo (or Tamo) and in Japan he is called Daruma. Little is known about the man himself and in researching his life, it is impossible to separate fact from myth and legend.

In paintings, he is usually depicted as a large monk with a black beard and a piercing gaze. Bodhidharma is clearly not Chinese and came from the West, probably India, though possibly Persia or Central Asia. Most sources have him coming from Pallava in Southern India, in what is now Tamil Nadu. He is often cited as being the son of a king or a nobleman, either a Brahmin priest or a member of the Kshatriya who were the warrior caste. His family name may have been Sardili.

The Shaolin Temple existed before his arrival in China around A.D. 520, but Bodhidharma is credited with introducing new methods and creating a center of excellence that grew and thrived until recent times. His method of meditation was called Dhyana in Sanskrit, which became Ch'an in Chinese and Zen in Japanese. Today, many Zen sects also trace their legendary origins to Bodhidharma and Shaolin.

Bodhidharma arrived at a time when Buddhism was in great demand in China. Indian missionaries and dedicated Chinese monks crossed paths on the dangerous trade routes known as the Silk Road that joined the two countries. The fantastical tale of Monkey is based on the true-life journey of Xuanzang, a Chinese pilgrim who traveled to India about a hundred years after the time of Bodhidharma.

The Silk Road skirted the Himalayas in a giant arc, passing through modern-day Pakistan, Afghanistan, and Uzbekistan before entering the deserts of western China. The journey took many months, often years, through high mountain passes and the barren wastes of the Taklamakan desert. However, in Bodhidharma's time the Huns occupied the territories of northern India, so he is commonly thought to have traveled by the long sea route to Southern China. Even this is far from certain and some sources suggest he took a more direct route through Tibet. In the writing of *A Sudden Dawn* there was no special reason to suppose that he did, other than it fitted neatly with his direct approach to life and made for a more dramatic narrative.

Most sources agree that Bodhidharma met with the Emperor Wu Di in Nanjing. The emperor asked who he was, and Bodhidharma replied that he had no idea. The emperor asked how much merit he had earned for all the good deeds he had done, and Bodhidharma told him "no merit." After this, Bodhidharma went north, crossing the Yangtze "on a single reed" and spent nine years in Shaolin, sitting in a nearby cave and gazing at the wall. His gaze was said to be so powerful that it penetrated the rock and the markings can still be seen today.

He found the monks of Shaolin too weak to meditate correctly and taught them exercises to make them fitter and stronger. There is no record of these being martial exercises and it is widely accepted that fighting methods were developed later. However, if Bodhidharma was born to Indian nobility, it is quite probable that he was highly trained in the battlefield arts.

What happened to him after he left Shaolin remains a mystery. Some say he was poisoned by a jealous monk and buried at Shaolin. Later, when his grave was exhumed, only a single sandal was found. Others say he was seen wandering in Central Asia. The Japanese like to think he paid them a visit too, and in a legend as big as Bodhidharma's, who's to say it's not true?

During his time in Shaolin, Bodhidharma ordained only two monks. One understood The Way but did not teach it. The other was his successor and the first Chinese patriarch of Zen, a one-armed man named Hui Ko.

Acknowledgements

I embarked on my first novel unaware of the enormity of the task ahead. The plot came quickly, as did the character of Bodhidharma, but as the months wore on I ground to a halt on more than one occasion. It was only through the encouragement of my wife Charmaigne that I succeeded, several years later, in putting Bodhidharma's epic story on paper. Thank you Charmaigne, for your patience, love, and support through some testing times.

I shared *A Sudden Dawn* with others whose opinion I value: my father Michael, my sister Sasha, my sister-in-law Charlie, my fellow writers Doug Woods, Diane Messidoro, and Ingrid Charles, and my Sensei, Gavin Mulholland. Their insights helped me to shape the book into what it has become, for which I am eternally grateful.

I received much-needed advice on Chinese names from Olivia Milburn of the School of Oriental and African Studies in London. Any errors and inconsistencies are entirely my own, my only defense being that, in places, I ignored her advice to make the names easier for a Western readership. I also received help with Chinese calligraphy from Wai Chung Chan and Ben Hung, two talented students from my karate club.

Finally I would like to acknowledge the personal support of my publisher David Ripianzi of YMAA and my editor, Leslie Takao, for her valuable comments and suggestions. To work with industry professionals who are experienced martial artists in their own right has been a rare and real pleasure.

About the Author

Goran Powell began his writing career in 1991 as an advertising copywriter, and, by 1995, he was creative director of a major London advertising agency. During this period, his work won ten national and international awards. He became a freelance writer in 1999 and currently works for many of London's top agencies.

He is a regular contributor to the martial arts press and was twice featured on the front cover of *Traditional Karate* magazine. His first book, *Waking Dragons*, published by Summersdale in 2006, became an instant bestseller on the Amazon Martial Arts listing and is now in its second edition. In 2008, he edited the widely acclaimed karate book *Four Shades of Black* written by his Sensei, Gavin Mulholland.

His martial arts training spans more than thirty-five years, and today he holds the rank of 4th dan black belt in Goju Ryu Karate. He is a qualified instructor with Daigaku Karate Kai (DKK), one of the United Kingdom's leading clubs, and assistant coach to the successful Mixed Martial Arts team, DKK Fighters.

Goran Powell resides in north London, in England, with his wife Charmaigne. He has three children, Harry, Hannah, and Autumn.

Printed in the USA
CPSIA information can be obtained
at www.ICGtesting.com
JSHW022202140824
68134JS00018B/816

9 781594 391989